COLERIDGE

Samuel Taylor Coleridge was born in 1772 at Ottery St Mary, Devon, the youngest son of a clergyman. He was educated at Christ's Hospital, London (where he began his friendship with Charles Lamb), and Jesus College, Cambridge, although he left without taking his degree. In 1794 he met Robert Southey, and during the following year they were occupied with the project of a Pantisocracy, an ideal community to be founded in America. But the scheme collapsed and this led to a break with Southey. In that same year Coleridge married Sara Fricker, but the marriage was unhappy. He first met Dorothy and William Wordsworth in 1797, and a close association developed between them. In 1799 he and Wordsworth published the *Lyrical Ballads*, which marked a conscious break with eighteenth-century tradition and included one of Coleridge's greatest poems, 'The Rime of the Ancient Mariner'. During a visit to the Wordsworths at County Durham in 1799 he met Sara Hutchinson, sister of Wordsworth's wife-to-be, Mary, who became his lifelong love. In the following year Coleridge and his family settled at Greta Hall, Keswick, and that year also saw the completion of the second part of 'Christabel'. In 1804 he separated from his wife, and he spent the following years in London or abroad, returning in 1808 to live with the Wordsworths in Grasmere. But in 1810, after a quarrel with Wordsworth, he left the Lake District for ever, and his life thereafter centred in London. In 1816, in an attempt to control his opium intake, he put himself in the care of Dr James Gillman and spent the remaining eighteen years of his life in his household.

Poet, philosopher and critic, Coleridge stands as one of the seminal figures of his time. In spite of great emotional stress in his personal affairs, he continued his literary work, gave lectures, founded and edited the *Friend*–a literary, moral and political weekly paper–wrote articles and travelled a good deal. His literary and philosophical theories were presented in *Biographia Literaria* (1817). The great flowering of his poetic genius took place within five years and above all in one year, from the summer of 1797, when he first met the Wordsworths, into the following spring. During this time he wrote 'The Ancient Mariner', the first part of 'Christabel', 'Kubla Khan' and many other less well-known poems. As William Hazlitt wrote: 'His thoughts did not seem to come with labour and effort; but as if borne on the gusts of genius, and as if the wings of his imagination lifted him from off his feet. . . His mind was clothed with wings; and raised on them, he lifted philosophy to heaven.'

Coleridge

Selected Poetry and Prose

Selected by Kathleen Raine

PENGUIN BOOKS

Published by the Penguin Group
Penguin Books Ltd, 27 Wrights Lane, London W8 5TZ, England
Penguin Books USA Inc., 375 Hudson Street, New York, New York 10014, USA
Penguin Books Australia Ltd, Ringwood, Victoria, Australia
Penguin Books Canada Ltd, 10 Alcorn Avenue, Toronto, Ontario, Canada M4V 3B2
Penguin Books (NZ) Ltd, 182–190 Wairau Road, Auckland 10, New Zealand

Penguin Books Ltd, Registered Offices: Harmondsworth, Middlesex, England

This selection first published 1957
13 15 17 19 20 18 16 14 12

Printed in England by Clays Ltd, St Ives plc
Typeset in Monotype Bembo

CONTENTS

POETRY

CONTENTS

PROSE

CONTENTS

CONTENTS

INTRODUCTION

THE difficulties of making a selection from the writings of Coleridge
are of a special kind. So many are the fields of thought in which
Coleridge's protean genius was active, that the first question that arises
is how to present him—as poet, as metaphysician, as critic, as theolo-
gian; as the dreamer of 'Kubla Khan', or as the philosopher of the
Romantic movement. During his life-time, readers of the *Morning Post*
knew him as a parliamentary reporter and an influential journalist;
subscribers to his two periodicals, The *Watchman* and The *Friend*, as a
political philosopher. We can no longer catch the echoes of his won-
derful talk, by which he dominated and enchanted private gatherings
and the public audiences who attended his extempore lectures; but to
regard Coleridge as purely and simply a poet would be an over-
simplification. He has been described as the last English thinker to at-
tempt that universality of knowledge characteristic of the Renaissance;
for science also was within his field of interest—he was a friend of
Humphry Davy—and his speculations on memory and association
point forward to the discoveries of Freud on the nature of the human
mind, and the unconscious.

Yet another Coleridge might be presented from his many letters,
that range over all these aspects of thought, and contain, besides,
minute observations of nature, mountain walks, waterfalls—Coleridge
the Lake-poet, although in fact all his important poems had been
written before he set foot in Cumberland. From these letters, besides,
emerges the story of a day-to-day life hampered by domestic unhap-
piness, financial anxiety, ill-health, and opium addiction—Coleridge
the failure, the procrastinator, the dreamer of great unfulfilled pro-
jects. What, in a small selection, should be included, what omitted?

One way would be to give a little of everything; to indicate the
range of his mind; but in a small volume, I doubt whether this could
be done adequately; for Coleridge's ideas require ample space for their
development; his conclusions cannot be separated from his method of
thought, from the building of those great edifices of orderly exposi-
tion, for which even in conversation he was famous—as de Quincey's
description recalls; 'Coleridge, like some great river, the Orellana, or
the St Lawrence, that, having been checked and fretted by rocks or
diverting islands, suddenly recovers its volume of waters, and its
mighty music, swept at once . . . into a continuous strain of orderly
dissertation, certainly the most novel, the most finely illustrated and

traversing the most spacious fields of thought by transitions the most just and logical that it was possible to conceive. What I mean by saying that his transitions were "just" is by contradistinction to that mode of conversation which courts variety through links of *verbal* connexions. Coleridge, to many people, and often I have heard the complaint, seemed to wander; and he seemed then to wander most when, in fact, his resistance to the wandering instinct was greatest—viz. when the compass and huge circuit by which his illustrations moved travelled farthest into remote regions before they began to revolve. Long before his coming round commenced, most people had lost him.'

Because of this 'huge circuit' of his thought, it is necessary to represent Coleridge by long passages; and in the present selection, I have thought it better to omit entirely whole fields of thought, and to represent as fully as space permits Coleridge as poet and as critic of poetry. I have omitted very few poems whose exclusion has caused me regret; of the criticism, there is enough to give a just idea of its full range, and from the letters and diaries, I have taken, with a few exceptions, only passages relating to literature. With great regret I have omitted whole chapters of psychological observation and metaphysical speculation; many passages that set forth a philosophy that would now be called existentialism; with less regret much 'theologico-metaphysical' material. Of all the fields in which his mind was active, Coleridge's theology alone seems to have little value outside its own time. His *Aids to Reflection* was an influential work in its day, in Anglican circles, but Coleridge was not, like his elder contemporary Blake, a great religious thinker. The present selection, therefore, while it is far from being representative of the whole of Coleridge, does, I hope, fairly represent those aspects of him that it is most important to include in a volume making part of a series of the English poets.

Coleridge the poet wrote his farewell to the Muse in his 'Ode to Dejection' in 1802. He did occasionally write poems later, some of them fine ones, but the great flowering of his poetic genius took place within five years, and, above all, in one single year, from the summer of 1797 when he first knew Dorothy and William Wordsworth, into the following spring. During that time he wrote 'The Ancient Mariner', the first part of 'Christabel', 'Kubla Khan', besides other poems only less great than these, the works not of his talent but of his genius. Coleridge had been a prolific writer of juvenilia, much of which is worthless, and which he himself was eager to discard, when he came into his full powers as a poet. The difference between Coleridge at his worst and at his best is that between smoke and fire.

To kindle the fire, some magical touch was needed, and that magic the circumstances of his life brought but once. When he made the third person of that trinity with a single soul, with Wordsworth and his sister Dorothy, he experienced for the last, and perhaps the first time in his life, what he himself names as the source of poetic inspiration; and soon he was to fall in love with Wordsworth's sister-in-law, Sara Huchinson, to whom the 'Ode to Melancholy' is addressed.

> O pure of heart! Thou need'st not ask of me
> What this strong music in the soul may be!
> What, and wherein it doth exist,
> This light, this glory, this fair luminous mist,
> This beautiful and beauty-making power.
> Joy, virtuous lady!

It is joy. 'Joys impregnate,' William Blake wrote, 'sorrows bring forth.' Poetic inspiration is too close to Eros to exist when natural love must for any reason be denied and stifled. Coleridge, in 1797, had already made a mistaken marriage; but this had not yet become intolerable to him, as it later did, because it made it impossible for him to marry the woman he loved. To the poet who as a child had been torn away from home for the eight years of his school-days, friendship had the power to release all his pent-up affections, to give him, perhaps, that sense of home-coming to his true spiritual next-of-kin, that could for a time heal in him that sense of exile from those he loved, that began in childhood, and returned more bitterly in his later years.

At the age of thirty, Coleridge the inspired poet was dead; for the years before him, that brought much fame, never again brought joy. But they brought wisdom. The main stream of his genius, diverted from poetry, flowed into other channels. The myth of failure, of promise unfulfilled, is largely untrue. 'Christabel' remained unfinished, and so did 'Kubla Khan'; scarcely anything Coleridge ever undertook was finished; but *finish* implies the realization of some finite end, and Coleridge's ends were ocean-like and boundless. Even as a child, Coleridge tells of himself, through the thought of the stars in the night sky, and his reading of fairy-tales and genii, 'my mind had been habituated *to the vast*'; and his thought is no more finished, or capable of completion, than the universe. His trains of thought lead often to a point at which Coleridge stops short, because of the very extent of the horizons that still open before him. He pauses in the *Biographia Literaria*, and inserts a letter of self-criticism, from that supposed friend who writes to him: 'imperfectly as I understand you in the present Chapter, I see clearly that you have done too much, yet not enough. You have been obliged to omit so many links, from the necessity of compression, that what remains looks like the fragments of the winding steps of an old ruined tower'–but adds, 'In that greater work to which you have devoted so many years, and study so intense and various, it will be in its proper place'–a work that remained unwritten because it was essentially unwriteable: Coleridge was hampered by the very vastness of his own mental processes.

Yet we have little reason to complain because, instead of an entire universe, we have only a few galaxies, for Coleridge's parts exceed the wholes of all but a few, and those few the greatest, minds. Besides this, although much may remain incomplete, all is consistent, coherent, as even a fragment of a Greek sculpture implies the perfection of the whole. All that he wrote was grounded in fundamental philosophical principles–or rather should one say, unwavering imaginative insight –that gives to the whole body of his thought, poetic, political, or critical, that consistency that is the mark of genius as contrasted with talent; the difference (to quote Sir Herbert Read, who so defines the difference between the romantic and the classical view of poetry) between 'form as proceeding' as contrasted with 'shape as superinduced'. His work has the coherence of a living organism; and such it is–for imagination, as runs his famous definition, 'is essentially *vital*, even as all objects (*as* objects) are essentially fixed and dead'.

Coleridge's thought–the philosophy of the Romantic movement– is essentially Platonic; or, rather, perhaps, Neoplatonic, for his Plato is the Plato of the Timaeus, and of Plotinus. To quote Professor I. A. Richards, it is 'an idealism, Platonic-Kantian in origins but very distinctively Coleridgean in actuality'. The poet he defined as one who 'brings the whole soul of man into activity, with the subordination of its faculties to each other, according to their relative worth and dignity'. With Plato, he places, of these faculties, reason as supreme, with emotion, will and understanding as its subordinates and instruments. He praises Milton's definition of poetry as 'simple, sensuous, and passionate', a definition that, like his own, defines poetry in terms of a vital experience, which transcends all definitions and laws. *Reason*, as Coleridge uses the word, is the equivalent of Plato's *noesis*; and the term is perhaps unfortunate, since the usual connotation of the word is the exact opposite of Coleridge's: *reason*, as Coleridge uses the word, is what William Blake calls *vision*; it is 'the mind's eye', a direct intuition of truth, 'an inward beholding, having a similar relation to the intelligible or spiritual, as sense has to the material or phenomenal'.

What is commonly called *reason*–in the modern sense of the word *rationalism*–Coleridge calls the *understanding*. By bearing in mind this difference in terminology, much confusion, in reading Coleridge can be avoided. Coleridge's reason, then, is at once the act of knowing, and that which is known; 'thus, God, the soul, eternal truth, etc., are the objects of reason; but they are themselves reason. We name God the Supreme Reason; and Milton says,

> ... whence the soul
> Reason receives, and reason is her being.

Whatever is conscious self-knowledge is reason: and in this sense it may be safely defined as the organ of the supersensuous; even as the understanding, wherever it does not possess or use the reason as its inward eye, may be defined the conception of the senses, or the faculty by which we generalize and arrange the *phaenomena* of perception.' Thus defined, reason is the inspiration alike of the poet and the scientist, and in it consists the genius of a Newton no less than of a Shakespeare; it is the intuition of reality.

All truth, for Coleridge, is drawn from that deep well; and the same imaginative intuition that made him a poet, made him supreme among critics; for in his application of this principle to the criticism of poetry, Coleridge raised that study once and for all above those purely mechanical supposed *rules* of art, that had been defined and redefined from the time of Aristotle, to Pope, Dryden, and Dr Johnson.

Coleridge's criticism of Shakespeare was, indeed, revolutionary. To the eighteenth century, Shakespeare was the 'wild', the 'irregular' child of 'nature'–of *nature* as contrasted with *art*. But, Coleridge pointed out, poetry is not unlike, but like nature because it is, like nature, a vital formative power, that no mechanical artifice can simulate. Art does not imitate the externals of nature, but its operation. Hence the transcendent genius of Shakespeare, who is, for Coleridge, the supreme example of the romantic poet. The form of his plays is neither 'wild' nor 'irregular' because they do not conform to the Unities of Aristotle: the form of each is inherent in its conception. Thus Coleridge leads us to the very heart of the motivation of Shakespeare's characters: for these, he says, are to be understood from within, by *meditation*; and not, like those of the classical Ben Jonson, by objective scrutiny. Coleridge points to a common characteristic of many of Shakespeare's villains–his Richard III, Thersites, Iago, Edmund, and even Falstaff–that they act from the discursive understanding alone: they are what we should call *rationalists* (using the word not in Coleridge's but in the common acceptance) who dismiss as idle nonsense the promptings of that deeper vision of truth that can be perceived, but not argued, the 'inward eye' of the soul. What makes Swift's Houyhnhnms monstrous is that they act rightly on rational grounds alone, and not from the deeper motivation of (Coleridgean and Platonic) *reason*. By a shifting of the focus of his thought from the general conception to the minutest detail of metre, or the choice and ordering of words in a single line, Coleridge applies the same principle to the parts as to the whole; for in true poetry, the same vital principle serves to organize the minute particulars, as inspires the general plan. Above all Coleridge's greatness as a critic lies, not (as in the clever journalist) in his power of pointing to the defects of a work, but in his power of illuminating its merits: not by easily accorded praise, for 'to exclude the great is to magnify the little'; but because 'He who tells me that there are *defects* in a new work, tells me nothing which I should not have taken for granted. . . But he who points out and elucidates the *beauties* of an original work, does indeed give me interesting information, such as experience would not have authorized me in anticipating.' Always he respects the work, according to his 'golden rule', *until you understand a writer's ignorance, presume yourself ignorant of his understanding*. By that same rule, he respects man; for to judge a man by his defects is to judge by what is accidental, not essential. For reasons of this kind, we must surely say that Coleridge was a good, as well as a great man.

Coleridge's poetry is, no less than his criticism, profoundly Platonic –as all great poetry must be; for his 'persons and characters supernatural' are no vulgar ghosts and phantoms, but archetypal figures from the depths of the mind itself, given 'a semblance of truth sufficient to procure for those shadows of imagination that willing suspension of disbelief for the moment, which constitutes poetic faith'. They are supernatural in the precise meaning of the word–they come from *above nature*, that is, from those regions of mind that find in merely natural forms the symbolic terms of an imaginative language: 'In looking at the objects of Nature while I am thinking, as at yonder moon dim-glimmering through the dewy window-pane, I seem rather to be seeking, as it were *asking* for, a symbolical language for something within me that already and forever exists, than observing anything new. Even when that latter is the case, yet still I have always a feeling as if that new phenomenon were the dim awakening of a forgotten or hidden truth of my inner nature.' For Coleridge, as for Plato, physical appearances are the shadows of ideas, projected upon the transient flux of nature, that Penelope's web that is forever woven and undone. Every landscape is, for him—even those described with a minuteness that recalls Wordsworth, or the drawings of Constable—a landscape of the mind.

Indeed Coleridge's debt to Plato and Plotinus cannot be exaggerated. If his philosophy was primarily that of Kant and Schelling, his poetry (the bulk of it written before he commenced his studies of German philosophy) is more purely Platonic. He platonized even in his dreams—if 'Kubla Khan' was entirely a dream; for the symbolism of the Neoplatonists is central to the poem. Nor is this surprising, for from his letters we know that Coleridge had been reading their works shortly before it was written. There is Plotinus' sea, or lake, of material existence, the 'non-entity' that is the term of a descending series of orders of being. This descent itself is symbolized by a river that, in the Orphic theology, issues from the night of the Unmanifest—(the same that in Cabbalistic writings flows from the *dark Aleph*) to the Stygian lake of matter:

> ... where waters white
> Burst from a fountain hid in depths of night,
> And thro' a dark and stony cavern glide,
> A cave profound, invisible ...

In tne mutable sea of material existence are reflected (according to the Platonic philosophers) the realities of the world of ideas.

> The shadow of the dome of pleasure
> Floated midway on the waves

is an image that must recall to any Platonist those shadows that, in Plato's famous fable, the prisoners saw cast upon the walls of the cave in which they were imprisoned, and mistook for realities; or, as Plotinus mythologizes the same concept (or conceptualizes the myth), the image that Narcissus saw in the flowing stream of Nature, and mistook for enduring reality. The symbol of a river flowing from a hidden and mysterious source is one to which Coleridge returns in his critical writings. The sense in which he uses it essentially is the same as 'Alph, the sacred river' of 'Kubla Khan'. *Knowing* and *being* he likens to two confluent streams that flow from the divine fountain of reason. The philospher is one who sails, 'still pushing upward and sounding as he goes, towards the common fountain head of both, the mysterious source whose being is knowledge, whose knowledge is being—the adorable I AM THAT I AM'. To realize the consistency alike of symbol and concept in Coleridge's most Sibylline poem and in his metaphysical writings is to understand both—for in his poems he was a philospher, and in his philosophy a poet.

Coleridge's symbolism is archetypal, drawn from the world of 'what eternally exists, really and unchangeably' within the human mind. His imagery, sensuous and minute, is nevertheless the vehicle of the faery-land of subjectivity. Typically, his landscapes are moonlit, or seen by the light of stars, or in the twilight, when objects perceived can most easily be detached from their utilitarian association, and become the figures of whatever dream the imagination may choose to elaborate—the eyes of hidden birds, the living mountains seen in the coals of a fire, glow-worms, the half-human voices of wind, cataract, or baying dog. In the same way, upon the fauna and flora of pre-Darwinian natural history, of unexplored oceans and new continents and tropical islands, as yet imperfectly charted by science, imagination may work its will, not by imprecision, but by the freedom of such images from common associations, or conformity with known general laws. What science has not yet made its own, may the more readily be interpreted according to those other laws that operate in the world of fancy.

There is no major poet who has not also been a man of the highest intelligence, and, in consequence, of wide knowledge beyond the frontiers of literature. Inspiration may fuse what is in the mind; but the more richly stored that mind may be, the more splendid the product of inspiration acting upon it. Coleridge was a man of vast erudition—'I have read almost everything,' so he wrote to a friend, when he was twenty-five, 'a library cormorant'. He continued to read everything, to the end of his life. Just how much went into the making of 'The Ancient Mariner', Professor Livingstone Lowes has shown in his remarkable study, *The Road to Xanadu*—and that study cannot, in its very nature, be complete. Poetry, the work of 'the *whole* man', can no more be created without wide knowledge and deep thought, than without profound feeling and senses alive to the minutest things.

Second only to his own poems is that part, imponderable, but very great, that he played in forming the genius of Wordsworth, and of proclaiming that genius to the world. Coleridge always deferred to Wordsworth as to one greater than himself; but he himself helped to create, or to evoke, that greatness. Had he not written one poem that, so long as the English language and the human imagination endure, can never lose its supernatural power, still he would remain the first of critics. His verdict upon himself, humble, yet just, must stand:

INTRODUCTION

I dare believe that in the mind of a competent Judge what I have per-
formed will excite more surprise than what I have omitted to do, or
failed in doing. . . By what I *have* effected, am I to be judged by my
fellow men; what I *could* have done is a question for my own con-
science.

KATHLEEN RAINE

CHRONOLOGY

1772 October 21. Samuel Taylor Coleridge born, tenth and youngest child of the vicar and schoolmaster of Ottery St Mary, Devonshire.

1782 July. Entered at Christ's Hospital, London, following the death of his father. He did not revisit home for eight years.

1791 October. Jesus College, Cambridge.

1793 December. Left Cambridge in a mood of despondency, and enlisted in the Light Dragoons under the same of Silas Tomkyns Comberbacke.

1794 April 10. Discharged, and returned to Cambridge.
Met Southey at Oxford.
December. Left Cambridge, without taking a degree.

1795 January. Lectures at Bristol. Southey and Coleridge occupied with the project of a Pantisocracy, an ideal community to consist of twelve young men and their wives, to be founded in the American colonies. The project was abandoned, and this led to a break with Southey.
October 4. Married Sara Fricker, sister of Southey's wife-to-be. This marriage was the unfortunate, and only, practical outcome of the Pantisocracy project. Coleridge and his wife moved to a cottage at Clevedon, Somerset.

1796 March–May. The *Watchman,* a periodical of democratic views, which failed after ten numbers.
September 19. Hartley Coleridge born.
December 31. Moved to Nether Stowey, to be near Coleridge's friend and patron, Thomas Poole.

1797 First met Dorothy and William Wordsworth, then living at Racedown, some forty miles from Nether Stowey. Coleridge stayed with the Wordsworths in June; in July they returned the visit, and in order to be near Coleridge moved into the large house of Alfoxden.
July 7. Charles Lamb an old school fellow visited Coleridge.
November 13. 'The Ancient Mariner' begun, on a walk with Dorothy and William Wordsworth.
First part of 'Christabel' completed.

1798 January. Thomas and Josiah Wedgwood offered Coleridge an annuity of one hundred and fifty pounds for life, which he accepted.
May 14. Birth of a second son, Berkeley, who died during Coleridge's absence in Germany.
'Kubla Khan'.
September (to July 1799) to Germany with the Wordsworths, there to study the language, and philosophy. Publication of the *Lyrical Ballads.*

1799 October. Visited the Wordsworths at Sockburn, County Durham, at the farm-house of the Hutchinson family. There Coleridge met Sara Hutchinson, sister of Wordsworth's wife-to-be, Mary. Sara was the *Astra* of Coleridge's poems, and his life-long love.

November. Took up work on the *Morning Post*, in London.

1800 July. Moved, with his family, to Greta Hall, Keswick.

September 14. Birth of Derwent Coleridge.

Second part of 'Christabel' completed.

1802 The Southeys, now reconciled, moved to Greta Hall to share the house with Coleridge and his family.

December 23. Birth of Sara Coleridge.

1803 Tour in Scotland, with William and Dorothy Wordsworth (described in Dorothy Wordsworth's *Journal*). Coleridge abandoned the tour, on account of ill-health. The habit of taking opium as a remedy for his many ailments was by now already a serious addiction.

1804 August. Returned to London.

December. Visited the Wordsworths at Coleorton, where Sara Hutchinson was also staying. With their encouragement, decided upon a separation from his wife.

1804–6 In Malta and the Mediterranean in an attempt to regain health. Secretary to Sir Robert Ball in Malta.

1806 Returned in no better health.

1808 January. First series of lectures at the Royal Institution.

September (to May 1810). Returned to the Lake District, to live with the Wordsworths at Grasmere.

1809 June (to March 1810). The *Friend*, which ran to twenty-seven numbers. Sara Hutchinson acted as Coleridge's amanuensis.

1810 March. Sara Hutchinson left the Wordsworths' household to live with a brother in Wales. After a few months at Greta Hall, Coleridge left the Lake District for ever, under the double grief of parting with Sara and a breach with Wordsworth, never entirely healed. His life thereafter was centred in London.

1811 November. Lectures to the London Philosophical Society.

1812 May. Lectures at Willis's Rooms.

November. Lectures at Surrey Institution.

1813 January 23. *Osorio*, a play projected many years earlier, and now revised under the title *Remorse*, ran for twenty nights at Drury Lane. (This was considered a successful run at that time.)

October (to April 1814). Lectures at Bristol.

1814 November. Living with the Morgans, at the village of Calne. Here he began work on his *Biographia Literaria*.

1816 April. Entered the household of James Gillman, a physician of Highgate, as a patient. In this kind refuge, Coleridge spent the last eighteen years of his life, with only a few breaks, in the company of friends who understood his condition.

1816 June. 'Christabel' and 'Kubla Khan' published.
1817 *Lay Sermons* and *Biographia Literaria*.
1818 December (to March 1819). Lectures on History of Philosophy, and on Shakespeare. From this time, Coleridge's interests shifted increasingly from poetry and politics, to 'theologico–metaphysical studies.
1825 *Aids to Reflection*.
1828 *Poetical Works*. A tour on the Continent with Wordsworth.
1830 *Church and State*.
1834 July 25. Died.

TEXTUAL NOTE
AND ACKNOWLEDGEMENTS

THE text of Coleridge's poems is from the edition of E. H. Coleridge, first published in 1912. *Anima Poetae,* a selection from the entries in Coleridge's notebooks, was also edited by E. H. Coleridge, in 1895. The *Notes and Lectures upon Shakespeare etc* were first edited and published by Coleridge's nephew and son-in-law, H. N. Coleridge, in Volumes i and ii of the *Literary Remains,* in 1836. In 1853 the poet's daughter, Mrs H. N. Coleridge, published a new and enlarged edition of the lectures and notes, and from this edition the present selection has been made. The Letters are from E. H. Coleridge's *Letters of Samuel Taylor Coleridge,* 1895, with the exception of a single extract (p. 132) which appears in Professor E. L. Griggs' *Unpublished Letters of Samuel Taylor Coleridge* (1932). For permission to make use of the single extract from the *Unpublished Letters,* my thanks are due to Professor Griggs, and to Mr A. H. B. Coleridge, on behalf of the Coleridge family, in whose possession remain the hitherto unpublished writings of Samuel Taylor Coleridge.

POETRY

SONNET

MILD Splendour of the various-vested Night!
   Mother of wildly-working visions! hail!
I watch thy gliding, while with watery light
   Thy weak eye glimmers through a fleecy veil;
And when thou lovest thy pale orb to shroud
   Behind the gather'd blackness lost on high;
And when thou dartest from the wind-rent cloud   5
   Thy placid lightning o'er the awaken'd sky.

Ah such is Hope! as changeful and as fair!
   Now dimly peering on the wistful sight;   10
Now hid behind the dragon-wing'd Despair:
   But soon emerging in her radiant might
She o'er the sorrow-clouded breast of Care
   Sails, like a meteor kindling in its flight.

1788

QUAE NOCENT DOCENT

[IN CHRIST'S HOSPITAL BOOK]

O! mihi praeteritos referat si Jupiter annos!

OH! might my ill-past hours return again!
No more, as then, should Sloth around me throw
   Her soul-enslaving, leaden chain!
No more the precious time would I employ
In giddy revels, or in thoughtless joy,   5
A present joy producing future woe.

But o'er the midnight Lamp I'd love to pore,
I'd seek with care fair Learning's depths to sound,
   And gather scientific Lore:
Or to mature the embryo thoughts inclin'd,   10
That half-conceiv'd lay struggling in my mind,
The cloisters' solitary gloom I'd round.

'Tis vain to wish, for Time has ta'en his flight –
For follies past be ceas'd the fruitless tears:

15   Let follies past to future care incite.
        Averse maturer judgements to obey
        Youth owns, with pleasure owns, the Passions' sway,
        But sage Experience only comes with years.

        1789 (First published in 1893)

SONNET

TO THE RIVER OTTER

DEAR native Brook! wild Streamlet of the West!
  How many various-fated years have past,
  What happy and what mournful hours, since last
I skimm'd the smooth thin stone along thy breast,
5 Numbering its light leaps! yet so deep imprest
Sink the sweet scenes of childhood, that mine eyes
  I never shut amid the sunny ray,
But straight with all their tints thy waters rise,
  Thy crossing plank, thy marge with willows grey,
10 And bedded sand that vein'd with various dyes
Gleam'd through thy bright transparence! On my way,
  Visions of Childhood! oft have ye beguil'd
Lone manhood's cares, yet waking fondest sighs:
  Ah! that once more I were a careless Child!

    ?1793

THE EOLIAN HARP

COMPOSED AT CLEVEDON, SOMERSETSHIRE

MY pensive Sara! thy soft cheek reclined·
Thus on mine arm, most soothing sweet it is
To sit beside our Cot, our Cot o'ergrown
With white-flower'd Jasmin, and the broad-leav'd Myrtle,
5 (Meet emblems they of Innocence and Love!)
And watch the clouds, that late were rich with light,
Slow saddening round, and mark the star of eve
Serenely brilliant (such should Wisdom be)
Shine opposite! How exquisite the scents
10 Snatch'd from yon bean-field! and the world *so* hush'd!

The stilly murmur of the distant Sea
Tells us of silence.

          And that simplest Lute,
Placed length-ways in the clasping casement, hark!
How by the desultory breeze caress'd,
Like some coy maid half yielding to her lover,   15
It pours such sweet upbraiding, as must needs
Tempt to repeat the wrong! And now, its strings
Boldlier swept, the long sequacious notes
Over delicious surges sink and rise,
Such a soft floating witchery of sound   20
As twilight Elfins make, when they at eve
Voyage on gentle gales from Fairy-Land,
Where Melodies round honey-dropping flowers,
Footless and wild, like birds of Paradise,
Nor pause, nor perch, hovering on untam'd wing!   25
O! the one Life within us and abroad,
Which meets all motion and becomes its soul,
A light in sound, a sound-like power in light,
Rhythm in all thought, and joyance every where –
Methinks, it should have been impossible   30
Not to love all things in a world so fill'd;
Where the breeze warbles, and the mute still air
Is Music slumbering on her instrument.

    And thus, my Love! as on the midway slope
Of yonder hill I stretch my limbs at noon,   35
Whilst through my half-clos'd eye-lids I behold
The sunbeams dance, like diamonds, on the main,
And tranquil muse upon tranquillity;
Full many a thought uncall'd and undetain'd,
And many idle flitting phantasies,   40
Traverse my indolent and passive brain,
As wild and various as the random gales
That swell and flutter on this subject Lute!
    And what if all of animated nature
Be but organic Harps diversely fram'd,   45
That tremble into thought, as o'er them sweeps
Plastic and vast, one intellectual breeze
At once the Soul of each, and God of all?
    But thy more serious eye a mild reproof

50 Darts, O belovéd Woman! nor such thoughts
     Dim and unhallow'd dost thou not reject
     And biddest me walk humbly with my God.
     Meek Daughter in the family of Christ!
     Well hast thou said and holily disprais'd
55 These shapings of the unregenerate mind;
     Bubbles that glitter as they rise and break
     On vain Philosophy's aye-babbling spring.
     For never guiltless may I speak of him,
     The Incomprehensible! save when with awe
60 I praise him, and with Faith that inly *feels*;
     Who with his saving mercies healéd me,
     A sinful and most miserable man,
     Wilder'd and dark, and gave me to possess
     Peace, and this Cot, and thee, heart-honour'd Maid!

     1795

REFLECTIONS ON HAVING LEFT A
PLACE OF RETIREMENT

Sermoni propriora. – HORACE

     Low was our pretty Cot: our tallest Rose
     Peep'd at the chamber-window. We could hear
     At silent noon, and eve, and early morn,
     The Sea's faint murmur. In the open air
5   Our Myrtles blossom'd; and across the porch
     Thick Jasmins twined: the little landscape round
     Was green and woody, and refresh'd the eye.
     It was a spot which you might aptly call
     The Valley of Seclusion! Once I saw
10   (Hallowing his Sabbath-day by quietness)
     A wealthy son of Commerce saunter by,
     Bristowa's citizen; methought, it calm'd
     His thirst of idle gold, and made him muse
     With wiser feelings: for he paus'd, and look'd
15   With a pleas'd sadness, and gaz'd all around,
     Then eyed our Cottage, and gaz'd round again,
     And sigh'd, and said, it was a Blesséd Place.
     And we *were* bless'd. Oft with patient ear

Long-listening to the viewless sky-lark's note
(Viewless, or haply for a moment seen   20
Gleaming on sunny wings) in whisper'd tones
I've said to my Belovéd, 'Such, sweet Girl!
The inobtrusive song of Happiness,
Unearthly minstrelsy! then only heard
When the Soul seeks to hear; when all is hush'd,   25
And the Heart listens!'

                         But the time, when first
From that low Dell, steep up the stony Mount
I climb'd with perilous toil and reach'd the top,
Oh! what a goodly scene! *Here* the bleak mount,
The bare bleak mountain speckled thin with sheep;   30
Grey clouds, that shadowing spot the sunny fields;
And river, now with bushy rocks o'er-brow'd,
Now winding bright and full, with naked banks;
And seats, and lawns, the Abbey and the wood,
And cots, and hamlets, and faint city-spire;   35
The Channel *there*, the Islands and white sails,
Dim coasts, and cloud-like hills, and shoreless Ocean –
It seem'd like Omnipresence! God, methought,
Had built him there a Temple: the whole World
Seem'd *imag'd* in its vast circumference: 40
No *wish* profan'd my overwhelméd heart.
Blest hour! It was a luxury, – to be!

   Ah! quiet Dell! dear Cot, and Mount sublime!
I was constrain'd to quit you. Was it right,
While my unnumber'd brethren toil'd and bled,   45
That I should dream away the entrusted hours
On rose-leaf beds, pampering the coward heart
With feelings all too delicate for use?
Sweet is the tear that from some Howard's eye
Drops on the cheek of one he lifts from earth: 50
And he that works me good with unmov'd face,
Does it but half: he chills me while he aids,
My benefactor, not my brother man!
Yet even this, this cold beneficence
Praise, praise it, O my Soul! oft as thou scann'st   55
The sluggard Pity's vision-weaving tribe!
Who sigh for Wretchedness, yet shun the Wretched,

Nursing in some delicious solitude
Their slothful loves and dainty sympathies!
60   I therefore go, and join head, heart, and hand,
Active and firm, to fight the bloodless fight
Of Science, Freedom, and the Truth in Christ.

Yet oft when after honourable toil
Rests the tir'd mind, and waking loves to dream,
65   My spirit shall revisit thee, dear Cot!
Thy Jasmin and thy window-peeping Rose,
And Myrtles fearless of the mild sea-air.
And I shall sigh fond wishes – sweet Abode!
Ah! – had none greater! And that all had such!
70   It might be so – but the time is not yet.
Speed it, O Father! Let thy Kingdom come!

1795

TO A YOUNG FRIEND

ON HIS PROPOSING TO DOMESTICATE WITH THE AUTHOR
Composed in 1796

A MOUNT, not wearisome and bare and steep,
   But a green mountain variously up-piled,
Where o'er the jutting rocks soft mosses creep,
Or colour'd lichens with slow oozing weep;
5   Where cypress and the darker yew start wild;
And, 'mid the summer torrent's gentle dash
Dance brighten'd the red clusters of the ash;
   Beneath whose boughs, by those still sounds beguil'd,
Calm Pensiveness might muse herself to sleep;
10   Till haply startled by some fleecy dam.
That rustling on the bushy cliff above
With melancholy bleat of anxious love,
   Made meek enquiry for her wandering lamb:
   Such a green mountain 'twere most sweet to climb,
15   E'en while the bosom ach'd with loneliness –
How more than sweet, if some dear friend should bless
   The adventurous toil, and up the path sublime
Now lead, now follow: the glad landscape round,
Wide and more wide, increasing without bound!

O then 'twere loveliest sympathy, to mark   20
The berries of the half-uprooted ash
Dripping and bright; and list the torrent's dash, –
   Beneath the cypress, or the yew more dark,
Seated at ease, on some smooth mossy rock;
In social silence now, and now to unlock   25
The treasur'd heart; arm linked in friendly arm,
Save if the one, his muse's witching charm
Muttering brow-bent, at unwatch'd distance lag;
   Till high o'er head his beckoning friend appears,
And from the forehead of the topmost crag   30
   Shouts eagerly: for haply *there* uprears
That shadowing Pine its old romantic limbs,
   Which latest shall detain the enamour'd sight
Seen from below, when eve the valley dims,
   Tinged yellow with the rich departing light;   35
   And haply, bason'd in some unsunn'd cleft,
A beauteous spring, the rock's collected tears,
Sleeps shelter'd there, scarce wrinkled by the gale!
   Together thus, the world's vain turmoil left,
Stretch'd on the crag, and shadow'd by the pine,   40
   And bending o'er the clear delicious fount,
Ah! dearest youth! it were a lot divine
To cheat our noons in moralising mood,
While west-winds fann'd our temples toil-bedew'd:
   Then downwards slope, oft pausing, from the mount,   45
To some lone mansion, in some woody dale,
Where smiling with blue eye, Domestic Bliss
Gives *this* the Husband's, *that* the Brother's kiss!

Thus rudely vers'd in allegoric lore,
The Hill of Knowledge I essayed to trace;   50
That verdurous hill with many a resting-place,
And many a stream, whose warbling waters pour
   To glad, and fertilise the subject plains;
That hill with secret springs, and nooks untrod,
And many a fancy-blest and holy sod   55
   Where Inspiration, his diviner strains
Low-murmuring, lay; and starting from the rock's
Stiff evergreens, (whose spreading foliage mocks
Want's barren soil, and the bleak frosts of age,

60 And Bigotry's mad fire-invoking rage!)
    O meek retiring spirit! we will climb,
    Cheering and cheered, this lovely hill sublime;
        And from the stirring world up-lifted high
        (Whose noises, faintly wafted on the wind,
65 To quiet musings shall attune the mind,
        And oft the melancholy *theme* supply),
        There, while the prospect through the gazing eye
        Pours all its healthful greenness on the soul,
    We'll smile at wealth, and learn to smile at fame,
70 Our hopes, our knowledge, and our joys the same,
        As neighbouring fountains image each the whole:
    Then when the mind hath drunk its fill of truth
        We'll discipline the heart to pure delight,
    Rekindling sober joy's domestic flame.
75 They whom I love shall love thee, honour'd youth!
        Now may Heaven realise this vision bright!

    1796

THIS LIME-TREE BOWER MY PRISON

[ADDRESSED TO CHARLES LAMB, OF THE INDIA HOUSE, LONDON]

In the June of 1797 some long-expected friends paid a visit to the
author's cottage; and on the morning of their arrival, he met with an
accident, which disabled him from walking during the whole time of
their stay. One evening, when they had left him for a few hours, he
composed the following lines in the garden-bower.

        WELL, they are gone, and here must I remain,
        This lime-tree bower my prison! I have lost
        Beauties and feelings, such as would have been
        Most sweet to my remembrance even when age
5   Had dimm'd mine eyes to blindness! They, meanwhile,
        Friends, whom I never more may meet again,
        On springy heath, along the hill-top edge
        Wander in gladness, and wind down, perchance,
        To that still roaring dell, of which I told;
10   The roaring dell, o'erwooded, narrow, deep,
        And only speckled by the mid-day sun;
        Where its slim trunk the ash from rock to rock
        Flings arching like a bridge; – that branchless ash,

Unsunn'd and damp, whose few poor yellow leaves
Ne'er tremble in the gale, yet tremble still,   15
Fann'd by the water-fall! and there my friends
Behold the dark green file of long lank weeds,
That all at once (a most fantastic sight!)
Still nod and drip beneath the dripping edge
Of the blue clay-stone.

                   Now, my friends emerge   20
Beneath the wide wide Heaven – and view again
The many-steepled tract magnificent
Of hilly fields and meadows, and the sea,
With some fair bark, perhaps, whose sails light up
The slip of smooth clear blue betwixt two Isles   25
Of purple shadow! Yes! they wander on
In gladness all; but thou, methinks, most glad,
My gentle-hearted Charles! for thou hast pined
And hunger'd after Nature, many a year,
In the great City pent, winning thy way   30
With sad yet patient soul, through evil and pain
And strange calamity! Ah! slowly sink
Behind the western ridge, thou glorious Sun!
Shine in the slant beams of the sinking orb,
Ye purple heath-flowers! richlier burn, ye clouds!   35
Live in the yellow light, ye distant groves!
And kindle, thou blue Ocean! So my friend
Struck with deep joy may stand, as I have stood,
Silent with swimming sense; yea, gazing round
On the wide landscape, gaze till all doth seem   40
Less gross than bodily; and of such hues
As veil the Almighty Spirit, when yet he makes
Spirits perceive his presence.

                  A delight
Comes sudden on my heart, and I am glad
As I myself were there! Nor in this bower,   45
This little lime-tree bower, have I not mark'd
Much that has sooth'd me. Pale beneath the blaze
Hung the transparent foliage; and I watch'd
Some broad and sunny leaf, and lov'd to see
The shadow of the leaf and stem above   50
Dappling its sunshine! And that walnut-tree

Was richly ting'd, and a deep radiance lay
Full on the ancient ivy, which usurps
Those fronting elms, and now, with blackest mass
55   Makes their dark branches gleam a lighter hue
Through the late twilight: and though now the bat
Wheels silent by, and not a swallow twitters,
Yet still the solitary humble-bee
Sings in the bean-flower! Henceforth I shall know
60   That Nature ne'er deserts the wise and pure;
No plot so narrow, be but Nature there,
No waste so vacant, but may well employ
Each faculty of sense, and keep the heart
Awake to Love and Beauty! and sometimes
65   'Tis well to be bereft of promis'd good,
That we may lift the soul, and contemplate
With lively joy the joys we cannot share.
My gentle-hearted Charles! when the last rook
Beat its straight path along the dusky air
70   Homewards, I blest it! deeming its black wing
(Now a dim speck, now vanishing in light)
Had cross'd the mighty Orb's dilated glory,
While thou stood'st gazing; or, when all was still,
Flew creeking o'er thy head, and had a charm
75   For thee, my gentle-hearted Charles, to whom
No sound is dissonant which tells of Life.

1797

THE DUNGEON

[From *Osorio*, Act V; and *Remorse*, Act V, Scene 1. The
title and text are here printed from *Lyrical Ballads*, 1798.]

AND this place our forefathers made for man!
This is the process of our love and wisdom,
To each poor brother who offends against us –
Most innocent, perhaps – and what if guilty?
5   Is this the only cure? Merciful God!
Each pore and natural outlet shrivell'd up
By Ignorance and parching Poverty,
His energies roll back upon his heart,
And stagnate and corrupt; till chang'd to poison,

They break out on him, like a loathsome plague-spot; 10
Then we call in our pamper'd mountebanks –
And this is their best cure! uncomforted
And friendless solitude, groaning and tears,
And savage faces, at the clanking hour,
Seen through the steams and vapour of his dungeon, 15
By the lamp's dismal twilight! So he lies
Circled with evil, till his very soul
Unmoulds its essence, hopelessly deform'd
By sights of ever more deformity!

With other ministrations thou, O Nature! 20
Healest thy wandering and distemper'd child:
Thou pourest on him thy soft influences,
Thy sunny hues, fair forms, and breathing sweets,
Thy melodies of woods, and winds, and waters,
Till he relent, and can no more endure 25
To be a jarring and a dissonant thing,
Amid this general dance and minstrelsy;
But, bursting into tears, wins back his way,
His angry spirit heal'd and harmoniz'd
By the benignant touch of Love and Beauty. 30

1797

THE RIME OF THE ANCIENT MARINER

IN SEVEN PARTS

Facile credo, plures esse Naturas invisibiles quam visibiles in rerum universitate. Sed horum omnium familiam quis nobis enarrabit? et gradus et cognationes et discrimina et singulorum munera? Quid agunt? quae loca habitant? Harum rerum notitiam semper ambivit ingenium humanum, nunquam attigit. Juvat, interea, non diffiteor, quandoque in animo, tanquam in tabula, majoris et melioris mundi imaginem contemplari: ne mens assuefacta hodiernae vitae minutiis se contrahat nimis, et tota subsidat in pusillas cogitationes. Sed veritati interea invigilandum est, modusque servandus, ut certa ab incertis, diem a nocte, distinguamus. – T. BURNET, *Archaeol. Phil.*, p. 68.

(I can well believe that there are more invisible than visible natures in the universe. But who shall describe their family? Who set forth the orders, kinships, respective stations, and functions of each? What do they do? Where is their habitation? The human mind has always sought after, but never attained, knowledge of these things. Meanwhile it is desirable, I grant, to contemplate in thought, as if in a picture, an image of a greater and better world; lest the mind, accustoming itself to the minutiae of daily life, should become too narrow, and lapse into mean thoughts. But at the same time we must be vigilant for truth, and set a limit, lest we fail to distinguish certain from uncertain, day from night.)

ARGUMENT

How a Ship having passed the Line was driven by storms to the cold Country towards the South Pole; and how from thence she made her course to the tropical Latitude of the Great Pacific Ocean; and of the strange things that befell; and in what manner the Ancyent Marinere came back to his own Country.

PART I

An ancient Mariner meeteth three Gallants bidden to a wedding-feast, and detaineth one.	It is an ancient Mariner, And he stoppeth one of three. 'By thy long grey beard and glittering eye, Now wherefore stopp'st thou me?

5

The Bridegroom's doors are opened wide,
And I am next of kin;
The guests are met, the feast is set:
May'st hear the merry din.'

The Wedding Guest is spell-bound by the eye of the old seafaring man, and constrained to hear his tale.

He holds him with his skinny hand,
'There was a ship,' quoth he.   10
'Hold off! unhand me, grey-beard loon!'
Eftsoons his hand dropt he.

He holds him with his glittering eye –
The Wedding-Guest stood still,
And listens like a three years' child: 15
The Mariner hath his will.

The Wedding-Guest sat on a stone:
He cannot choose but hear;
And thus spake on that ancient man,
The bright-eyed Mariner.   20

The Mariner tells how the ship sailed southward with a good

'The ship was cheered, the harbour cleared,
Merrily did we drop
Below the kirk, below the hill,
Below the lighthouse top.

wind and fair
weather, till it
reached the
line.

The Sun came up upon the left,　　　　　　25
Out of the sea came he!
And he shone bright, and on the right
Went down into the sea.

Higher and higher every day,
Till over the mast at noon –'　　　　　　30
The Wedding-Guest here beat his breast,
For he heard the loud bassoon.

The Wedding-
Guest heareth
the bridal
music; but
the Mariner
continueth
his tale.

The bride hath paced into the hall,
Red as a rose is she;
Nodding their heads before her goes　　　35
The merry minstrelsy.

The Wedding-Guest he beat his breast,
Yet he cannot choose but hear;
And thus spake on that ancient man,
The bright-eyed Mariner.　　　　　　40

The ship
driven by a
storm toward
the south pole.

'And now the STORM-BLAST came, and he
Was tyrannous and strong:
He struck with his o'ertaking wings,
And chased us south along.

With sloping masts and dipping prow,　　45
As who pursued with yell and blow
Still treads the shadow of his foe,
And forward bends his head,
The ship drove fast, loud roared the blast,
And southward aye we fled.　　　　　　50

And now there came both mist and snow,
And it grew wondrous cold:
And ice, mast-high, came floating by,
As green as emerald.

The land of
ice, and of
fearful sounds
where no
living thing
was to be seen.

And through the drifts the snowy clifts　55
Did send a dismal sheen:
Nor shapes of men nor beasts we ken –
The ice was all between.

The ice was here, the ice was there,
The ice was all around:　　　　　　　60

It cracked and growled, and roared and howled,
Like noises in a swound!

Till a great
sea-bird,
called the
Albatross,
came through
the snow-fog,
and was
received with
great joy and
hospitality.

At length did cross an Albatross,
Thorough the fog it came;
As if it had been a Christian soul,
We nailed it in God's name.   65

It ate the food it ne'er had eat,
And round and round it flew.
The ice did split with a thunder-fit;
The helmsman steered us through!   70

And lo! the
Albatross
proveth a bird
of good omen,
and followeth
the ship as it
returned
northward
through fog
and floating
ice.

And a good south wind sprung up behind;
The Albatross did follow,
And every day, for food or play,
Came to the mariner's hollo!

In mist or cloud, on mast or shroud,   75
It perched for vespers nine;
Whiles all the night, through fog-smoke white,
Glimmered the white Moon-shine.'

The ancient
Mariner
inhospitably
killeth the
pious bird of
good omen.

'God save thee, ancient Mariner!
From the fiends, that plague thee thus! –   80
Why look'st thou so?' – With my cross-bow
I shot the ALBATROSS.

PART II

The Sun now rose upon the right:
Out of the sea came he,
Still hid in mist, and on the left   85
Went down into the sea.

And the good south wind still blew behind,
But no sweet bird did follow,
Nor any day for food or play
Came to the mariners' hollo!   90

His shipmates
cry out against
the ancient
Mariner, for
killing the

And I had done a hellish thing,
And it would work 'em woe:
For all averred, I had killed the bird
That made the breeze to blow.

bird of good luck.

Ah wretch! said they, the bird to slay, 95
That made the breeze to blow!

But when the fog cleared off, they justify the same, and thus make themselves accomplices in the crime.

Nor dim nor red, like God's own head,
The glorious Sun uprist:
Then all averred, I had killed the bird
That brought the fog and mist. 100
'Twas right, said they, such birds to slay,
That bring the fog and mist.

The fair breeze continues; the ship enters the Pacific Ocean, and sails northward, even till it reaches the Line.

The fair breeze blew, the white foam flew,
The furrow followed free;
We were the first that ever burst 105
Into that silent sea.

Down dropt the breeze, the sails dropt down,
'Twas sad as sad could be;
And we did speak only to break

The ship hath been suddenly becalmed.

The silence of the sea! 110

All in a hot and copper sky,
The bloody Sun, at noon,
Right up above the mast did stand,
No bigger than the Moon.

Day after day, day after day, 115
We stuck, nor breath nor motion;
As idle as a painted ship
Upon a painted ocean.

And the Albatross begins to be avenged.

Water, water, every where,
And all the boards did shrink; 120
Water, water, every where,
Nor any drop to drink.

The very deep did rot: O Christ!
That ever this should be!
Yea, slimy things did crawl with legs 125
Upon the slimy sea.

About, about, in reel and rout
The death-fires danced at night;
The water, like a witch's oils,
Burnt green, and blue and white. 130

A Spirit had followed them; one of the invisible inhabitants of this planet,

And some in dreams assuréd were
Of the Spirit that plagued us so;
Nine fathom deep he had followed us
From the land of mist and snow.

neither departed souls nor angels; concerning whom the learned Jew, Josephus, and the Platonic Constantinopolitan, Michael Psellus, may be consulted. They are very numerous, and there is no climate or element without one or more.

And every tongue, through utter drought,   135
Was withered at the root;
We could not speak, no more than if
We had been choked with soot.

The shipmates, in their sore distress, would fain throw the whole guilt on the ancient

Ah! well a-day! what evil looks
Had I from old and young!   140
Instead of the cross, the Albatross
About my neck was hung.

Mariner: in sign whereof they hang the dead sea-bird round his neck.

PART III

There passed a weary time. Each throat
Was parched, and glazed each eye.
A weary time! a weary time!   145
How glazed each weary eye,

The ancient Mariner beholdeth a sign in the element afar off.

When looking westward, I beheld
A something in the sky.

At first it seemed a little speck,
And then it seemed a mist;   150
It moved and moved, and took at last
A certain shape, I wist.

A speck, a mist, a shape, I wist!
And still it neared and neared:
As if it dodged a water-sprite,   155
It plunged and tacked and veered.

At its nearer approach, it seemeth him to be a ship; and at a dear ransom he freeth his speech from

With throats unslaked, with black lips baked,
We could nor laugh nor wail;
Through utter drought all dumb we stood!
I bit my arm, I sucked the blood,   160
And cried, A sail! a sail!

the bonds of thirst.	With throats unslaked, with black lips baked, Agape they heard me call:	
A flash of joy;	Gramercy! they for joy did grin, And all at once their breath drew in, As they were drinking all.	165

With throats unslaked, with black lips baked,
Agape they heard me call:
Gramercy! they for joy did grin,
And all at once their breath drew in,
As they were drinking all.

See! see! (I cried) she tacks no more!
Hither to work us weal;
Without a breeze, without a tide,
She steadies with upright keel!

The western wave was all a-flame.
The day was well nigh done!
Almost upon the western wave
Rested the broad bright Sun;
When that strange shape drove suddenly
Betwixt us and the Sun.

And straight the Sun was flecked with bars,
(Heaven's Mother send us grace!)
As if through a dungeon-grate he peered
With broad and burning face.

Alas! (thought I, and my heart beat loud)
How fast she nears and nears!
Are those *her* sails that glance in the Sun,
Like restless gossameres?

Are those *her* ribs through which the Sun
Did peer, as through a grate?
And is that Woman all her crew?
Is that a DEATH? and are there two?
Is DEATH that woman's mate?

Her lips were red, *her* looks were free,
Her locks were yellow as gold:
Her skin was as white as leprosy,
The Night-mare LIFE-IN-DEATH was she,
Who thicks man's blood with cold.

The naked hulk alongside came,
And the twain were casting dice;
'The game is done! I've won! I've won!'
Quoth she, and whistles thrice.

the bonds of thirst.

A flash of joy;

And horror follows. For can it be a ship that comes onward without wind or tide?

It seemeth him but the skeleton of a ship.

And its ribs are seen as bars on the face of the setting Sun. The Spectre-Woman and her Death-mate, and no other on board the skeleton ship.

Like vessel, like crew! Death and Life-in-Death have diced for the ship's crew, and she (the latter) winneth the ancient Mariner.

No twilight
within the
courts of the
Sun.

The Sun's rim dips; the stars rush out:
At one stride comes the dark;   200
With far-heard whisper, o'er the sea,
Off shot the spectre-bark.

At the rising
of the Moon,

We listened and looked sideways up!
Fear at my heart, as at a cup,
My life-blood seemed to sip!   205
The stars were dim, and thick the night,
The steersman's face by his lamp gleamed white;
From the sails the dew did drip –
Till clomb above the eastern bar
The hornéd Moon, with one bright star   210
Within the nether tip.

One after
another,

One after one, by the star-dogged Moon,
Too quick for groan or sigh,
Each turned his face with a ghastly pang,
And cursed me with his eye.   215

His shipmates
drop down
dead.

Four times fifty living men,
(And I heard nor sigh nor groan)
With heavy thump, a lifeless lump,
They dropped down one by one.

But Life-in-
Death begins
her work on
the ancient
Mariner.

The souls did from their bodies fly, –   220
They fled to bliss or woe!
And every soul, it passed me by,
Like the whizz of my cross-bow!

PART IV

The Wedding-
Guest feareth
that a Spirit
is talking to
him;

'I fear thee, ancient Mariner!
I fear thy skinny hand!   225
And thou art long, and lank, and brown,
As is the ribbed sea-sand.

But the
ancient Ma-
riner assureth
him of his
bodily life, and
proceedeth to

I fear thee and thy glittering eye,
And thy skinny hand, so brown.' –
Fear not, fear not, thou Wedding-Guest!   230
This body dropt not down.

Alone, alone, all, all alone,
Alone on a wide wide sea!

relate his hor-
rible penance.

And never a saint took pity on
My soul in agony.

He despiseth
the creatures
of the calm,

The many men, so beautiful!
And they all dead did lie:
And a thousand thousand slimy things
Lived on; and so did I.

And envieth
that *they*
should live,
and so many
lie dead.

I looked upon the rotting sea,
And drew my eyes away;
I looked upon the rotting deck,
And there the dead men lay.

I looked to heaven, and tried to pray;
But or ever a prayer had gusht,
A wicked whisper came, and made
My heart as dry as dust.

I closed my lids, and kept them close,
And the balls like pulses beat;
For the sky and the sea, and the sea and the sky
Lay like a load on my weary eye,
And the dead were at my feet.

But the curse
liveth for him
in the eye of
the dead men.

The cold sweat melted from their limbs,
Nor rot nor reek did they:
The look with which they looked on me
Had never passed away.

An orphan's curse would drag to hell
A spirit from on high;
But oh! more horrible than that
Is the curse in a dead man's eye!
Seven days, seven nights, I saw that curse,
And yet I could not die.

In his lone-
liness and
fixedness he
yearneth to-
wards the
journeying
Moon, and the
stars that still
sojourn, yet
still move
onward; and

The moving Moon went up the sky,
And no where did abide:
Softly she was going up,
And a star or two beside –

Her beams bemocked the sultry main,
Like April hoar-frost spread;
But where the ship's huge shadow lay,

235

240

245

250

255

260

265

every where
the blue sky
belongs to

The charméd water burnt alway   270
A still and awful red.

them, and is their appointed rest, and their native country and their own
natural homes, which they enter unannounced, as lords that are certainly ex-
pected and yet there is a silent joy at their arrival.

By the light
of the Moon he
beholdeth
God's crea-
tures of the
great calm.

Beyond the shadow of the ship,
I watched the water-snakes:
They moved in tracks of shining white,
And when they reared, the elfish light   275
Fell off in hoary flakes.

Within the shadow of the ship
I watched their rich attire:
Blue, glossy green, and velvet black,   280
They coiled and swam; and every track
Was a flash of golden fire.

Their beauty
and their
happiness.

He blesseth
them in his
heart.

O happy living things! no tongue
Their beauty might declare:
A spring of love gushed from my heart,
And I blessed them unaware: 285
Sure my kind saint took pity on me,
And I blessed them unaware.

The spell
begins to
break.

The self-same moment I could pray;
And from my neck so free
The Albatross fell off, and sank   290
Like lead into the sea.

PART V

Oh sleep! it is a gentle thing,
Beloved from pole to pole!
To Mary Queen the praise be given!
She sent the gentle sleep from Heaven,   295
That slid into my soul.

By grace of
the holy
Mother, the
ancient
Mariner is
refreshed with
rain.

The silly buckets on the deck,
That had so long remained,
I dreamt that they were filled with dew;
And when I awoke, it rained.   300

My lips were wet, my throat was cold,
My garments all were dank;

Sure I had drunken in my dreams,
And still my body drank.

I moved, and could not feel my limbs: 305
I was so light – almost
I thought that I had died in sleep,
And was a blessèd ghost.

He heareth
sounds and
seeth strange
sights and
commotions in
the sky and
the element.

And soon I heard a roaring wind:
It did not come anear;   310
But with its sound it shook the sails,
That were so thin and sere.

The upper air burst into life!
And a hundred fire-flags sheen,
To and fro they were hurried about!   315
And to and fro, and in and out,
The wan stars danced between.

And the coming wind did roar more loud,
And the sails did sigh like sedge;
And the rain poured down from one black cloud; 320
The Moon was at its edge.

The thick black cloud was cleft, and still
The Moon was at its side:
Like waters shot from some high crag,
The lightning fell with never a jag,   325
A river steep and wide.

The bodies of
the ship's crew
are inspirited,
and the ship
moves on;

The loud wind never reached the ship,
Yet now the ship moved on!
Beneath the lightning and the Moon
The dead men gave a groan.   330

They groaned, they stirred, they all uprose,
Nor spake, nor moved their eyes;
It had been strange, even in a dream,
To have seen those dead men rise.

The helmsman steered, the ship moved on;   335
Yet never a breeze up-blew;
The mariners all 'gan work the ropes,
Where they were wont to do;

They raised their limbs like lifeless tools –
We were a ghastly crew.   340

The body of my brother's son
Stood by me, knee to knee:
The body and I pulled at one rope,
But he said nought to me.

'I fear thee, ancient Mariner!'   345
Be calm, thou Wedding-Guest!
'Twas not those souls that fled in pain,
Which to their corses came again,
But a troop of spirits blest:

For when it dawned – they dropped their arms,   350
And clustered round the mast;
Sweet sounds rose slowly through their mouths,
And from their bodies passed.

Around, around, flew each sweet sound,
Then darted to the Sun;   355
Slowly the sounds came back again,
Now mixed, now one by one.

Sometimes a-dropping from the sky
I heard the sky-lark sing;
Sometimes all little birds that are,   360
How they seemed to fill the sea and air
With their sweet jargoning!

And now 'twas like all instruments,
Now like a lonely flute;
And now it is an angel's song,   365
That makes the heavens be mute.

It ceased; yet still the sails made on
A pleasant noise till noon,
A noise like of a hidden brook
In the leafy month of June,   370
That to the sleeping woods all night
Singeth a quiet tune.

Till noon we quietly sailed on,
Yet never a breeze did breathe:

Marginal gloss: But not by the souls of the men, nor by daemons of earth or middle air, but by a blessed troop of angelic spirits, sent down by the invocation of the guardian saint.

48

Slowly and smoothly went the ship,   375
Moved onward from beneath.

The lonesome Spirit from the south-pole carries on the ship as far as the Line, in obedience to the angelic troop, but still requireth vengeance.

Under the keel nine fathom deep,
From the land of mist and snow,
The spirit slid: and it was he
That made the ship to go.   380
The sails at noon left off their tune,
And the ship stood still also.

The Sun, right up above the mast,
Had fixed her to the ocean:
But in a minute she 'gan stir,   385
With a short uneasy motion –
Backwards and forwards half her length
With a short uneasy motion.

Then like a pawing horse let go,
She made a sudden bound: 390
It flung the blood into my head,
And I fell down in a swound.

The Polar Spirit's fellow-daemons, the invisible inhabitants of the element, take part in his wrong; and two of them relate, one to the other, that penance long and heavy for the ancient Mariner hath been accorded to the Polar Spirit, who returneth southward.

How long in that same fit I lay,
I have not to declare;
But ere my living life returned,   395
I heard and in my soul discerned
Two voices in the air.

'Is it he?' quoth one, 'Is this the man?
By him who died on cross,
With his cruel bow he laid full low   400
The harmless Albatross.

The spirit who bideth by himself
In the land of mist and snow,
He loved the bird that loved the man
Who shot him with his bow.'   405

The other was a softer voice,
As soft as honey-dew:
Quoth he, 'The man hath penance done,
And penance more will do.'

PART VI

First Voice

'But tell me, tell me! speak again,   410
Thy soft response renewing –
What makes that ship drive on so fast?
What is the ocean doing?'

Second Voice

'Still as a slave before his lord,
The ocean hath no blast;   415
His great bright eye most silently
Up to the Moon is cast –

If he may know which way to go;
For she guides him smooth or grim.
See, brother, see! how graciously   420
She looketh down on him.'

First Voice

The Mariner hath been cast into a trance; for the angelic power causeth the vessel to drive northward faster than human life could endure.

'But why drives on that ship so fast,
Without or wave or wind?'

Second Voice

'The air is cut away before,
And closes from behind.   425

Fly, brother, fly! more high, more high!
Or we shall be belated:
For slow and slow that ship will go,
When the Mariner's trance is abated.'

The supernatural motion is retarded; the Mariner awakes, and his penance begins anew.

I woke, and we were sailing on   430
As in a gentle weather:
'Twas night, calm night, the moon was high;
The dead men stood together.

All stood together on the deck,
For a charnel-dungeon fitter: 435
All fixed on me their stony eyes,
That in the Moon did glitter.

The pang, the curse, with which they died,
Had never passed away:

I could not draw my eyes from theirs,   440
Nor turn them up to pray.

The curse is
finally ex-
piated.
And now this spell was snapt: once more
I viewed the ocean green,
And looked far forth, yet little saw
Of what had else been seen –   445

Like one, that on a lonesome road
Doth walk in fear and dread,
And having once turned round walks on,
And turns no more his head;
Because he knows, a frightful fiend   450
Doth close behind him tread.

But soon there breathed a wind on me,
Nor sound nor motion made:
Its path was not upon the sea,
In ripple or in shade.   455

It raised my hair, it fanned my cheek
Like a meadow-gale of spring –
It mingled strangely with my fears,
Yet it felt like a welcoming.

Swiftly, swiftly flew the ship,   460
Yet she sailed softly too:
Sweetly, sweetly blew the breeze –
On me alone it blew.

And the
ancient
Mariner be-
holdeth his
native
country.
Oh! dream of joy! is this indeed
The light-house top I see?   465
Is this the hill? is this the kirk?
Is this mine own countree?

We drifted o'er the harbour-bar,
And I with sobs did pray –
O let me be awake, my God!   470
Or let me sleep alway.

The harbour-bar was clear as glass,
So smoothly it was strewn!
And on the bay the moonlight lay,
And the shadow of the Moon.   475

The rock shone bright, the kirk no less,
That stands above the rock:
The moonlight steeped in silentness
The steady weathercock.

And the bay was white with silent light,   480
Till rising from the same,
Full many shapes, that shadows were,
In crimson colours came.

The angelic
spirits leave
the dead
bodies,
And appear in
their own
forms of light.

A little distance from the prow
Those crimson shadows were: 485
I turned my eyes upon the deck –
Oh, Christ! what saw I there!

Each corse lay flat, lifeless and flat,
And, by the holy rood!
A man all light, a seraph-man,   490
On every corse there stood.

This seraph-band, each waved his hand:
It was a heavenly sight!
They stood as signals to the land,
Each one a lovely light;   495

This seraph-band, each waved his hand,
No voice did they impart –
No voice; but oh! the silence sank
Like music on my heart.

But soon I heard the dash of oars,   500
I heard the Pilot's cheer;
My head was turned perforce away
And I saw a boat appear.

The Pilot and the Pilot's boy,
I heard them coming fast: 505
Dear Lord in Heaven! it was a joy
The dead men could not blast.

I saw a third – I heard his voice:
It is the Hermit good!
He singeth loud his godly hymns   510
That he makes in the wood.
He'll shrieve my soul, he'll wash away
The Albatross's blood.

PART VII

The Hermit of
the Wood,

This Hermit good lives in that wood
Which slopes down to the sea.
How loudly his sweet voice he rears!　　515
He loves to talk with marineres
That come from a far countree.

He kneels at morn, and noon, and eve –
He hath a cushion plump:　　520
It is the moss that wholly hides
The rotted old oak-stump.

The skiff-boat neared: I heard them talk,
'Why, this is strange, I trow!
Where are those lights so many and fair,　　525
That signal made but now?'

Approacheth
the ship with
wonder.

'Strange, by my faith!' the Hermit said –
'And they answered not our cheer!
The planks looked warped! and see those sails,
How thin they are and sere!　　530
I never saw aught like to them,
Unless perchance it were

Brown skeletons of leaves that lag
My forest-brook along;
When the ivy-tod is heavy with snow,　　535
And the owlet whoops to the wolf below,
That eats the she-wolf's young.'

'Dear Lord! it hath a fiendish look –
(The Pilot made reply)
I am a-feared' – 'Push on, push on!'　　540
Said the Hermit cheerily.

The boat came closer to the ship,
But I nor spake nor stirred;
The boat came close beneath the ship,
And straight a sound was heard.　　545

The ship
suddenly
sinketh.

Under the water it rumbled on,
Still louder and more dread:
It reached the ship, it split the bay;
The ship went down like lead.

The ancient
Mariner is
saved in the
Pilot's boat.

Stunned by that loud and dreadful sound,   550
Which sky and ocean smote,
Like one that hath been seven days drowned
My body lay afloat;
But swift as dreams, myself I found
Within the Pilot's boat.   555

Upon the whirl, where sank the ship,
The boat spun round and round;
And all was still, save that the hill
Was telling of the sound.

I moved my lips – the Pilot shrieked   560
And fell down in a fit;
The holy Hermit raised his eyes,
And prayed where he did sit.

I took the oars: the Pilot's boy,
Who now doth crazy go,   565
Laughed loud and long, and all the while
His eyes went to and fro.
'Ha! ha!' quoth he, 'full plain I see,
The Devil knows how to row.'

And now, all in my own countree,   570
I stood on the firm land!
The Hermit stepped forth from the boat,
And scarcely he could stand.

The ancient
Mariner
earnestly en-
treateth the
Hermit to
shrieve him;
and the
penance of
life falls on
him.

'O shrieve me, shrieve me, holy man!'
The Hermit crossed his brow.   575
'Say quick,' quoth he, 'I bid thee say –
What manner of man art thou?'

Forthwith this frame of mine was wrenched
With a woful agony,
Which forced me to begin my tale;   580
And then it left me free.

And ever and
anon through-
out his future
life an agony
constraineth

Since then, at an uncertain hour,
That agony returns:
And till my ghastly tale is told,
This heart within me burns.   585

him to travel
from land to
land;

I pass, like night, from land to land;
I have strange power of speech;
That moment that his face I see,
I know the man that must hear me:
To him my tale I teach.   590

What loud uproar bursts from that door!
The wedding-guests are there:
But in the garden-bower the bride
And bride-maids singing are:
And hark the little vesper bell,   595
Which biddeth me to prayer!

O Wedding-Guest! this soul hath been
Alone on a wide wide sea:
So lonely 'twas, that God himself
Scarce seeméd there to be.   600

O sweeter than the marriage-feast,
'Tis sweeter far to me,
To walk together to the kirk
With a goodly company! –

To walk together to the kirk,   605
And all together pray,
While each to his great Father bends,
Old men, and babes, and loving friends
And youths and maidens gay!

And to teach,
by his own
example, love
and reverence
to all things
that God made
and loveth.

Farewell, farewell! but this I tell   610
To thee, thou Wedding-Guest!
He prayeth well, who loveth well
Both man and bird and beast.

He prayeth best, who loveth best
All things both great and small;   615
For the dear God who loveth us,
He made and loveth all.

The Mariner, whose eye is bright,
Whose beard with age is hoar,
Is gone: and now the Wedding-Guest   620
Turned from the bridegroom's door.

He went like one that hath been stunned,
And is of sense forlorn:
A sadder and a wiser man,
He rose the morrow morn.   625

1797–1798

CHRISTABEL

PREFACE

The first part of the following poem was written in the year 1797, at
Stowey, in the county of Somerset. The second part, after my return
from Germany, in the year 1800, at Keswick, Cumberland. It is prob-
able that if the poem had been finished at either of the former periods,
or if even the first and second part had been published in the year 1800,
the impression of its originality would have been much greater than I
dare at present expect. But for this I have only my own indolence to
blame. The dates are mentioned for the exclusive purpose of precluding
charges of plagiarism or servile imitation from myself. For there is
amongst us a set of critics, who seem to hold, that every possible thought
and image is traditional; who have no notion that there are such things
as fountains in the world, small as well as great; and who would there-
fore charitably derive every rill they behold flowing, from a perforation
made in some other man's tank. I am confident, however, that as far as
the present poem is concerned, the celebrated poets* whose writings I
might be suspected of having imitated, either in particular passages, or
in the tone and the spirit of the whole, would be among the first to
vindicate me from the charge, and who, on any striking coincidence,
would permit me to address them in this doggerel version of two
monkish Latin hexameters.

'Tis mine and it is likewise yours;
But an if this will not do;
Let it be mine, good friend! for I
Am the poorer of the two.

I have only to add that the metre of Christabel is not, properly speak-
ing, irregular, though it may seem so from its being founded on a new
principle: namely, that of counting in each line the accents, not the
syllables. Though the latter may vary from seven to twelve, yet in each
line the accents will be found to be only four. Nevertheless, this occa-
sional variation in number of syllables is not introduced wantonly, or for
the mere ends of convenience, but in correspondence with some transi-
tion in the nature of the imagery or passion.

* Sir Walter Scott and Lord Byron.

PART I

'TIS the middle of night by the castle clock,
And the owls have awakened the crowing cock;
Tu – whit! – – Tu – whoo!
And hark, again! the crowing cock,
How drowsily it crew.   5

Sir Leoline, the Baron rich,
Hath a toothless mastiff bitch;
From her kennel beneath the rock
She maketh answer to the clock,
Four for the quarters, and twelve for the hour;   10
Ever and aye, by shine and shower,
Sixteen short howls, not over loud;
Some say, she sees my lady's shroud.

Is the night chilly and dark?
The night is chilly, but not dark.   15
The thin gray cloud is spread on high,
It covers but not hides the sky.
The moon is behind, and at the full;
And yet she looks both small and dull.
The night is chill, the cloud is gray: 20
'Tis a month before the month of May,
And the Spring comes slowly up this way.

The lovely lady, Christabel,
Whom her father loves so well,
What makes her in the wood so late,   25
A furlong from the castle gate?
She had dreams all yesternight
Of her own betrothéd knight;
And she in the midnight wood will pray
For the weal of her lover that's far away.   30

She stole along, she nothing spoke,
The sighs she heaved were soft and low,
And naught was green upon the oak
But moss and rarest misletoe:
She kneels beneath the huge oak tree,   35
And in silence prayeth she.

The lady sprang up suddenly,
The lovely lady, Christabel!
It moaned as near, as near can be,
But what it is she cannot tell. –
On the other side it seems to be,
Of the huge, broad-breasted, old oak tree.

The night is chill; the forest bare;
Is it the wind that moaneth bleak?
There is not wind enough in the air
To move away the ringlet curl
From the lovely lady's cheek –
There is not wind enough to twirl
The one red leaf, the last of its clan,
That dances as often as dance it can,
Hanging so light, and hanging so high,
On the topmost twig that looks up at the sky.

Hush, beating heart of Christabel!
Jesu, Maria, shield her well!
She folded her arms beneath her cloak,
And stole to the other side of the oak.
　　　What sees she there?

There she sees a damsel bright,
Drest in a silken robe of white,
That shadowy in the moonlight shone:
The neck that made that white robe wan,
Her stately neck, and arms were bare;
Her blue-veined feet unsandal'd were,
And wildly glittered here and there
The gems entangled in her hair.

I guess, 'twas frightful there to see
A lady so richly clad as she –
Beautiful exceedingly!

Mary mother, save me now!
(Said Christabel,) And who art thou?

The lady strange made answer meet,
And her voice was faint and sweet: –
Have pity on my sore distress,
I scarce can speak for weariness:

40
45
50
55
60
65
70

Stretch forth thy hand, and have no fear!   75
Said Christabel, How camest thou here?
And the lady, whose voice was faint and sweet,
Did thus pursue her answer meet: –

My sire is of a noble line,
And my name is Geraldine: 80
Five warriors seized me yestermorn,
Me, even me, a maid forlorn:
They choked my cries with force and fright,
And tied me on a palfrey white.
The palfrey was as fleet as wind,   85
And they rode furiously behind.
They spurred amain, their steeds were white:
And once we crossed the shade of night.
As sure as Heaven shall rescue me,
I have no thought what men they be;   90
Nor do I know how long it is
(For I have lain entranced I wis)
Since one, the tallest of the five,
Took me from the palfrey's back,
A weary woman, scarce alive.   95
Some muttered words his comrades spoke:
He placed me underneath this oak;
He swore they would return with haste;
Whither they went I cannot tell –
I thought I heard, some minutes past,   100
Sounds as of a castle bell.
Stretch forth thy hand (thus ended she),
And help a wretched maid to flee.

Then Christabel stretched forth her hand,
And comforted fair Geraldine: 105
O well, bright dame! may you command
The service of Sir Leoline;
And gladly our stout chivalry
Will he send forth and friends withal
To guide and guard you safe and free   110
Home to your noble father's hall.

She rose: and forth with steps they passed
That strove to be, and were not, fast.
Her gracious stars the lady blest,

115 And thus spake on sweet Christabel:
All our household are at rest,
The hall as silent as the cell;
Sir Leoline is weak in health,
And may not well awakened be,
120 But we will move as if in stealth,
And I beseech your courtesy,
This night, to share your couch with me.

They crossed the moat, and Christabel
Took the key that fitted well;
125 A little door she opened straight,
All in the middle of the gate;
The gate that was ironed within and without,
Where an army in battle array had marched out.
The lady sank, belike through pain,
130 And Christabel with might and main
Lifted her up, a weary weight,
Over the threshold of the gate:
Then the lady rose again,
And moved, as she were not in pain.

135 So free from danger, free from fear,
They crossed the court: right glad they were.
And Christabel devoutly cried
To the lady by her side,
Praise we the Virgin all divine
140 Who hath rescued thee from thy distress!
Alas, alas! said Geraldine,
I cannot speak for weariness.
So free from danger, free from fear,
They crossed the court: right glad they were.

145 Outside her kennel, the mastiff old
Lay fast asleep, in moonshine cold.
The mastiff old did not awake,
Yet she an angry moan did make!
And what can ail the mastiff bitch?
150 Never till now she uttered yell
Beneath the eye of Christabel.
Perhaps it is the owlet's scritch:
For what can ail the mastiff bitch?

They passed the hall, that echoes still,
Pass as lightly as you will!   155
The brands were flat, the brands were dying,
Amid their own white ashes lying;
But when the lady passed, there came
A tongue of light, a fit of flame;
And Christabel saw the lady's eye,   160
And nothing else saw she thereby,
Save the boss of the shield of Sir Leoline tall,
Which hung in a murky old niche in the wall.
O softly tread, said Christabel,
My father seldom sleepeth well.   165

Sweet Christabel her feet doth bare,
And jealous of the listening air
They steal their way from stair to stair,
Now in glimmer, and now in gloom,
And now they pass the Baron's room,   170
As still as death, with stifled breath!
And now have reached her chamber door;
And now doth Geraldine press down
The rushes of the chamber floor.

The moon shines dim in the open air,   175
And not a moonbeam enters here.
But they without its light can see
The chamber carved so curiously,
Carved with figures strange and sweet,
All made out of the carver's brain,   180
For a lady's chamber meet:
The lamp with twofold silver chain
Is fastened to an angel's feet.

The silver lamp burns dead and dim;
But Christabel the lamp will trim.   185
She trimmed the lamp, and made it bright,
And left it swinging to and fro,
While Geraldine, in wretched plight,
Sank down upon the floor below.

O weary lady, Geraldine,   190
I pray you, drink this cordial wine!

It is a wine of virtuous powers;
My mother made it of wild flowers.

And will your mother pity me,
195 Who am a maiden most forlorn?
Christabel answered – Woe is me!
She died the hour that I was born.
I have heard the grey-haired friar tell
How on her death-bed she did say,
200 That she should hear the castle-bell
Strike twelve upon my wedding-day.
O mother dear! that thou wert here!
I would, said Geraldine, she were!
But soon with altered voice, said she –
205 'Off, wandering mother! Peak and pine!
I have power to bid thee flee.'
Alas! what ails poor Geraldine?
Why stares she with unsettled eye?
Can she the bodiless dead espy?
210 And why with hollow voice cries she,
'Off, woman, off! this hour is mine –
Though thou her guardian spirit be,
Off, woman, off! 'tis given to me.'

Then Christabel knelt by the lady's side,
215 And raised to heaven her eyes so blue –
Alas! said she, this ghastly ride –
Dear lady! it hath wildered you!
The lady wiped her moist cold brow,
And faintly said, ''tis over now!'

220 Again the wild-flower wine she drank:
Her fair large eyes 'gan glitter bright,
And from the floor whereon she sank,
The lofty lady stood upright:
She was most beautiful to see,
225 Like a lady of a far countrée.

And thus the lofty lady spake –
'All they who live in the upper sky,
Do love you, holy Christabel!
And you love them, and for their sake
230 And for the good which me befel,

Even I in my degree will try,
Fair maiden, to requite you well.
But now unrobe yourself; for I
Must pray, ere yet in bed I lie.'

Quoth Christabel, So let it be!   235
And as the lady bade, did she.
Her gentle limbs did she undress,
And lay down in her loveliness.

But through her brain of weal and woe
So many thoughts moved to and fro,   240
That vain it were her lids to close;
So half-way from the bed she rose,
And on her elbow did recline
To look at the lady Geraldine.

Beneath the lamp the lady bowed,   245
And slowly rolled her eyes around;
Then drawing in her breath aloud,
Like one that shuddered, she unbound
The cincture from beneath her breast:
Her silken robe, and inner vest,   250
Dropt to her feet, and full in view,
Behold! her bosom, and half her side – –
A sight to dream of, not to tell!
O shield her! shield sweet Christabel!

Yet Geraldine nor speaks nor stirs;   255
Ah! what a stricken look was hers!
Deep from within she seems half-way
To lift some weight with sick assay,
And eyes the maid and seeks delay;
Then suddenly, as one defied,   260
Collects herself in scorn and pride,
And lay down by the Maiden's side! –
And in her arms the maid she took,
        Ah wel-a-day!
And with low voice and doleful look   265
These words did say:
'In the touch of this bosom there worketh a spell,
Which is lord of thy utterance, Christabel!
Thou knowest to-night, and wilt know to-morrow,

270 This mark of my shame, this seal of my sorrow;
    But vainly thou warrest,
      For this is alone in
    Thy power to declare,
      That in the dim forest
275   Thou heard'st a low moaning,
And found'st a bright lady, surpassingly fair;
And didst bring her home with thee in love and in charity,
To shield her and shelter her from the damp air.'

THE CONCLUSION TO PART I

It was a lovely sight to see
280 The lady Christabel, when she
Was praying at the old oak tree.
    Amid the jaggéd shadows
    Of mossy leafless boughs,
    Kneeling in the moonlight,
285   To make her gentle vows;
Her slender palms together prest,
Heaving sometimes on her breast;
Her face resigned to bliss or bale –
Her face, oh call it fair not pale,
290 And both blue eyes more bright than clear,
Each about to have a tear.

With open eyes (ah woe is me!)
Asleep, and dreaming fearfully,
Fearfully dreaming, yet, I wis,
295 Dreaming that alone, which is –
O sorrow and shame! Can this be she,
The lady, who knelt at the old oak tree?
And lo! the worker of these harms,
That holds the maiden in her arms,
300 Seems to slumber still and mild,
As a mother with her child.

A star hath set, a star hath risen,
O Geraldine! since arms of thine
305 Have been the lovely lady's prison.
O Geraldine! one hour was thine –
Thou'st had thy will! By tairn and rill,

The night-birds all that hour were still.
But now they are jubilant anew,
From cliff and tower, tu – whoo! tu – whoo!
Tu – whoo! tu – whoo! from wood and fell!   310

And see! the lady Christabel
Gathers herself from out her trance;
Her limbs relax, her countenance
Grows sad and soft; the smooth thin lids
Close o'er her eyes; and tears she sheds –   315
Large tears that leave the lashes bright!
And oft the while she seems to smile
As infants at a sudden light!

Yea, she doth smile, and she doth weep,
Like a youthful hermitess,   320
Beauteous in a wilderness,
Who, praying always, prays in sleep.
And, if she move unquietly,
Perchance, 'tis but the blood so free
Comes back and tingles in her feet.   325
No doubt, she hath a vision sweet.
What if her guardian spirit 'twere,
What if she knew her mother near?
But this she knows, in joys and woes,
That saints will aid if men will call: 330
For the blue sky bends over all!

  1797

PART II

Each matin bell, the Baron saith,
Knells us back to a world of death.
These words Sir Leoline first said,
When he rose and found his lady dead: 335
These words Sir Leoline will say
Many a morn to his dying day!

And hence the custom and law began
That still at dawn the sacristan,
Who duly pulls the heavy bell,   340
Five and forty beads must tell
Between each stroke – a warning knell,

Which not a soul can choose but hear
From Bratha Head to Wyndermere.

345   Saith Bracy the bard, So let it knell!
And let the drowsy sacristan
Still count as slowly as he can!
There is no lack of such, I ween,
As well fill up the space between.
350   In Langdale Pike and Witch's Lair,
And Dungeon-ghyll so foully rent,
With ropes of rock and bells of air
Three sinful sextons' ghosts are pent,
Who all give back, one after t'other,
355   The death-note to their living brother;
And oft too, by the knell offended,
Just as their one! two! three! is ended,
The devil mocks the doleful tale
With a merry peal from Borodale.

360   The air is still! through mist and cloud
That merry peal comes ringing loud;
And Geraldine shakes off her dread,
And rises lightly from the bed;
Puts on her silken vestments white,
365   And tricks her hair in lovely plight,
And nothing doubting of her spell
Awakens the lady Christabel.
'Sleep you, sweet lady Christabel?
I trust that you have rested well.'

370   And Christabel awoke and spied
The same who lay down by her side –
O rather say, the same whom she
Raised up beneath the old oak tree!
Nay, fairer yet! and yet more fair!
375   For she belike hath drunken deep
Of all the blessedness of sleep!
And while she spake, her looks, her air
Such gentle thankfulness declare,
That (so it seemed) her girded vests
380   Grew tight beneath her heaving breasts.
'Sure I have sinn'd!' said Christabel,

'Now heaven be praised if all be well!'
And in low faltering tones, yet sweet,
Did she the lofty lady greet
With such perplexity of mind
As dreams too lively leave behind.   385

So quickly she rose, and quickly arrayed
Her maiden limbs, and having prayed
That He, who on the cross did groan,
Might wash away her sins unknown,   390
She forthwith led fair Geraldine
To meet her sire, Sir Leoline.

The lovely maid and the lady tall
Are pacing both into the hall,
And pacing on through page and groom,   395
Enter the Baron's presence-room.

The Baron rose, and while he prest
His gentle daughter to his breast,
With cheerful wonder in his eyes
The lady Geraldine espies,   400
And gave such welcome to the same,
As might beseem so bright a dame!

But when he heard the lady's tale,
And when she told her father's name,
Why waxed Sir Leoline so pale,   405
Murmuring o'er the name again,
Lord Roland de Vaux of Tryermaine?

Alas! they had been friends in youth;
But whispering tongues can poison truth;
And constancy lives in realms above;   410
And life is thorny; and youth is vain;
And to be wroth with one we love
Doth work like madness in the brain.
And thus it chanced, as I divine,
With Roland and Sir Leoline.   415
Each spake words of high disdain
And insult to his heart's best brother:
They parted – ne'er to meet again!
But never either found another

420 To free the hollow heart from paining –
They stood aloof, the scars remaining,
Like cliffs which had been rent asunder;
A dreary sea now flows between; –
But neither heat, nor frost, nor thunder,
425 Shall wholly do away, I ween,
The marks of that which once hath been.

Sir Leoline, a moment's space,
Stood gazing on the damsel's face:
And the youthful Lord of Tryermaine
430 Came back upon his heart again.

O then the Baron forgot his age,
His noble heart swelled high with rage;
He swore by the wounds in Jesu's side
He would proclaim it far and wide,
435 With trump and solemn heraldry,
That they, who thus had wronged the dame,
Were base as spotted infamy!
'And if they dare deny the same,
My herald shall appoint a week,
440 And let the recreant traitors seek
My tourney court – that there and then
I may dislodge their reptile souls
From the bodies and forms of men!'
He spake: his eye in lightning rolls!
445 For the lady was ruthlessly seized; and he kenned
In the beautiful lady the child of his friend!

And now the tears were on his face,
And fondly in his arms he took
Fair Geraldine, who met the embrace,
450 Prolonging it with joyous look.
Which when she viewed, a vision fell
Upon the soul of Christabel,
The vision of fear, the touch and pain!
She shrunk and shuddered, and saw again –
455 (Ah, woe is me! Was it for thee,
Thou gentle maid! such sights to see?)

Again she saw that bosom old,
Again she felt that bosom cold,

And drew in her breath with a hissing sound:
Whereat the Knight turned wildly round,   460
And nothing saw, but his own sweet maid
With eyes upraised, as one that prayed.

The touch, the sight, had passed away,
And in its stead that vision blest,
Which comforted her after-rest   465
While in the lady's arms she lay,
Had put a rapture in her breast,
And on her lips and o'er her eyes
Spread smiles like light!
                            With new surprise,
'What ails then my belovéd child?'   470
The Baron said – His daughter mild
Made answer, 'All will yet be well!'
I ween, she had no power to tell
Aught else: so mighty was the spell.

Yet he, who saw this Geraldine,   475
Had deemed her sure a thing divine:
Such sorrow with such grace she blended,
As if she feared she had offended
Sweet Christabel, that gentle maid!
And with such lowly tones she prayed   480
She might be sent without delay
Home to her father's mansion.
                            'Nay!
Nay, by my soul!' said Leoline.
'Ho! Bracy the bard, the charge be thine!
Go thou, with music sweet and loud,   485
And take two steeds with trappings proud,
And take the youth whom thou lov'st best
To bear thy harp, and learn thy song,
And clothe you both in solemn vest,
And over the mountains haste along,   490
Lest wandering folk, that are abroad,
Detain you on the valley road.

'And when he has crossed the Irthing flood,
My merry bard! he hastes, he hastes
Up Knorren Moor, through Halegarth Wood,   495

And reaches soon that castle good
Which stands and threatens Scotland's wastes.

'Bard Bracy! bard Bracy! your horses are fleet,
Ye must ride up the hall, your music so sweet,
500 More loud than your horses' echoing feet!
And loud and loud to Lord Roland call,
Thy daughter is safe in Langdale hall!
Thy beautiful daughter is safe and free –
Sir Leoline greets thee thus through me!
565 He bids thee come without delay
With all thy numerous array
And take thy lovely daughter home:
And he will meet thee on the way
With all his numerous array
510 White with their panting palfreys' foam:
And, by mine honour! I will say,
That I repent me of the day
When I spake words of fierce disdain
To Roland de Vaux of Tryermaine! –
515 – For since that evil hour hath flown,
Many a summer's sun hath shone;
Yet ne'er found I a friend again
Like Roland de Vaux of Tryermaine.

The lady fell, and clasped his knees,
520 Her face upraised, her eyes o'erflowing;
And Bracy replied, with faltering voice,
His gracious Hail on all bestowing! –
'Thy words, thou sire of Christabel,
Are sweeter than my harp can tell;
525 Yet might I gain a boon of thee,
This day my journey should not be,
So strange a dream hath come to me,
That I had vowed with music loud
To clear yon wood from thing unblest,
530 Warned by a vision in my rest!
For in my sleep I saw that dove,
That gentle bird, whom thou dost love,
And call'st by thy own daughter's name –
Sir Leoline! I saw the same
535 Fluttering, and uttering fearful moan,

Among the green herbs in the forest alone.
Which when I saw and when I heard,
I wonder'd what might ail the bird;
For nothing near it could I see,
Save the grass and green herbs underneath the old tree.   540

'And in my dream methought I went
To search out what might there be found;
And what the sweet bird's trouble meant,
That thus lay fluttering on the ground.
I went and peered, and could descry   545
No cause for her distressful cry;
But yet for her dear lady's sake
I stooped, methought, the dove to take,
When lo! I saw a bright green snake
Coiled around its wings and neck.   550
Green as the herbs on which it crouched,
Close by the dove's its head it crouched;
And with the dove it heaves and stirs,
Swelling its neck as she swelled hers!
I woke; it was the midnight hour,   555
The clock was echoing in the tower;
But though my slumber was gone by,
This dream it would not pass away –
It seems to live upon my eye!
And thence I vowed this self-same day   560
With music strong and saintly song
To wander through the forest bare,
Lest aught unholy loiter there.'

Thus Bracy said: the Baron, the while,
Half-listening heard him with a smile;   565
Then turned to Lady Geraldine,
His eyes made up of wonder and love;
And said in courtly accents fine,
'Sweet maid, Lord Roland's beauteous dove,
With arms more strong than harp or song,   570
Thy sire and I will crush the snake!'
He kissed her forehead as he spake,
And Geraldine in maiden wise
Casting down her large bright eyes,
With blushing cheek and courtesy fine   575

She turned her from Sir Leoline;
Softly gathering up her train,
That o'er her right arm fell again;
And folded her arms across her chest,
580 And couched her head upon her breast,
And looked askance at Christabel – –
Jesu, Maria, shield her well!

A snake's small eye blinks dull and shy;
And the lady's eyes they shrunk in her head,
585 Each shrunk up to a serpent's eye,
And with somewhat of malice, and more of dread,
At Christabel she looked askance! –
One moment – and the sight was fled!
But Christabel in dizzy trance
590 Stumbling on the unsteady ground
Shuddered aloud, with a hissing sound;
And Geraldine again turned round,
And like a thing, that sought relief,
Full of wonder and full of grief,
595 She rolled her large bright eyes divine
Wildly on Sir Leoline.

The maid, alas! her thoughts are gone,
She nothing sees – no sight but one!
The maid, devoid of guile and sin,
600 I know not how, in fearful wise,
So deeply had she drunken in
That look, those shrunken serpent eyes
That all her features were resigned
To this sole image in her mind:
605 And passively did imitate
That look of dull and treacherous hate!
And thus she stood, in dizzy trance,
Still picturing that look askance
With forced unconscious sympathy
610 Full before her father's view – –
As far as such a look could be
In eyes so innocent and blue!

And when the trance was o'er, the maid
Paused awhile, and inly prayed:

Then falling at the Baron's feet, 615
'By my mother's soul do I entreat
That thou this woman send away!'
She said: and more she could not say:
For what she knew she could not tell,
O'er-mastered by the mighty spell. 620

Why is thy cheek so wan and wild,
Sir Leoline? Thy only child
Lies at thy feet, thy joy, thy pride,
So fair, so innocent, so mild;
The same, for whom thy lady died! 625
O by the pangs of her dear mother
Think thou no evil of thy child!
For her, and thee, and for no other,
She prayed the moment ere she died:
Prayed that the babe for whom she died, 630
Might prove her dear lord's joy and pride!
    That prayer her deadly pangs beguiled,
        Sir Leoline!
    And wouldst thou wrong thy only child,
        Her child and thine? 635

Within the Baron's heart and brain
If thoughts, like these, had any share,
They only swelled his rage and pain,
And did but work confusion there.
His heart was cleft with pain and rage, 640
His cheeks they quivered, his eyes were wild,
Dishonoured thus in his old age;
Dishonoured by his only child,
And all his hospitality
To the wronged daughter of his friend 645
By more than woman's jealousy
Brought thus to a disgraceful end –
He rolled his eye with stern regard
Upon the gentle minstrel bard,
And said in tones abrupt, austere – 650
'Why, Bracy! dost thou loiter here?
I bade thee hence!' The bard obeyed;
And turning from his own sweet maid,

The agéd knight, Sir Leoline,
655   Led forth the lady Geraldine!

    1800

THE CONCLUSION TO PART II

A little child, a limber elf,
Singing, dancing to itself,
A fairy thing with red round cheeks,
That always finds, and never seeks,
660   Makes such a vision to the sight
As fills a father's eyes with light;
And pleasures flow in so thick and fast
Upon his heart, that he at last
Must needs express his love's excess
665   With words of unmeant bitterness.
Perhaps 'tis pretty to force together
Thoughts so all unlike each other;
To mutter and mock a broken charm,
To dally with wrong that does no harm.
670   Perhaps 'tis tender too and pretty
At each wild word to feel within
A sweet recoil of love and pity.
And what, if in a world of sin
(O sorrow and shame should this be true!)
675   Such giddiness of heart and brain
Comes seldom save from rage and pain,
So talks as it's most used to do.

    1801

FROST AT MIDNIGHT

THE Frost performs its secret ministry,
Unhelped by any wind. The owlet's cry
Came loud – and hark, again! loud as before.
The inmates of my cottage, all at rest,
5   Have left me to that solitude, which suits
Abstruser musings: save that at my side
My cradled infant slumbers peacefully.
'Tis calm indeed! so calm, that it disturbs

And vexes meditation with its strange
And extreme silentness. Sea, hill, and wood,   10
This populous village! Sea, and hill, and wood,
With all the numberless goings-on of life,
Inaudible as dreams! the thin blue flame
Lies on my low-burnt fire, and quivers not;
Only that film, which fluttered on the grate,   15
Still flutters there, the sole unquiet thing.
Methinks, its motion in this hush of nature
Gives it dim sympathies with me who live,
Making it a companionable form,
Whose puny flaps and freaks the idling Spirit   20
By its own moods interprets, every where
Echo or mirror seeking of itself,
And makes a toy of Thought.

                  But O! how oft,
How oft, at school, with most believing mind,
Presageful, have I gazed upon the bars,   25
To watch that fluttering *stranger*! and as oft
With unclosed lids, already had I dreamt
Of my sweet birth-place, and the old church-tower,
Whose bells, the poor man's only music, rang
From morn to evening, all the hot Fair-day,   30
So sweetly, that they stirred and haunted me
With a wild pleasure, falling on mine ear
Most like articulate sounds of things to come!
So gazed I, till the soothing things, I dreamt,
Lulled me to sleep, and sleep prolonged my dreams!   35
And so I brooded all the following morn,
Awed by the stern preceptor's face, mine eye
Fixed with mock study on my swimming book:
Save if the door half opened, and I snatched
A hasty glance, and still my heart leaped up,   40
For still I hoped to see the *stranger's* face,
Townsman, or aunt, or sister more beloved,
My play-mate when we both were clothed alike!

    Dear Babe, that sleepest cradled by my side,
Whose gentle breathings, heard in this deep calm,   45
Fill up the interspersèd vacancies
And momentary pauses of the thought!

My babe so beautiful! it thrills my heart
With tender gladness, thus to look at thee,
50   And think that thou shalt learn far other lore,
And in far other scenes! For I was reared
In the great city, pent 'mid cloisters dim,
And saw nought lovely but the sky and stars.
But *thou*, my babe! shalt wander like a breeze
55   By lakes and sandy shores, beneath the crags
Of ancient mountain, and beneath the clouds,
Which image in their bulk both lakes and shores
And mountain crags: so shalt thou see and hear
The lovely shapes and sounds intelligible
60   Of that eternal language, which thy God
Utters, who from eternity doth teach
Himself in all, and all things in himself.
Great universal Teacher! he shall mould
Thy spirit, and by giving make it ask.

65   Therefore all seasons shall be sweet to thee,
Whether the summer clothe the general earth
With greenness, or the redbreast sit and sing
Betwixt the tufts of snow on the bare branch
Of mossy apple-tree, while the nigh thatch
70   Smokes in the sun-thaw; whether the eave-drops fall
Heard only in the trances of the blast,
Or if the secret ministry of frost
Shall hang them up in silent icicles,
    Quietly shining to the quiet Moon.

    February 1798

LEWTI

OR THE CIRCASSIAN LOVE-CHAUNT

At midnight by the stream I roved,
To forget the form I loved.
Image of Lewti! from my mind
Depart; for Lewti is not kind.
5   The Moon was high, the moonlight gleam
    And the shadow of a star
Heaved upon Tamaha's stream;

But the rock shone brighter far,
The rock half sheltered from my view
By pendent boughs of tressy yew. –   10
So shines my Lewti's forehead fair,
Gleaming through her sable hair.
Image of Lewti! from my mind
Depart; for Lewti is not kind.

I saw a cloud of palest hue,   15
   Onward to the moon it passed;
Still brighter and more bright it grew,
With floating colours not a few,
   Till it reached the moon at last:
Then the cloud was wholly bright,   20
With a rich and amber light!
And so with many a hope I seek,
   And with such joy I find my Lewti;
And even so my pale wan cheek
   Drinks in as deep a flush of beauty!   25
Nay, treacherous image! leave my mind,
If Lewti never will be kind.

The little cloud – it floats away,
   Away it goes; away so soon!
Alas! it has no power to stay: 30
Its hues are dim, its hues are grey –
   Away it passes from the moon!
How mournfully it seems to fly,
   Ever fading more and more,
To joyless regions of the sky –   35
   And now 'tis whiter than before!
As white as my poor cheek will be,
   When, Lewti! on my couch I lie,
A dying man for love of thee.
Nay, treacherous image! leave my mind –   40
And yet, thou didst not look unkind.

I saw a vapour in the sky,
Thin, and white, and very high;
I ne'er beheld so thin a cloud:
   Perhaps the breezes that can fly   45
   Now below and now above,

Have snatched aloft the lawny shroud
   Of Lady fair – that died for love.
For maids, as well as youths, have perished
50 From fruitless love too fondly cherished.
Nay, treacherous image! leave my mind –
For Lewti never will be kind.

Hush! my heedless feet from under
   Slip the crumbling banks for ever:
55 Like echoes to a distant thunder,
   They plunge into the gentle river.
The river-swans have heard my tread,
And startle from their reedy bed.
O beauteous birds! methinks ye measure
60   Your movements to some heavenly tune!
O beauteous birds! 'tis such a pleasure
   To see you move beneath the moon,
I would it were your true delight
To sleep by day and wake all night.

65 I know the place where Lewti lies,
When silent night has closed her eyes:
   It is a breezy jasmine-bower,
The nightingale sings o'er her head:
   Voice of the Night! had I the power
70 That leafy labyrinth to thread,
And creep, like thee, with soundless tread,
I then might view her bosom white
Heaving lovely to my sight,
   As these two swans together heave
75 On the gently-swelling wave.

Oh! that she saw me in a dream,
   And dreamt that I had died for care;
All pale and wasted I would seem,
   Yet fair withal, as spirits are!
80 I'd die indeed, if I might see
Her bosom heave, and heave for me!
Soothe, gentle image! soothe my mind!
To-morrow Lewti may be kind.

1798

THE NIGHTINGALE

A CONVERSATION POEM, APRIL 1798

No cloud, no relique of the sunken day
Distinguishes the West, no long thin slip
Of sullen light, no obscure trembling hues.
Come, we will rest on this old mossy bridge!
You see the glimmer of the stream beneath,   5
But hear no murmuring: it flows silently,
O'er its soft bed of verdure. All is still,
A balmy night! and though the stars be dim,
Yet let us think upon the vernal showers
That gladden the green earth, and we shall find   10
A pleasure in the dimness of the stars.
And hark! the Nightingale begins its song,
'Most musical, most melancholy' bird!
A melancholy bird? Oh! idle thought!
In Nature there is nothing melancholy.   15
But some night-wandering man whose heart was pierced
With the remembrance of a grievous wrong,
Or slow distemper, or neglected love,
(And so, poor wretch! filled all things with himself,
And made all gentle sounds tell back the tale   20
Of his own sorrow) he, and such as he,
First named these notes a melancholy strain.
And many a poet echoes the conceit;
Poet who hath been building up the rhyme
When he had better far have stretched his limbs   25
Beside a brook in mossy forest-dell,
By sun or moon-light, to the influxes
Of shapes and sounds and shifting elements
Surrendering his whole spirit, of his song
And of his fame forgetful! so his fame   30
Should share in Nature's immortality,
A venerable thing! and so his song
Should make all Nature lovelier, and itself
Be loved like Nature! But 'twill not be so;
And youths and maidens most poetical,   35
Who lose the deepening twilights of the spring
In ball-rooms and hot theatres, they still

Full of meek sympathy must heave their sighs
O'er Philomela's pity-pleading strains.

40   My Friend, and thou, our Sister! we have learnt
A different lore: we may not thus profane
Nature's sweet voices, always full of love
And joyance! 'Tis the merry Nightingale
That crowds, and hurries, and precipitates
45   With fast thick warble his delicious notes,
As he were fearful that an April night
Would be too short for him to utter forth
His love-chant, and disburthen his full soul
Of all its music!
             And I know a grove
50   Of large extent, hard by a castle huge,
Which the great lord inhabits not; and so
This grove is wild with tangling underwood,
And the trim walks are broken up, and grass,
Thin grass and king-cups grow within the paths.
55   But never elsewhere in one place I knew
So many nightingales; and far and near,
In wood and thicket, over the wide grove,
They answer and provoke each other's song,
With skirmish and capricious passagings,
60   And murmurs musical and swift jug jug,
And one low piping sound more sweet than all –
Stirring the air with such a harmony,
That should you close your eyes, you might almost
Forget it was not day! On moon-lit bushes,
65   Whose dewy leaflets are but half-disclosed,
You may perchance behold them on the twigs,
Their bright, bright eyes, their eyes both bright and full,
Glistening, while many a glow-worm in the shade
Lights up her love-torch.
             A most gentle Maid,
70   Who dwelleth in her hospitable home
Hard by the castle, and at latest eve
(Even like a Lady vowed and dedicate
To something more than Nature in the grove)
Glides through the pathways; she knows all their notes,
75   That gentle Maid! and oft, a moment's space,

What time the moon was lost behind a cloud,
Hath heard a pause of silence; till the moon
Emerging, hath awakened earth and sky
With one sensation, and those wakeful birds
Have all burst forth in choral minstrelsy,   80
As if some sudden gale had swept at once
A hundred airy harps! And she hath watched
Many a nightingale perch giddily
On blossomy twig still swinging from the breeze,
And to that motion tune his wanton song   85
Like tipsy Joy that reels with tossing head.

Farewell, O Warbler! till to-morrow eve,
And you, my friends! farewell, a short farewell!
We have been loitering long and pleasantly,
And now for our dear homes. – That strain again!   90
Full fain it would delay me! My dear babe,
Who, capable of no articulate sound,
Mars all things with his imitative lisp,
How he would place his hand beside his ear,
His little hand, the small forefinger up,   95
And bid us listen! And I deem it wise
To make him Nature's play-mate. He knows well
The evening-star; and once, when he awoke
In most distressful mood (some inward pain
Had made up that strange thing, an infant's dream –)   100
I hurried with him to our orchard-plot.
And he beheld the moon, and, hushed at once,
Suspends his sobs, and laughs most silently,
While his fair eyes, that swam with undropped tears,
Did glitter in the yellow moon-beam! Well! –   105
It is a father's tale: But if that Heaven
Should give me life, his childhood shall grow up
Familiar with these songs, that with the night
He may associate joy. – Once more, farewell,
Sweet Nightingale! once more, my friends! farewell.   110

1798

THE WANDERINGS OF CAIN

PREFATORY NOTE

A Prose composition, one not in metre at least, seems *prima facie* to require explanation or apology. It was written in the year 1798, near Nether Stowey, in Somersetshire, at which place (*sanctum et amabile nomen!* rich by so many associations and recollections) the author had taken up his residence in order to enjoy the society and close neighbourhood of a dear and honoured friend, T. Poole, Esq. The work was to have been written in concert with another [Wordsworth], whose name is too venerable within the precincts of genius to be unnecessarily brought into connection with such a trifle, and who was then residing at a small distance from Nether Stowey. The title and subject were suggested by myself, who likewise drew out the scheme and the contents for each of the three books or cantos, of which the work was to consist, and which, the reader is to be informed, was to have been finished in one night! My partner undertook the first canto: I the second: and which ever had *done first*, was to set about the third. Almost thirty years have passed by; yet at this moment I cannot without something more than a smile moot the question which of the two things was the more impracticable, for a mind so eminently original to compose another man's thoughts and fancies, or for a taste so austerely pure and simple to imitate the Death of Abel? Methinks I see his grand and noble countenance as at the moment when having despatched my own portion of the task at full finger-speed, I hastened to him with my manu script – that look of humorous despondency fixed on his almost blank sheet of paper, and then its silent mock-piteous admission of failure struggling with the sense of the exceeding ridiculousness of the whole scheme – which broke up in a laugh: and the Ancient Mariner was written instead.

Years afterward, however, the draft of the plan and proposed incidents, and the portion executed, obtained favour in the eyes of more than one person, whose judgement on a poetic work could not but have weighed with me, even though no parental partiality had been thrown into the same scale, as a make-weight: and I determined on commencing anew, and composing the whole in stanzas, and made some progress in realising this intention, when adverse gales drove my bark off the 'Fortunate Isles' of the Muses: and then other and more momentous interests prompted a different voyage, to firmer anchorage and a securer port. I have in vain tried to recover the lines from the palimpsest tablet of my memory: and I can only offer the introductory stanza, which had been committed to writing for the purpose of procuring a friend's judgement on the metre, as a specimen:

Encinctured with a twine of leaves,
That leafy twine his only dress!
A lovely Boy was plucking fruits,
By moonlight, in a wilderness.
The moon was bright, the air was free,
And fruits and flowers together grew
On many a shrub and many a tree:
And all put on a gentle hue,
Hanging in the shadowy air
Like a picture rich and rare.
It was a climate where, they say,
The night is more belov'd than day.
But who that beauteous Boy beguil'd,
That beauteous Boy to linger here?
Alone, by night, a little child,
In place so silent and so wild –
Has he no friend, no loving mother near?

I have here given the birth, parentage, and premature decease of the
'Wanderings of Cain, a poem', – intreating, however, my Readers, not
to think so meanly of my judgement as to suppose that I either regard
or offer it as any excuse for the publication of the following fragment
(and I may add, of one or two others in its neighbourhood) in its primi-
tive crudity. But I should find still greater difficulty in forgiving myself
were I to record pro *taedio* publico a set of petty mishaps and annoy-
ances which I myself wish to forget. I must be content therefore with
assuring the friendly Reader, that the less he attributes its appearance to
the Author's will, choice, or judgement, the nearer to the truth he
will be.

S. T. COLERIDGE (1828)

CANTO II

'A LITTLE further, O my father, yet a little further, and we shall come
into the open moonlight.' Their road was through a forest of fir-
trees; at its entrance the trees stood at distances from each other, and
the path was broad, and the moonlight and the moonlight shadows
reposed upon it, and appeared quietly to inhabit that solitude. But
soon the path winded and became narrow; the sun at high noon some-
times speckled, but never illumined it, and now it was dark as a cavern.

'It is dark, O my father!' said Enos, 'but the path under our feet is
smooth and soft, and we shall soon come out into the open moonlight.'

'Lead on, my child!' said Cain; 'guide me, little child!' And the
innocent little child clasped a finger of the hand which had murdered
the righteous Abel, and he guided his father. 'The fir branches drip

upon thee, my son.' 'Yea, pleasantly, father, for I ran fast and eagerly
to bring thee the pitcher and the cake, and my body is not yet cool.
How happy the squirrels are that feed on these fir-trees! they leap
from bough to bough, and the old squirrels play round their young
ones in the nest. I clomb a tree yesterday at noon, O my father, that I
might play with them, but they leaped away from the branches, even
to the slender twigs did they leap, and in a moment I beheld them on
another tree. Why, O my father, would they not play with me? I
would be good to them as thou art good to me: and I groaned to
them even as thou groanest when thou givest me to eat, and when
thou coverest me at evening, and as often as I stand at thy knee and
thine eyes look at me?' Then Cain stopped, and stifling his groans he
sank to the earth, and the child Enos stood in the darkness beside him.

And Cain lifted up his voice and cried bitterly, and said, 'The
Mighty One that persecuteth me is on this side and on that; he pur-
sueth my soul like the wind, like the sand-blast he passeth through me;
he is around me even as the air! O that I might be utterly no more! I
desire to die – yea, the things that never had life, neither move they
upon the earth – behold! they seem precious to mine eyes. O that a
man might live without the breath of his nostrils. So I might abide in
darkness, and blackness, and an empty space! Yea, I would lie down,
I would not rise, neither would I stir my limbs till I became as the
rock in the den of the lion, on which the young lion resteth his head
whilst he sleepeth. For the torrent that roareth far off hath a voice:
and the clouds in heaven look terribly on me; the Mighty One who
is against me speaketh in the wind of the cedar grove; and in silence
am I dried up.' Then Enos spake to his father, 'Arise, my father, arise,
we are but a little way from the place where I found the cake and the
pitcher.' And Cain said, 'How knowest thou!' and the child answered
– 'Behold the bare rocks are a few of thy strides distant from the forest;
and while even now thou wert lifting up thy voice, I heard the echo.'
Then the child took hold of his father, as if he would raise him: and
Cain being faint and feeble rose slowly on his knees and pressed him-
self against the trunk of a fir, and stood upright and followed the child.

The path was dark till within three strides' length of its termina-
tion, when it turned suddenly; the thick black trees formed a low
arch, and the moonlight appeared for a moment like a dazzling portal.
Enos ran before and stood in the open air; and when Cain, his father,
emerged from the darkness, the child was affrighted. For the mighty
limbs of Cain were wasted as by fire; his hair was as the matted curls
on the bison's forehead, and so glared his fierce and sullen eye beneath:

and the black abundant locks on either side, a rank and tangled mass, were stained and scorched, as though the grasp of a burning iron hand had striven to rend them; and his countenance told in a strange and terrible language of agonies that had been, and were, and were still to continue to be.

The scene around was desolate; as far as the eye could reach it was desolate: the bare rocks faced each other, and left a long and wide interval of thin white sand. You might wander on and look round and round, and peep into the crevices of the rocks and discover nothing that acknowledged the influence of the seasons. There was no spring, no summer, no autumn: and the winter's snow, that would have been lovely, fell not on these hot rocks and scorching sands. Never morning lark had poised himself over this desert; but the huge serpent often hissed there beneath the talons of the vulture, and the vulture screamed, his wings imprisoned within the coils of the serpent. The pointed and shattered summits of the ridges of the rocks made a rude mimicry of human concerns, and seemed to prophesy mutely of things that then were not; steeples, and battlements, and ships with naked masts. As far from the wood as a boy might sling a pebble of the brook, there was one rock by itself at a small distance from the main ridge. It had been precipitated there perhaps by the groan which the Earth uttered when our first father fell. Before you approached, it appeared to lie flat on the ground, but its base slanted from its point, and between its point and the sands a tall man might stand upright. It was here that Enos had found the pitcher and cake, and to this place he led his father. But ere they had reached the rock they beheld a human shape: his back was towards them, and they were advancing unperceived, when they heard him smite his breast and cry aloud, 'Woe is me! woe is me! I must never die again, and yet I am perishing with thirst and hunger.'

Pallid, as the reflection of the sheeted lightning on the heavy-sailing night-cloud, became the face of Cain; but the child Enos took hold of the shaggy skin, his father's robe, and raised his eyes to his father, and listening whispered, 'Ere yet I could speak, I am sure, O my father, that I heard that voice. Have not I often said that I remembered a sweet voice? O my father! this is it': and Cain trembled exceedingly. The voice was sweet indeed, but it was thin and querulous, like that of a feeble slave in misery, who despairs altogether, yet can not refrain himself from weeping and lamentation. And, behold! Enos glided forward, and creeping softly round the base of the rock, stood before the stranger, and looked up into his face. And the Shape shrieked, and turned round, and Cain beheld him, that his limbs and his face were those of his brother Abel whom he had killed! And Cain stood like one who struggles in his sleep because of the exceeding terribleness of a dream.

Thus as he stood in silence and darkness of soul, the Shape fell at his feet, and embraced his knees, and cried out with a bitter outcry, 'Thou eldest born of Adam, whom Eve, my mother, brought forth, cease to torment me! I was feeding my flocks in green pastures by the side of quiet rivers, and thou killedst me; and now I am in misery.' Then Cain closed his eyes, and hid them with his hands; and again he opened his eyes, and looked around him, and said to Enos, 'What beholdest thou? Didst thou hear a voice, my son?' 'Yes, my father, I beheld a man in unclean garments, and he uttered a sweet voice, full of lamentation.' Then Cain raised up the Shape that was like Abel, and said: – 'The Creator of our father, who had respect unto thee, and unto thy offering, wherefore hath he forsaken thee?' Then the Shape shrieked a second time, and rent his garment, and his naked skin was like the white sands beneath their feet; and he shrieked yet a third time, and threw himself on his face upon the sand that was black with the shadow of the rock, and Cain and Enos sate beside him; the child by his right hand, and Cain by his left. They were all three under the rock, and within the shadow. The Shape that was like Abel raised himself up, and spake to the child, 'I know where the cold waters are, but I may not drink, wherefore didst thou then take away my pitcher?' But Cain said, 'Didst thou not find favour in the sight of the Lord thy God?' The Shape answered, 'The Lord is God of the living only, the dead have another God.' Then the child Enos lifted up his eyes and prayed; but Cain rejoiced secretly in his heart. 'Wretched shall they be all the days of their mortal life,' exclaimed the Shape, 'who sacrifice worthy and acceptable sacrifices to the God of the dead; but after death their toil ceaseth. Woe is me, for I was well beloved by the God of the living, and cruel wert thou, O my brother, who didst snatch me away from his power and his dominion.' Having uttered these words, he rose suddenly, and fled over the sands: and Cain said in his heart, 'The curse of the Lord is on me; but who is the God of the dead?' and he ran after the Shape, and the Shape fled shrieking over the sands, and the sands rose like white mists behind the steps of Cain, but the feet of him that was like Abel disturbed not the sands. He greatly outran Cain, and turning short, he wheeled round, and came again to the rock where they had been sitting, and where Enos still stood; and the child caught hold of his garment as he passed by, and he fell upon the ground. And Cain stopped, and beholding him not, said, 'he has passed into the dark woods,' and he walked slowly back to the rocks; and when he reached it the child told him that he had caught hold of his garment as he passed by, and that the man had fallen upon the ground: and Cain once more sate beside him, and said, 'Abel, my brother, I would lament for thee, but that the spirit within me is withered, and burnt up with extreme agony. Now, I pray thee, by thy flocks, and by thy pastures, and by the quiet rivers which thou lovedst, that thou tell me all that thou knowest. Who is the God of the dead? where doth he make his dwelling? what sacrifices are acceptable unto him? for I have offered, but have not been received; I have prayed, and have not been heard; and how can I be afflicted more than I already am?' The Shape arose and answered, 'O that thou hadst had pity on me as I will have pity on thee. Follow me, Son of Adam! and bring thy child with thee!'

And they three passed over the white sands between the rocks, silent as the shadows.

1798

TO —

I MIX in life, and labour to seem free,
     With common persons pleas'd and common things,
While every thought and action tends to thee,
     And every impulse from thy influence springs.

? 1798

KUBLA KHAN:

OR, A VISION IN A DREAM. A FRAGMENT

The following fragment is here published at the request of a poet of great and deserved celebrity [Lord Byron], and, as far as the Author's own opinions are concerned, rather as a psychological curiosity, than on the ground of any supposed *poetic* merits.

In the summer of the year 1797, the Author, then in ill health, had retired to a lonely farm-house between Porlock and Linton, on the Exmoor confines of Somerset and Devonshire. In consequence of a slight indisposition, an anodyne had been prescribed, from the effects of which he fell asleep in his chair at the moment that he was reading the following sentence, or words of the same substance, in 'Purchas's Pilgrimage': 'Here the Khan Kubla commanded a palace to be built, and a stately garden thereunto. And thus ten miles of fertile ground were inclosed with a wall.' The Author continued for about three hours in a profound sleep, at least of the external senses, during which time he has the most vivid confidence, that he could not have composed less than from two to three hundred lines; if that indeed can be called composition in which all the images rose up before him as *things*, with a parallel production of the correspondent expressions, without any sensation or consciousness of effort. On awaking he appeared to himself to have a distinct recollection of the whole, and taking his pen, ink, and paper, instantly and eagerly wrote down the lines that are here preserved. At this moment he was unfortunately called out by a person on business from Porlock, and detained by him above an hour, and on his return to his room, found, to his no small surprise and mortification, that though he still retained some vague and dim recollection of the general purport of the vision, yet, with the exception of some eight or ten scattered lines and images, all the rest had passed away like the images on the surface of a stream into which a stone has been cast, but, alas! without the after restoration of the latter!

> In Xanadu did Kubla Khan
> A stately pleasure-dome decree:
> Where Alph, the sacred river, ran
> Through caverns measureless to man
>   Down to a sunless sea.
> So twice five miles of fertile ground
> With walls and towers were girdled round:
> And there were gardens bright with sinuous rills,
> Where blossomed many an incense-bearing tree;
> And here were forests ancient as the hills,
> Enfolding sunny spots of greenery.
>
> But oh! that deep romantic chasm which slanted
> Down the green hill athwart a cedarn cover!
> A savage place! as holy and enchanted
> As e'er beneath a waning moon was haunted
> By woman wailing for her demon-lover!
> And from this chasm, with ceaseless turmoil seething,
> As if this earth in fast thick pants were breathing,
> A mighty fountain momently was forced:
> Amid whose swift half-intermitted burst
> Huge fragments vaulted like rebounding hail,
> Or chaffy grain beneath the thresher's flail:
> And 'mid these dancing rocks at once and ever
> It flung up momently the sacred river.

5

10

15

20

Five miles meandering with a mazy motion
Through wood and dale the sacred river ran,   25
Then reached the caverns measureless to man,
And sank in tumult to a lifeless ocean:
And 'mid this tumult Kubla heard from far
Ancestral voices prophesying war!
   The shadow of the dome of pleasure   30
   Floated midway on the waves;
   Where was heard the mingled measure
   From the fountain and the caves.
It was a miracle of rare device,
A sunny pleasure-dome with caves of ice!   35

   A damsel with a dulcimer
   In a vision once I saw:
   It was an Abyssinian maid,
   And on her dulcimer she played,
   Singing of Mount Abora.   40
   Could I revive within me
   Her symphony and song,
   To such a deep delight 'twould win me,
That with music loud and long,
I would build that dome in air,   45
That sunny dome! those caves of ice!
And all who heard should see them there,
And all should cry, Beware! Beware!
His flashing eyes, his floating hair!   50
Wave a circle round him thrice,
And close your eyes with holy dread,
For he on honey-dew hath fed,
And drunk the milk of Paradise.

  1798

FRAGMENT

SEA-WARD, white gleaming thro' the busy scud
With arching Wings, the sea-mew o'er my head
Posts on, as bent on speed, now passaging
Edges the stiffer Breeze, now, yielding, drifts,
Now floats upon the air, and sends from far
A wildly-wailing Note.

THE HOMERIC HEXAMETER

DESCRIBED AND EXEMPLIFIED

STRONGLY it bears us along in swelling and limitless billows,
Nothing before and nothing behind but the sky and the ocean.

1799

THE OVIDIAN ELEGIAC METRE

DESCRIBED AND EXEMPLIFIED

In the hexameter rises the fountain's silvery column;
In the pentameter aye falling in melody back.

1799

LOVE

ALL thoughts, all passions, all delights,
Whatever stirs this mortal frame,
All are but ministers of Love,
  And feed his sacred flame.

5 Oft in my waking dreams do I
Live o'er again that happy hour,
When midway on the mount I lay,
  Beside the ruined tower.

The moonshine, stealing o'er the scene
10 Had blended with the lights of eve;
And she was there, my hope, my joy,
  My own dear Genevieve!

She leant against the arméd man,
The statue of the arméd knight;
15 She stood and listened to my lay,
  Amid the lingering light.

Few sorrows hath she of her own,
My hope! my joy! my Genevieve!
She loves me best, whene'er I sing
20 The songs that make her grieve.

I played a soft and doleful air,
I sang an old and moving story –
An old rude song, that suited well
    That ruin wild and hoary.

She listened with a flitting blush,   25
With downcast eyes and modest grace;
For well she knew, I could not choose
    But gaze upon her face.

I told her of the Knight that wore
Upon his shield a burning brand;   30
And that for ten long years he wooed
    The Lady of the Land.

I told her how he pined: and ah!
The deep, the low, the pleading tone
With which I sang another's love,   35
    Interpreted my own.

She listened with a flitting blush,
With downcast eyes, and modest grace;
And she forgave me, that I gazed
    Too fondly on her face!   40

But when I told the cruel scorn
That crazed that bold and lovely Knight,
And that he crossed the mountain-woods,
    Nor rested day nor night;

That sometimes from the savage den,   45
And sometimes from the darksome shade,
And sometimes starting up at once
    In green and sunny glade, –

There came and looked him in the face
An angel beautiful and bright;   50
And that he knew it was a Fiend,
    This miserable Knight!

And that unknowing what he did,
He leaped amid a murderous band,
And saved from outrage worse than death   55
    The Lady of the Land!

And how she wept, and clasped his knees;
And how she tended him in vain –
And ever strove to expiate
    The scorn that crazed his brain; –

And that she nursed him in a cave;
And how his madness went away,
When on the yellow forest-leaves
    A dying man he lay; –

His dying words – but when I reached
That tenderest strain of all the ditty,
My faultering voice and pausing harp
    Disturbed her soul with pity!

All impulses of soul and sense
Had thrilled my guileless Genevieve;
The music and the doleful tale,
    The rich and balmy eve;

And hopes, and fears that kindle hope,
An undistinguishable throng,
And gentle wishes long subdued,
    Subdued and cherished long!

She wept with pity and delight,
She blushed with love, and virgin-shame;
And like the murmur of a dream,
    I heard her breathe my name.

Her bosom heaved – she stepped aside,
As conscious of my look she stepped –
Then suddenly, with timorous eye
    She fled to me and wept.

She half enclosed me with her arms,
She pressed me with a meek embrace;
And bending back her head, looked up,
    And gazed upon my face.

'Twas partly love, and partly fear,
And partly 'twas a bashful art,
That I might rather feel, than see,
    The swelling of her heart.

I calmed her fears, and she was calm,
And told her love with virgin pride;
And so I won my Genevieve,   95
    My bright and beauteous Bride.

1799

APOLOGIA PRO VITA SUA

THE poet in his lone yet genial hour
Gives to his eyes a magnifying power:
Or rather he emancipates his eyes
From the black shapeless accidents of size –
In unctuous cones of kindling coal,   5
Or smoke upwreathing from the pipe's trim bole,
    His gifted ken can see
    Phantoms of sublimity.

1800

A THOUGHT SUGGESTED BY A VIEW

OF SADDLEBACK IN CUMBERLAND

ON stern Blencartha's perilous height
  The winds are tyrannous and strong;
And flashing forth unsteady light
From stern Blencartha's skiey height,
  As loud the torrents throng!   5
Beneath the moon, in gentle weather,
  They bind the earth and sky together.
But oh! the sky and all its forms, how quiet!
The things that seek the earth, how full of noise and riot!

1800

DEJECTION: AN ODE

[WRITTEN APRIL 4, 1802]

Late, late yestreen I saw the new Moon,
With the old Moon in her arms;
And I fear, I fear, my Master dear!
We shall have a deadly storm.

Ballad of Sir Patrick Spence

I

WELL! If the Bard was weather-wise, who made
  The grand old ballad of Sir Patrick Spence,
  This night, so tranquil now, will not go hence
Unroused by winds, that ply a busier trade
5 Than those which mould yon cloud in lazy flakes,
Or the dull sobbing draft, that moans and rakes
Upon the strings of this Aeolian lute,
  Which better far were mute.
For lo! the New-moon winter-bright!
10 And overspread with phantom light,
  (With swimming phantom light o'erspread
  But rimmed and circled by a silver thread)
I see the old Moon in her lap, foretelling
  The coming-on of rain and squally blast.
15 And oh! that even now the gust were swelling,
  And the slant night-shower driving loud and fast!
Those sounds which oft have raised me, whilst they awed,
  And sent my soul abroad,
Might now perhaps their wonted impulse give,
20 Might startle this dull pain, and make it move and live!

II

A grief without a pang, void, dark, and drear,
A stifled, drowsy, unimpassioned grief,
Which finds no natural outlet, no relief,
  In word, or sigh, or tear –
25 O Lady! in this wan and heartless mood,
To other thoughts by yonder throstle woo'd,
  All this long eve, so balmy and serene,
Have I been gazing on the western sky,
  And its peculiar tint of yellow green:

And still I gaze – and with how blank an eye! 30
And those thin clouds above, in flakes and bars,
That give away their motion to the stars;
Those stars, that glide behind them or between,
Now sparkling, now bedimmed, but always seen:
Yon crescent Moon, as fixed as if it grew 35
In its own cloudless, starless lake of blue;
I see them all so excellently fair,
I see, not feel, how beautiful they are!

III

My genial spirits fail;
And what can these avail 40
To lift the smothering weight from off my breast?
It were a vain endeavour,
Though I should gaze for ever
On that green light that lingers in the west:
I may not hope from outward forms to win 45
The passion and the life, whose fountains are within.

IV

O Lady! we receive but what we give,
And in our life alone does Nature live:
Ours is her wedding garment, ours her shroud!
And would we aught behold, of higher worth, 50
Than that inanimate cold world allowed
To the poor loveless ever-anxious crowd,
Ah! from the soul itself must issue forth
A light, a glory, a fair luminous cloud
Enveloping the Earth – 55
And from the soul itself must there be sent
A sweet and potent voice, of its own birth
Of all sweet sounds the life and element!

V

O pure of heart! thou need'st not ask of me
What this strong music in the soul may be! 60
What, and wherein it doth exist,
This light, this glory, this fair luminous mist,
This beautiful and beauty-making power.
Joy, virtuous Lady! Joy that ne'er was given,

65 Save to the pure, and in their purest hour,
    Life, and Life's effluence, cloud at once and shower,
    Joy, Lady! is the spirit and the power,
    Which wedding Nature to us gives in dower
        A new Earth and new Heaven,
70 Undreamt of by the sensual and the proud –
    Joy is the sweet voice, Joy the luminous cloud –
            We in ourselves rejoice!
    And thence flows all that charms or ear or sight,
        All melodies the echoes of that voice,
75 All colours a suffusion from that light.

VI

There was a time when, though my path was rough,
    This joy within me dallied with distress,
And all misfortunes were but as the stuff
    Whence Fancy made me dreams of happiness:
80 For hope grew round me, like the twining vine,
And fruits, and foliage, not my own, seemed mine.
But now afflictions bow me down to earth:
Nor care I that they rob me of my mirth;
            But oh! each visitation
85 Suspends what nature gave me at my birth,
    My shaping spirit of Imagination.
For not to think of what I needs must feel,
    But to be still and patient, all I can;
And haply by abstruse research to steal
90   From my own nature all the natural man –
    This was my sole resource, my only plan:
Till that which suits a part infects the whole,
And now is almost grown the habit of my soul.

VII

Hence, viper thoughts, that coil around my mind,
95   Reality's dark dream!
I turn from you, and listen to the wind,
    Which long has raved unnoticed. What a scream
Of agony by torture lengthened out
That lute sent forth! Thou Wind, that rav'st without,
100   Bare crag, or mountain-tairn, or blasted tree,
    Or pine-grove whither woodman never clomb,

Or lonely house, long held the witches' home,
  Methinks were fitter instruments for thee,
Mad Lutanist! who in this month of showers,
Of dark-brown gardens, and of peeping flowers,   105
Mak'st Devils' yule, with worse than wintry song,
The blossoms, buds, and timorous leaves among.
    Thou Actor, perfect in all tragic sounds!
Thou mighty Poet, e'en to frenzy bold!
      What tell'st thou now about?   110
     'Tis of the rushing of an host in rout,
  With groans, of trampled men, with smarting wounds –
At once they groan with pain, and shudder with the cold!
But hush! there is a pause of deepest silence!
    And all that noise, as of a rushing crowd,   115
With groans, and tremulous shudderings – all is over –
  It tells another tale, with sounds less deep and loud!
    A tale of less affright,
And tempered with delight,
As Otway's self had framed the tender lay, –   120
    'Tis of a little child
     Upon a lonesome wild,
Not far from home, but she hath lost her way:
And now moans low in bitter grief and fear,
And now screams loud, and hopes to make her mother hear.

VIII

'Tis midnight, but small thoughts have I of sleep: 126
Full seldom may my friend such vigils keep!
Visit her, gentle Sleep! with wings of healing,
  And may this storm be but a mountain-birth,
May all the stars hang bright above her dwelling,   130
  Silent as though they watched the sleeping Earth!
    With light heart may she rise,
    Gay fancy, cheerful eyes,
  Joy lift her spirit, joy attune her voice;
To her may all things live, from pole to pole,   135
Their life the eddying of her living soul!
  O simple spirit, guided from above,
Dear Lady! friend devoutest of my choice,
Thus mayest thou ever, evermore rejoice.

1802

INSCRIPTION FOR A FOUNTAIN ON A HEATH

THIS Sycamore, oft musical with bees, –
Such tents the Patriarchs loved! O long unharmed
May all its agéd boughs o'er-canopy
The small round basin, which this jutting stone
5   Keeps pure from falling leaves! Long may the Spring,
Quietly as a sleeping infant's breath,
Send up cold waters to the traveller
With soft and even pulse! Nor ever cease
Yon tiny cone of sand its soundless dance,
10   Which at the bottom, like a Fairy's Page,
As merry and no taller, dances still,
Nor wrinkles the smooth surface of the Fount.
Here Twilight is and Coolness: here is moss,
A soft seat, and a deep and ample shade.
15   Thou may'st toil far and find no second tree.
Drink, Pilgrim, here; Here rest! and if thy heart
Be innocent, here too shalt thou refresh
Thy spirit, listening to some gentle sound,
Or passing gale or hum of murmuring bees!

1802

ANSWER TO A CHILD'S QUESTION

Do you ask what the birds say? The Sparrow, the Dove,
The Linnet and Thrush say, 'I love and I love!'
In the winter they're silent – the wind is so strong;
What it says, I don't know, but it sings a loud song.
5   But green leaves, and blossoms, and sunny warm weather,
And singing, and loving – all come back together.
But the Lark is so brimful of gladness and love,
The green fields below him, the blue sky above,
That he sings, and he sings; and for ever sings he –
10   'I love my Love, and my Love loves me!'

1802

THE PAINS OF SLEEP

ERE on my bed my limbs I lay,
It hath not been my use to pray
With moving lips or bended knees;
But silently, by slow degrees,
My spirit I to Love compose, 5
In humble trust mine eye-lids close,
With reverential resignation,
No wish conceived, no thought exprest,
Only a sense of supplication;
A sense o'er all my soul imprest 10
That I am weak, yet not unblest,
Since in me, round me, every where
Eternal Strength and Wisdom are.

But yester-night I prayed aloud
In anguish and in agony, 15
Up-starting from the fiendish crowd
Of shapes and thoughts that tortured me:
A lurid light, a trampling throng,
Sense of intolerable wrong,
And whom I scorned, those only strong! 20
Thirst of revenge, the powerless will
Still baffled, and yet burning still!
Desire with loathing strangely mixed
On wild or hateful objects fixed.
Fantastic passions! maddening brawl! 25
And shame and terror over all!
Deeds to be hid which were not hid,
Which all confused I could not know
Whether I suffered, or I did:
For all seemed guilt, remorse or woe, 30
My own or others still the same
Life-stifling fear, soul-stifling shame.

So two nights passed: the night's dismay
Saddened and stunned the coming day.
Sleep, the wide blessing, seemed to me 35
Distemper's worst calamity.
The third night, when my own loud scream

Had waked me from the fiendish dream,
O'ercome with sufferings strange and wild,
40   I wept as I had been a child;
And having thus by tears subdued
My anguish to a milder mood,
Such punishments, I said, were due
To natures deepliest stained with sin, –
45   For aye entempesting anew
The unfathomable hell within,
The horror of their deeds to view,
To know and loathe, yet wish and do!
Such griefs with such men well agree,
50   But wherefore, wherefore fall on me?
To be beloved is all I need,
And whom I love, I love indeed.

1803

A BECK IN WINTER

OVER the broad, the shallow, rapid stream,
The Alder, a vast hollow Trunk, and ribb'd –
All mossy green with mosses manifold,
And ferns still waving in the river-breeze
5   Sent out, like fingers, five projecting trunks –
The shortest twice 6 (?) of a tall man's strides. –
One curving upward in its middle growth
Rose straight with grove of twigs – a pollard tree: –
The rest more backward, gradual in descent –
10   One in the brook and one befoamed its waters:
One ran along the bank in the elk-like head
And pomp of antlers –

January 1804

PHANTOM*

ALL look and likeness caught from earth
All accident of kin and birth,
Had pass'd away. There was no trace
Of aught on that illumined face,

Uprais'd beneath the rifted stone 5
But of one spirit all her own; —
She, she herself, and only she,
Shone through her body visibly.

1805

*Coleridge wrote this poem in his notebook on 8 February 1805, together with the following entry:
On Friday Night, 8th Feb. 1805, my feeling, in sleep, of exceeding great love for my infant, seen by me in the dream! — yet so as it might be Sara, Derwent, or Berkley, and still it was an individual babe and mine.

This abstract self is, indeed, in its nature a Universal personified, as Life, Soul, Spirit, etc. Will not this *prove* it to be a *deeper* feeling, and of such intimate affinity with ideas, so as to modify them and become one with them; whereas the appetites and the feelings of revenge and anger co-exist with the ideas, not combine with them, and alter the apparent effect of this form, not the forms themselves? Certain modifications of fear seem to approach nearest to this love-sense in its manner of acting.

A SUNSET

Upon the mountain's edge with light touch resting,
There a brief while the globe of splendour sits
  And seems a creature of the earth; but soon
    More changeful than the Moon,
To wane fantastic his great orb submits, 5
Or cone or mow of fire: till sinking slowly
Even to a star at length he lessens wholly.

Abrupt, as Spirits vanish, he is sunk!
A soul-like breeze possesses all the wood.
  The boughs, the sprays have stood 10
As motionless as stands the ancient trunk!
But every leaf through all the forest flutters,
And deep the cavern of the fountain mutters.

1805

WHAT IS LIFE?

RESEMBLES life what once was deem'd of light,
Too ample in itself for human sight?
An absolute self – an element ungrounded –
All that we see, all colours of all shade
5   By encroach of darkness made? –
Is very life by consciousness unbounded?
And all the thoughts, pains, joys of mortal breath,
A war-embrace of wrestling life and death?

1805

FRAGMENT

THE spruce and limber yellow-hammer
In the dawn of spring and sultry summer,
In hedge or tree the hours beguiling
With notes as of one who brass is filing.

1807

TO WILLIAM WORDSWORTH

COMPOSED ON THE NIGHT AFTER HIS RECITATION OF A POEM ON THE GROWTH OF AN INDIVIDUAL MIND

FRIEND of the wise! and Teacher of the Good!
Into my heart have I received that Lay
More than historic, that prophetic Lay
Wherein (high theme by thee first sung aright)
5   Of the foundations and the building up
Of a Human Spirit thou hast dared to tell
What may be told, to the understanding mind
Revealable; and what within the mind
By vital breathings secret as the soul
10   Of vernal growth, oft quickens in the heart
Thoughts all too deep for words! –

                                    Theme hard as high!
Of smiles spontaneous, and mysterious fears
(The first-born they of Reason and twin-birth),

Of tides obedient to external force,
And currents self-determined, as might seem,   15
Or by some inner Power; of moments awful,
Now in thy inner life, and now abroad,
When power streamed from thee, and thy soul received
The light reflected, as a light bestowed –
Of fancies fair, and milder hours of youth,   20
Hyblean murmurs of poetic thought
Industrious in its joy, in vales and glens
Native or outland, lakes and famous hills!
Or on the lonely high-road, when the stars
Were rising; or by secret mountain-streams,   25
The guides and the companions of thy way!

Of more than Fancy, of the Social Sense
Distending wide, and man beloved as man,
Where France in all her towns lay vibrating
Like some becalméd bark beneath the burst   30
Of Heaven's immediate thunder, when no cloud
Is visible, or shadow on the main.
For thou wert there, thine own brows garlanded,
Amid the tremor of a realm aglow,
Amid a mighty nation jubilant,   35
When from the general heart of human kind
Hope sprang forth like a full-born Deity!
– – Of that dear Hope afflicted and struck down,
So summoned homeward, thenceforth calm and sure
From the dread watch-tower of man's absolute self,   40
With light unwaning on her eyes, to look
Far on – herself a glory to behold,
The Angel of the vision! Then (last strain)
Of Duty, chosen Laws controlling choice,
Action and joy! – An Orphic song indeed,   45
A song divine of high and passionate thoughts
To their own music chaunted!

                    O great Bard!
Ere yet that last strain dying awed the air,
With stedfast eye I viewed thee in the choir
Of ever-enduring men. The truly great   50
Have all one age, and from one visible space
Shed influence! They, both in power and act,

Are permanent, and Time is not with them,
Save as it worketh for them, they in it.
55 Nor less a sacred Roll, than those of old,
And to be placed, as they, with gradual fame
Among the archives of mankind, thy work
Makes audible a linked lay of Truth,
Of Truth profound a sweet continuous lay,
60 Not learnt, but native, her own natural notes!
Ah! as I listened with a heart forlorn,
The pulses of my being beat anew:
And even as Life returns upon the drowned,
Life's joy rekindling roused a throng of pains –
65 Keen pangs of Love, awakening as a babe
Turbulent, with an outcry in the heart;
And fears self-willed, that shunned the eye of Hope;
And Hope that scarce would know itself from Fear;
Sense of past Youth, and Manhood come in vain,
70 And Genius given, and Knowledge won in vain;
And all which I had culled in wood-walks wild,
And all which patient toil had reared, and all,
Commune with thee had opened out – but flowers
Strewed on my corse, and borne upon my bier
75 In the same coffin, for the self-same grave!

That way no more! and ill beseems it me,
Who came a welcomer in herald's guise,
Singing of Glory, and Futurity,
To wander back on such unhealthful road,
80 Plucking the poisons of self-harm! And ill
Such intertwine beseems triumphal wreaths
Strew'd before thy advancing!

Nor do thou,
Sage Bard! impair the memory of that hour
Of thy communion with my nobler mind
85 By pity or grief, already felt too long!
Nor let my words import more blame than needs.
The tumult rose and ceased: for Peace is nigh
Where Wisdom's voice has found a listening heart.
Amid the howl of more than wintry storms,
90 The Halcyon hears the voice of vernal hours
Already or. the wing.

Eve following eve,
Dear tranquil time, when the sweet sense of Home
Is sweetest! moments for their own sake hailed
And more desired, more precious, for thy song,
In silence listening, like a devout child,   95
My soul lay passive, by thy various strain
Driven as in surges now beneath the stars,
With momentary stars of my own birth,
Fair constellated foam, still darting off
Into the darkness; now a tranquil sea,   100
Outspread and bright, yet swelling to the moon.

And when – O Friend! my comforter and guide!
Strong in thyself, and powerful to give strength! –
Thy long sustainéd Song finally closed,
And thy deep voice had ceased – yet thou thyself   105
Wert still before my eyes, and round us both
That happy vision of belovéd faces –
Scarce conscious, and yet conscious of its close
I sate, my being blended in one thought
(Thought was it? or aspiration? or resolve?)   110
Absorbed, yet hanging still upon the sound –
And when I rose, I found myself in prayer.

January 1807

PSYCHE

THE butterfly the ancient Grecians made
The soul's fair emblem, and its only name –
But of the soul, escaped the slavish trade
Of mortal life! – For in this earthly frame
Ours is the reptile's lot, much toil, much blame,   5
Manifold motions making little speed,
And to deform and kill the things whereon we feed.

1808

FRAGMENT

THE body,
Eternal Shadow of the finite Soul,
The Soul's self-symbol, its image of itself.
Its own yet not itself.

TIME, REAL AND IMAGINARY

AN ALLEGORY

On the wide level of a mountain's head,
(I knew not where, but 'twas some faery place)
Their pinions, ostrich-like, for sails out-spread,
Two lovely children run an endless race,
5   A sister and a brother!
       This far outstripp'd the other;
Yet ever runs she with reverted face,
And looks and listens for the boy behind:
       For he, alas! is blind!
10 O'er rough and smooth with even step he passed,
And knows not whether he be first or last.

?1812

SONG

FROM *Zapolya*

A sunny shaft did I behold,
    From sky to earth it slanted:
And poised therein a bird so bold –
    Sweet bird, thou wert enchanted!

5 He sank, he rose, he twinkled, he trolled
    Within that shaft of sunny mist;
His eyes of fire, his beak of gold,
    All else of amethyst!

And thus he sang: 'Adieu! adieu!
10 Love's dreams prove seldom true.
The blossoms they make no delay:
The sparkling dew-drops will not stay.
    Sweet month of May,
      We must away;
15   Far, far away!
          To-day! to-day!'

1815

HUNTING SONG

FROM *Zapolya*

UP, up! ye dames, and lasses gay!
To the meadows trip away.
'Tis you must tend the flocks this morn,
And scare the small birds from the corn.
    Not a soul at home may stay: 5
      For the shepherds must go
      With lance and bow
    To hunt the wolf in the woods to-day.

Leave the hearth and leave the house
To the cricket and the mouse: 10
Find grannam out a sunny seat,
With babe and lambkin at her feet.
    Not a soul at home must stay:
      For the shepherds must go
      With lance and bow   15
    To hunt the wolf in the woods to-day.

    1815

THE KNIGHT'S TOMB

WHERE is the grave of Sir Arthur O'Kellyn?
Where may the grave of that good man be? –
By the side of a spring, on the breast of Helvellyn,
Under the twigs of a young birch tree!
The oak that in summer was sweet to hear,   5
And rustled its leaves in the fall of the year,
And whistled and roared in the winter alone,
Is gone, – and the birch in its stead is grown. –
The Knight's bones are dust,
And his good sword rust; –   10
His soul is with the saints, I trust.

    ?1817

ON DONNE'S POETRY

WITH Donne, whose muse on dromedary trots,
Wreathe iron pokers into true-love knots;
Rhyme's sturdy cripple, fancy's maze and clue,
Wit's forge and fire-blast, meaning's press and screw.

?1818

WORK WITHOUT HOPE

LINES COMPOSED 21ST FEBRUARY 1825

ALL Nature seems at work. Slugs leave their lair –
The bees are stirring – birds are on the wing –
And Winter slumbering in the open air,
Wears on his smiling face a dream of Spring!
5   And I the while, the sole unbusy thing,
Nor honey make, nor pair, nor build, nor sing.

   Yet well I ken the banks where amaranths blow,
Have traced the fount whence streams of nectar flow.
Bloom, O ye amaranths! bloom for whom ye may,
10 For me ye bloom not! Glide, rich, streams, away!
With lips unbrightened, wreathless brow, I stroll:
And would you learn the spells that drowse my soul?
Work without Hope draws nectar in a sieve,
And Hope without an object cannot live.

1825

SONG

THOUGH veiled in spires of myrtle-wreath,
Love is a sword which cuts its sheath,
And through the clefts itself has made,
We spy the flashes of the blade!

5 But through the clefts itself has made
We likewise see Love's flashing blade,
By rust consumed, or snapt in twain;
And only hilt and stump remain.

?1825

DESIRE

Ἔρως ἀεὶ λάληθρος ἑταῖρος

IN many ways does the full heart reveal
The presence of the love it would conceal;
But in far more th' estrangéd heart lets know
The absence of the love, which yet it fain would shew.

1826

COLOGNE

IN Köhln, a town of monks and bones,
And pavements fang'd with murderous stones
And rags, and hags, and hideous wenches;
I counted two and seventy stenches,
All well defined, and several stinks!   5
Ye Nymphs that reign o'er sewers and sinks,
The river Rhine, it is well known,
Doth wash your city of Cologne;
But tell me, Nymphs, what power divine
Shall henceforth wash the river Rhine?   10

1828

THE NETHERLANDS

WATER and windmills, greenness, Islets green; –
Willows whose Trunks beside the shadows stood
Of their own higher half, and willowy swamp: –
Farmhouses that at anchor seem'd – in the inland sky
The fog-transfixing Spires –   5
Water, wide water, greenness and green banks,
And water seen –

June 1828

DESIRE

WHERE true Love burns Desire is Love's pure flame;
It is the reflex of our earthly frame,
That takes its meaning from the nobler part,
And but translates the language of the heart.

?1830

SELF-KNOWLEDGE

– E coelo descendit γνῶθι σεαυτόν

Juvenal, XI, 27

Γνῶθι σεαυτόν ! – and is this the prime
And heaven-sprung adage of the olden time! –
Say, canst thou make thyself? – Learn first that trade; –
Haply thou mayst know what thyself had made.
5   What hast thou, Man, that thou dar'st call thine own? –
What is there in thee, Man, that can be known? –
Dark fluxion, all unfixable by thought,
A phantom dim of past and future wrought,
Vain sister of the worm, – life, death, soul, clod –
10   Ignore thyself, and strive to know thy God!

1832

EPITAPH

Stop, Christian passer-by! – Stop, child of God,
And read with gentle breast. Beneath this sod
A poet lies, or that which once seem'd he.
O, lift one thought in prayer for S. T. C.;
5   That he who many a year with toil of breath
Found death in life, may here find life in death!
Mercy for praise – to be forgiven for fame
He ask'd, and hoped, through Christ. Do thou the same!

9 November 1833

PROSE

ON READERS

READERS may be divided into four classes:

1. Sponges, who absorb all they read, and return it nearly in the same state, only a little dirtied.

2. Sand-glasses, who retain nothing, and are content to get through a book for the sake of getting through the time.

3. Strain-bags, who retain merely the dregs of what they read.

4. Mogul diamonds, equally rare and valuable, who profit by what they read, and enable others to profit by it also.

Lectures, 1811-12

LETTERS

TO THOMAS POOLE

February, 1797

MY DEAR POOLE,

I could inform the dullest author how he might write an interesting book. Let him relate the events of his own life with honesty, not disguising the feelings that accompanied them. I never yet read even a Methodist's Experience in the *Gospel Magazine* without receiving instruction and amusement; and I should almost despair of that man who could peruse the *Life of John Woolman* without an amelioration of heart. As to my Life, it has all the charms of variety, – high life and low life, vices and virtues, great folly and some wisdom. However, what I am depends on what I have been; and you, *my best Friend!* have a right to the narration. To me the task will be a useful one. It will renew and deepen my reflections on the past; and it will perhaps make you behold with no unforgiving or impatient eye those weaknesses and defects in my character, which so many untoward circumstances have concurred to plant there. . . .

TO THOMAS POOLE

March, 1797

MY DEAR POOLE,

My father (Vicar of, and Schoolmaster at, Ottery St Mary, Devon) was a profound mathematician, and well versed in the Latin, Greek, and Oriental Languages. He published, or rather attempted to publish, several works; 1st, Miscellaneous Dissertations arising from the 17th and 18th Chapters of the Book of Judges; 2d, *Sententiae excerptae*, for the use of his own school; and 3d, his best work, a Critical Latin Grammar; in the preface to which he proposes a bold innovation in the names of the cases. My father's new nomenclature was not likely to become popular, although it must be allowed to be both sonorous and expressive. *Exempli gratia*, he calls the ablative the *quippe-quare-quale-quia-quidditive case*! My father made the world his confidant with respect to his learning and ingenuity, and the world seems to have kept the secret very faithfully. His various works, uncut, unthumbed, have been preserved free from all pollution. This piece of good luck promises to be hereditary; for all *my* compositions have the same amiable *home-studying* propensity. The truth is, my father was not a first-rate genius; he was, however, a first-rate Christian. I need not detain you with his character. In learning, good-heartedness, absentness of mind, and excessive ignorance of the world, he was a perfect Parson Adams.

My mother was an admirable economist, and managed exclusively. My eldest brother's name was John. He went over to the East Indies in the Company's service; he was a successful officer and a brave one, I have heard. He died of a consumption there about eight years ago. My second brother was called William. He went to Pembroke College, Oxford, and afterwards was assistant to Mr Newcome's School, at Hackney. He died of a putrid fever the year before my father's death, and just as he was on the eve of marriage with Miss Jane Hart, the eldest daughter of a very wealthy citizen of Exeter. My third brother, James, has been in the army since the age of sixteen, has married a woman of fortune, and now lives at Ottery St Mary, a respectable man. My brother Edward, the wit of the family, went to Pembroke College, and afterwards to Salisbury, as assistant to Dr Skinner. He married a woman twenty years older than his mother. She is dead, and he now lives at Ottery St Mary. My fifth brother, George, was educated at Pembroke College, Oxford, and from there went to Mr Newcome's, Hackney, on the death of William. He stayed there fourteen years, when the living of Ottery St Mary was given him. There he has now a fine school, and has lately married Miss Jane Hart, who with beauty and wealth had remained a faithful widow to the memory of William for sixteen years. My brother George is a man of reflective mind and elegant genius. He possesses learning in a greater degree than any of the family, excepting myself. His manners are grave and hued over with a tender sadness. In his moral character he approaches every way nearer to perfection than any man I ever yet knew; indeed, he is worth the whole family in a lump. My sixth brother, Luke (indeed, the seventh, for one brother, the second, died in his infancy, and I had forgot to mention him), was bred as a medical man. He married Miss Sara Hart, and died at the age of twenty-two, leaving one child, a lovely boy, still alive. My brother Luke was a man of uncommon genius, a severe student, and a good man. The eighth child was a sister, Anne. She died a little after my brother Luke, aged twenty-one;

> Rest, gentle Shade! and wait thy Maker's will;
> Then rise *unchanged*, and be an Angel still!

The ninth child was called Francis. He went out as a midshipman, under Admiral Graves. His ship lay on the Bengal coast, and he accidentally met his brother John, who took him to land, and procured him a commission in the Army. He died from the effects of a delirious fever brought on by his excessive exertions at the siege of Seringapatam, at which his conduct had been so gallant, that Lord Cornwallis paid him a high compliment in the presence of the army, and presented him with a valuable gold watch, which my mother now has. All my brothers are remarkably handsome; but they were as inferior to Francis as I am to them. He went by the name of 'the handsome Coleridge'. The tenth and last child was S. T. Coleridge, the subject of these epistles, born (as I told you in my last) October 20, 1772. . . .

TO THOMAS POOLE

October 9, 1797

My Dearest Poole,

From March to October – a long silence! But (as) it is possible that I may have been preparing materials for future letters, the time cannot be considered as altogether subtracted from you.

From October, 1775, to October, 1778. These three years I continued at the Reading School, because I was too little to be trusted among my father's schoolboys. After breakfast I had a halfpenny given me, with which I bought three cakes at the baker's close by the school of my old mistress; and these were my dinner on every day except Saturday and Sunday, when I used to dine at home, and wallowed in a beef and pudding dinner. I am remarkably fond of beans and bacon; and this fondness I attribute to my father having given me a penny for having eat a large quantity of beans on Saturday. For the other boys did not like them, and as it was an economic food, my father thought that my attachment and penchant for it ought to be encouraged. My father was very fond of me, and I was my mother's darling; in consequence I was very miserable. For Molly, who had nursed my brother Francis, and was immoderately fond of him, hated me because my mother took more notice of me than of Frank, and Frank hated me because my mother gave me now and then a bit of cake, when he had none, – quite forgetting that for one bit of cake which I had and he had not, he had twenty sops in the pan, and pieces of bread and butter with sugar on them from Molly, from whom I received only thumps and ill names.

So I became fretful and timorous, and a tell-tale; and the schoolboys drove me from play, and were always tormenting me, and hence I took no pleasure in boyish sports, but read incessantly. My father's sister kept an *everything* shop at Crediton, and there I read through all the gilt-cover little books that could be had at that time, and likewise all the uncovered tales of Tom Hickathrift, Jack the Giant-killer, &c., &c., &c., &c. And I used to lie by the wall and *mope*, and my spirits used to come upon me suddenly; and in a flood of them I was accustomed to race up and down the churchyard, and act over all I had been reading, on the docks, the nettles, and the rank grass. At six years old I remember to have read Belisarius, Robinson Crusoe, and Philip Quarles; and then I found the Arabian Nights' Entertainments, one tale of which (the tale of a man who was compelled to seek for a pure virgin) made so deep an impression on me (I had read it in the evening while my mother was mending stockings), that I was haunted by spectres, whenever I was in the dark; and I distinctly remember the anxious and fearful eagerness with which I used to watch the window in which the books lay, and whenever the sun lay upon them, I would seize it, carry it by the wall, and bask and read. My father found out the effect which these books had produced, and burnt them.

So I became a *dreamer*, and acquired an indisposition to all bodily activity; and I was fretful, and inordinately passionate, and as I could not play at anything, and was slothful, I was despised and hated by the boys; and because I could read and spell and had, I may truly say, a memory and understanding forced into almost an unnatural ripeness, I was flattered and wondered at by all the old women. And so I became very vain, and despised most of the boys that were at all near my own age, and before I was eight years old I was a *character*. Sensibility, imagination, vanity, sloth, and feelings of deep and bitter contempt for all who traversed the orbit of my understanding, were even then prominent and manifest.

From October, 1778, to 1779. That which I began to be from three to six I continued from six to nine. In this year (1778) I was admitted into the Grammar School, and soon outstripped all of my age. I had a dangerous putrid fever this year. My brother George lay ill of the same fever in the next room. My poor brother Francis, I remember, stole up in spite of orders to the contrary, and sat by my bedside and read Pope's Homer to me. Frank had a violent love of beating me; but whenever that was superseded by any humour or circumstances, he was always very fond of me, and used to regard me with a strange mixture of admiration and contempt. Strange it was not, for he hated books, and loved climbing, fighting, playing and robbing orchards, to distraction.

My mother relates a story of me, which I repeat here, because it must be regarded as my first piece of wit. During my fever, I asked why Lady Northcote (our neighbour) did not come and see me. My mother said she was afraid of catching the fever. I was piqued, and answered, 'Ah, Mamma! the four Angels round my bed an't afraid of catching it!' I suppose you know the prayer:

> Matthew! Mark! Luke and John!
> God bless the bed which I lie on.
> Four angels round me spread,
> Two at my foot, and two at my head.

This prayer I said nightly, and most firmly believed the truth of it. Frequently have I (half-awake and half-asleep, my body diseased and fevered by my imagination) seen armies of ugly things bursting in upon me, and these four angels keeping them off. In my next I shall carry on my life to my father's death.

God bless you, my dear Poole, and your affectionate

S. T. COLERIDGE

TO THOMAS POOLE

October 16, 1797

DEAR POOLE

From October, 1779, to October, 1781. I had asked my mother one evening to cut my cheese entire, so that I might toast it. This was no easy matter, it being a *crumbly* cheese. My mother, however, did it. I went into the garden for something or other, and in the mean time my brother Frank *minced* my cheese 'to disappoint the favorite'. I returned, saw the exploit, and in an agony of passion flew at Frank. He pretended to have been seriously hurt by my blow, flung himself on the ground, and there lay with outstretched limbs. I hung over him moaning, and in a great fright; he leaped up, and with a horse-laugh gave me a severe blow in the face. I seized a knife, and was running at him, when my mother came in and took me by the arm. I expected a flogging, and struggling from her I ran away to a hill at the bottom of which the Otter flows, about one mile from Ottery. There I stayed; my rage died away, but my obstinacy vanquished my fears, and taking out a little shilling book which had, at the end, morning and evening prayers, I very devoutly repeated them – thinking at the *same time* with inward and gloomy satisfaction how miserable my mother must be! I distinctly remember my feelings when I saw a Mr Vaughan pass over the bridge, at about a furlong's distance, and how I watched the calves in the fields beyond the river. It grew dark and I fell asleep. It was towards the latter end of October, and it proved a dreadful stormy night. I felt the cold in my sleep, and dreamt that I was pulling the blanket over me, and actually pulled over me a dry thorn bush which lay on the hill. In my sleep I had rolled from the top of the hill to within three yards of the river, which flowed by the unfenced edge at the bottom. I awoke several times, and finding myself wet and stiff and cold, closed my eyes again that I might forget it.

In the mean time my mother waited about half an hour, expecting my return when the *sulks* had evaporated. I not returning, she sent into the churchyard and round the town. Not found! Several men and all the boys were sent to ramble about and seek me. In vain! My mother was almost distracted; and at ten o'clock at night I was *cried* by the crier in Ottery, and in two villages near it, with a reward offered for me. No one went to bed; indeed, I believe half the town were up all the night. To return to myself. About five in the morning, or a little after, I was broad awake, and attempted to get up and walk; but I could not move. I saw the shepherds and workmen at a distance, and cried, but so faintly that it was impossible to hear me thirty yards off. And there I might have lain and died; for I was now almost given over, the ponds and even the river, near where I was lying, having been dragged. But by good luck, Sir Stafford Northcote, who had been out all night, resolved to make one other trial, and came so near that he heard me crying. He carried me in his arms for near a quarter of a mile, when we met my father and Sir Stafford's servants. I remember and never shall forget my father's face as he looked upon me while I lay in the servant's arms – so calm, and the tears stealing down his face; for I was the child of his old age. My mother, as you may suppose, was outrageous with joy. (Meantime) in rushed a *young lady*, crying out, 'I hope you'll whip him, Mrs Coleridge!' This woman still lives in Ottery; and neither philosophy or religion have been able to conquer the antipathy which I feel towards her whenever I see her. I was put to bed and recovered in a day or so, but I was certainly injured. For I was weakly and subject to the ague for many years after.

My father (who had so little of parental ambition in him, that he had destined his children to be blacksmiths, &c., and had accomplished his intention but for my mother's pride and spirit of aggrandizing her family) – my father had, however, resolved that I should be a parson. I read every book that came in my way without distinction; and my father was fond of me, and used to take me on his knee and hold long conversations with me. I remember that at eight years old I walked with him one winter evening from a farmer's house, a mile from Ottery, and he told me the names of the stars and how Jupiter was a thousand times larger than our world, and that the other twinkling stars were suns that had worlds rolling round them; and when I came home he shewed me how they rolled round. I heard him with a profound delight and admiration: but without the least mixture of wonder or incredulity. For from my early reading of fairy tales and genii, &c., &c., my mind had been habituated *to the Vast*, and I never regarded *my senses* in any way as the criteria of my belief. I regulated all my creeds by my conceptions, not by my *sight*, even at that age. Should children be permitted to read romances, and relations of giants and magicians and genii? I know all that has been said against it; but I have formed my faith in the affirmative. I know no other way of giving the mind a love of the Great and the Whole. Those who have been led to the same truths step by step, through the constant testimony of their senses, seem to me to want a sense which I possess. They contemplate nothing but *parts*, and all *parts* are necessarily little. And the universe to them is but a mass of *little things*. It is true, that the mind may become credulous and prone to superstition by the former method; but are not the experimentalists credulous even to madness in believing any absurdity, rather than believe the grandest truths, if they have not the testimony of their own senses in their favour? I have known some who have been *rationally* educated, as it is styled. They were marked by a microscopic acuteness, but when they looked at great things, all became a blank and they saw nothing, and denied (very illogically) that anything could be seen, and uniformly put the negation of a power for the possession of a power, and called the want of imagination judgement and the never being moved to rapture philosophy!

Towards the latter end of September, 1781, my father went to Plymouth with my brother Francis, who was to go as midshipman under Admiral Graves, who was a friend of my father's. My father settled my brother, and returned October 4, 1781. He arrived at Exeter about six o'clock, and was pressed to take a bed there at the Harts', but he refused, and, to avoid their entreaties, he told them, that he had never been superstitious, but that the night before he had had a dream which had made a deep impression. He dreamt that Death had appeared to him as he is commonly painted, and touched him with his dart. Well, he returned home, and all his family, I excepted, were up. He told my mother his dream; but he was in high health and good spirits, and there was a bowl of punch made, and my father gave a long and particular account of his travel, and that he had placed Frank under a religious captain, &c. At length he went to bed, very well and in high spirits. A short time after he had lain down he complained of a pain in his bowels. My mother got him some peppermint water, and, after a pause, he said, 'I am much better now, my dear!' and lay down again. In a minute my mother heard a noise in his throat, and spoke to him, but he did not answer; and she spoke repeatedly in vain. Her *shriek* awaked me, and I said, 'Papa is dead!' I did not know of my father's return, but I knew that he was expected. How I came to think of his death I cannot tell; but so it was. Dead he was. Some said it was the gout in the heart; – probably it was a fit of apoplexy. He was an Israelite without guile, simple, generous, and taking some Scripture texts in their literal sense, he was conscientiously indifferent to the good and the evil of this world.

God love you and

S. T. COLERIDGE

TO JOHN THELWALL

May 13, 1796

... YOUR remarks on my poems are, I think, just in general; there is a rage and affectation of double epithets. 'Unshuddered, unaghasted' is, indeed, *truly* ridiculous. But why so violent against *metaphysics* in poetry? Is not Akenside's a metaphysical poem? Perhaps you do not like Akenside? Well, but *I do*, and so do a great many others. Why pass an act of *uniformity* against poets? I received a letter from a very sensible friend abusing love verses; another blaming the introduction of politics, 'as wider from true poetry than the equator from the poles'. 'Some for each' is my motto. That poetry pleases which interests. My religious poetry interests the *religious*, who read it with rapture. Why? Because it awakes in them all the associations connected with a love of future existence, etc. A very dear friend of mine, who is, in my opinion, the best poet of the age (I will send you his poem when published), thinks that the lines from 364 to 375 and from 403 to 428 the best in the volume, – indeed, worth all the rest. And this man is a republican, and, at least a *semi*-atheist. Why do you object to 'shadowy of truth'? It is, I acknowledge, a Grecism, but, I think, an elegant one. Your remarks on the della-crusca place of emphasis are just in part. Where we wish to point out the *thing*, and the *quality* is mentioned merely as a decoration, this mode of emphasis is indeed absurd; therefore, I very patiently give up to critical vengeance '*high* tree', '*sore* wounds', and '*rough* rock'; but when you wish to dwell chiefly on the *quality* rather than the *thing*, then this mode is proper, and, indeed, is used in common conversation. Who says good *man*? Therefore, '*big* soul', '*cold* earth', '*dark* womb', and '*flamy* child' are all right, and introduce a variety into the versification, (which is) an advantage where you can attain it without any sacrifice of sense. As to harmony, it is all *association*. Milton is *harmonious* to me, and I absolutely nauseate Darwin's poems.

> Yours affectionately,
> S. T. COLERIDGE

TO JOHN THELWALL

Oxford Street, Bristol, Saturday, November 19 (1796)

... YOUR portrait of yourself interested me. As to me, my face, unless when animated by immediate eloquence, expresses great sloth, and great, indeed, almost idiotic good-nature. 'T is a mere carcass of a face; fat, flabby, and expressive chiefly of inexpression. Yet I am told that my eyes, eyebrows, and forehead are physiognomically good; but of this the deponent knoweth not. As to my shape, 't is a good shape enough if measured, but my gait is awkward, and the walk of the whole man indicates *indolence capable of energies*. I am, and ever have been, a great reader, and have read almost everything – a library cormorant. I am *deep* in all out of the way books, whether of the monkish times, or of the puritanical era. I have read and digested most of the historical writers; but I do not like *history*. Metaphysics and poetry and 'facts of mind', that is, accounts of all the strange phantasms that ever possessed 'your philosophy'; dreamers, from Thoth the Egyptian to Taylor the English pagan, are my darling studies. In short, I seldom read except to amuse myself, and I am almost always reading. Of useful knowledge, I am a so-so chemist, and I love chemistry. All else is *blank*; but I *will* be (please God) an horticulturalist and a farmer. I compose very little, and I absolutely hate composition, and such is my dislike that even a sense of duty is sometimes too weak to overpower it.

I cannot breathe through my nose, so my mouth, with sensual thick lips, is almost always open. In conversation I am impassioned, and oppose what I deem error with an eagerness which is often mistaken for personal asperity; but I am ever so swallowed up in the *thing* that I perfectly forget my *opponent*. Such am I. I am just going to read Dupuis' twelve octavos, which I have got from London. I shall read only one octavo a week, for I cannot *speak* French at all and I read it slowly.

My wife is well and desires to be remembered to you and your *Stella* and little ones. N.B. Stella (among the Romans) was a man's name. All the *classics* are against you; but our Swift, I suppose, is authority for this unsexing.

Write on the receipt of this, and believe me as ever, with affectionate esteem,

Your sincere friend,

S. T. COLERIDGE

P.S. I have enclosed a five-guinea note. The five shillings over please to lay out for me thus. In White's (of Fleet Street or the Strand, I forget which – O! the Strand I believe, but I don't know which), well, in White's catalogue are the following books:

4674. *Iamblichus, Proclus, Porphyrius*, etc., one shilling and sixpence, one little volume.

4686. *Juliani Opera*, three shillings: which two books you will be so kind as to purchase for me, and send down with the twenty-five pamphlets. But if they should unfortunately be sold, in the same catalogue are:

2109. *Juliani Opera*, 12s. 6d.

676. *Iamblichus de Mysteriis*, 10s. 6d.

2681. *Sidonius Apollinaris*, 6s.

And in the catalogue of Robson, the bookseller in New Bond Street, *Politini Opera*, a *Ficino*, £1.1.0, making altogether £2.10.0.

If you can get the two former little books, costing only four and sixpence, I will rest content with them; if they are gone, be so kind as to purchase for me the others I mentioned to you, amounting to two pounds, ten shillings; and, as in the course of next week I shall send a small parcel of books and manuscripts to my very dear Charles Lamb of the India House, I shall be enabled to convey the money to you in a letter, which he will leave at your house. I make no apology for this commission, because I feel (to use a vulgar phrase) that I would do as much for you.

TO JOSEPH COTTLE

Spring, 1797

... I SEE they have reviewed Southey's Poems and my Ode in the *Monthly Review*. Notwithstanding the Reviews, I, who in the sincerity of my heart am *jealous* for Robert Southey's fame, regret the publication of that volume. Wordsworth complains, with justice, that Southey writes *too much at his ease* – that he seldom

> feels his burthened breast
> Heaving beneath th' incumbent Deity.

He certainly will make literature more *profitable to him* from the fluency with which he writes, and the facility with which he pleases himself. But I fear, that to posterity his wreath will look unseemly – here an ever living amaranth, and close by its side some weed of an hour, sere, yellow, and shapeless – his exquisite beauties will lose half their effect from the bad company they keep. Besides I am fearful that he will begin to rely too much on *story* and *event* in his poems, to the neglect of those *lofty imaginings*, that are peculiar to, and definitive of, the poet. The *story* of Milton might be told in two pages – it is this which distinguishes an *Epic Poem* from a *Romance in metre*. Observe the march of Milton – his severe application, his laborious polish, his deep metaphysical researches, his prayers to God before he began his great poem, all that could lift and swell his intellect, became his daily food. I should not think of devoting less than 20 years to an Epic Poem. Ten to collect materials and warm my mind with universal science. I would be a tolerable Mathematician, I would thoroughly know Mechanics, Hydrostatics, Optics, and Astronomy, Botany, Metallurgy, Fossilism, Chemistry, Geology, Anatomy, Medicine – then the *mind of man* – then the *minds* of *men* – in all Travels, Voyages and Histories. So I would spend ten years – the next five to the composition of the poem – and the five last to the correction of it.

So I would write haply not unhearing of that divine and rightly-whispering Voice, which speaks to mighty minds of predestinated Garlands, starry and unwithering. God love you,

S. T. COLERIDGE

TO ROBERT SOUTHEY

July, 1797

Dear Southey,

You are acting kindly in your exertions for Chatterton's sister; but I doubt the success. Chatterton's or Rowley's poems were never popular. The very circumstance which made them so much talked of, their *ancientness*, prevented them from being generally read, in the degree, I mean, that Goldsmith's poems or even Rogers' thing upon memory has been. ... I am almost inclined to think a *subscription* simply would be better. It is unpleasant to cast a damp on anything; but that benevolence alone is likely to be beneficent which *calculates*. If, however, you continue to entertain higher hopes than I, believe me, I will shake off my sloth, and use my best muscles in gaining subscribers. I will certainly write a preliminary essay, and I will *attempt* to write a poem on the life and death of Chatterton, but the 'Monody' *must not be reprinted*. Neither this nor the 'Pixies' Parlour' would have been in the second edition, but for dear Cottle's solicitous importunity. Excepting the last eighteen lines of the 'Monody', which, though deficient in chasteness and severity of diction, breathe a pleasing spirit of romantic feeling, there are not five lines in either poem which might not have been written by a man who had lived and died in the self-same St Giles' cellar, in which he had been first suckled by a drab with milk and gin. The 'Pixies' is the least disgusting, because the subject leads you to expect nothing, but on a life and death so full of heart-going *realities* as poor Chatterton's, to find such shadowy nobodies as cherub-winged *Death*, Trees of *Hope*, bare-bosomed *Affection* and simpering *Peace*, makes one's blood circulate like ipecacuanha. But so it is. A young man by strong feelings is impelled to write on a particular subject, and this is all his feelings do for him. They set him upon the business and then they leave him. He has such a high idea of what poetry ought to be, that he cannot conceive that such things as his natural emotions may be allowed to find a place in it; his learning therefore, his fancy, or rather conceit, and all his powers of buckram are put on the stretch. It appears to me that strong feeling is not so requisite to an author's being profoundly pathetic as taste and good sense. ...

I had been on a visit to Wordsworth's at Racedown, near Crewkerne, and I brought him and his sister back with me, and here I have *settled them*. By a combination of curious circumstances a gentleman's seat, with a park and woods, elegantly and completely furnished, with nine lodging rooms, three parlours, and a hall, in the most beautiful and romantic situation by the seaside, four miles from Stowey, – this we have got for Wordsworth at the *rent of twenty-three pounds a year, taxes included*! The park and woods are *his* for all purposes *he* wants them, and the large gardens are altogether and entirely his. Wordsworth is a very great man, the only man to whom *at all times* and *in all modes of excellence* I feel myself inferior, the only one, I mean, whom *I have yet met with*, for the London *literati* appear to me to be very much like little potatoes, that is, *no great things*, a compost of nullity and dullity.

Charles Lamb has been with me for a week. He left me Friday morning. The second day after Wordsworth came to me, dear Sara accidentally emptied a skillet of boiling milk on my foot, which confined me during the whole time of C. Lamb's stay and still prevents me from all *walks* longer than a furlong. While Wordsworth, his sister, and Charles Lamb were out one evening, sitting in the arbour of T. Poole's garden which communicates with mine I wrote these lines, with which I am pleased . . .

(Here follows the poem entitled 'This lime-tree bower my prison'.)

TO JOSEPH COTTLE

July, 1797

. . . WORDSWORTH & his exquisite Sister are with me – She is a woman indeed! – in mind, I mean, & heart – for her person is such, that if you expected to see a pretty woman, you would think her ordinary – if you expected to find an ordinary woman, you would think her pretty! – But her manners are simple, ardent, impressive –

> In every motion her most innocent soul
> Outbeams so brightly, that who saw would say,
> Guilt was a thing impossible in her.

Her information various – her eye watchful in minutest observation of nature – and her taste a perfect electrometer – it bends, protrudes, and draws in, at subtlest beauties & most recondite faults. . . .

TO THOMAS POOLE

March 23, 1801

... MY opinion is this: that deep thinking is attainable only by a man of deep feeling, and that all truth is a species of revelation. The more I understand of Sir Isaac Newton's works, the more boldly I dare utter to my own mind, and therefore to *you*, that I believe the souls of five hundred Sir Isaac Newtons would go to the making up of a Shakespeare or a Milton. But if it please the Almighty to grant me health, hope, and a steady mind (always the three clauses of my hourly prayers), before my thirtieth year I will thoroughly understand the whole of Newton's works. At present I must content myself with endeavouring to make myself entire master of his easier work, that on Optics. I am exceedingly delighted with the beauty and neatness of his experiments, and with the accuracy of his *immediate* deductions from them; but the opinions founded on these deductions, and indeed his whole theory is, I am persuaded, so exceedingly superficial as without impropriety to be deemed false. Newton was a mere materialist. *Mind*, in his system, is always *passive*, – a lazy *Looker-on* on an external world. If the mind be not *passive*, if it be indeed made in God's Image, and that, too, in the sublimest sense, the *Image of the Creator*, there is ground for suspicion that any system built on the passiveness of the mind must be false, as a system. I need not observe, my dear friend, how unutterably silly and contemptible these opinions would be if written to any but to another self. I assure you, solemnly assure you, that you and Wordsworth are the only men on earth to whom I would have uttered a word on this subject. ...

TO W. SOTHEBY

Greta Hall, Keswick, September 10th, 1802

... IT has struck me with great force lately that the Psalms afford a most complete answer to those who state the Jehovah of the Jews, as a personal and national God, and the Jews as differing from the Greeks only in calling the minor Gods Cherubim and Seraphim, and confining the word 'God' to their Jupiter. It must occur to every reader that the Greeks in their religious poems address always the Numina Loci, the Genii, the Dryads, the Naiads, etc., etc. All natural objects were *dead*, mere hollow statues, but there was a Godkin or Goddessling *included* in each. In the Hebrew poetry you find nothing of this poor stuff, as poor in genuine imagination as it is mean in intellect. At best, it is but fancy, or the aggregating faculty of the mind, not *imagination* or the *modifying* and *coadunating* faculty. This the Hebrew poets appear to me to have possessed beyond all others, and next to them the English. In the Hebrew poets each thing has a life of its own, and yet they are all one life. In God they move and live and *have* their being; not *had*, as the cold system of Newtonian Theology represents, but *have*. Great pleasure indeed, my dear sir, did I receive from the latter part of your letter. If there be any two subjects which have in the very depths of my nature interested me, it has been the Hebrew and Christian Theology, and the Theology of Plato. Last winter I read the Parmenides and the Timaeus with great care, and oh, that you were here – even in this howling rainstorm that dashes itself against my windows – on the other side of my blazing fire, in that great armchair there! I guess we should encroach on the morning before we parted. How little the commentators of Milton have availed themselves of the writings of Plato, Milton's darling! But alas, commentators only hunt out verbal parallelisms – *numen abest*. I was much impressed with this in all the many notes on that beautiful passage in Comus from l. 629 to 641. All the puzzle is to find out what plant Haemony is; which they discover to be the English spleenwort, and decked out as a mere play and licence of poetic fancy with all the strange properties suited to the purpose of the drama. They thought little of Milton's platonizing spirit, who wrote nothing without an interior meaning. 'Where more is meant than meets the ear', is true of himself beyond all writers. He was so great a man that he seems to have considered fiction as profane unless where it is consecrated by being emblematic of some truth. What an unthinking and ignorant man we must have supposed Milton to be, if, without any hidden meaning, he had described it as growing in such abundance that the dull swain treads on it daily, and yet as never *flowering*. Such blunders Milton of all others was least likely to commit. Do look at the passage. Apply it as an allegory of Christianity, or, to speak more precisely, of the Redemption by the Cross, every syllable is full of light! '*A small unsightly root*' – 'To the Greeks folly, to the Jews a stumbling-block' – '*The leaf was darkish and had prickles on it*' – 'If in this life only we have hope, we are of all men the most miserable', and a score of other texts. '*But in another country, as he said, Bore a bright golden flower*' – 'The exceeding weight of glory prepared for us hereafter' – '*But not in this soil; Unknown and like esteemed and the dull swain Treads on it daily with his clouted shoon'* – The promises of Redemption offered daily and hourly, and to all, but accepted scarcely by any – '*He called it Haemony*'. Now what is Haemony? αἷμα οἶνος, Blood-wine. 'And he took the wine and blessed it and said, "This is my Blood," ' – the great symbol of the Death on the Cross. There is a general ridicule cast on all allegorizing of poets. Read Milton's prose works, and observe whether he was one of those who joined in this ridicule. There is a very curious passage in Josephus [De Bello Jud. 6, 7, cap. 25 (vi. § 3)] which is, in its literal meaning, more wild and fantastically absurd than the passage in Milton; so much so, that Lardner quotes it in exultation and says triumphantly, 'Can any man who reads it think it any disparagement to the Christian Religion that it was not embraced by a man who would believe such stuff as this? God forbid that it should affect Christianity, that it is not believed by the learned of this world!' But the passage in Josephus, I have no doubt, is wholly allegorical. . . .

TO RICHARD SHARP

January 15th, 1804

. . . MR WORDSWORTH does not excite that almost painfully profound moral admiration which the sense of the exceeding difficulty of a given virtue can alone call forth, and which therefore I feel exclusively towards T. Wedgwood; but, on the other hand, he is an object to be contemplated with greater complacency, because he both deserves to be, and *is*, a happy man; and a happy man, not from natural temperament, for therein lies his main obstacle, not by enjoyment of the good things of this world – for even to this day, from the first dawn of his manhood, he has purchased independence and leisure for great and good pursuits by austere frugality and daily self-denials; nor yet by an accidental confluence of amiable and happy-making friends and relatives, for every one near to his heart has been placed there by choice and after knowledge and deliberation; but he is a happy man, because he is a Philosopher, because he knows the intrinsic value of the different objects of human pursuit, and regulates his wishes in strict subordination to that knowledge; because he feels, and with a *practical* faith, the truth of that which you, more than once, my dear sir, have with equal good sense and kindness pressed upon me, that we can do but one thing well, and that therefore we must make a choice. He has made that choice from his early youth, has pursued and is pursuing it; and certainly no small part of his happiness is owing to this unity of interest and that homogeneity of character which is the natural consequence of it, and which that excellent man, the poet Sotheby, noticed to me as the characteristic of Wordsworth.

Wordsworth is a poet, a most original poet. He no more resembles Milton than Milton resembles Shakespeare – no more resembles Shakespeare than Shakespeare resembles Milton. He is himself; and I dare affirm that he will hereafter be admitted as the first and greatest philosophical poet, the only man who has effected a complete and constant synthesis of thought and feeling and combined them with poetic forms, with the music of pleasurable passion, and with Imagination or the *modifying* power in that highest sense of the word in which I have ventured to oppose it to Fancy, or the *aggregating* power – in that sense in which it is a dim analogue of creation – not all that we can believe, but all that we can *conceive* of creation. – Wordsworth is a poet, and I feel myself a better poet, in knowing how to honour *him* than in all my own poetic compositions, all I have done or hope to do; and I prophesy immortality to his 'Recluse', as the first and finest philosophical poem, if only it be (as it undoubtedly will be) a faithful transcript of his own most august and innocent life, of his own habitual feelings and modes of seeing and hearing. . . .

TO SIR GEORGE BEAUMONT

Feb. 1, 1804

. . . In explaining what I shall do with Shakespeare, I explain the nature of the other five (projected Essays). Each scene of each play I read as if it were the whole of Shakespeare's works – the sole thing extant. I ask myself what are the characteristics, the diction, the cadences, and metre, the character, the passion, the moral or metaphysical inherencies and fitness for theatric effect, and in what sort of theatres. All these I write down with great care and precision of thought and language (and when I have gone through the whole, I then shall collect my papers, and observe how often such and such expressions recur), and thus shall not only know what the characteristics of Shakespeare's plays are, but likewise what proportion they bear to each other. Then, not carelessly, though of course with far less care, I shall read through the old plays, just before Shakespeare's time, Sir Phillip Sidney's *Arcadia*, Ben Jonson, Beaumont and Fletcher, and Massinger in the same way; so as to see, and to be able to prove, what of Shakespeare belonged to his age, and was common to all *the first-rate men* of that true *saeculum aureum* of English poetry, and what is his own, and his only. Thus I shall both exhibit the characteristics of the plays and of the mind of Shakespeare, and a philosophical analysis and justification of almost every character, at greater or less length, in the spirit of that analysis of the character of Hamlet, with which you were much pleased, and by being so, I solemnly assure, gave me heart and hope, and did me much good. For much as I loathe flattery from the bottom of my very *stomach*, and much as I *wriggle* under the burden and discomfort of the praise of people, for whose heads, hearts, and specific competence I have small respect, yet I own myself no self-subsisting mind. I know, I feel, that I am weak, apt to faint away, inwardly self-deserted, and bereft of the confidence in my own powers; and that the approbation and sympathy of good and intelligent men is my sea-breeze, without which I should languish from morn to evening, – a very trade-wind to me, in which my bark drives on regularly and lightly. . . .

TO WILLIAM WORDSWORTH

Calne, May 30, 1815

. . . WHATEVER in Lucretius is poetry is not philosophical, whatever is philosophical is not poetry; and in the very pride of confident hope I looked forward to 'The Recluse' as the *first* and *only* true Philosophical poem in existence. Of course, I expected the colours, music, imaginative life, and passion of *poetry*; but the matter and arrangement of *philosophy*; not doubting from the advantages of the subject that the totality of a system was not only capable of being harmonized with, but even calculated to aid, the unity (beginning, middle, and end) of a poem. Thus, whatever the length of the work might be, still it was a *determinate* length; of the subjects announced, each would have its own appointed place, and excluding repetitions, each would relieve and rise in interest above the other. I supposed you first to have meditated the faculties of man in the abstract, in their correspondence with his sphere of action, and, first in the feeling, touch, and taste, then in the eye, and last in the ear, – to have laid a solid and immovable foundation for the edifice by removing the sandy sophisms of Locke, and the mechanic dogmatists, and demonstrating that the senses were living growths and developments of the mind and spirit, in a much juster as well as higher sense, than the mind can be said to be formed by the senses. Next, I understood that you would take the human race in the concrete, have exploded the absurd notion of Pope's 'Essay on Man', Darwin, and all the countless believers even (strange to say) among Christians of man's having progressed from an ourang-outang state – so contrary to all history, to all religion, nay, to all possibility – to have affirmed a Fall in some sense, as a fact, the possibility of which cannot be understood from the nature of the will, but the reality of which is attested by experience and conscience. Fallen men contemplated in the different ages of the world, and in the different states – savage, barbarous, civilized, the lonely cot, or borderer's wigwam, the village, the manufacturing town, seaport, city, universities, and, not disguising the sore evils under which the whole creation groans, to point out, however, a manifest scheme of redemption, of reconciliation from this enmity with Nature – what are the obstacles, the *Antichrist* that must be and already is – and to conclude by a grand didactic swell on the necessary identity of a true philosophy with true religion, agreeing in the results and differing only as the analytic and synthetic process, as discursive from intuitive, the former chiefly useful as perfecting the latter; in short, the necessity of a general revolution in the modes of developing and disciplining the human mind by the substitution of life and intelligence (considered in its different powers from the plant up to that state in which the difference of degree becomes a new kind (man, self-consciousness), but yet not by essential opposition) for the philosophy of mechanism, which, in everything that is most worthy of the human intellect, strikes *Death*, and cheats itself by mistaking clear images for distinct conceptions, and which idly demands conceptions where intuitions alone are possible or adequate to the majesty of the Truth. In short, facts elevated into theory – theory into laws – and laws into living and intelligent powers – true idealism necessarily perfecting itself in realism, and realism refining itself into idealism.

Such or something like this was the plan I had supposed that you were engaged on. Your own words will therefore explain my feelings, *viz.*, that your object 'was not to convey recondite, or refined truths, but to place commonplace truths in an interesting point of view'. Now this I suppose to have been in your two volumes of poems, as far as was desirable or possible, without an insight into the whole truth. How can common truths be made permanently interesting but by being *bottomed* on our common nature? It is only by the profoundest insight into numbers and quantity that a sublimity and even religious wonder become attached to the simplest operations of arithmetic, the most evident properties of the circle or triangle. I have only to finish a preface, which I shall have done in two, or, at farthest, three days; and I will then, dismissing all comparison either with the poem on the growth of your own support, or with the imagined plan of 'The Recluse', state fairly my main objections to 'The Excursion' as it is. But it would have been alike unjust both to you and to myself, if I had led you to suppose that any disappointment I may have felt arose wholly or chiefly from the passages I do not like, or from the poem considered irrelatively. . . .

TO THE REV. H. F. CARY

LITTLE HAMPTON, ARUNDEL, SUSSEX

Highgate, February 6, 1818

. . . PS. I have this morning been reading a strange publication – *viz.* Poems with very wild and interesting pictures, as the swathing, etched (I suppose) but it is said – printed and painted by the Author, W. Blake. He is a man of Genius – and I apprehend, a Swedenborgian – certainly, a mystic *emphatically*. You perhaps smile at *my* calling another Poet, a *Mystic*; but verily I am in the very mire of commonplace common-place compared with Mr Blake, apo- or rather anacalyptic Poet, and Painter!

TO CHARLES AUGUSTUS TULK

Highgate, Thursday evening, 1818

. . . Blake's Poems. – I begin with my dyspathies that I may forget them, and have uninterrupted space for loves and sympathies. Title-page and the following emblem contain all the faults of the drawings with as few beauties as could be in the compositions of a man who was capable of such faults and such beauties. The faulty despotism in symbols amounting in the title-page to the μισητόν, and occasionally, irregular unmodified lines of the inanimate, sometimes as the effect of rigidity and sometimes of exossation like a wet tendon. So likewise the ambiguity of the drapery. Is it a garment or the body incised and scored out? The lumpness (the effect of vinegar on an egg) in the upper one of the two prostrate figures in the title-page, and the straight line down the waistcoat of pinky goldbeaters' skin in the next drawing, with the I don't-know-whatness of the countenance, as if the mouth had been formed by the habit of placing the tongue not contemptuously, but stupidly, between the lower gums and the lower jaw – these are the only *repulsive* faults I have noticed. The figure, however, of the second leaf, abstracted from the *expression* of the countenance given it by something about the mouth, and the interspace from the lower lip to the chin, is such as only a master learned in his art could produce.

N.B. I signifies 'It gave me great pleasure'. ‡, 'Still greater'. ‡‡, 'And greater still'. Θ , 'In the highest degree'. O, 'In the lowest'.

Shepherd, I; Spring, I (last stanza, ‡); Holy Thursday, ‡‡; Laughing Song, ‡; Nurse's Song, I; The Divine Image, Θ ; The Lamb, ‡; The little black Boy, Θ , yea Θ + Θ ; Infant Joy, ‡‡ (N.B. For the three last lines I should write, 'When wilt thou smile', or 'O smile, O smile! I'll sing the while'. For a babe two days old does not, cannot smile, and innocence and the very truth of Nature must go together. Infancy is too holy a thing to be ornamented). 'The Echoing Green', I, (the figures ‡, and of the second leaf, ‡‡); 'The Cradle Song', I; 'The School Boy', ‡‡; Night, Θ ; 'On another's Sorrow', I; 'A Dream', ?; 'The little boy lost', I (the drawing, ‡); 'The little boy found', I; 'The Blossom', O; 'The Chimney Sweeper', O; 'The Voice of the Ancient Bard', O.

Introduction, ‡; Earth's Answer, ‡; Infant Sorrow, I; 'The Clod and the Pebble', I; 'The Garden of Love', ‡; 'The Fly', I; 'The Tyger', ‡; 'A little boy lost', ‡; 'Holy Thursday', I; (p. 13, O; 'Nurse's Song', O?); 'The little girl lost and found' (the ornaments most exquisite! the poem, I); 'Chimney Sweeper in the Snow', O; 'To Tirzah, and the Poison Tree', I – and yet O; 'A little Girl lost', O. (I would have had it omitted, not for the want of innocence in the poem, but from the too probable want of it in many readers.) 'London', I; 'The Sick Rose', I; 'The little Vagabond', O. Though I cannot approve altogether of this last poem, and have been inclined to think that the error which is most likely to beset the scholars of Emmanuel Swedenborg is that of utterly demerging the tremendous incompatibilities with an evil will that arise out of the essential Holiness of the abysmal A-seity in the love of the Eternal *Person*, and thus giving temptation to weak minds to sink this love and itself into *Good Nature*, yet still I disapprove the mood of mind in this wild poem so much less than I do the servile blind-worm, wrap-rascal scurf-coat of *fear* of the *modern* Saint (whose whole being is a lie, to themselves as well as to their brethren), that I should laugh with good conscience in watching a Saint of the new stamp, one of the first stars of our eleemosynary advertisements, groaning in wind-pipe! and with the whites of his eyes upraised at the *audacity* of this poem! Anything rather than this degradation I of Humanity, and therein of the Incarnate Divinity!

S.T.C.

O means that I am perplexed and have no opinion.
I, with which how can we utter 'Our Father'?

TO T. ALLSOP

January, 1821

... To the completion of these four works I have literally nothing more to do than *to transcribe*; but, as I before hinted, from so many scraps and *Sibylline* leaves, including margins of books and blank pages, that, unfortunately, I must be my own scribe, and not done by myself, they will be all but lost; or perhaps (as has been too often the case already) furnish feathers for the caps of others; some for this purpose, and some to plume the arrows of detraction, to be let fly against the luckless bird from whom they had been plucked or moulted.

In addition to these – of my GREAT WORK, to the preparation of which more than twenty years of my life have been devoted, and on which my hopes of extensive and permanent utility, of fame, in the noblest sense of the word, mainly rest – that by which I might,

> As now by thee, by all the good be known,
>   When this weak frame lies mouldered in the grave,
> Which self-surviving I might call my own,
>   Which Folly cannot mar, nor Hate deprave –
> The incense of those powers, which, risen in flame,
> Might make me dear to Him from whom they came –

of this work, to which all my other writings (unless I except my Poems, and these I can exclude in part only) are introductory and preparative; and the result of which (if the premises be, as I with the most tranquil assurance am convinced they are – insubvertible, the deductions legitimate, and the conclusions commensurate, and only commensurate, with both), must finally be a revolution of all that has been called *Philosophy* or Metaphysics in England and France since the era of the commencing predominance of the mechanical system at the restoration of our second Charles, and with this the present fashionable views, not only of religion, morals, and politics, but even of the modern physics and physiology. You will not blame the earnestness of my expressions, nor the high importance which I attach to this work; for how, with less noble objects, and less faith in their attainment, could I stand acquitted of folly, and abuse of time, talents, and learning, in a labour of three-fourths of my *intellectual* life? Of this work, something more than a volume has been dictated by me, so as to exist fit for the press, to my friend and enlightened pupil, Mr Green; and more than as much again would have been evolved and delivered to paper, but that, for the last six or eight months, I have been compelled to break off our weekly meeting, from the necessity of writing (alas! alas! of *attempting* to write) for purposes, and on the subjects of the passing day. – Of my poetic works, I would fain finish the 'Christabel'. Alas! for the proud time when I planned, when I had present to my mind, the materials, as well as the scheme, of the Hymns entitled Spirit, Sun, Earth, Air, Water, Fire, and Man: and the Epic Poem on – what still appears to me the one only fit subject remaining for an Epic Poem – Jerusalem besieged and destroyed by Titus. . . .

From ANIMA POETAE

THE elder languages were fitter for poetry because they expressed only prominent ideas with clearness, the others but darkly. . . . Poetry gives most pleasure when only generally and not perfectly understood. It was so by me with Gray's 'Bard' and Collins' Odes. The 'Bard' once intoxicated me, and now I read it without pleasure. From this cause it is that what I call metaphysical poetry gives me so much delight.

Poetry which excites us to artificial feelings makes us callous to real ones.

May 20, 1799
The nightingales in a cluster or little wood of blossomed trees, and a bat wheeling incessantly round and round! The noise of the frogs was not unpleasant, like the humming of spinning wheels in a large manufactory – now and then a distinct sound, sometimes like a duck, and, sometimes, like the shrill notes of sea-fowl.

O heavens! when I think how perishable things, how imperishable thoughts seem to be! For what is forgetfulness? Renew the state of affection or bodily feeling (so as to be the) same or similar, sometimes dimly similar, and, instantly, the trains of forgotten thoughts rise from their living catacombs!

Nov. 27, 1799
The immoveableness of all things through which so many men were moving – a harsh contrast compared with the universal motion, the harmonious system of motions in the country, and everywhere in Nature. In the dim light London appeared to be a huge place of sepulchres through which hosts of spirits were gliding.

Slanting pillars of misty light moved along under the sun hid by clouds.

Leaves of trees upturned by the stirring wind in twilight – an image of paleness, wan affright.

Dec. 19, 1800
The thin scattered rain-clouds were scudding along the sky; above them, with a visible interspace, the crescent moon hung, and partook

not of the motion; her own hazy light filled up the concave, as if it had been painted and the colours had run.

The spring with the little tiny cone of loose sand ever rising and sinking at the bottom, but its surface without a wrinkle.

Sept. 14, 1801
Northern lights remarkably fine – chiefly a purple-blue – in shooting pyramids, moved from over Bassenthwaite behind Skiddaw. Derwent's birthday, one year old.

Sept. 15, 1801
Observed the great half moon setting behind the mountain ridge, and watched the shapes its various segments presented as it slowly sunk – first the foot of a boot, all but the heel – then a little pyramid △ – then a star of the first magnitude – indeed, it was not distinguishable from the evening star at its largest – then rapidly a smaller, a small, a very small star – and, as it diminished in size, so it grew paler in tint. And now where is it? Unseen – but a little fleecy cloud hangs above the mountain ridge, and is rich in amber light.

October 22, 1801
All the mountains black and tremendously obscure, except Swinside. At this time I saw, one after the other, nearly in the same place, two perfect moon-rainbows, the one foot in the field below my garden, the other in the field nearest but two to the church. It was grey-moonlight-mist-colour. Friday morning, Mary Hutchinson arrives.

A kind-hearted man who is obliged to give a refusal or the like which will inflict great pain, finds a relief in doing it roughly and fiercely. Explain this and use it in Christabel.

Never to lose an opportunity of reasoning against the head-dimming, heart-damping principle of judging a work by its defects, not its beauties. Every work must have the former – we know it *a priori* – but every work has not the latter, and he, therefore, who discovers them, tells you something that you could not with certainty, or even with probability, have anticipated.

Nothing affects me much at the moment it happens. It either stupefies me, and I, perhaps, look at a merry-make and dance-the-hay of flies, or listen entirely to the loud click of the great clock, or I am simply indifferent, not without some sense of philosophical self-complacency. For a thing at the moment is but a thing of the moment; it must be taken up into the mind, diffuse itself through the whole multitude of shapes and thoughts, not one of which it leaves untinged, between (not one of) which and it some new thought is not engendered. Now this is a work of time, but the body feels it quicker with me.

On St Herbert's Island, I saw a large spider with most beautiful legs, floating in the air on his back by a single thread which he was spinning out, and still, as he spun, heaving on the air, as if the air beneath was a pavement elastic to his strokes. From the top of a very high tree he had spun his line; at length reached the bottom, tied his thread round a piece of grass, and reascended to spin another – a net to hang, as a fisherman's sea-net hangs, in the sun and wind to dry.

October 21, 1803
A drizzling rain. Heavy masses of shapeless vapour upon the mountains (O the perpetual forms of Borrowdale!) yet it is no unbroken tale of dull sadness. Slanting pillars travel across the lake at long intervals, the vaporous mass whitens in large stains of light – on the lakeward ridge of that huge arm-chair of Lodore fell a gleam of softest light, that brought out the rich hues of the late autumn. The woody Castle Crag between me and Lodore is a rich flower-garden of colours – the brightest yellows with the deepest crimsons and the infinite shades of brown and green, the *infinite* diversity of which blends the whole, so that the brighter colours seem to be colours upon a ground, not coloured things. Little woolpacks of white bright vapour rest on different summits and declivities. The vale is narrowed by the mist and cloud, yet through the wall of mist you can see into a bower of sunny light, in Borrowdale; the birds are singing in the tender rain, as if it were the rain of April, and the decaying foliage were flowers and blossoms. The pillar of smoke from the chimney rises up in the mist, and is just distinguishable from it, and the mountain forms in the gorge of Borrowdale consubstantiate with the mist and cloud, even as the pillar'd smoke – a shade deeper and a determinate form.

A pretty optical fact occurred this morning. As I was returning from Fletcher's, up the back lane and just in sight of the river, I saw, floating high in the air, somewhere over Mr Banks', a noble kite. I continued gazing at it for some time, when, turning suddenly round, I saw at an equi-distance on my right, that is, over the middle of our field, a pair of kites floating about. I looked at them for some seconds, when it occurred to me that I had never before seen two kites together and instantly the vision disappeared. It was neither more nor less than two pair of leaves, each pair on a separate stalk, on a young fruit tree that grew on the other side of the wall, not two yards from my eye. The leaves being alternate, did, when I looked at them as leaves, strikingly resemble wings, and they were the only leaves on the tree. The magnitude was given by the imagined distance, that distance by the former adjustment of the eye, which *remained* in consequence of the deep impression, the length of time I had been looking at the kite, the pleasure, &c., and (the fact that) a new object (had) impressed itself on the eye.

My nature requires another nature for its support, and reposes only in another from the necessary indigence of its being. Intensely similar yet not the same (must that other be); or, may I venture to say, the same indeed, but dissimilar, as the same breath sent with the same force, the same pauses, and the same melody pre-imaged in the mind, into the flute and the clarion shall be the same *soul diversely incarnate*.

The soul within the body – can I, any way, compare this to the reflection of the fire seen through my window on the solid wall, seeming, of course, within the solid wall, as deep within as the distance of the fire from the wall. I fear I can make nothing out of it; but why do I always hurry away from any interesting thought to do something uninteresting? As, for instance, when this thought struck me, I turned off my attention suddenly and went to look for the copy of Wolff which I had missed. Is it a cowardice of all deep feeling, even though pleasurable? or is it laziness? or is it something less obvious than either? is it connected with my epistolary embarrassments?

The stedfast rainbow in the fast-moving, fast-hurrying hail-mist! What a congregation of images and feelings, of fantastic permanence amidst the rapid change of tempest – quietness the daughter of storm.

I would make a pilgrimage to the deserts of Arabia to find the man who could make me understand how the *one can be many*. Eternal, universal mystery! It seems as if it were impossible, yet it *is*, and it is everywhere! It is indeed a contradiction in *terms*, and only in terms. It is the co-presence of feeling and life, limitless by their very essence, with form by its very essence limited, determinable, definite.

A time will come when passiveness will attain the dignity of worthy activity, when men shall be as proud within themselves of having remained in a state of deep tranquil emotion, whether in reading or in hearing or in looking, as they now are in having figured away for an hour! Oh! how few can transmute activity of mind into emotion! Yet there are as active as the stirring tempest and playful as the may-blossom in a breeze of May, who can yet for hours together remain with *hearts* broad awake, and the *understanding* asleep in all but its retentiveness and *receptivity*. Yea, and (in) the latter (state of mind) evince as great genius as in the former.

1804

To deduce instincts from obscure recollections of a pre-existing state – I have often thought of it. 'Ey!' I have said, when I have seen certain tempers and actions in Hartley, 'that is I in my future state.' So I think, oftentimes, that my children are my soul – that multitude and division are not (O mystery!) necessarily subversive of unity. I am sure that two very different meanings, if not more, lurk in the word One.

1804

One travels along with the lines of a mountain. Years ago I wanted to make Wordsworth sensible of this. How fine is Keswick vale! Would I repose, my soul lies and is quiet upon the broad level vale. Would it act? it darts up into the mountain-top like a kite, and like a chamois-goat runs along the ridge – or like a boy that makes a sport on the road of running along a wall or narrow fence!

1804

How opposite to nature and the fact to talk of the 'one moment' of Hume, of our whole being an aggregate of successive single sensations! Who ever felt a single sensation? Is not every one at the same moment conscious that there co-exist a thousand others, a darker shade, or less light, even as when I fix my attention on a white house or a grey bare hill or rather long ridge that runs out of sight each way (how often I want the German *unübersetzbar!*) (untranslatable) – the pretended sight-sensation, is it anything more than the light-point in every picture either of nature or of a good painter? and, again, subordinately, in every component part of the picture? And what is a moment? Succession with interspace? Absurdity! It is evidently only the *licht-punct* in the indivisible undivided duration.

1804

Everyone of tolerable education feels the *imitability* of Dr Johnson's and other-such's style, the inimitability of Shakespere's, &c. Hence, I believe, arises the partiality of thousands for Johnson. They can imagine *themselves* doing the same. Vanity is at the bottom of it. The number of imitators proves this in some measure.

1805

The question should be fairly stated, how far a man can be an adequate, or even a good (as far as he goes) though inadequate critic of poetry who is not a poet, at least, *in posse?* Can he be an adequate, can he be a good critic, though not commensurate (with the poet criticized)? But there is yet another distinction. Supposing he is not only not a poet, but is a bad poet! What then?

1805

In looking at objects of Nature while I am thinking, as at yonder moon dim-glimmering through the dewy window-pane, I seem rather to be seeking, as it were *asking* for, a symbolical language for something within me that already and for ever exists, than observing anything new. Even when that latter is the case, yet still I have always an obscure feeling as if that new phenomena were the dim awaking of a forgotten or hidden truth of my inner nature. It is still interesting as a word – a symbol. It is Λόγος the Creator, and the Evolver! (Now) what is the right, the virtuous feeling, and consequent action when a man having long meditated on and perceived a certain truth, finds another, a foreign writer, who has handled the same with an approximation to the truth as he had previously conceived it? Joy! Let Truth make her voice audible! While I was preparing the pen to write this remark, I lost the train of thought which had led me to it. I meant to have asked something else now forgotten. For the above answers itself. It needed no answer, I trust, in my heart.

1805

Mem. always to bear in mind that profound sentence of Leibnitz that men's intellectual errors consist chiefly in *denying*. What they *affirm* with *feeling* is, for the most part, right – if it be a real affirmation, and not affirmative in form, negative in reality. As, for instance, when a man praises the French stage, meaning and implying his dislike of Shakespeare (and the Elizabethan dramatists).

1805

The confusion of metaphor with reality is one of the fountains of the many-headed Nile of credulity, which, overflowing its banks, covers the world with miscreations and reptile monsters, and feeds by its many mouths the sea of blood.

1805

Our mortal existence, what is it but a stop-page in the blood of life, a brief eddy from wind or concourse of currents in the ever-flowing ocean of pure Activity, who beholds pyramids, yea, Alps and Andes, giant pyramids, the work of fire that raiseth monuments, like a generous victor o'er its own conquest, the tombstones of a world destroyed! Yet these, too, float down the sea of Time, and melt away as mountains of floating ice.

1806

To you there are many like me, yet to me there is none like you, and you are always like yourself. There are groves of night-flowers, yet the night-flower sees only the moon.

1806

What a swarm of thoughts and feelings, endlessly minute fragments, and, as it were, representations of all preceding and embryos of all future thought, lie compact in any one moment! So, in a single drop of water, the microscope discovers what motions, what tumult, what wars, what pursuits, what stratagems, what a circle-dance of death and life, death-hunting life, and life renewed and invigorated by death! The whole world seems here in a many-meaning cypher. What if our existence was but that moment? What an unintelligible, affrightful riddle, what a chaos of limbs and trunk, tailless, headless, nothing begun and nothing ended, would it not be? And yet scarcely more than that other moment of fifty or sixty years, were that our all? Each part throughout infinite diminution adapted to some other, and yet the whole a means to nothing – ends everywhere, and yet an end nowhere.

1811-12

I am persuaded that we love what is above us more than what is under us.

1811–12

The first man of science was he who looked into a thing, not to learn whether it could furnish him with food, or shelter, or weapons, or tools, or ornaments, or *playwiths*, but who sought to know it for the gratification of *knowing*; while he that first sought to *know* in order to *be* was the first philosopher. I have read of two rivers passing through the same lake, yet all the way preserving their streams visibly distinct – if I mistake not, the Rhone and the Adar, through the Lake of Geneva. In a far finer distinction, yet in a subtler union, such, for the contemplative mind, are the streams of knowing and being. The lake is formed by the two streams in man and nature as it exists in and for man; and up this lake the philosopher sails on the junction-line of the constituent streams, still pushing upward and sounding as he goes, towards the common fountain-head of both, the mysterious source whose being is knowledge, whose knowledge is being – the adorable I AM IN THAT I AM.

1814

The sentimental *cantilena* respecting the benignity and loveliness of nature – how does it not sink before the contemplation of the pravity of nature, on whose reluctance and inaptness a form is forced (the mere reflex of that form which is itself absolute substance!) and which it struggles against, bears but for a while and then sinks with the alacrity of self-seeking into dust or *sanies*, which falls abroad into endless nothings or creeps and cowers in poison or explodes in havock! What is the beginning? what the end? And how evident an alien is the supernatural in the brief interval!

If a man could pass through Paradise in a dream, and have a flower presented to him as a pledge that his soul had really been there, and if he found that flower in his hand when he awoke – Aye! and what then?

1816

Few die of a *broken heart*, and these few (the surgeons tell us) know nothing of it, and, dying suddenly, leave to the dissector the first discovery. O this is but the shallow remark of a hard and unthinking prosperity! Have you never seen a stick broken in the middle, and yet cohering by the rind? The fibres, half of them actually broken and the rest sprained and, though tough, unsustaining? O many, many are the broken-hearted for those who know what the moral and practical heart of the man is!

1824

THE FRIEND
(1809)

From ESSAY III

PROBLEMS OF COMMUNICATION

... A MAN long accustomed to silent and solitary meditation, in proportion as he increases the power of thinking in long and connected trains, is apt to lose or lessen the talent of communicating his thoughts with grace and perspicuity. Doubtless too, I have in some measure injured my style, in respect to its facility and popularity, from having almost confined my reading, of late years, to the works of the ancients and those of the elder writers in the modern languages. We insensibly imitate what we habitually admire; and an aversion to the epigrammatic unconnected periods of the fashionable Anglo-gallican taste has too often made me willing to forget, that the stately march and difficult evolutions, which characterize the eloquence of Hooker, Bacon, Milton, and Jeremy Taylor, are, notwithstanding their intrinsic excellence, still less suited to a periodical essay. This fault I am now endeavouring to correct; though I can never so far sacrifice my judgement to the desire of being immediately popular, as to cast my sentences in the French moulds, or affect a style which an ancient critic would have deemed purposely invented for persons troubled with asthma to read, and for those to comprehend who labour under the more pitiable asthma of a short-witted intellect. It cannot but be injurious to the human mind never to be called into effort: the habit of receiving pleasure without any exertion of thought, by the mere excitement of curiosity and sensibility, may be justly ranked among the worst effects of habitual novel reading. It is true that these short and unconnected sentences are easily and instantly understood: but it is equally true, that wanting all the cement of thought as well as of style, all the connections, and (if you will forgive so trivial a metaphor) all the hooks-and-eyes of the memory, they are as easily forgotten: or rather, it is scarcely possible that they should be remembered. – Nor is it less true, that those who confine their reading to such books dwarf their own faculties, and finally reduce their understandings to a deplorable imbecility: the fact you mention, and which I shall hereafter make use of, is a fair instance and a striking illustration. Like idle morning visitors, the brisk and breathless periods hurry in and hurry off in quick and profitless succession; each indeed for the moments of its stay prevents the pain of vacancy, while it indulges the love of sloth; but all together they leave the mistress of the house (the soul I mean) flat and exhausted, incapable of attending to her own concerns, and unfitted for the conversation of more rational guests. . . .

Hitherto, my dear sir, I have been employed in laying the foundations of my work. But the proper merit of a foundation is its massiveness and solidity. The conveniences and ornaments, the gilding and stucco work, the sunshine and sunny prospects, will come with the superstructure. Yet I dare not flatter myself, that any endeavours of mine, compatible with the duty I owe to truth and the hope of permanent utility, will render The Friend agreeable to the majority of what is called the reading public. I never expected it. How indeed could I, when I was to borrow so little from the influence of passing events, and when I had absolutely excluded from my plan all appeals to personal curiosity and personal interests? Yet even this is not my greatest impediment. No real information can be conveyed, no important errors rectified, no widely injurious prejudices rooted up, without requiring some effort of thought on the part of the reader. But the obstinate (and toward a contemporary writer, the contemptuous) aversion to all intellectual effort is the mother evil of all which I had proposed to war against, the queen bee in the hive of our errors and misfortunes, both private and national. To solicit the attention of those, on whom these debilitating causes have acted to their full extent, would be no less absurd than to recommend exercise with the dumb bells, as the only mode of cure, to a patient paralytic in both arms.

From INTRODUCTION TO SECTION 2

PROGRESS

THERE are two errors into which we easily slip when thinking of past times. One lies in forgetting in the excellence of what remains, the large overbalance of worthlessness that has been swept away. Ranging over the wide tracts of antiquity, the situation of the mind may be likened to that of a traveller in some unpeopled part of America, who is attracted to the burial-place of one of the primitive inhabitants. It is conspicuous upon an eminence, 'a mount upon a mount!' He digs into it, and finds that it contains the bones of a man of mighty stature; and he is tempted to give way to a belief, that as there were giants in those days, so all men were giants. But a second and wiser thought may suggest to him, that this tomb would never have forced itself upon his notice if it had not contained a body that was distinguished from others, that of a man who had been selected as a chieftain or ruler for the very reason that he surpassed the rest of his tribe in stature, and who now lies thus conspicuously inhumed upon the mountain-top, while the bones of his followers are laid unobtrusively together in their burrows upon the plain below. The second habitual error is, that in this comparison of ages we divide time merely into past and present, and place these in the balance to be weighed against each other, not considering that the present is in our estimation not more than a period of thirty years, or half a century at most, and that the past is a mighty accumulation of many such periods, perhaps the whole of recorded time, or at least the whole of that portion of it in which our own country has been distinguished. We may illustrate this by the familiar use of the words ancient and modern, when applied to poetry: what can be more inconsiderate or unjust than to compare a few existing writers with the whole succession of their progenitors? The delusion, from the moment that our thoughts are directed to it, seems too gross to deserve mention; yet men will talk for hours upon poetry, balancing against each other the words ancient and modern, and be unconscious that they have fallen into it.

These observations are not made as implying a dissent from the belief of my correspondent, that the moral spirit and intellectual powers of this country are declining; but to guard against unqualified admiration, even in cases where admiration has been rightly fixed, and to prevent that depression which must necessarily follow, where the notion of the peculiar unfavourableness of the present times to dignity of mind has been carried too far. For in proportion as we imagine obstacles to exist out of ourselves to retard our progress, will, in fact, our progress be retarded. Deeming then, that in all ages an ardent mind will be baffled and led astray in the manner under contemplation, though in various degrees, I shall at present content myself with a few practical and desultory comments upon some of those general causes, to which my correspondent justly attributes the errors in opinion, and the lowering or deadening of sentiment to which ingenuous and aspiring youth is exposed. And first, for the heart-cheering belief in the perpetual progress of the species towards a point of unattainable perfection. If the present age do indeed transcend the past in what is most beneficial and honourable, he that perceives this, being in no error, has no cause for complaint; but if it be not so, a youth of genius might, it should seem, be preserved from any wrong influence of this faith, by an insight into a simple truth, namely, that it is not necessary, in order to satisfy the desires of our nature, or to reconcile us to the economy of Providence, that there should be at all times a continuous advance in what is of highest worth. In fact it is not, as a writer of the present day has admirably observed, in the power of fiction to portray in words, or of the imagination to conceive in spirit, actions or characters of more exalted virtue than those which thousands of years ago have existed upon earth, as we know from the records of authentic history. Such is the inherent dignity of human nature, that there belong to it sublimities of virtues which all men may attain, and which no man can transcend; and though this be not true, in an equal degree, of intellectual power, yet in the persons of Plato, Demosthenes, and Homer, – and in those of Shakespeare, Milton, and Lord Bacon, – were enshrined as much of the divinity of intellect as the inhabitants of this planet can hope will ever take up its abode among them. But the question is not of the power or worth of individual minds, but of the general moral or intellectual merits of an age, or a people, or of the human race. Be it so; let us allow and believe that there is a progress in the species towards unattainable perfection, or whether this be so or not, that it is a necessity of a good and greatly-gifted nature to believe it; surely it does not follow, that this progress should be constant in those virtues and intellectual qualities, and in those departments of knowledge, which in themselves absolutely considered are of most value – things independent and in their degree indispensable. The progress of the species neither is nor can be like that of a Roman road in a right line. It may be more justly compared to that of a river, which, both in its smaller reaches and larger turnings, is frequently forced back towards its fountains by objects which cannot otherwise be eluded or overcome; yet with an accompanying impulse that will insure its advancement hereafter, it is either gaining strength every hour, or conquering in secret some difficulty, by a labour that contributes as effectually to further it in its course, as when it moves forward uninterrupted in a line, direct as that of the Roman road with which we began the comparison.

From SECTION 2, ESSAY IV

ON METHOD

WHAT is that which first strikes us, and strikes us at once, in a man of education; and which among educated men so instantly distinguishes the man of superior mind, that (as was observed with eminent propriety of the late Edmund Burke) 'we cannot stand under the same archway during a shower of rain, without finding him out'? Not the weight or novelty of his remarks; not any unusual interest of facts communicated by him; for we may suppose both the one and the other precluded by the shortness of our intercourse and the triviality of the subjects. The difference will be impressed and felt, though the conversation should be confined to the state of the weather or the pavement. Still less will it arise from any peculiarity in his words and phrases. For if he be, as we now assume, a well-educated man as well as a man of superior powers, he will not fail to follow the golden rule of Julius Caesar, *Insolens verbum, tanquam scopulum, evitare*. Unless where new things necessitate new terms, he will avoid an unusual word as a rock. It must have been among the earliest lessons of his youth that the breach of this precept – at all times hazardous – becomes ridiculous in the topics of ordinary conversation. There remains but one other point of distinction possible, and this must be, and in fact is, the true cause of the impression made on us. It is the unpremeditated and evidently habitual arrangement of his words, grounded on the habit of foreseeing in each integral part, or (more plainly) in every sentence, the whole that he then intends to communicate. However irregular and desultory his talk, there is method in the fragments.

Listen, on the other hand, to an ignorant man, though perhaps shrewd and able in his particular calling, whether he be describing or relating. We immediately perceive, that his memory alone is called into action; and that the objects and events recur in the narration in the same order, and with the same accompaniments, however accidental or impertinent, as they had first occurred to the narrator. The necessity of taking breath, the efforts of recollection, and the abrupt rectification of its failures, produce all his pauses; and with exception of the 'and then', the 'and there', and the still less significant 'and so', they constitute likewise all his connections.

Our discussion, however, is confined to method as employed in the formation of the understanding, and in the constructions of science and literature. It would indeed be superfluous to attempt a proof of its importance in the business and economy of active or domestic life. From the cotter's hearth or the workshop of the artisan to the palace of the arsenal, the first merit, that which admits neither substitute nor equivalent, is, that *every* thing is in its place. Where this charm is wanting, every other merit either loses its name, or becomes an additional ground of accusation and regret. Of one by whom it is eminently possessed, we say, proverbially, he is like clock-work. The resemblance extends beyond the point of regularity, and yet falls short of the truth. Both do, indeed, at once divide and announce the silent and otherwise indistinguishable lapse of time. But the man of methodical industry and honourable pursuits does more; he realizes its ideal divisions, and gives a character and individuality to its moments. If the idle are described as killing time, he may be justly said to call it into life and moral being, while he makes it the distinct object not only of the consciousness but of the conscience. He organizes the hours and gives them a soul; and that, the very essence of which is to fleet away, and evermore to have been, he takes up into his own permanence, and communicates to it the imperishableness of a spiritual nature. Of the good and faithful servant, whose energies, thus directed, are thus methodized, it is less truly affirmed that he lives in time, than that time lives in him. His days, months, and years, as the stops and punctual marks in the records of duties performed, will survive the wreck of worlds, and remain extant when time itself shall be no more.

But as the importance of method in the duties of social life is incomparably greater, so are its practical elements proportionably obvious, and such as relate to the will far more than to the understanding. Henceforward, therefore, we contemplate its bearings on the latter.

The difference between the products of a well disciplined and those of an uncultivated understanding, in relation to what we will now venture to call the *Science of Method*, is often and admirably exhibited by our great dramatist. We scarcely need refer our readers to the Clown's evidence, in the first scene of the second act of *Measure for Measure*, or to the Nurse in *Romeo and Juliet*. But not to leave the position, without an instance to illustrate it, we will take the 'easy-yielding' Mrs Quickly's relation of the circumstances of Sir John Falstaff's debt to her:

FALSTAFF. What is the gross sum that I owe thee?

MRS QUICKLY. Marry, if you wert an honest man, thyself and the money too. Thou didst swear to me upon a parcel-gilt goblet, sitting in my Dolphin chamber, at the round table, by a sea-coal fire, on Wednesday in Whitsun week, when the prince broke thy head for liking his father to a singing-man of Windsor – thou didst swear to me then, as I was washing thy wound, to marry me and make me my lady thy wife. Canst thou deny it? Did not goodwife Keech, the butcher's wife, come in then and call me gossip Quickly? – coming in to borrow a mess of vinegar: telling us she had a good dish of prawns – whereby thou didst desire to eat some – whereby I told thee they were ill for a green wound, &c. &c. &c.

Henry IV, 2nd pt., Act ii, sc. 1

And this, be it observed, is so far from being carried beyond the bounds of a fair imitation, that 'the poor soul's' thoughts and sentences are more closely interlinked than the truth of nature would have required, but that the connections and sequence, which the habit of method can alone give, have in this instance a substitute in the fusion of passion. For the absence of method, which characterizes the uneducated, is occasioned by an habitual submission of the understanding to mere events and images as such, and independent of any power in the mind to classify or appropriate them. The general accompaniments of time and place are the only relations which persons of this class appear to regard in their statements. As this constitutes their leading feature, the contrary excellence, as distinguishing the well-educated man, must be referred to the contrary habit. Method, therefore, becomes natural to the mind which has been accustomed to contemplate not things only, or for their own sake alone, but likewise and chiefly the relations of things, either their relations to each other, or to the observer, or to the state and apprehension of the hearers. To enumerate and analyse these relations, with the conditions under which alone they are discoverable, is to teach the science of method.

The enviable results of this science, when knowledge has been ripened into those habits which at once secure and evince its possession, can scarcely be exhibited more forcibly as well as more pleasingly, than by contrasting with the former extract from Shakespeare the narration given by Hamlet to Horatio of the occurrences during his proposed transportation to England, and the events that interrupted his voyage:

> HAMLET. Sir, in my heart there was a kind of fighting
> That would not let me sleep: methought I lay
> Worse than the mutines in the bilboes. Rashly,
> And prais'd be rashness for it – Let us know,
> Our indiscretion sometimes serves us well,
> When our deep plots do pall: and that should teach us,
> There's a divinity that shapes our ends,
> Rough-hew them how we will.
> HORATIO. That is most certain.
> HAMLET. Up from my cabin,
> My sea-gown scarf'd about me, in the dark
> Grop'd I to find out them; had my desire
> Finger'd their packet; and, in fine, withdrew
> To my own room again: making so bold,
> My fears forgetting manners, to unseal
> Their grand commission; where I found, Horatio,

O royal knavery! an exact command,
Larded with many several sorts of reasons,
Importing Denmark's health, and England's too,
With, ho! such bugs and goblins in my life,
That on the supervise, no leisure bated,
No, not to stay the grinding of the axe
My head should be struck off!
HORATIO. Is't possible?
HAMLET. Here's the commission. – Read it at more leisure.

Act v, sc. 2

Here the events, with the circumstances of time and place, are all
stated with equal compression and rapidity, not one introduced which
could have been omitted without injury to the intelligibility of the
whole process. If any tendency is discoverable, as far as the mere facts
are in question, it is the tendency to omission; and, accordingly, the
reader will observe that the attention of the narrator is afterwards
called back to one material circumstance, which he was hurrying by,
by a direct question from the friend to whom the story is communi-
cated, 'How was this sealed?' But by a trait which is indeed peculiarly
characteristic of Hamlet's mind, ever disposed to generalize, and
meditative to excess (but which, with due abatement and reduction,
is distinctive of every powerful and methodizing intellect), all the
digressions and enlargements consist of reflections, truths, and prin-
ciples of general and permanent interest, either directly expressed or
disguised in playful satire.

... I sat me down:
Devis'd a new commission; wrote it fair.
I once did hold it, as our statists do,
A baseness to write fair, and laboured much
How to forget that learning; but, sir, now
It did me yeoman's service. Wilt thou know
The effect of what I wrote?
HORATIO. Aye, good my lord.
HAMLET. An earnest conjuration from the king,
As England was his faithful tributary;
As love between them, like the palm, might flourish;
As peace should still her wheaten garland wear,
And many such like As'es of great charge –
That on the view and knowing of these contents
He should the bearers put to sudden death,
Not shriving time allowed.
HORATIO. How was this sealed?
HAMLET. Why, even in that was heaven ordinant.

I had my father's signet in my purse,
Which was the model of that Danish seal:
Folded the writ up in form of the other;
Subscribed it; gave't the impression; placed it safely,
The changeling never known. Now, the next day
Was our sea-fight; and what to this was sequent,
Thou knowest already.

HORATIO. So Guildenstern and Rosencrantz go to't?

HAMLET. Why, man, they did make love to this employment.
They are not near my conscience: their defeat
Doth by their own insinuation grow.
'Tis dangerous when the baser nature comes
Between the pass and fell incensed points
Of mighty opposites.

It would, perhaps be sufficient to remark of the preceding passage, in connection with the humorous specimen of narration,

Fermenting o'er with frothy circumstance,

in *Henry IV*, that if overlooking the different value of matter in each, we considered the form alone, we should find both immethodical; Hamlet from the excess, Mrs Quickly from the want, of reflection and generalization; and that method, therefore, must result from the due mean or balance between our passive impressions and the mind's own reaction on the same. (Whether this reaction does not suppose or imply a primary act positively originating in the mind itself, and prior to the object in order of nature, though co-instantaneous in its manifestation, will be hereafter discussed.) But we had a further purpose in thus contrasting these extracts from our 'myriad-minded bard', (μυριονοῦς ἀνηρ). We wished to bring forward, each for itself, these two elements of method, or (to adopt an arithmetical term) its two main factors.

Instances of the want of generalization are of no rare occurrence in real life; and the narrations of Shakespeare's Hostess and the Tapster differ from those of the ignorant and unthinking in general by their superior humour, the poet's own gift and infusion, not by their want of method, which is not greater than we often meet with in that class of which they are the dramatic representatives. Instances of the opposite fault, arising from the excess of generalization and reflection in minds of the opposite class, will, like the minds themselves, occur less frequently in the course of our own personal experience. Yet they will not have been wanting to our readers, nor will they have passed unobserved, though the great poet himself (ὁ τὴν ἑαυτοῦ ψυχὴν ὡσεὶ ὕλην τίνα ἀσώματον μορφαῖς ποικιλαῖς μορφώσας*) has more conveniently supplied the illustrations. To complete, therefore, the purpose aforementioned, that of presenting each of the two components as separately as possible, we chose an instance in which, by the surplus of its own activity, Hamlet's mind disturbs the arrangement, of which that very activity had been the cause and impulse.

Thus exuberance of mind, on the one hand, interferes with the forms of method; but sterility of mind, on the other, wanting the spring and impulse to mental action, is wholly destructive of method itself. For in attending too exclusively to the relations which the past or passing events and objects bear to general truth, and the moods of his own thought, the most intelligent man is sometimes in danger of overlooking that other relation in which they are likewise to be placed to the apprehension and sympathies of his hearers. His discourse appears like soliloquy intermixed with dialogue. But the uneducated and unreflecting talker overlooks all mental relations, both logical and psychological; and consequently precludes all method that is not purely accidental. Hence the nearer the things and incidents in time and place, the more distant, disjointed, and impertinent to each other, and to any common purpose, will they appear in his narration; and this from the want of a staple, or starting-post, in the narrator himself; from the absence of the leading thought, which, borrowing a phrase from the nomenclature of legislation, we may not inaptly call the initiative. On the contrary, where the habit of method is present and effective, things the most remote and diverse in time, place, and outward circumstance, are brought into mental contiguity and succession, the more striking as the less expected. But while we would impress the necessity of this habit, the illustrations adduced give proof that in undue preponderance, and when the prerogative of the mind is stretched into despotism, the discourse may degenerate into the grotesque or the fantastical.

With what a profound insight into the constitution of the human soul is this exhibited to us in the character of the Prince of Denmark, where flying from the sense of reality, and seeking a reprieve from the pressure of its duties in that ideal activity, the overbalance of which, with the consequent indisposition to action, is his disease, he compels the reluctant good sense of the high yet healthful-minded Horatio, to follow him in his wayward meditation amid the graves! 'To what base uses we may return, Horatio! Why may not imagination trace

* (*Translation*) – He that moulded his own soul, as some incorporeal material, into various forms. – THEMISTIUS.

the noble dust of Alexander, till he find it stopping a bung-hole? HOR. 'Twere to consider too curiously to consider so. HAM. No, faith, not a jot; but to follow him thither with modesty enough and likelihood to lead it. As thus: Alexander died, Alexander was buried, Alexander returneth to dust – the dust is earth; of earth we make loam: and why of that loam, whereto he was converted, might they not stop a beer-barrel?

> Imperial Caesar, dead and turn'd to clay,
> Might stop a hole to keep the wind away!'

Act v, sc. I

But let it not escape our recollection, that when the objects thus connected are proportionate to the connecting energy, relatively to the real, or at least to the desirable sympathies of mankind; it is from the same character that we derive the genial method in the famous soliloquy, 'To be? or not to be?' which, admired as it is, and has been, has yet received only the first-fruits of the admiration due to it.

We have seen that from the confluence of innumerable impressions in each moment of time the mere passive memory must needs tend to confusion – a rule, the seeming exceptions to which (the thunder-bursts in *Lear*, for instance) are really confirmations of its truth. For, in many instances, the predominance of some mighty passion takes the place of the guiding thought, and the result presents the method of nature, rather than the habit of the individual. For thought, imagination (and we may add passion), are, in their very essence, the first, connective, the latter, co-adunative; and it has been shown, that if the excess lead to method misapplied, and to connections of the moment, the absence, or marked deficiency, either precludes method altogether, both form and substance, or (as the following extract will exemplify) retains the outward form only.

> My liege and madam, to expostulate
> What majesty should be, what duty is,
> Why day is day, night night, and time is time,
> Were nothing but to waste night, day and time.
> Therefore – since brevity is the soul of wit,
> And tediousness the limbs and outward flourishes,
> I will be brief. Your noble son is mad:
> Mad call I it – for to define true madness,
> What is't, but to be nothing else but mad?
> But let that go.

QUEEN. More matter with less art.

POLONIUS. Madam! I swear, I use no art at all.

That he is mad, 'tis true: 'tis true, 'tis pity:
And pity 'tis, 'tis true (a foolish figure!
But farewell it, for I will use no art)
Mad let us grant him then: and now remains,
That we find out the cause of this effect,
Or rather say the cause of this defect:
For this effect defective comes by cause.
Thus it remains, and the remainder thus
Perpend!

Hamlet, Act ii, sc. 2

Does not the irresistible sense of the ludicrous in this flourish of the soul-surviving body of old Polonius's intellect, not less than in the endless confirmations and most undeniable matters of fact, of Tapster Pompey or 'the hostess of the tavern' prove to our feelings, even before the word is found which presents the truth to our understandings, that confusion and formality are but the opposite poles of the same nullpoint?

It is Shakespeare's peculiar excellence, that throughout the whole of his splendid picture gallery (the reader will excuse the confessed inadequacy of this metaphor), we find individuality everywhere, mere portrait nowhere. In all his various characters, we still feel ourselves communing with the same human nature, which is everywhere present as the vegetable sap in the branches, sprays, leaves, buds, blossoms, and fruits, their shapes, tastes, and odours. Speaking of the effect, *i.e.* his works themselves, we may define the excellence of their method as consisting in that just proportion, that union and interpenetration of the universal and the particular, which must ever pervade all works of decided genius and true science. For method implies a progressive transition, and it is the meaning of the word in the original language. The Greek Μέθοδος, is literally a way, or path of transit. Thus we extol the Elements of Euclid, or Socrates' discourse with the slave in the Menon, as methodical, a term which no one who holds himself bound to think or speak correctly would apply to the alphabetical order or arrangement of a common dictionary. But as, without continuous transition, there can be no method, so without a pre-conception there can be no transition with continuity. The term, method, cannot therefore, otherwise than by abuse, be applied to a mere dead arrangement, containing in itself no principle of progression.

From SECTION 2, ESSAY II

EXISTENCE

Hast thou ever raised thy mind to the consideration of existence, in and by itself, as the mere act of existing? Hast thou ever said to thyself thoughtfully, It is! heedless in that moment, whether it were a man before thee, or a flower, or a grain of sand? without reference, in short, to this or that particular mode or form of existence? If thou hast indeed attained to this, thou wilt have felt the presence of a mystery, which must have fixed thy spirit in awe and wonder. The very words, There is nothing! or, There was a time when there was nothing! are self-contradictory. There is that within us which repels the proposition with as full and instantaneous a light, as if it bore evidence against the fact in the right of its own eternity.

Not to be, then, is impossible; to be, incomprehensible. If thou hast mastered this intuition of absolute existence, thou wilt have learnt likewise that it was this, and no other, which in the earlier ages seized the nobler minds, the elect among men, with a sort of sacred horror. This it was which first caused them to feel within themselves a something ineffably greater than their own individual nature. It was this which, raising them aloft, and projecting them to an ideal distance from themselves, prepared them to become the lights and awakening voices of other men, the founders of law and religion, the educators and foster-gods of mankind. The power, which evolved this idea of being, being in its essence, being limitless, comprehending its own limits in its dilatation, and condensing itself into its own apparent mounds – how shall we name it? The idea itself, which, like a mighty billow, at once overwhelms and bears aloft – what is it? Whence did it come? In vain would we derive it from the organs of sense; for these supply only surfaces, undulations, phantoms! In vain from the instruments of sensation; for these furnish only the chaos, the shapeless elements of sense! And least of all may we hope to find its origin, or sufficient cause, in the moulds and mechanism of the understanding, the whole purport and functions of which consist in individualization, in outlines and differencings by quantity, quality, and relation. It were wiser to seek substance in shadow, than absolute fulness in mere negation.

We have asked then for its birth-place in all that constitutes our relative individuality, in all that each man calls exclusively himself. It is an alien of which they know not; and for them the question itself is purposeless, and the very words that convey it are as sounds in an unknown language, or as the vision of heaven and earth expanded by the rising sun, which falls but as warmth on the eyelids of the blind. To no class of phaenomena or particulars can it be referred, itself being none; therefore, to no faculty by which these alone are apprehended. As little dare we refer it to any form of abstraction or generalization, for it has neither co-ordinate or analogon! It is absolutely one, and that it is, and affirms itself to be, is its only predicate. And yet this power, nevertheless, is! In eminence of being it is! And he for whom it manifests itself in its adequate idea, dare as little arrogate it to himself as his own, can as little appropriate it either totally or by partition, as he can claim ownership in the breathing air, or make an enclosure in the cope of heaven. He bears witness of it to his own mind, even as he describes life and light; and, with the silence of light, it describes itself and dwells in *us* only as far as we dwell in *it*. The truths which it manifests are such as it alone can manifest, and in all truth it manifests itself. By what name then canst thou call a truth so manifested? Is it not revelation? Ask thyself whether thou canst attach to that latter word any consistent meaning not included in the idea of the former. And the manifesting power, the source and the correlative of the idea thus manifested – is it not God? Either thou knowest it to be God, or thou hast called an idol by that awful name! Therefore in the most appropriate, no less than in the highest, sense of the word were the earliest teachers of humanity inspired. They alone were the true seers of God, and therefore prophets of the human race.

BIOGRAPHIA LITERARIA

From CHAPTER I

The motives of the present work – Reception of the Author's first publication – The discipline of his taste at school – The effect of contemporary writers on youthful minds – Bowles's Sonnets – Comparison between the poets before and since Pope.

IT has been my lot to have had my name introduced, both in conversation and in print, more frequently than I find it easy to explain, whether I consider the fewness, unimportance, and limited circulation of my writings, or the retirement and distance in which I have lived, both from the literary and political world. Most often it has been connected with some charge which I could not acknowledge, or some principle which I had never entertained. Nevertheless, had I had no other motive or incitement, the reader would not have been troubled with this exculpation. What my additional purposes were will be seen in the following pages. It will be found that the least of what I have written concerns myself personally. I have used the narration chiefly for the purpose of giving a continuity to the work, in part for the sake of the miscellaneous reflections suggested to me by particular events; but still more as introductory to the statement of my principles in Politics, Religion, and Philosophy, and the application of the rules, deduced from philosophical principles, to poetry and criticism. But of the objects which I proposed to myself, it was not the least important to effect, as far as possible, a settlement of the long-continued controversy concerning the true nature of poetic diction, and at the same time to define with the utmost impartiality the real *poetic* character of the poet, by whose writings this controversy was first kindled, and has been since fuelled and fanned.

In 1794, when I had barely passed the verge of manhood, I published a small volume of juvenile poems. They were received with a degree of favour which, young as I was, I well knew was bestowed on them not so much for any positive merit, as because they were considered buds of hope and promises of better works to come. The critics of that day, the most flattering equally with the severest, concurred in objecting to them obscurity, a general turgidness of diction, and a profusion of new-coined double epithets. The first is the fault which a writer is the least able to detect in his own compositions; and my mind was not then sufficiently disciplined to receive the authority of others as a substitute for my own conviction. Satisfied that the thoughts, such as they were, could not have been expressed otherwise, or at least more perspicuously, I forgot to inquire whether the thoughts themselves did not demand a degree of attention unsuitable to the nature and objects of poetry. This remark, however, applies chiefly, though not exclusively, to the *Religious Musings*. The remainder of the charge I admitted to its full extent, and not without sincere acknowledgements to both my private and public censors for their friendly admonitions. In the after editions I pruned the double epithets with no sparing hand, and used my best efforts to tame the swell and glitter both of thought and diction; though, in truth, these parasite plants of youthful poetry had insinuated themselves into my longer poems with such intricacy of union, that I was often obliged to omit disentangling the weed, from the fear of snapping the flower. From that period to the date of the present work I have published nothing with my name which could by any possibility have come before the board of anonymous criticism. Even the three or four poems, printed with the works of a friend, as far as they were censured at all, were charged with the same or similar defects, though I am persuaded, not with equal justice; with an *excess of ornament*, in addition to *strained and elaborate diction*. May I be permitted to add, that, even at the early period of my juvenile poems, I saw and admitted the superiority of an austerer and more natural style, with an insight not less clear than I at present possess. My judgement was stronger than were my powers of realizing its dictates, and the faults of my language, though indeed partly owing to a wrong choice of subjects, and the desire of giving a poetic colouring to abstract and metaphysical truths, in which a new world then seemed to open upon me, did yet, in part likewise, originate in unfeigned diffidence of my own comparative talent. During several years of my youth and early manhood, I reverenced those who had reintroduced the manly simplicity of the Grecian, and of our own elder poets, with such enthusiasm, as made the hope seem presumptuous of writing successfully in the same style. Perhaps a similar process has happened to others; but my earliest poems were marked by an ease and simplicity, which I have studied, perhaps with inferior success, to impress on my later compositions.

At school I enjoyed the inestimable advantage of a very sensible, though at the same time, a very severe master. He early moulded my taste to the preference of Demosthenes to Cicero, of Homer and Theocritus to Virgil, and again of Virgil to Ovid. He habituated me to compare Lucretius (in such extracts as I then read), Terence, and, above all, the chaster poems of Catullus, not only with the Roman poets of the so-called silver and brazen ages, but with even those of the Augustan era; and, on grounds of plain sense and universal logic, to see and assert the superiority of the former, in the truth and native-ness both of their thoughts and diction. At the same time that we were studying the Greek Tragic Poets, he made us read Shakespeare and Milton as lessons; and they were the lessons, too, which required most time and trouble to *bring up*, so as to escape his censure. I learnt from him that poetry, even that of the loftiest, and, seemingly, that of the wildest odes, had a logic of its own as severe as that of science, and more difficult, because more subtle, more complex, and dependent on more and more fugitive causes. In the truly great poets, he would say, there is a reason assignable, not only for every word, but for the posi-tion of every word; and I well remember that, availing himself of the synonymes to the Homer of Didymus, he made us attempt to show, with regard to each, *why* it would not have answered the same pur-pose, and wherein consisted the peculiar fitness of the word in the original text.

In our own English compositions (at least for the last three years of our school education) he showed no mercy to phrase, metaphor, or image, unsupported by a sound sense, or where the same sense might have been conveyed with equal force and dignity in plainer words. Lute, harp, and lyre, muse, muses, and inspirations, Pegasus, Parnassus and Hippocrene, were all an abomination to him. In fancy I can almost hear him now, exclaiming, '*Harp? Harp? Lyre? Pen and ink, boy, you mean! Muse, boy, muse? Your Nurse's daughter you mean! Pierian spring? Oh, aye! the cloister-pump, I suppose!*' Nay, certain introductions, similes, and examples were placed by name on a list of interdiction. Among the similes there was, I remember, that of the manchineel fruit, as suiting equally well with too many subjects, in which, how-ever, it yielded the palm at once to the example of Alexander and Clytus, which was equally good and apt whatever might be the theme. Was it ambition? Alexander and Clytus! Flattery? Alexander and Clytus! Anger? Drunkenness? Pride? Friendship? Ingratitude? Late repentance? Still, still Alexander and Clytus! At length the praises of agriculture having been exemplified in the sagacious ob-servation, that, had Alexander been holding the plough, he would not have run his friend Clytus through with a spear; this tried and ser-viceable old friend was banished by public edict in *saecula saeculorum*. I have sometimes ventured to think that a list of this kind, or an *index expurgatorius* of certain well-known and ever returning phrases, both introductory and transitional, including the large assortment of modest egotisms and flattering illeisms, &c., &c., might be hung up in our law courts and both Houses of Parliament, with great advantage to the public as an important saving of national time, an incalculable relief to his Majesty's ministers; but, above all, as insuring the thanks of country attorneys and their clients, who have private bills to carry through the House.

Be this as it may, there was one custom of our master's, which I cannot pass over in silence, because I think it imitable and worthy of imitation. He would often permit our theme exercises, under some pretext of want of time, to accumulate, till each lad had four or five to be looked over. Then placing the whole number *abreast* on his desk, he would ask the writer why this or that sentence might not have found as appropriate a place under this or that other thesis; and if no satisfying answer could be returned, and two faults of the same kind were found in one exercise, the irrevocable verdict followed, the exercise was torn up, and another on the same subject to be produced, in addition to the tasks of the day. The reader will, I trust, excuse this tribute of recollection to a man, whose severities, even now, not seldom furnish the dreams by which the blind fancy would fain interpret to the mind the painful sensations of distempered sleep; but neither lessen nor dim the deep sense of my moral and intellectual obligations. He sent us to the University excellent Latin and Greek scholars, and tolerable Hebraists. Yet our classical knowledge was the least of the good gifts which we derived from his zealous and conscientious tutorage. He is now gone to his final reward, full of years and full of honours, even of those honours which were dearest to his heart, as gratefully bestowed by that school, and still binding him to the interests of that school in which he had been himself educated, and to which during his whole life he was a dedicated thing.

From causes which this is not the place to investigate, no models of past times, however perfect, can have the same vivid effect on the youthful mind, as the productions of contemporary genius. The discipline my mind had undergone '*Ne falleretur rotundo sono et versuum cursu, cincinnis et floribus; sed ut inspiceret quidnam subesset, quae sedes, quod firmamentum, quis fundus verbis; an figurae essent mera ornatura et orationis fucus: vel sanguinis e materiae ipsius corde effluentis rubor quidam nativus et incalescentia genuina;*' removed all obstacles to the appreciation of excellence in style without diminishing my delight. That I was thus prepared for the perusal of Mr Bowles's sonnets and earlier poems, at once increased *their* influence and *my* enthusiasm. The great works of past ages seem to a young man things of another race, in respect to which his faculties must remain passive and submiss, even as to the stars and mountains. But the writings of a contemporary, perhaps not many years older than himself, surrounded by the same circumstances, and disciplined by the same manners, possess a reality for him, and inspire an actual friendship as of a man for a man. His very admiration is the wind which fans and feeds his hope. The poems themselves assume the properties of flesh and blood. To recite, to extol, to contend for them is but the payment of a debt due to one, who exists to receive it.

There are indeed modes of teaching which have produced, and are producing, youths of a very different stamp; modes of teaching, in comparison with which we have been called on to despise our great public schools, and universities,

> in whose halls are hung
> Armoury of the invincible knights of old –

modes, by which children are to be metamorphosed into prodigies. And prodigies with a vengeance have I known thus produced! Prodigies of self-conceit, shallowness, arrogance, and infidelity! Instead of storing the memory during the period when the memory is the predominant faculty, with facts for the after exercise of the judgement; and instead of awakening by the noblest models the fond and unmixed *Love* and *Admiration* which is the natural and graceful temper of early youth, *these* nurslings of improved pedagogy are taught to dispute and decide; to suspect all, but their own and their lecturer's wisdom; and to hold nothing sacred from their contempt but their own contemptible arrogance: boy-graduates in all the technicals, and in all the dirty passions and impudence, of anonymous criticism. To such dispositions alone can the admonition of Pliny be requisite, '*Neque enim debet operibus ejus obesse, quod vivit. An si inter eos, quos nunquam vidimus, floruisset, non solum libros ejus, verum etiam imagines conquireremus, ejusdem nunc honor praesentis, et gratia quasi satietate languescet? At hoc pravum, malignumque est, non admirari hominem admiratione dignissimum, quia videre, complecti, nec laudare tantum, verum etiam amare contingit.*' Plin. Epist. Lib. I.

I had just entered on my seventeenth year, when the sonnets of Mr Bowles, twenty in number, and just then published in a quarto pamphlet, were first made known and presented to me by a schoolfellow, who had quitted us for the University, and who, during the whole time that he was in our first form (or in our school language a Grecian), had been my patron and protector. I refer to Dr Middleton, the truly learned, and every way excellent Bishop of Calcutta. . . .

It was a double pleasure to me, and still remains a tender recollection, that I should have received from a friend so revered the first knowledge of a poet, by whose works, year after year, I was so enthusiastically delighted and inspired. My earliest acquaintances will not have forgotten the undisciplined eagerness and impetuous zeal with which I laboured to make proselytes, not only of my companions, but of all with whom I conversed, of whatever rank, and in whatever place. As my school finances did not permit me to purchase copies, I made, within less than a year and a half, more than forty transcriptions, as the best presents I could offer to those who had in any way won my regard. And with almost equal delight did I receive the three or four following publications of the same author.

Though I have seen and known enough of mankind to be well aware that I shall perhaps stand alone in my creed, and that it will be well if I subject myself to no worse charge than that of singularity; I am not, therefore, deterred from avowing that I regard, and ever have regarded the obligations of intellect among the most sacred of the claims of gratitude. A valuable thought, or a particular train of thoughts, gives me additional pleasure when I can safely refer and attribute it to the conversation or correspondence of another. My obligations to Mr Bowles were indeed important, and for radical good. At a very premature age, even before my fifteenth year, I had bewildered myself in metaphysics, and in theological controversy. Nothing else pleased me. History, and particular facts, lost all interest in my mind. Poetry (though for a schoolboy of that age I was above par in English versification, and had already produced two or three compositions which, I may venture to say, without reference to my age, were somewhat above mediocrity, and which had gained me more credit than the sound good sense of my old master was at all pleased with) poetry itself, yea novels and romances, became insipid to me. In my friendless wanderings on our *leave-days* (for I was an orphan, and had scarce any connections in London), highly was I delighted if any passenger, especially if he were dressed in black, would enter into conversation with me. For I soon found the means of directing it to my favourite subjects

> Of providence, fore-knowledge, will, and fate,
> Fixed fate, free will, fore-knowledge absolute,
> And found no end in wandering mazes lost.

This preposterous pursuit was, beyond doubt, injurious, both to my natural powers, and to the progress of my education. It would, perhaps, have been destructive had it been continued; but from this I was auspiciously withdrawn, partly, indeed, by an accidental introduction to an amiable family, chiefly, however, by the genial influence of a style of poetry, so tender and yet so manly, so natural and real, and yet so dignified and harmonious, as the sonnets, &c., of Mr Bowles! Well were it for me, perhaps, had I never relapsed into the same mental disease; if I had continued to pluck the flower and reap the harvest from the cultivated surface, instead of delving in the unwholesome quicksilver mines of metaphysic depths. But if in after time I have sought a refuge from bodily pain and mismanaged sensibility in abstruse researches, which exercised the strength and subtlety of the understanding without awakening the feelings of the heart, still there was a long and blessed interval, during which my natural faculties were allowed to expand, and my original tendencies to develop themselves; my fancy, and the love of nature, and the sense of beauty in forms and sounds.

The second advantage, which I owe to my early perusal and admiration of these poems (to which, let me add, though known to me at a somewhat later period, the Lewesdon Hill of Mr Crowe), bears more immediately on my present subject. Among those with whom I conversed, there were, of course, very many who had formed their taste and their notions of poetry from the writings of Pope and his followers; or, to speak more generally, in that school of French poetry, condensed and invigorated by English understanding, which had predominated from the last century. I was not blind to the merits of this school; yet, as from inexperience of the world, and consequent want of sympathy with the general subjects of these poems, they gave me little pleasure, I doubtless undervalued the *kind*, and, with the presumption of youth, withheld from its masters the legitimate name of poets. I saw that the excellence of this kind consisted in just and acute observations on men and manners in an artificial state of society, as its matter and substance; and, in the logic of wit, conveyed in smooth and strong epigrammatic couplets as its *form*. Even when the subject was addressed to the fancy or the intellect, as in the *Rape of the Lock*, or the *Essay on Man*; nay, when it was a consecutive narration, as in that astonishing product of matchless talent and ingenuity, Pope's *Translation of the Iliad*; still a *point* was looked for at the end of each second line, and the whole was as it were a sorites, or, if I may exchange a logical for a grammatical metaphor, a *conjunction disjunctive* of epigrams. Meantime the matter and diction seemed to me characterized not so much by poetic thoughts, as by thoughts *translated* into the language of poetry. On this last point I had occasion to render my own thoughts gradually more and more plain to myself by frequent amicable disputes concerning Darwin's *Botanic Garden*, which for some years was greatly extolled, not only by the *reading* public in general, but even by those whose genius and natural robustness of understanding enabled them afterwards to act foremost in dissipating these 'painted mists' that occasionally rise from the marshes at the foot of Parnassus. During my first Cambridge vacation I assisted a friend in a contribution for a literary society in Devonshire, and in this I remember to have compared Darwin's work to the Russian palace of ice, glittering, cold, and transitory. In the same essay, too, I assigned sundry reasons, chiefly drawn from a comparison of passages in the Latin poets with the original Greek from which they were borrowed, for the preference of Collins's odes to those of Gray, and of the simile in Shakespeare:

> How like a younker or a prodigal
> The scarfed bark puts from her native bay
> Hugg'd and embraced by the strumpet wind!
> How like the prodigal doth she return,
> With over-weather'd ribs and ragged sails,
> Lean, rent and beggar'd by the strumpet wind!

to the imitation in the bard:

> Fair laughs the morn, and soft the zephyr blows
> While proudly riding o'er the azure realm
> In gallant trim the gilded vessel goes,
> YOUTH at the prow and PLEASURE at the helm,
> Regardless of the sweeping whirlwind's sway,
> That hush'd in grim repose, expects its evening prey.

(In which, by-the-by, the words 'realm' and 'sway' are rhymes dearly purchased.) I preferred the original on the ground that, in the imitation, it depended wholly in the compositor's putting, or not putting, a *small Capital* both in this and in many other passages of the same poet, whether the words should be personifications or mere abstracts. I mention this because, in referring various lines in Gray to their original in Shakespeare and Milton – and in the clear perception how completely all the propriety was lost in the transfer – I was, at that early period, led to a conjecture which, many years afterwards, was recalled to me from the same thought having been started in conversation, but far more ably, and developed more fully, by Mr

Wordsworth, namely, that this style of poetry, which I have characterized above as translations of prose thoughts into poetic language, had been kept up by, if it did not wholly arise from, the custom of writing Latin verses, and the great importance attached to these exercises in our public schools. Whatever might have been the case in the fifteenth century, when the use of the Latin tongue was so general among learned men, that Erasmus is said to have forgotten his native language; yet in the present day it is not to be supposed that a youth can *think* in Latin, or that he can have any other reliance on the force or fitness of his phrases but the authority of the author from whence he has adopted them. Consequently he must first prepare his thoughts, and then pick out from Virgil, Horace, Ovid, or perhaps more compendiously, from his 'Gradus', halves and quarters of lines in which to embody them.

I never object to a certain degree of disputatiousness in a young man from the age of seventeen to that of four or five and twenty, provided I find him always arguing on one side of the question. The controversies, occasioned by my unfeigned zeal for the honour of a favourite contemporary, then known to me only by his works, were of great advantage in the formation and establishment of my taste and critical opinions. In my defence of the lines running into each other, instead of closing at each couplet; and of natural language, neither bookish nor vulgar, neither redolent of the lamp or of the kennel, such as *I will remember thee*; instead of the same thought tricked up in the rag-fair finery of

> Thy image on her wing
> Before my *Fancy's* eye shall *Memory* bring,

I had continually to adduce the metre and diction of the Greek poets from Homer to Theocritus inclusive; and still more of our elder English poets from Chaucer to Milton. Nor was this all. But as it was my constant reply to authorities brought against me from later poets of great name, that no authority could avail in opposition to *Truth*, *Nature*, *Logic*, and the *Laws of Universal Grammar*; actuated too by my former passion for metaphysical investigations, I laboured at a solid foundation, on which permanently to ground my opinions, in the component faculties of the human mind itself, and their comparative dignity and importance. According to the faculty or source from which the pleasure given by any poem or passage was derived, I estimated the merit of such poem or passage. As the result of all my reading and meditation, I abstracted two critical aphorisms, deeming them to comprise the conditions and *criteria* of poetic style; first, that not the poem which we have *read*, but that to which we *return*, with the greatest pleasure, possesses the genuine power and claims the name of *essential poetry*. Second, that whatever lines can be translated into other words of the same language, without diminution of their significance, either in sense or association, or in any worthy feeling, are so far vicious in their diction. Be it, however, observed, that I excluded from the list of worthy feelings the pleasure derived from mere novelty in the reader, and the desire of exciting wonderment at his powers in the author. Oftentimes since then, in perusing French tragedies, I have fancied two marks of admiration at the end of each line, as hieroglyphics of the author's own admiration at his own cleverness. Our genuine admiration of a great poet is a continuous *undercurrent* of feeling; it is everywhere present, but seldom anywhere as a separate excitement. I was wont boldly to affirm that it would be scarcely more difficult to push a stone out from the pyramids with the bare hand, than to alter a word, or the position of a word, in Milton or Shakespeare (in their most important works at least) without making the author say something else, or something worse, than he does say. One great distinction I appeared to myself to see plainly, between even the characteristic faults of our elder poets and the false beauties of the moderns. In the former, from Donne to Cowley, we find the most fantastic out-of-the-way thoughts, but in the most pure and genuine mother English; in the latter, the most obvious thoughts, in language the most fantastic and arbitrary. Our faulty elder poets sacrificed the passion, and passionate flow of poetry, to the subtleties of intellect and to the starts of wit; the moderns to the glare and glitter of a perpetual yet broken and heterogeneous imagery, or rather to an amphibious something, made up, half of image and half of abstract meaning. The one sacrificed the heart to the head, the other both heart and head to point and drapery.

The reader must make himself acquainted with the general style of composition that was at that time deemed poetry, in order to understand and account for the effect produced on me by the Sonnets, the Monody at Matlock, and the Hope, of Mr Bowles; for it is peculiar to original genius to become less and less *striking*, in proportion to its success in improving the taste and judgement of its contemporaries. The poems of West, indeed, had the merit of chaste and manly diction, but they were cold, and, if I may so express it, only dead-coloured; while in the best of Warton's there is a stiffness, which too often gives them the appearance of imitations from the Greek. Whatever relation, therefore, of cause or impulse Percy's collection of

Ballads may bear to the most popular poems of the present day, yet in the more sustained and elevated style of the then living poets Bowles and Cowper were, to the best of my knowledge, the first who combined natural thoughts with natural diction; the first who reconciled the heart with the head. . . .

From CHAPTER II

Supposed irritability of men of genius – Brought to the test of facts – Causes and occasions of the charge – its injustice.

I HAVE often thought, that it would be neither uninstructive nor un-amusing to analyse, and bring forward into distinct consciousness, that complex feeling, with which readers in general take part against the author, in favour of the critic; and the readiness with which they apply to *all* poets the old sarcasm of Horace upon the scribblers of his time: '*Genus irritabile vatum.*' A debility and dimness of the imaginative power, and a consequent necessity of reliance on the immediate impressions of the senses, do, we well know, render the mind liable to superstition and fanaticism. Having a deficient portion of internal and proper warmth, minds of this class seek in the crowd *circum fana* for a warmth in common, which they do not possess singly. Cold and phlegmatic in their own nature, like damp hay, they heat and inflame by co-acervation; or like bees they become restless and irritable through the increased temperature of collected multitudes. Hence the German word for fanaticism (such at least was its original import) is derived from the swarming of bees, namely, *schwärmen, schwärmerei.* The passion being in an inverse proportion to the insight, *that* the more vivid, as *this* the less distinct; anger is the inevitable consequence. The absence of all foundation within their own minds for that which they yet believe both true and indispensable for their safety and happiness, cannot but produce an uneasy state of feeling, an involuntary sense of fear from which nature has no means of rescuing herself but by anger. Experience informs us that the first defence of weak minds is to recriminate.

> There's no philosopher but sees,
> That rage and fear are one disease,
> Though that may burn, and this may freeze.
> They're both alike the ague.
>
> MAD OX

But where the ideas are vivid, and there exists an endless power of combining and modifying them, the feelings and affections blend more easily and intimately with these ideal creations than with the objects of the senses; the mind is affected by thoughts rather than by things; and only then feels the requisite interest even for the most important events, and accidents, when by means of meditation they have passed into *thoughts*. The sanity of the mind is between superstition with fanaticism on the one hand and enthusiasm with indifference and a diseased slowness to action on the other. For the conceptions of the mind may be so vivid and adequate, as to preclude that impulse to the realizing of them, which is strongest and most restless in those who possess more than mere *talent* (or the faculty of appropriating and applying the knowledge of others) yet still want something of the creative, and self-sufficing power of *absolute* genius. For this reason, therefore, they are men of *commanding* genius. While the former rest content between thought and reality, as it were in an *intermundium* of which their own living spirit supplies the *substance*, and their imagination the ever-varying *form*; the latter must impress their preconceptions on the world without, in order to present them back to their own view with the satisfying degree of clearness, distinctness, and individuality. These in tranquil times are formed to exhibit a perfect poem in palace or temple or landscape-garden; or a tale of romance in canals that join sea with sea, or in walls of rock, which shouldering back the billows, imitate the power, and supply the benevolence of nature to sheltered navies; or in aqueducts that, arching the wide vale from mountain to mountain, give a Palmyra to the desert. But alas! in times of tumult they are the men destined to come forth as the shaping spirit of Ruin, to destroy the wisdom of ages in order to substitute the fancies of a day, and to change kings and kingdoms, as the wind shifts and shapes the clouds. The records of biography seem to confirm this theory. The men of the greatest genius, as far as we can judge from their own works or from the accounts of their contemporaries, appear to have been of calm and tranquil temper, in all that related to themselves. In the inward assurance of permanent fame, they seem to have been either indifferent or resigned, with regard to immediate reputation. Through all the works of Chaucer there reigns a cheerfulness, a manly hilarity, which makes it almost impossible to doubt a correspondent habit of feeling in the author himself. Shakespeare's evenness and sweetness of temper were almost proverbial in his own age. That this did not arise from ignorance of his own comparative greatness, we have abundant proof in his Sonnets, which could scarcely have been known to Pope, when he asserted, that our great bard 'grew immortal in his own despite.' . . .

In Spenser, indeed, we trace a mind constitutionally tender, delicate, and, in comparison with his three great compeers, I had almost said, *effeminate*; and this additionally saddened by the unjust persecution of Burleigh, and the severe calamities, which overwhelmed his latter days. These causes have diffused over all his compositions 'a melancholy grace', and have drawn forth occasional strains, the more pathetic from their gentleness. But nowhere do we find the least trace of irritability, and still less of quarrelsome or affected contempt of his censurers.

The same calmness, and even great self-possession, may be affirmed of Milton, as far as his poems and poetic character are concerned. He reserved his anger for the enemies of religion, freedom, and his country. My mind is not capable of forming a more august conception than arises from the contemplation of this great man in his latter days: – poor, sick, old, blind, slandered, persecuted:

> Darkness before, and danger's voice behind,

in an age in which he was as little understood by the party *for* whom, as by that *against* whom, he had contended, and among men before whom he strode so far as to *dwarf* himself by the distance; yet still listening to the music of his own thoughts; or, if additionally cheered, yet cheered only by the prophetic faith of two or three solitary individuals, he did nevertheless

> argue not
> Against Heaven's hand or will, nor bate a jot
> Of heart or hope; but still bore up and steer'd
> Right onward.

From others only do we derive our knowledge that Milton, in his latter day, had his scorners and detractors; and even in his day of youth and hope, that he had enemies would have been unknown to us, had they not been likewise the enemies of his country.

I am well aware that in advanced stages of literature, when there exist many and excellent models, a high degree of talent, combined with taste and judgement, and employed in works of imagination, will acquire for a man the *name* of a great genius; though even that *analogon* of genius which, in certain states of society, may even render his writings more popular than the absolute reality could have done, would be sought for in vain in the mind and temper of the author himself. Yet even in instances of this kind, a close examination will often detect that the irritability which has been attributed to the author's *genius* as its cause, did really originate in an ill conformation of body, obtuse pain, or constitutional defect of pleasurable sensation. What is charged to the *author* belongs to the *man*, who would probably have been still more impatient but for the humanizing influences of the very pursuit which yet bears the blame of his irritability.

How then are we to explain the easy credence generally given to this charge, if the charge itself be not, as we have endeavoured to show, supported by experience? This seems to me of no very difficult solution. In whatever country literature is widely diffused, there will be many who mistake an intense desire to possess the reputation of poetic genius for the actual powers and original tendencies which constitute it. But men, whose dearest wishes are fixed on objects wholly out of their own power, become in all cases more or less impatient and prone to anger. Besides, though it may be paradoxical to assert, that a man can know one thing and believe the opposite; yet, assuredly, a vain person may have so habitually indulged the wish, and persevered in the attempt to appear what he is not, as to become himself one of his own proselytes. Still, as this counterfeit and artificial persuasion must differ even in the person's own feelings, from a real sense of inward power, what can be more natural than that this difference should betray itself in suspicious and jealous irritability? Even as the flowery sod which covers a hollow may be often detected by its shaking and trembling. . . .

For myself, if from my own feelings, or from the less suspicious test of the observations of others, I had been made aware of any literary testiness or jealousy; I trust that I should have been, however, neither silly or arrogant enough to have burthened the imperfection on genius. But an experience (and I should not need documents in abundance to prove my words if I added) a tried experience of twenty years has taught me that the original sin of my character consists in a careless indifference to public opinion, and to the attacks of those who influence it; that praise and admiration have become yearly less and less desirable, except as marks of sympathy; nay, that it is difficult and distressing to me to think with any interest, even about the sale and profit of my works, important as, in my present circumstances, such considerations must needs be. Yet it never occurred to me to believe or fancy, that the *quantum* of intellectual power bestowed on me by nature or education was in any way connected with this habit of my feelings, or that it needed any other parents or fosterers than constitutional indolence, aggravated into languor by ill-health; the accumulating embarrassments of procrastination; the mental cowardice, which is the inseparable companion of procrastination, and which makes us anxious to think and converse on anything rather than on what concerns ourselves: in fine, all those close vexations, whether chargeable on my faults or my fortunes, which leave me but little grief to spare for evils comparatively distant and alien.

Indignation at literary wrongs I leave to men born under happier stars. I cannot *afford* it. But so far from condemning those who can, I deem it a writer's duty, and think it creditable to his heart, to feel and express a resentment proportioned to the grossness of the provocation, and the importance of the object. There is no profession on earth which requires an attention so early, so long, or so unintermitting, as that of poetry; and, indeed, as that of literary composition in general, if it be such as at all satisfies the demands both of taste and of sound logic. How difficult and delicate a task even the mere mechanism of verse is, may be conjectured from the failure of those who have attempted poetry late in life. Where, then, a man has, from his earliest youth, devoted his whole being to an object, which by the admission of all civilized nations, in all ages, is honourable as a pursuit and glorious as an attainment; what of all that relates to himself and his family, if only we except his moral character, can have fairer claims to his protection, or more authorize acts of self-defence, than the elaborate products of his intellect, and intellectual industry? Prudence itself would command us to *show*, even if defect or diversion of natural sensibility had prevented us from *feeling*, a due interest and qualified anxiety for the offspring and representatives of our nobler being. I know it, alas! by woeful experience! I have laid too many eggs in the hot sands of this wilderness, the world, with ostrich carelessness and ostrich oblivion. The greater part, indeed, have been trod under foot, and are forgotten; but yet no small number have crept forth into life, some to furnish feathers for the caps of others, and still more to plume the shafts in the quivers of my enemies, of them that unprovoked have lain in wait against my soul.

Sic vos, non vobis mellificatis, apes!

From CHAPTER III

The author's obligations to critics, and the probable occasion – Principles of modern criticism – Mr Southey's works and character.

To anonymous critics in reviews, magazines, and news-journals of various name and rank, and to satirists with or without a name, in verse or prose, or in verse-text aided by prose-comment, I do seriously believe and profess, that I owe full two-thirds of whatever reputation and publicity I happen to possess. For when the name of an individual has occurred so frequently, in so many works, for so great a length of time, the readers of these works (which with a shelf or two of Beauties, Elegant Extracts, and Anas, form nine-tenths of the reading of the reading public*) cannot but be familiar with the name, without distinctly remembering whether it was introduced for eulogy or for censure. And this becomes the more likely, if (as I believe) the habit of perusing periodical works may be properly added to Averroes' catalogue of Anti-mnemonics, or weakeners of the memory. But where this has not been the case, yet the reader will be apt to suspect that there must be something more than usually strong and extensive in a reputation, that could either require or stand so merciless and long continued a cannonading. Without any feeling of *anger* therefore (for which, indeed, on my own account, I have no pretext) I may yet be allowed to express some degree of *surprise*, that after having run the critical gauntlet for a certain class of faults which I *had*, nothing having come before the judgement-seat in the interim, I should, year after year, quarter after quarter, month after month (not to mention sundry petty periodicals of still quicker revolution, 'or weekly or diurnal') have been for at least seventeen years consecutively, dragged forth by them into the foremost ranks of the *proscribed*, and forced to abide the brunt of abuse, for faults directly opposite, and which I certainly had not. How shall I explain this?

* For as to the devotees of the circulating libraries, I dare not compliment their pass-time, or rather kill-time, with the name of reading. Call it rather a sort of beggarly day-dreaming, during which the mind of the dreamer furnishes for itself nothing but laziness and a little mawkish sensibility; while the whole *materiel* and imagery of the doze is supplied *ab extra* by a sort of mental *camera obscura* manufactured at the printing office, which *pro tempore* fixes, reflects and transmits the moving phantasms of one man's delirium, so as to people the barrenness of an hundred other brains afflicted with the same trance or suspension of all common sense and all definite purpose. We should therefore transfer this species of amusement, (if indeed those can be said to retire *a musis*, who were never in their company, or relaxation be attributable to those, whose bows are never bent) from the genus, reading, to that comprehensive class characterized by the power of reconciling the two contrary yet co-existing propensities of human nature, namely; indulgence of sloth, and hatred of vacancy. In addition to novels and tales of chivalry in prose or rhyme, (by which last I mean neither rhythm nor metre) this genus comprises as its species, gaming, swinging, or swaying on a chair or gate; spitting over a bridge; smoking; snuff-taking; tête-a-tête quarrels after dinner between husband and wife; conning word by word all the advertisements of the Daily Advertiser in a public house on a rainy day, &c, &c, &c.

Whatever may have been the case with others, I certainly cannot attribute this persecution to personal dislike, or to envy, or to feelings of vindictive animosity. Not to the former, for, with the exception of a very few who are my intimate friends, and were so before they were known as authors, I have had little other acquaintance with literary characters, than what may be implied in an accidental introduction, or casual meeting in a mixed company. And, as far as words and looks can be trusted, I must believe that, even in these instances, I had excited no unfriendly disposition. Neither by letter, or in conversation, have I ever had dispute or controversy beyond the common social interchange of opinions. Nay, where I had reason to suppose my convictions fundamentally different, it has been my habit, and I may add, the impulse of my nature, to assign the grounds of my belief, rather than the belief itself; and not to express dissent till I could establish some points of complete sympathy, some grounds common to both sides, from which to commence its explanation.

Still less can I place these attacks to the charge of envy. The few pages which I have published are of too distant a date, and the extent of their sale a proof too conclusive against their having been popular at any time, to render probable, I had almost said possible, the excitement of envy on *their* account; and the man who should envy me on any *other*, verily he must be *envy-mad*!

Lastly, with as little semblance of reason, could I suspect any animosity towards me from vindictive feelings as the cause. I have before said, that my acquaintance with literary men has been limited and distant, and that I have had neither dispute nor controversy. From my first entrance into life, I have, with few and short intervals, lived either abroad or in retirement. My different essays on subjects of national interest, published at different times, first in the *Morning Post* and then in the *Courier*, with my courses of lectures on the principles of criticism as applied to Shakespeare and Milton, constitute my whole publicity; the only occasions on which I *could* offend any member of the republic of letters. With one solitary exception, in which my words were first misstated, and then wantonly applied to an individual, I could never learn that I had excited the displeasure of any among my literary contemporaries. Having announced my intention to give a course of lectures on the characteristic merits and defects of English poetry in its different eras; first, from Chaucer to Milton; second, from Dryden inclusive to Thomson; and third, from Cowper to the present day; I changed my plan, and confined my disquisition to the two former eras that I might furnish no possible pretext for the unthinking to misconstrue, or the malignant to misapply my words, and having stamped their own meaning on them, to pass them as current coin in the marts of garrulity or detraction.

Praises of the unworthy are felt by ardent minds as robberies of the deserving; and it is too true, and too frequent, that Bacon, Harrington, Machiavel, and Spinoza are not read, because Hume, Condillac, and Voltaire *are*. But in promiscuous company no prudent man will oppugn the merits of a contemporary in his own supposed department; contenting himself with praising in his turn those whom *he* deem excellent. If I should ever deem it my duty at all to oppose the pretensions of individuals, I would oppose them in books which could be weighed and answered, in which I could evolve the whole of my reasons and feelings, with their requisite limits and modifications; not in irrecoverable conversation, where, however strong the reasons might be, the feelings that prompted them would assuredly be attributed by some one or other to envy and discontent. Besides, I well know, and I trust have acted on that knowledge, that it must be the ignorant and injudicious who extol the unworthy; and the eulogies of critics without taste or judgement are the natural reward of authors without feeling or genius. *Sint unicuique sua praemia.*

How then, dismissing, as I do, these three causes, am I to account for attacks, the long continuance and inveteracy of which it would require all three to explain. The solution may seem to have been given, or at least suggested, in a note to a preceding page. *I was in habits of intimacy with Mr Wordsworth and Mr Southey!* This, however, transfers rather than removes the difficulty. Be it, that by an unconscionable extension of the old adage, *noscitur a socio*, my literary friends are never under the waterfall of criticism, but I must be wet through with the spray; yet how came the torrent to descend upon *them?*

First, then, with regard to Mr Southey. I well remember the general reception of his earlier publications: viz., the poems published with Mr Lovell under the names of Moschus and Bion (1795), the two volumes of poems under his own name (1797), and the Joan of Arc (1796). The censures of the critics by profession are extant, and may be easily referred to: – careless lines, inequality in the merit of the different poems, and (in the lighter works) a predilection for the strange and whimsical; in short, such faults as might have been anticipated in a young and rapid writer, were indeed sufficiently enforced. Nor was there at that time wanting a party spirit to aggravate the defects of a poet, who, with all the courage of uncorrupted youth, had avowed his zeal for a cause which he deemed that of liberty, and his abhorrence of oppression by whatever name consecrated. But it was as little objected by others, as dreamt of by the poet himself, that he *preferred* careless and prosaic lines on rule and of forethought, or indeed that he pretended to any other art or theory of poetic diction, besides that which we may all learn from Horace, Quintilian, the admirable dialogue *De Causis Corruptae Eloquentiae*, or Strada's *Prolusions*; if indeed natural good sense and the early study of the best models in his own language had not infused the same maxims more securely, and, if I may venture the expression, more vitally. All that could have been fairly deduced was, that in his taste and estimation of writers Mr Southey agreed far more with Warton than with Johnson. Nor do I mean to deny, that at all times Mr Southey was of the same mind with Sir Philip Sidney in preferring an excellent ballad in the *humblest* style of poetry to twenty indifferent poems that strutted in the *highest*. And by what have his works, published since then, been characterized, each more strikingly than the preceding, but by greater splendour, a deeper pathos, profounder reflections, and a more sustained dignity of language and of metre? Distant may the period be, but whenever the time shall come, when all his works shall be collected by some editor worthy to be his biographer, I trust that an *excerpta* of all the passages in which his writings, name, and character have been attacked, from the pamphlets and periodical works of the last twenty years, may be an accompaniment. Yet that it would prove medicinal in after times I dare not hope; for as long as there are readers to be delighted with calumny, there will be found reviewers to calumniate. And such readers will become in all probability more numerous, in proportion as a still greater diffusion of literature shall produce an increase of sciolists; and sciolism bring with it petulance and presumption. In times of old, books were as religious oracles; as literature advanced, they next became venerable preceptors; they then descended to the rank of instructive friends; and as their numbers increased, they sank still lower to that of entertaining companions; and at present they seem degraded into culprits to hold up their hands at the bar of every self-elected, yet not the less peremptory, judge, who chooses to write from humour or interest, from enmity or arrogance, and to abide the decision (in the words of Jeremy Taylor) 'of him that reads in malice, or him that reads after dinner'.

The same gradual retrograde movement may be traced in the relation which the authors themselves have assumed towards their readers. From the lofty address of Bacon: 'These are the meditations of Francis of Verulam, which, that posterity should be possessed of, he deemed *their* interest'; or from dedication to Monarch or Pontiff, in which the honour given was asserted in equipoise to the patronage acknowledged; ... There was a gradual sinking in the etiquette of allowed style of pretension.

Poets and Philosophers, rendered diffident by their very number, addressed themselves to 'learned readers'; then, aimed to conciliate the graces of 'the *candid* reader'; till, the critic still rising as the author sank, the amateurs of literature collectively were erected into a municipality of judges, and addressed as the Town! And now finally, all men being supposed able to read, and all readers able to judge, the multitudinous public, shaped into personal unity by the magic of abstraction, sits nominal despot on the throne of criticism. But, alas! as in other despotisms, it but echoes the decisions of its invisible ministers, whose intellectual claims to the guardianship of the Muses seem, for the greater part, analogous to the physical qualifications which adapt their Oriental brethren for the superintendence of the Harem. Thus it is said that St Nepomuc was installed the guardian of bridges, because he had fallen over one, and sunk out of sight. Thus, too, St Cecilia is said to have been first propitiated by musicians, because, having failed in her own attempts, she had taken a dislike to the art and all its successful professors. But I shall probably have occasions hereafter to deliver my convictions more at large concerning this state of things, and its influences on taste, genius, and morality.

In the Thalaba, the Madoc, and still more evidently, in the unique Cid, the Kehama, and as last, so best, the Don Roderick, Southey has given abundant proof:

Se cogitasse quam sit magnum dare aliquid in manus hominum; nec persuadere sibi posse, non saepe tractandum quod placere et semper et omnibus cupiat.

Plin. Ep. Lib. 7, Ep. 17

But, on the other hand, I guess that Mr Southey was quite unable to comprehend wherein could consist the crime or mischief of printing half a dozen or more playful poems; or, to speak more generally, compositions which would be enjoyed or passed over, according as the taste and humour of the reader might chance to be, provided they contained nothing immoral. In the present age 'periturae parcere chartae' is emphatically an unreasonable demand. The merest trifle he ever sent abroad had tenfold better claims to its ink and paper, than all the silly criticisms which prove no more than that the critic was not one of those for whom the trifle was written, and than all the grave exhortations to a greater reverence for the public. As if the passive page of a book, by having an epigram or doggerel tale impressed on it, instantly assumed at once locomotive power and a sort of ubiquity, so as to flutter and buz in the ear of the public, to the sore annoyance of the said mysterious personage. But what gives an additional and more ludicrous absurdity to these lamentations is the curious fact, that if, in a volume of poetry, the critic should find poem or passage which he deems more especially worthless, he is sure to select and reprint it in the review; by which, on his own grounds, he wastes as much more paper than the author, as the copies of a fashionable review are more numerous than those of the original book; in some, and those the most prominent instances, as ten thousand to five hundred. I know nothing that surpasses the liveness of deciding on the merits of a poet or painter – not by characteristic defects, for where there is genius, *these* always point to his characteristic *beauties* – but by accidental failures or faulty passages; except the imprudence of defending it, as the proper duty and most instructive part of criticism. Omit, or pass slightly over, the expression, grace, and grouping of Raphael's *figures*; but ridicule in *detail* the knitting-needles and broom-twigs that are to represent trees in his backgrounds, and never let him hear the last of his *gallipots*! Admit that the 'Allegro' and 'Penseroso' of Milton are not without merit; but repay yourself for this concession by reprinting at length the *two poems on the University Carrier*! As a fair specimen of his Sonnets, quote:

A Book was writ of late called Tetrachordon;

and as characteristic of his rhythm and metre, cite his literal translation of the first and second Psalm! In order to justify yourself, you need only assert that, had you dwelt chiefly on the beauties and excellencies of the poet, the admiration of these might seduce the attention of future writers from the objects of their love and wonder, to an imitation of the few poems and passages in which the poet was most unlike himself.

But till reviews are conducted on far other principles, and with far other motives; till in the place of arbitrary dictation and petulant sneers, the reviewers support their decisions by reference to fixed canons of criticism, previously established and deduced from the nature of man; reflecting minds will pronounce it arrogance in them thus to announce themselves to men of letters as the guides of their taste and judgement. To the purchaser and mere reader it is, at all events, an injustice. He who tells me that there are *defects* in a new work, tells me nothing which I should not have taken for granted without his information. But he who points out and elucidates the *beauties* of an original work, does indeed give me interesting information, such as experience would not have authorized me in anticipating. . . .

From CHAPTER IV

DURING the last year of my residence at Cambridge, I became acquainted with Mr Wordworth's first publication, entitled, *Descriptive Sketches*; and seldom, if ever, was the emergence of an original poetic genius above the literary horizon more evidently announced. In the form, style, and manner of the whole poem, and in the structure of the particular lines and periods, there is a harshness and acerbity connected and combined with words and images all a-glow, which might recall those products of the vegetable world, where gorgeous blossoms rise out of the hard and thorny rind and shell, within which the rich fruit was elaborating. The language was not only peculiar and strong, but at times knotty and contorted, as by its own impatient strength; while the novelty and struggling crowd of images acting in conjunction with the difficulties of the style, demanded always a greater closeness of attention than poetry (at all events than descriptive poetry) has a right to claim. It not seldom, therefore, justified the complaint of obscurity. In the following extract I have sometimes fancied that I saw an emblem of the poem itself and of the author's genius as it was then displayed:

> 'Tis storm; and hid in mist from hour to hour,
> All day the floods a deepening murmur pour;
> The sky is veiled, and every cheerful sight:
> Dark is the region as with coming night;
> And yet what frequent bursts of overpowering light!
> Triumphant on the bosom of the storm,
> Glances the fire-clad eagle's wheeling form;
> Eastward, in long perspective glittering, shine
> The wood-crowned cliffs that o'er the lake recline;
> Wide o'er the Alps a hundred streams unfold,
> At once to pillars turn'd that flame with gold;
> Behind his sail the peasant strives to shun
> The West, that burns like one dilated sun,
> Where in a mighty crucible expire
> The mountains, glowing hot, like coals of fire.

The poetic Psyche, in its process to full development, undergoes as many changes as its Greek namesake, the Butterfly. And it is remarkable how soon genius clears and purifies itself from the faults and errors of its earliest products; faults which, in its earliest compositions, are the more obtrusive and confluent, because, as heterogeneous elements which had only a temporary use, they constitute the very *ferment* by which themselves are carried off. Or we may compare them to some diseases, which must work on the humours, and be thrown out on the surface, in order to secure the patient from their future recurrence. I was in my twenty-fourth year when I had the happiness of knowing Mr Wordsworth personally; and, while memory lasts, I shall hardly forget the sudden effect produced on my mind by his recitation of a manuscript poem which still remains unpublished, but of which the stanza and tone of style were the same as those of 'The Female Vagrant', as originally printed in the first volume of the *Lyrical Ballads*. There was here no mark of strained thought or forced diction, no crowd or turbulence of imagery; and, as the poet hath himself well described in his 'Lines on re-visiting the Wye', manly reflection and human associations had given both variety and an additional interest to natural objects, which in the passion and appetite of the first love they had seemed to him neither to need or permit. The occasional obscurities which had risen from an imperfect control over the resources of his native language had almost wholly disappeared, together with that worse defect of arbitrary and illogical phrases, at once hackneyed and fantastic, which hold so distinguished a place in the *technique* of ordinary poetry, and will, more or less, alloy the earlier poems of the truest genius, unless the attention has been specifically directed to their worthlessness and incongruity. I did not perceive anything particular in the mere style of the poem alluded to during its recitation, except indeed such difference as was not separable from the thought and manner; and the Spenserian stanza, which always, more or less, recalls to the reader's mind Spenser's own style, would doubtless have authorized, in my then opinion, a more frequent descent to the phrases of ordinary life, than could, without an ill effect, have been hazarded in the heroic couplet. It was not, however, the freedom from false taste, whether as to common defects or to those more properly his own, which made so unusual an impression on my feelings immediately, and subsequently on my judgement. It was the union of deep feeling with profound thought; the fine balance of truth in observing, with the imaginative faculty in modifying, the objects observed; and, above all, the original gift of spreading the tone, the *atmosphere*, and with it the depth and height of the ideal world, around forms, incidents, and situations of which, for the common view, custom had bedimmed all the lustre, had dried up the sparkle and the dew-drops. 'To find no contradiction in the union of old and new; to contemplate the Ancient of days and all his works with feelings as fresh as if all had then sprang forth at the first creative fiat; characterizes the mind that feels the riddle of the world, and may help to unravel it. To carry on the feelings of childhood into the powers of manhood; to combine the child's sense of wonder and novelty with the appearances which every day for perhaps forty years had rendered familiar:

> With sun and moon and stars throughout the year,
> And man and woman;

this is the character and privilege of genius, and one of the marks which distinguish genius from talents. And, therefore, it is the prime merit of genius, and its most unequivocal mode of manifestation, so to represent familiar objects, as to awaken in the minds of others a kindred feeling concerning them, and that freshness of sensation which is the constant accompaniment of mental, no less than of bodily, convalescence. Who has not a thousand times seen snow fall on water? Who has not watched it with a new feeling from the time that he has read Burns' comparison of sensual pleasure:

> To snow that falls upon a river
> A moment white – then gone for ever!

'In poems, equally as in philosophic disquisitions, genius produces the strongest impressions of novelty, whilst it rescues the most admitted truths from the impotence caused by the very circumstance of their universal admission. Truths of all others the most awful and mysterious, yet being at the same time of universal interest, are too often considered as *so* true, that they lose all the life and efficiency of truth, and lie bed-ridden in the dormitory of the soul side by side with the most despised and exploded errors.'

This excellence, which in all Mr Wordsworth's writings is more or less predominant, and which constitutes the character of his mind, I no sooner felt, than I sought to understand. Repeated meditations led me first to suspect (and a more intimate analysis of the human faculties, their appropriate marks, functions, and effects, matured my conjecture into full conviction), that fancy and imagination were two distinct and widely different faculties, instead of being, according to the general belief, either two names with one meaning, or, at furthest, the lower and higher degree of one and the same power. It is not, I own, easy to conceive a more opposite translation of the Greek *Phantasia* than the Latin *imaginatio*; but it is equally true that in all societies there exists an instinct of growth, a certain collective unconscious good sense, working progressively to desynonymize those words originally of the same meaning, which the conflux of dialects had supplied to the more homogeneous languages, as the Greek and German, and which the same cause, joined with accidents of translation from original works of different countries, occasion in mixed languages like our own. The first and most important point to be proved is, that two conceptions perfectly distinct are confused under one and the same word, and (this done) to appropriate that word exclusively to one meaning, and the synonyme, should there be one, to the other. But if (as will be often the case in the arts and sciences) no synonyme exists, we must either invent or borrow a word. In the present instance the appropriation had already begun, and been legitimated in the derivative adjective: Milton had a highly *imaginative*, Cowley a very *fanciful*, mind. If, therefore, I should succeed in establishing the actual existences of two faculties generally different, the nomenclature would be at once determined. To the faculty by which I had characterized Milton, we should confine the term *imagination*; while the other would be contra-distinguished as *fancy*. Now were it once fully ascertained, that this division is no less grounded in nature than that of delirium from mania, or Otway's:

> Lutes, laurels, seas of milk, and ships of amber,

from Shakespeare's:

> What! have his daughters brought him to this pass?

or from the preceding apostrophe to the elements, the theory of the fine arts, and of poetry in particular, could not, I thought, but derive some additional and important light. It would, in its immediate effects, furnish a torch of guidance to the philosophical critic, and ultimately to the poet himself. In energetic minds truth soon changes by domestication into power; and, from directing in the discrimination and appraisal of the product, becomes influencive in the production. To admire on principle is the only way to imitate without loss of originality.

It has been already hinted that metaphysics and psychology have long been my hobby-horse. But to have a hobby-horse, and to be vain of it, are so commonly found together, that they pass almost for the same. I trust, therefore, that there will be more good humour than contempt in the smile with which the reader chastises my self-complacency, if I confess myself uncertain whether the satisfaction for the perception of a truth new to myself may not have been rendered more poignant by the conceit that it would be equally so to the public. There was a time, certainly, in which I took some little credit to myself in the belief that I had been the first of my countrymen who had pointed out the diverse meaning of which the two terms were capable, and analyzed the faculties to which they should be appropriated. Mr W. Taylor's recent volume of synonymes I have not yet seen; but his specification of the terms in question has been clearly shown to be both insufficient and erroneous by Mr Wordsworth, in the preface added to the late collection of his Lyrical Ballads, and other poems. The explanation which Mr Wordsworth has himself given will be found to differ from mine chiefly, perhaps, as our objects are different. It could scarcely indeed happen otherwise, from the advantage I have enjoyed of frequent conversation with him, on a subject to which a poem of his own first directed my attention, and my conclusions concerning which he had made more lucid to myself by many happy instances drawn from the operation of natural objects on the mind. But it was Mr Wordsworth's purpose to consider the influences of fancy and imagination as they are manifested in poetry, and from the different effects to conclude their diversity in kind; while it is my object to investigate the seminal principle, and then from the kind to deduce the degree. My friend has drawn a masterly sketch of the branches, with their *poetic* fruitage. I wish to add the trunk, and even the roots, as far as they lift themselves above ground, and are visible to the naked eye of our common consciousness. . . .

From CHAPTER X

'*Esemplastic*. The word is not in Johnson, nor have I met with it elsewhere.' Neither have I! I constructed it myself from the Greek words, εἰς ἓν πλάττειν, i.e. to shape into one; because, having to convey a new sense, I thought that a new term would both aid the recollection of my meaning, and prevent its being confounded with the usual import of the word, imagination. 'But this is pedantry!' Not necessarily so, I hope. If I am not misinformed, pedantry consists in the use of words unsuitable to the time, place, and company. The language of the market would be in the schools as *pedantic*, though it might not be reprobated by that name, as the language of the schools in the market. The mere man of the world, who insists that no other terms but such as occur in common conversation should be employed in a scientific disquisition, and with no greater precision, is as truly a *pedant* as the man of letters, who either over-rating the acquirements of his auditors, or misled by his own familiarity with technical or scholastic terms, converses at the wine-table with his mind fixed on his museum or laboratory; even though the latter pedant instead of desiring his wife to *make the tea*, should bid her add to the *quant. suff.* of *thea Sinensis* the oxyd of hydrogen saturated with caloric. To use the colloquial (and in truth somewhat vulgar) metaphor, if the pedant of the cloister, and the pedant of the lobby, both *smell equally of the shop*, yet the odour from the Russian binding of good old *authentic-looking* folios and quartos is less annoying than the steams from the tavern or bagnio. Nay, though the pedantry of the scholar should betray a little ostentation, yet a well-conditioned mind would more easily, methinks, tolerate the *fox brush* of learned vanity, than the *sans culotterie* of a contemptuous ignorance, that assumes a merit from mutilation in the self-consoling sneer at the pompous incumbrance of tails.

The first lesson of philosophic discipline is to wean the student's attention from the *Degrees* of things, which alone form the vocabulary of common life, and to direct it to the kind abstracted from degree. Thus the chemical student is taught not to be startled at disquisitions on the heat in ice, or on latent and fixible light. In such discourse the instructor has no other alternative than either to use old words with new meanings (the plan adopted by Darwin in his *Zoonomia*;) or to introduce new terms, after the example of Linnaeus, and the framers of the present chemical nomenclature. The latter mode is evidently preferable, were it only that the former demands a twofold exertion of thought in one and the same act. For the reader (or hearer) is required not only to learn and bear in mind the new definition; but to unlearn, and keep out of his view, the old and habitual meaning; a far more difficult and perplexing task, and for which the mere *semblance* of eschewing pedantry seems to me an inadequate compensation. Where indeed, it is in our power to recall an appropriate term that had without sufficient reason become obsolete, it is doubtless a less evil to restore than to coin anew. Thus to express in one word all that appertains to the perception considered as passive, and merely recipient, I have adopted from our elder classics the word *sensuous*; because *sensual* is not at present used, except in a bad sense, or at least as a moral distinction, while *sensitive* and *sensible* would each convey a different meaning. Thus too I have followed Hooker, Sanderson, Milton, &c. in designating the *immediateness* of any act or object of knowledge by the word *intuition*, used sometimes subjectively, sometimes objectively, even as we use the word thought; now as *the* thought, or act of thinking, and now as *a* thought, or the object of our reflection; and we do this without confusion or obscurity. The very words, *objective* and *subjective*, of such constant recurrence in the schools of yore, I have ventured to reintroduce, because I could not so briefly or conveniently, by any more familiar terms, distinguish the *percipere* from the *percipi*. Lastly, I have cautiously discriminated the terms, the reason, and the understanding, encouraged and confirmed by the authority of our genuine divines, and philosophers, before the Revolution.

> . . . both life, and sense,
> Fancy, and *understanding*: whence the soul
> Reason receives, and reason is her *being*.
> *Discursive* or *Intuitive*. Discourse
> Is oftest your's, the latter most is our's,
> Differing but in *degree*, in *kind* the same.

> Paradise Lost, Book v

I say, that I was *confirmed* by authority so venerable: for I had previous and higher motives in my own conviction of the importance, nay, of the necessity of the distinction, as both an indispensable condition and a vital part of all sound speculation in metaphysics, ethical or theological. . . .

From CHAPTER XII

IN the perusal of philosophical works I have been greatly benefitted by a resolve which, in the antithetic form and with the allowed quaintness of an adage or maxim, I have been accustomed to word thus: 'Until you understand a writer's ignorance, presume yourself ignorant of his understanding.' This golden rule of mine does, I own, resemble those of Pythagoras in its obscurity rather than in its depth. If, however, the reader will permit me to be my own Hierocles, I trust that he will find its meaning fully explained by the following instances. I have now before me a treatise of a religious fanatic, full of dreams and supernatural *experiences*. I see clearly the writer's grounds, and their hollowness. I have a complete insight into the causes which, through the medium of his body, had acted on his mind; and by application of received and ascertained laws, I can satisfactorily explain to my own reason all the strange incidents which the writer records of himself. And this I can do without suspecting him of any intentional falsehood. As when in broad daylight a man tracks the steps of a traveller who had lost his way in a fog, or by treacherous moonshine; even so, and with the same tranquil sense of certainty, can I follow the traces of this bewildered visionary. I *Understand his Ignorance.*

On the other hand, I have been re-perusing with the best energies of my mind the *Timaeus* of Plato. Whatever I comprehend impresses me with a reverential sense of the author's genius; but there is a considerable portion of the work to which I can attach no consistent meaning. In other treatises of the same philosopher, intended for the average comprehensions of men, I have been delighted with the masterly good sense, with the perspicuity of the language, and the aptness of the inductions. I recollect, likewise, that numerous passages in this author, which I thoroughly comprehend, were formerly no less unintelligible to me than the passages now in question. It would, I am aware, be quite *fashionable* to dismiss them at once as Platonic jargon. But this I cannot do with satisfaction to my own mind, because I have sought in vain for causes adequate to the solution of the assumed inconsistency. I have no insight into the possibility of a man so eminently wise, using words with such half-meanings to himself as must, perforce, pass into no meaning to his readers. When, in addition to the motives thus suggested by my own reason, I bring into distinct remembrance the number and the series of great men who, after long and zealous study of these works, had joined in honouring the name of Plato with epithets that almost transcend humanity, I feel that a contemptuous verdict on my part might argue want of modesty, but would hardly be received by the judicious as evidence of superior penetration. Therefore, utterly baffled in all my attempts to understand the ignorance of Plato, *I conclude myself ignorant of his understanding*.

In lieu of the various requests which the anxiety of authorship addresses to the unknown reader, I advance but this one: that he will either pass over the following chapter altogether, or read the whole connectedly. The fairest part of the most beautiful body will appear deformed and monstrous, if dissevered from its place in the organic whole. Nay, on delicate subjects, where a seemingly trifling difference of more or less may constitute a difference in *kind*, even a *faithful* display of the main and supporting ideas, if yet they are separated from the forms by which they are at once clothed and modified, may perchance present a skeleton indeed, but a skeleton to alarm and deter. Though I might find numerous precedents, I shall not desire the reader to strip his mind of all prejudices, nor to keep all prior systems out of view during his examination of the present. For, in truth, such requests appear to me not much unlike the advance given to hypochondriacal patients in Dr Buchan's domestic medicine; videlicet, to preserve themselves uniformly tranquil and in good spirits. Till I had discovered the art of destroying the memory *a parte post*, without injury to its future operations, and without detriment to the judgement, I should suppress the request as premature; and, therefore, however much I may *wish* to be read with an unprejudiced mind, I do not presume to state it as a necessary condition.

The extent of my daring is to suggest one criterion by which it may be rationally conjectured beforehand whether or no a reader would lose his time, and perhaps his temper, in the perusal of this or any other treatise constructed on similar principles. But it would be cruelly misinterpreted, as implying the least disrespect either for the moral or intellectual qualities of the individuals thereby precluded. The criterion is this: if a man receives as fundamental facts, and therefore of course indemonstrable and incapable of further analysis, the general notions of matter, spirit, soul, body, action, passiveness, time, space, cause and effect, consciousness, perception, memory and habit; if he feels his mind completely at rest concerning all these, and is satisfied, if only he can analyse all other notions into some one or more of these supposed elements with plausible subordination and apt arrangement; to such a mind I would as courteously as possible convey the hint that for him the chapter was not written.

Vir bonus es, doctus, prudens! ast haud tibi spiro.

For these terms do in truth *include* all the difficulties which the human mind can propose for solution. Taking them therefore in mass and unexamined, it requires only a decent apprenticeship in logic to draw forth their contents in all forms and colours, as the professors of legerdemain at our village fairs pull out ribbon after ribbon from their mouths. And not more difficult is it to reduce them back again to their different genera. But though this analysis is highly useful in rendering our knowledge more distinct, it does not really add to it. It does not increase, though it gives us a greater mastery over, the wealth which we before possessed. For forensic purposes, for all the established professions of society, this is sufficient. But for philosophy in its highest sense, as the science of ultimate truths, and therefore *scientia scientiarum*, this mere analysis of terms is preparative only, though, as a preparative discipline, indispensable.

Still less dare a favourable perusal be anticipated from the prose-lytes of that compendious philosophy, which, talking of mind but thinking of brick and mortar, or other images equally abstracted from body, contrives a theory of spirit by nicknaming matter, and in a few hours can qualify its dullest disciples to explain the *omne scibile* by reducing all things to impressions, ideas, and sensations.

But it is time to tell the truth, though it requires some courage to avow it in an age and country in which disquisitions on all subjects not privileged to adopt technical terms or scientific symbols must be addressed to the public. I say, then, that it is neither possible or necessary for all men, or for many, to be *Philosophers*. There is a *philosophic* (and inasmuch as it is actualized by an effort of freedom, an *artificial*) *consciousness*, which lies beneath or (as it were) *behind* the spontaneous consciousness natural to all reflecting beings. As the elder Romans distinguished their northern provinces into Cis-Alpine and Trans-Alpine, so may we divide all the objects of human knowledge into those on this side, and those on the other side of the spontaneous consciousness; *citra et trans conscientiam communem*. The latter is exclusively the domain of pure philosophy, which is therefore properly entitled *transcendental*, in order to discriminate it at once both from mere reflection and *re*-presentation on the one hand, and on the other from those flights of lawless speculation which, abandoned by *all* distinct consciousness, because transgressing the bounds and purposes of our intellectual faculties, are justly condemned as *transcendent*. The first range of hills that encircles the scanty vale of human life is the horizon for the majority of its inhabitants. On *its* ridges the common sun is born and departs. From *them* the stars rise, and touching *them* they vanish. By the many even this range, the natural limit and bulwark of the vale, is but imperfectly known. Its higher ascents are too often hidden by mists and clouds from uncultivated swamps, which few have courage or curiosity to penetrate. To the multitude below these vapours appear, now as the dark haunts of terrific agents, on which none may intrude with impunity; and now all *aglow* with colours not their own, they are gazed at as the splendid palaces of happiness and power. But in all ages there have been a few who, measuring and sounding the rivers of the vale at the feet of their furthest inaccessible falls, have learnt that the sources must be far higher and far inward; a few, who even in the level streams have detected elements which neither the vale itself nor the surrounding mountains contained or could supply. How and whence to these thoughts, these strong probabilities, the ascertaining vision, the intuitive knowledge, may finally supervene, can be learnt only by the fact. I might oppose to the question the words with which Plotinus supposes nature to answer a similar difficulty: 'Should any one interrogate her, how she works, if graciously she vouchsafe to listen and speak, she will reply, it behoves thee not to disquiet me with interrogatories, but to understand in silence, even as I am silent, and work without words.'

Likewise in the fifth book of the fifth Ennead, speaking of the highest and intuitive knowledge as distinguished from the discursive, or in the language of Wordsworth:

> The vision and the faculty divine;

he says: 'it is not lawful to inquire from whence it sprang, as if it were a thing subject to place and motion; for it neither approached hither, nor again departs from hence to some other place; but it either appears to us or it does not appear. So that we ought not to pursue it with a view of detecting its secret source, but to watch in quiet till it suddenly shines upon us; preparing ourselves for the blessed spectacle, as the eye waits patiently for the rising sun.' They, and they only, can acquire the philosophic imagination, the sacred power of self-intuition, who within themselves can interpret and understand the symbol, that the wings of the air-sylph are forming within the skin of the caterpillar; those only, who feel in their own spirits the same instinct which impels the chrysalis of the horned fly to leave room in its involucrum for antennae yet to come. They know and feel that the *potential* works *in* them, even as the actual works on them! In short, all the organs of sense are framed for a corresponding world of sense, and we have it. All the organs of spirit are framed for a correspondent world of spirit: though the latter organs are not developed in all alike. But they exist in all, and their first appearance discloses itself in the *moral* being. How else could it be, that even worldlings, not wholly debased, will contemplate the man of simple and disinterested goodness with contradictory feelings of pity and respect? 'Poor man! he is not made for *this* world.' Oh! herein they utter a prophecy of universal fulfilment; for man must either rise or sink. . . .

From CHAPTER XIII

THE *Imagination* then, I consider either as primary, or secondary. The primary imagination I hold to be the living power and prime agent of all human perception, and as a repetition in the finite mind of the eternal act of creation in the infinite I AM. The secondary I consider as an echo of the former, co-existing with the conscious will, yet still as identical with the primary in the *kind* of its agency, and differing only in *degree*, and in the *mode* of its operation. It dissolves, diffuses, dissipates, in order to re-create; or where this process is rendered impossible, yet still, at all events, it struggles to idealize and to unify. It is essentially *vital*, even as all objects (as objects) are essentially fixed and dead.

Fancy, on the contrary, has no other counters to play with, but fixities and definites. The Fancy is indeed no other than a mode of memory emancipated from the order of time and space; and blended with, and modified by that empirical phenomenon of the will, which we express by the word choice. But equally with the ordinary memory, it must receive all its materials ready made from the law of association.

Whatever more than this, I shall think it fit to declare concerning the powers and privileges of the imagination in the present work, will be found in the Critical Essay on the uses of the Supernatural in poetry and the principles that regulate its introduction: which the reader will find prefixed to the poem of The Ancient Mariner.

CHAPTER XIV

Occasion of the Lyrical Ballads, and the objects originally proposed – Preface to the second edition – The ensuing controversy, its causes and acrimony – Philosophic definitions of a Poem and Poetry, with scholia.

DURING the first year that Mr Wordsworth and I were neighbours, our conversations turned frequently on the two cardinal points of poetry, the power of exciting the sympathy of the reader by a faithful adherence to the truth of nature, and the power of giving the interest of novelty by the modifying colours of imagination. The sudden charm, which accidents of light and shade, which moonlight or sunset, diffused over a known and familiar landscape, appeared to represent the practicability of combining both. These are the poetry of nature. The thought suggested itself (to which of us I do not recollect) that a series of poems might be composed of two sorts. In the one, the incidents and agents were to be, in part at least, supernatural; and the excellence aimed at was to consist in the interesting of the affections by the dramatic truth of such emotions, as would naturally accompany such situations, supposing them real. And real in *this* sense they have been to every human being who, from whatever source of delusion, has at any time believed himself under supernatural agency. For the second class, subjects were to be chosen from ordinary life; the characters and incidents were to be such as will be found in every village and its vicinity where there is a meditative and feeling mind to seek after them, or to notice them when they present themselves.

In this idea originated the plan of the *Lyrical Ballads;* in which it was agreed that my endeavours should be directed to persons and characters supernatural, or at least romantic; yet so as to transfer from our inward nature a human interest and a semblance of truth sufficient to procure for these shadows of imagination that willing suspension of disbelief for the moment, which constitutes poetic faith. Mr Wordsworth, on the other hand, was to propose to himself as his object, to give the charm of novelty to things of every day, and to excite a feeling analogous to the supernatural, by awakening the mind's attention from the lethargy of custom, and directing it to the loveliness and the wonders of the world before us; an inexhaustible treasure, but for which, in consequence of the film of familiarity and selfish solicitude, we have eyes, yet see not, ears that hear not, and hearts that neither feel nor understand.

With this view I wrote the *Ancient Mariner*, and was preparing, among other poems, the *Dark Ladie*, and the *Christabel*, in which I should have more nearly realized my ideal than I had done in my first attempt. But Mr Wordsworth's industry had proved so much more successful, and the number of his poems so much greater, that my compositions, instead of forming a balance, appeared rather an interpolation of heterogeneous matter. Mr Wordsworth added two or three poems written in his own character, in the impassioned, lofty, and sustained diction which is characteristic of his genius. In this form the 'Lyrical Ballads' were published; and were presented by him, as an *experiment*, whether subjects, which from their nature rejected the usual ornaments and extra-colloquial style of poems in general, might not be so managed in the language of ordinary life as to produce the pleasurable interest which it is the peculiar business of poetry to impart. To the second edition he added a preface of considerable length; in which, notwithstanding some passages of apparently a contrary import, he was understood to contend for the extension of this style to poetry of all kinds, and to reject as vicious and indefensible all phrases and forms of style that were not included in what he (unfortunately, I think, adopting an equivocal expression) called the language of *real* life. From this preface, prefixed to poems in which it was impossible to deny the presence of original genius, however mistaken its direction might be deemed, arose the whole long-continued controversy. For from the conjunction of perceived power with supposed heresy I explain the inveteracy, and in some instances, I grieve to say, the acrimonious passions, with which the controversy has been conducted by the assailants.

Had Mr Wordsworth's poems been the silly, the childish things which they were for a long time described as being; had they been really distinguished from the compositions of other poets merely by meanness of language and inanity of thought; had they indeed contained nothing more than what is found in the parodies and pretended imitations of them; they must have sunk at once, a dead weight, into the slough of oblivion, and have dragged the preface along with them. But year after year increased the number of Mr Wordsworth's admirers. They were found, too, not in the lower classes of the reading public, but chiefly among young men of strong sensibility and meditative minds; and their admiration (inflamed perhaps in some degree by opposition) was distinguished by its intensity, I might almost say, by its *religious* fervour. These facts, and the intellectual energy of the author, which was more or less consciously felt, where it was outwardly and even boisterously denied, meeting with sentiments of aversion to his opinions, and of alarm at their consequences, produced an eddy of criticism, which would of itself have borne up the poems by the violence with which it whirled them round and round. With many parts of this preface, in the sense attributed to them, and which the words undoubtedly seem to authorize, I never concurred; but, on the contrary, objected to them as erroneous in principle, and as contradictory (in appearance at least) both to other parts of the same preface and to the author's own practice in the greater number of the poems themselves. Mr Wordsworth, in his recent collection, has, I find, degraded this prefatory disquisition to the end of his second volume, to be read or not at the reader's choice. But he has not, as far as I can discover, announced any change in his poetic creed. At all events, considering it as the source of a controversy, in which I have been honoured more than I deserve by the frequent conjunction of my name with his, I think it expedient to declare, once for all, in what points I coincide with his opinions, and in what points I altogether differ. But in order to render myself intelligible, I must previously, in as few words as possible, explain my ideas, first, of a *Poem*; and secondly, of *Poetry* itself, in *kind* and in *essence*.

The office of philosophical *disquisition* consists in just *distinction*;

while it is the privilege of the philosopher to preserve himself constantly aware that distinction is not division. In order to obtain adequate notions of any truth, we must intellectually separate its distinguishable parts; and this is the technical process of philosophy. But having so done, we must then restore them in our conceptions to the unity in which they actually co-exist; and this is the *result* of philosophy. A poem contains the same elements as a prose composition; the difference, therefore, must consist in a different combination of them, in consequence of a different object proposed. According to the difference of the object will be the difference of the combination. It is possible that the object may be merely to facilitate the recollection of any given facts or observations by artificial arrangement; and the composition will be a poem, merely because it is distinguished from prose by metre, or by rhyme, or by both conjointly. In this, the lowest sense, a man might attribute the name of a poem to the well-known enumeration of the days in the several months:

> Thirty days hath September,
> April, June, and November, &c.

and others of the same class and purpose. And as a particular pleasure is found in anticipating the recurrence of sounds and quantities, all compositions that have this charm superadded, whatever be their contents, *may* be entitled poems.

So much for the superficial *form*. A difference of object and contents supplies an additional ground of distinction. The immediate purpose may be the communication of truths; either of truth absolute and demonstrable, as in works of science; or of facts experienced and recorded, as in history. Pleasure, and that of the highest and most permanent kind, may *result* from the *attainment* of the end; but it is not itself the immediate end. In other works the communication of pleasure may be the immediate purpose; and though truth, either moral or intellectual, ought to be the *ultimate* end, yet this will distinguish the character of the author, not the class to which the work belongs. Blest indeed is that state of society, in which the immediate purpose would be baffled by the perversion of the proper ultimate end; in which no charm of diction or imagery could exempt the Bathyllus even of an Anacreon, or the Alexis of Virgil, from disgust and aversion!

But the communication of pleasure may be the immediate object of a work not metrically composed; and that object may have been in a high degree attained, as in novels and romances. Would then the mere superaddition of metre, with or without rhyme, entitle *these* to the name of poems? The answer is, that nothing can permanently please, which does not contain in itself the reason why it is so, and not otherwise. If metre be superadded, all other parts must be made consonant with it. They must be such as to justify the perpetual and distinct attention to each part, which an exact correspondent recurrence of accent and sound are calculated to excite. The final definition then, so deduced, may be thus worded. A poem is that species of composition, which is opposed to works of science, by proposing for its *immediate* object pleasure, not truth; and from all other species (having *this* object in common with it) it is discriminated by proposing to itself such delight from the *whole*, as is compatible with a distinct gratification from each component *part*.

Controversy is not seldom excited in consequence of the disputants attaching each a different meaning to the same word; and in few instances has this been more striking than in disputes concerning the present subject. If a man chooses to call every composition a poem, which is rhyme, or measure, or both, I must leave his opinion uncontroverted. The distinction is at least competent to characterize the writer's intention. If it were subjoined, that the whole is likewise entertaining or affecting, as a tale, or as a series of interesting reflections, I of course admit this as another fit ingredient of a poem, and an additional merit. But if the definition sought for be that of a *legitimate* poem, I answer, it must be one the parts of which mutually support and explain each other; all in their proportion harmonizing with, and supporting the purpose and known influences of metrical arrangement. The philosophic critics of all ages coincide with the ultimate judgement of all countries, in equally denying the praises of a just poem, on the one hand to a series of striking lines or distichs, each of which absorbing the whole attention of the reader to itself, disjoins it from its context, and makes it a separate whole, instead of a harmonizing part; and on the other hand, to an unsustained composition, from which the reader collects rapidly the general result unattracted by the component parts. The reader should be carried forward, not merely or chiefly by the mechanical impulse of curiosity, or by a restless desire to arrive at the final solution; but by the pleasurable activity of mind excited by the attractions of the journey itself. Like the motion of a serpent, which the Egyptians made the emblem of intellectual power; or like the path of sound through the air, at every step he pauses and half recedes, and from the retrogressive movement collects the force which again carries him onward. *Praecipitandus est liber spiritus,* says Petronius Arbiter most happily. The epithet, *liber*, here balances the preceding verb: and it is not easy to conceive more meaning condensed in fewer words.

But if this should be admitted as a satisfactory character of a poem, we have still to seek for a definition of poetry. The writings of Plato, and Bishop Taylor, and the *Theoria Sacra* of Burnet, furnish undeniable proofs that poetry of the highest kind may exist without metre, and even without the contradistinguishing objects of a poem. The first chapter of Isaiah (indeed a very large proportion of the whole book) is poetry in the most emphatic sense; yet it would be not less irrational than strange to assert, that pleasure, and not truth, was the immediate object of the prophet. In short, whatever *specific* import we attach to the word poetry, there will be found involved in it, as a necessary consequence, that a poem of any length neither can be, nor ought to be, all poetry. Yet if a harmonious whole is to be produced, the remaining parts must be preserved *in keeping* with the poetry; and this can be no otherwise effected than by such a studied selection and artificial arrangement as will partake of *one*, though not a *peculiar*, property of poetry. And this again can be no other than the property of exciting a more continuous and equal attention than the language of prose aims at, whether colloquial or written.

My own conclusions on the nature of poetry, in the strictest use of the word, have been in part anticipated in the preceding disquisition on the fancy and imagination. What is poetry? is so nearly the same question with, what is a poet? that the answer to the one is involved in the solution of the other. For it is a distinction resulting from the poetic genius itself, which sustains and modifies the images, thoughts, and emotions of the poet's own mind.

The poet, described in *ideal* perfection, brings the whole soul of man into activity, with the subordination of its faculties to each other, according to their relative worth and dignity. He diffuses a tone and spirit of unity, that blends, and (as it were) *fuses*, each into each, by that synthetic and magical power to which we have exclusively appropriated the name of imagination. This power, first put in action by the will and understanding, and retained under their irremissive, though gentle and unnoticed, control (*laxis effertur habenis*) reveals itself in the balance or reconciliation of opposite or discordant qualities: of sameness, with difference; of the general, with the concrete; the idea, with the image; the individual, with the representative; the sense of novelty and freshness, with old and familiar objects; a more than usual state of emotion, with more than usual order; judgement

ever awake and steady self-possession, with enthusiasm and feeling
profound or vehement; and while it blends and harmonizes the natu-
ral and the artificial, still subordinates art to nature; the manner to the
matter; and our admiration of the poet to our sympathy with the
poetry. 'Doubtless', as Sir John Davies observes of the soul (and his
words may with slight alteration be applied, and even more appro-
priately, to the poetic *Imagination*),

> Doubtless this could not be, but that she turns
> Bodies to spirit by sublimation strange,
> As fire converts to fire the things it burns,
> As we our food into our nature change.
>
> From their gross matter she abstracts their forms,
> And draws a kind of quintessence from things;
> Which to her proper nature she transforms
> To bear them light on her celestial wings.
>
> Thus does she, when from individual states
> She doth abstract the universal kinds;
> Which then re-clothed in divers names and fates
> Steal access through our senses to our minds.

Finally, *Good Sense* is the body of poetic genius, *Fancy* its *Drapery*,
Motion its *Life*, and *Imagination* the *Soul* that is everywhere, and in
each; and forms all into one graceful and intelligent whole.

CHAPTER XV

The specific symptoms of poetic power elucidated in a critical analysis
of Shakespeare's Venus and Adonis, and Rape of Lucrece.

IN the application of these principles to purposes of practical criticism
as employed in the appraisal of works more or less imperfect, I have
endeavoured to discover what the qualities in a poem are, which may
be deemed promises and specific symptoms of poetic power, as dis-
tinguished from general talent determined to poetic composition by
accidental motives, by an act of the will, rather than by the inspiration
of a genial and productive nature. In this investigation, I could not, I
thought, do better, than keep before me the earliest work of the
greatest genius, that perhaps human nature has yet produced, our
myriad-minded Shakespeare. I mean the *Venus and Adonis*, and the
Lucrece; works which give at once strong promises of the strength,

and yet obvious proofs of the immaturity, of his genius. From these I abstracted the following marks, as characteristics of original poetic genius in general.

1. In the *Venus and Adonis*, the first and most obvious excellence is the perfect sweetness of the versification; its adaptation to the subject; and the power displayed in varying the march of the words without passing into a loftier and more majestic rhythm than was demanded by the thoughts, or permitted by the propriety of preserving a sense of melody predominant. The delight in richness and sweetness of sound, even to a faulty excess, if it be evidently original, and not the result of an easily imitable mechanism, I regard as a highly favourable promise in the compositions of a young man. 'The man that hath not music in his soul' can indeed never be a genuine poet. Imagery (even taken from nature, much more when transplanted from books, as travels, voyages, and works of natural history); affecting incidents; just thoughts; interesting personal or domestic feelings; and with these the art of their combination or intertexture in the form of a poem; may all by incessant effort be acquired as a trade, by a man of talents and much reading, who, as I once before observed, has mistaken an intense desire of poetic reputation for a natural poetic genius; the love of the arbitrary end for a possession of the peculiar means. But the sense of musical delight, with the power of producing it, is a gift of imagination; and this, together with the power of reducing multitude into unity of effect, and modifying a series of thoughts by some one predominant thought or feeling, may be cultivated and improved, but can never be learnt. It is in these that '*Poeta nascitur non fit*'.

2. A second promise of genius is the choice of subjects very remote from the private interests and circumstances of the writer himself. At least I have found, that where the subject is taken immediately from the author's personal sensations and experiences, the excellence of a particular poem is but an equivocal mark, and often a fallacious pledge, of genuine poetic power. We may perhaps remember the tale of the statuary, who had acquired considerable reputation for the legs of his goddesses, though the rest of the statue accorded but indifferently with ideal beauty; till his wife, elated by her husband's praises, modestly acknowledged that she herself had been his constant model. In the *Venus and Adonis*, this proof of poetic power exists even to excess. It is throughout as if a superior spirit, more intuitive, more intimately conscious even than the characters themselves, not only of every outward look and act, but of the flux and reflux of the mind in all its subtlest thoughts and feelings, were placing the whole before

our view; himself meanwhile unparticipating in the passions, and actuated only by that pleasurable excitement which had resulted from the energetic fervour of his own spirit, in so vividly exhibiting what it had so accurately and profoundly contemplated. I think I should have conjectured from these poems, that even then the great instinct which impelled the poet to the drama was secretly working in him, prompting him by a series and never-broken chain of imagery, always vivid, and because unbroken, often minute; by the highest effort of the picturesque in words, of which words are capable, higher perhaps than was ever realized by any other poet, even Dante not excepted; to provide a substitute for that visual language, that constant intervention and running comment by tone, look, and gesture, which, in his dramatic works, he was entitled to expect from the players. His Venus and Adonis seem at once the characters themselves, and the whole representation of those characters by the most consummate actors. You seem to be told nothing, but to see and hear everything. Hence it is, that from the perpetual activity of attention required on the part of the reader; from the rapid flow, the quick change, and the playful nature of the thoughts and images; and, above all, from the alienation, and, if I may hazard such an expression, the utter *aloofness* of the poet's own feelings from those of which he is at once the painter and the analyst; that though the very subject cannot but detract from the pleasure of a delicate mind, yet never was poem less dangerous on a moral account. Instead of doing as Ariosto, and as, still more offensively, Wieland has done; instead of degrading and deforming passion into appetite, the trials of love into the struggles of concupiscence, Shakespeare has here represented the animal impulse itself, so as to preclude all sympathy with it, by dissipating the reader's notice among the thousand outward images, and now beautiful, now fanciful circumstances, which form its dresses and its scenery; or by diverting our attention from the main subject by those frequent witty or profound reflections which the poet's ever active mind has deduced from, or connected with, the imagery and the incidents. The reader is forced into too much action to sympathise with the merely passive of our nature. As little can a mind thus roused and awakened be brooded on by mean and instinct emotion, as the low, lazy mist can creep upon the surface of a lake while a strong gale is driving it onward in waves and billows.

3. It has been before observed that images, however beautiful, though faithfully copied from nature, and as accurately represented in words, do not of themselves characterize the poet. They become

proofs of original genius only as far as they are modified by a predominant passion; or by associated thoughts or images awakened by that passion; or when they have the effect of reducing multitude to unity, or succession to an instant; or lastly, when a human and intellectual life is transferred to them from the poet's own spirit,

> Which shoots its being through earth, sea, and air.

In the following lines, for instance, there is nothing objectionable, nothing which would preclude them from forming, in their proper place, part of a descriptive poem:

> Behold yon row of pines, that shorn and bow'd
> Bend from the sea-blast, seen at twilight eve.

But with the small alteration of rhythm, the same words would be equally in their place in a book of topography, or in a descriptive tour. The same image will rise into a semblance of poetry if thus conveyed:

> Yon row of bleak and visionary pines,
> By twilight-glimpse discerned, mark! how they flee
> From the fierce sea-blast, all their tresses wild
> Streaming before them.

I have given this as an illustration, by no means as an instance, of that particular excellence which I had in view, and in which Shakespeare, even in his earliest as in his latest works, surpasses all other poets. It is by this that he still gives a dignity and a passion to the objects which he presents. Unaided by any previous excitement, they burst upon us at once in life and in power.

> Full many a glorious morning have I seen
> *Flatter* the mountain-tops with sovereign eye.
>
> Shakespeare's 33rd Sonnet

> Not mine own fears, nor the prophetic soul
> Of the wide world dreaming on things to come –
>
>   .   .   .   .
>   .   .   .   .
>
> The mortal moon hath her eclipse endured,
> And the sad augurs mock their own presage:
> Incertainties now crown themselves assured,
> And peace proclaims olives of endless age.
> Now with the drops of this most balmy time
> My love looks fresh: and Death to me subscribes,
> Since, spite of him, I'll live in this poor rhyme.

> While he insults o'er dull and speechless tribes.
> And thou in this shalt find thy monument,
> When tyrants' crests, and tombs of brass are spent.

Sonnet 107

As of higher worth, so doubtless still more characteristic of poetic genius does the imagery become, when it moulds and colours itself to the circumstances, passion, or character, present and foremost in the mind. For unrivalled instances of this excellence, the reader's own memory will refer him to the *Lear, Othello*, in short to which not of the '*great, ever living, dead man's*' dramatic works? *Inopem me copia fecit.* How true it is to nature, he has himself finely expressed in the instance of love in Sonnet 98:

> From you have I been absent in the spring,
> When proud-pied April drest in all his trim
> Hath put a spirit of youth in every thing;
> That heavy Saturn laugh'd and leap'd with him.
> Yet nor the lays of birds, nor the sweet smell
> Of different flowers in odour and in hue,
> Could make me any summer's story tell,
> Or from their proud lap pluck them where they grew:
> Nor did I wonder at the lily's white,
> Nor praise the deep vermilion in the rose;
> They were, but sweet, but figures of delight,
> Drawn after you, you pattern of all those.
> Yet seem'd it winter still, and you away,
> *As with your shadow I with these did play!*

Scarcely less sure, or if a less valuable, not less indispensable mark

> Γόνιμου μεν ποιητοῦ . . .
> . . . ὅστις ῥῆμα γενναῖον λάκοι

will the imagery supply, when, with more than the power of the painter, the poet gives us the liveliest image of succession with the feeling of simultaneousness!

> With this he breaketh from the sweet embrace
> Of those fair arms, that bound him to her breast,
> And homeward through the dark laund runs apace:
> *Look how a bright star shooteth from the sky!*
> *So glides he in the night from Venus' eye.*

Venus and Adonis, l. 811

4. The last character I shall mention, which would prove indeed but little, except as taken conjointly with the former; yet without

which the former could scarce exist in a high degree, and (even if this were possible) would give promises only of transitory flashes and a meteoric power; – is *Depth* and *Energy* of *Thought*. No man was ever yet a great poet, without being at the same time a profound philosopher. For poetry is the blossom and the fragrancy of all human knowledge, human thoughts, human passions, emotions, language. In Shakespeare's *poems*, the creative power and the intellectual energy wrestle as in a war embrace. Each in its excess of strength seems to threaten the extinction of the other. At length, in the *Drama* they were reconciled, and fought each with its shield before the breast of the other. Or like two rapid streams that, at their first meeting within narrow and rocky banks, mutually strive to repel each other, and intermix reluctantly and in tumult, but soon finding a wider channel and more yielding shores, blend and dilate, and flow on in one current and with one voice. The *Venus and Adonis* did not perhaps allow the display of the deeper passions. But the story of Lucretia seems to favour, and even demand, their intensest workings. And yet we find in *Shakespeare's* management of the tale neither pathos nor any other *dramatic* quality. There is the same minute and faithful imagery as in the former poem, in the same vivid colours, inspirited by the same impetuous vigour of thought, and diverging and contracting with the same activity of the assimilative and of the modifying faculties; and with a yet larger display, a yet wider range of knowledge and reflection; and lastly, with the same perfect dominion, often *domination*, over the whole world of language. What, then, shall we say? even this, that Shakespeare, no mere child of nature; no automaton of genius; no passive vehicle of inspiration possessed by the spirit, not possessing it; first studied patiently, meditated deeply, understood minutely, till knowledge, become habitual and intuitive, wedded itself to his habitual feelings, and at length gave birth to that stupendous power, by which he stands alone, with no equal or second in his own class; to that power which seated him on one of the two glory-smitten summits of the poetic mountain, with Milton as his compeer, not rival. While the former darts himself forth, and passes into all the forms of human character and passion, the one Proteus of the fire and the flood; the other attracts all forms and things to himself, into the unity of his own *Ideal*. All things and modes of action shape themselves anew in the being of *Milton*; while *Shakespeare* becomes all things, yet for ever remaining himself. O what great men hast thou not produced, England! my country! Truly, indeed,

Must *we* be free or die, who speak the tongue,
Which *Shakespeare* spake; the faith and morals hold,
Which *Milton* held. In every thing we are sprung
Of earth's first blood, have titles manifold!

WORDSWORTH

CHAPTER XVII

Examination of the tenets peculiar to Mr Wordsworth – Rustic life (above all, low and rustic life) especially unfavourable to the formation of a human diction – The best parts of language the products of philosophers, not of clowns or shepherds – Poetry essentially ideal and generic – The language of Milton as much the language of real life, yea, incomparably more so, than that of the cottager.

As far, then, as Mr Wordsworth in his preface contended, and most ably contended, for a reformation in our poetic diction; as far as he has evinced the truth of passion, and the *dramatic* propriety of those figures and metaphors in the original poets, which, stripped of their justifying reasons and converted into mere artifices of connection or ornament, constitute the characteristic falsity in the poetic style of the moderns; and as far as he has, with equal acuteness and clearness, pointed out the process by which this change was effected, and the resemblances between that state into which the reader's mind is thrown by the pleasurable confusion of thought from an unaccustomed train of words and images, and that state which is induced by the natural language of impassioned feeling; he undertook a useful task, and deserves all praise, both for the attempt and for the execution. The provocations to this remonstrance in behalf of truth and nature were still of perpetual recurrence before and after the publication of this preface. I cannot likewise but add that the comparison of such poems of merit as have been given to the public within the last ten or twelve years, with the majority of those produced previously to the appearance of that preface, leave no doubt on my mind that Mr Wordsworth is fully justified in believing his efforts to have been by no means ineffectual. Not only in the verses of those who have professed their admiration of his genius, but even of those who have distinguished themselves by hostility to his theory and depreciation of his writings, are the impressions of his principles plainly visible. It is possible that with these principles others may have been blended, which are not equally evident, and some which are unsteady and subvertible from the narrowness or imperfection of their basis. But it is more than possible that these errors of defect or exaggeration, by kindling and feeding the controversy, may have conduced not only to the wider propagation of the accompanying truths, but that, by their frequent presentation to the mind in an excited state, they may have won for them a more permanent and practical result. A man will borrow a part from his opponent the more easily, if he feel himself justified in continuing to reject a part. While there remain important points in which he can still feel himself in the right, in which he still finds firm footing for continued resistance, he will gradually adopt those opinions which were the least remote from his own convictions, as not less congruous with his own theory than with that which he reprobates. In like manner, with a kind of instinctive prudence, he will abandon by little and little his weakest posts, till at length he seems to forget that they had ever belonged to him, or affects to consider them at most as accidental and 'petty annexments', the removal of which leaves the citadel unhurt and unendangered.

My own differences from certain supposed parts of Mr Wordsworth's theory ground themselves on the assumption that his words had been rightly interpreted, as purporting that the proper diction for poetry in general consists altogether in a language taken, with due exceptions, from the mouths of men in real life, a language which actually constitutes the natural conversation of men under the influence of natural feelings. My objection is, first, that in *any* sense this rule is applicable only to *certain* classes of poetry; secondly, that even to these classes it is not applicable, except in such a sense as hath never by any one (as far as I know or have read) been denied, or doubted; and, lastly, that as far as and in that degree in which it is *practicable*, it is yet, as a *rule*, useless, if not injurious, and, therefore, either need not or ought not to be practised. The poet informs his reader that he had generally chosen *low and rustic* life, but not *as* low and rustic, or in order to repeat that pleasure of doubtful moral effect which persons of elevated rank and of superior refinement oftentimes derive from a happy *imitation* of the rude unpolished manners and discourse of their inferiors. For the pleasure so derived may be traced to three exciting causes. The first is the naturalness, in *fact*, of the things represented. The second is the apparent naturalness of the *representation*, as raised and qualified by an imperceptible infusion of the author's own knowledge and talent, which infusion does indeed constitute it an *imitation*, as distinguished from a mere *copy*. The third cause may be found in the reader's conscious feeling of his superiority, awakened by the contrast presented to him; even as for the same purpose the kings and great barons of yore retained sometimes *actual* clowns and fools but more frequently shrewd and witty fellows in that *character*. These, however, were not Mr Wordsworth's objects. *He* chose low and rustic life, 'because in that condition the essential passions of the heart find a better soil in which they can attain their maturity, are less under restraint, and speak a plainer and more emphatic language; because in that condition of life our elementary feelings co-exist in a state of greater simplicity, and consequently may be more accurately contemplated and more forcibly communicated; because the manners of rural life germinate from those elementary feelings, and from the necessary character of rural occupations are more easily comprehended and are more durable; and, lastly, because in that condition the passions of men are incorporated with the beautiful and permanent forms of nature'.

Now it is clear to me that in the most interesting of the poems, in which the author is more or less dramatic, as The Brothers, Michael, Ruth, The Mad Mother, &c., the persons introduced are by no means taken *from low or rustic life* in the common acceptation of those words; and it is not less clear, that the sentiments and language, as far as they can be conceived to have been really transferred from the minds and conversation of such persons, are attributable to causes and circumstances not necessarily connected with 'their occupations and abode'. The thoughts, feelings, language, and manners of the shepherd-farmers in the vales of Cumberland and Westmoreland, as far as they are actually adopted in those poems, may be accounted for from causes which will and do produce the same results in *every* state of life, whether in town or country. As the two principal, I rank that *Independence* which raises a man above servitude or daily toil for the profit of others, yet not above the necessity of industry and a frugal simplicity of domestic life, and the accompanying unambitious, but solid and religious, *Education* which has rendered few books familiar but the Bible and the liturgy or hymn-book. To this latter cause indeed, which is so far *accidental* that it is the blessing of particular countries and a particular age, not the product of particular places or employments, the poet owes the show of probability that his personages might really feel, think, and talk with any tolerable resemblance to his representation. It is an excellent remark of Dr Henry More's, that 'a man of confined education, but of good parts, by constant reading of the Bible, will naturally form a more winning and commanding rhetoric than those that are learned, the intermixture of tongues and of artificial phrases debasing *their* style'.

It is, moreover, to be considered, that to the formation of healthy feelings, and a reflecting mind, *negations* involve impediments not less formidable than sophistication and vicious intermixture. I am convinced that for the human soul to prosper in rustic life a certain vantage-ground is pre-requisite. It is not every man that is likely to be improved by a country life or by country labours. Education, or original sensibility, or both, must pre-exist, if the changes, forms, and incidents of nature are to prove a sufficient stimulant. And where these are not sufficient, the mind contracts and hardens by want of stimulants, and the man becomes selfish, sensual, gross, and hard-hearted. Let the management of the Poor Laws in Liverpool, Manchester, or Bristol, be compared with the ordinary dispensation of the poor rates in agricultural villages, where the *farmers* are the overseers and guardians of the poor. If my own experience has not been particularly unfortunate, as well as that of the many respectable country clergymen with whom I have conversed on the subject, the result would engender more than scepticism concerning the desirable influences of low and rustic life in and for itself. Whatever may be concluded on the other side, from the stronger local attachments and enterprising spirit of the Swiss, and other mountaineers, applies to a particular mode of pastoral life, under forms of property that permit and beget manners truly republican, not to rustic life in general, or to the absence of artificial cultivation. On the contrary the mountaineers, whose manners have been so often eulogized, are in general better educated and greater readers than men of equal rank elsewhere. But where this is not the case, as among the peasantry of North Wales, the ancient mountains, with all their terrors and all their glories, are pictures to the blind and music to the deaf.

I should not have entered so much into detail upon this passage, but here seems to be the point to which all the lines of difference converge as to their source and centre. (I mean, as far as, and in whatever respect, my poetic creed *does* differ from the doctrines promulged in this preface.) I adopt with full faith the principle of Aristotle, that poetry as poetry is essentially *ideal*, that it avoids and excludes all *accident*; that its apparent individualities of rank, character, or occupation must be *representative* of a class; and that the persons of poetry must be clothed with *generic* attributes, with the *common* attributes of the class; not with such as one gifted individual might *possibly* possess, but such as from his situation it is most probable beforehand that he *would* possess. If my premises are right, and my deductions legitimate, it follows that there can be no *poetic* medium

between the swains of Theocritus and those of an imaginary golden
age. . . .

If then I am compelled to doubt the theory, by which the choice of
characters was to be directed, not only *a priori*, from grounds of reason,
but both from the few instances in which the poet himself *need* be sup-
posed to have been governed by it, and from the comparative inferi-
ority of those instances; still more must I hesitate in my assent to the
sentence which immediately follows the former citation, and which I
can neither admit as particular fact, or as general rule. 'The language
too of these men is adopted (purified indeed from what appear to be
its real defects, from all lasting and rational causes of dislike or disgust)
because such men hourly communicate with the best objects from
which the best part of language is originally derived; and because,
from their rank in society, and the sameness and narrow circle of their
intercourse, being less under the action of social vanity, they convey
their feelings and notions in simple and unelaborated expressions'. To
this I reply, that a rustic's language, purified from all provincialism
and grossness, and so far reconstructed as to be made consistent with
the rules of grammar (which are in essence no other than the laws of
universal logic, applied to psychological materials), will not differ from
the language of any other man of common sense, however learned or
refined he may be, except as far as the notions which the rustic has to
convey are fewer and more indiscriminate. This will become still
clearer, if we add the consideration (equally important though less
obvious) that the rustic, from the more imperfect development of his
faculties, and from the lower state of their cultivation, aims almost
solely to convey *insulated facts*, either those of his scanty experience
or his traditional belief; while the educated man chiefly seeks to dis-
cover and express those *connections* of things, or those relative *bear-
ings* of fact to fact, from which some more or less general law is
deducible. For *facts* are valuable to a wise man, chiefly as they lead to
the discovery of the indwelling *law*, which is the true being of things,
the sole solution of their modes of existence, and in the knowledge of
which consists our dignity and our power.

As little can I agree with the assertion, that from the objects with
which the rustic hourly communicates the best part of language is
formed. For, first, if to communicate with an object implies such an
acquaintance with it as renders it capable of being discriminately re-
flected on, the distinct knowledge of an uneducated rustic would fur-
nish a very scanty vocabulary. The few things, and modes of action,
requisite for his bodily conveniences would alone be individualized;

while all the rest of nature would be expressed by a small number of confused general terms. Secondly, I deny that the words and combinations of words derived from the objects with which the rustic is familiar, whether with distinct or confused knowledge, can be justly said to form the *best* part of language. It is more than probable, that many classes of the brute creation possess discriminating sounds, by which they can convey to each other notices of such objects as concern their food, shelter, or safety. Yet we hesitate to call the aggregate of such sounds a language otherwise than metaphorically. The best part of human language, properly so called, is derived from reflection on the acts of the mind itself. It is formed by a voluntary appropriation of fixed symbols to internal acts, to processes and results of imagination, the greater part of which have no place in the consciousness of uneducated man; though in civilized society, by imitation and passive remembrance of what they hear from their religious instructors and other superiors, the most uneducated share in the harvest which they neither sowed or reaped. If the history of the phrases in hourly currency among our peasants were traced, a person not previously aware of the fact would be surprised at finding so large a number, which three or four centuries ago were the exclusive property of the universities and the schools, and at the commencement of the Reformation had been transferred from the school to the pulpit, and thus gradually passed into common life. The extreme difficulty, and often the impossibility, of finding words for the simplest moral and intellectual processes in the languages of uncivilized tribes has proved perhaps the weightiest obstacle to the progress of our most zealous and adroit missionaries. Yet these tribes are surrounded by the same nature as our peasants are; but in still more impressive forms; and they are, moreover, obliged to *particularize* many more of them. When therefore Mr Wordsworth adds, 'accordingly such a language' (meaning, as before, the language of rustic life purified from provincialism), 'arising out of repeated experience and regular feelings, is a more permanent, and a far more philosophical, language than that which is frequently substituted for it by poets, who think they are conferring honour upon themselves and their art in proportion as they indulge in arbitrary and capricious habits of expression'; it may be answered, that the language which he has in view can be attributed to rustics with no greater right than the style of Hooker or Bacon to Tom Brown or Sir Roger L'Estrange. Doubtless, if what is peculiar to each were omitted in each, the result must needs be the same. Further, that the poet who uses an illogical diction, or a style fitted to excite only the low and changeable pleasure of wonder by means of groundless novelty, substitutes a language of *folly* and *vanity*, not for that of the *rustic*, but for that of *good sense* and *natural feeling*.

Here let me be permitted to remind the reader, that the positions which I controvert are contained in the sentences – 'a selection of the *real* language of men;' – 'the language of these men (*i.e.*, men in low and rustic life) I propose to myself to imitate, and as far as possible to adopt the very language of men'. 'Between the language of prose and that of metrical composition there neither is, nor can be, any essential difference.' It is against these exclusively that my opposition is directed.

I object, in the very first instance, to an equivocation in the use of the word 'real'. Every man's language varies, according to the extent of his knowledge, the activity of his faculties, and the depth or quickness of his feelings. Every man's language has, first, its *individualities*; secondly, the common properties of the class to which he belongs; and thirdly, words and phrases of *universal* use. The language of Hooker, Bacon, Bishop Taylor, and Burke, differs from the common language of the learned class only by the superior number and novelty of the thoughts and relations which they had to convey. The language of Algernon Sidney differs not at all from that which every well-educated gentleman would wish to write, and (with due allowances for the undeliberateness, and less connected train of thinking natural and proper to conversation) such as he would wish to talk. Neither one or the other differ half as much from the general language of cultivated society as the language of Mr Wordsworth's homeliest composition differs from that of a common peasant. For 'real', therefore, we must substitute *ordinary*, or *lingua communis*. And this, we have proved, is no more to be found in the phraseology of low and rustic life than in that of any other class. Omit the peculiarities of each, and the result of course must be common to all. And assuredly the omissions and changes to be made in the language of rustics, before it could be transferred to any species of poem, except the drama or other professed imitation, are at least as numerous and weighty as would be required in adapting to the same purpose the ordinary language of tradesmen and manufacturers. Not to mention that the language so highly extolled by Mr Wordsworth varies in every county, nay, in every village, according to the accidental character of the clergyman, the existence or non-existence of schools; or even, perhaps, as the exciseman, publican, or barger, happen to be, or not to be, zealous politicians, and readers of the weekly newspaper *pro bono publico*. Anterior to cultivation the *lingua communis* of every country, as Dante has well observed, exists everywhere in parts, and nowhere as a whole.

Neither is the case rendered at all more tenable by the addition of the words, 'in a state of excitement'. For the nature of a man's words, when he is strongly affected by joy, grief, or anger, must necessarily depend on the number and quality of the general truths, conceptions, and images, and of the words expressing them, with which his mind had been previously stored. For the property of passion is not to *create*, but to set in increased activity. At least, whatever new connections of thoughts or images, or (which is equally, if not more than equally, the appropriate effect of strong excitement) whatever generalizations of truth or experience the heat of passion may produce, yet the terms of their conveyance must have pre-existed in his former conversations, and are only collected and crowded together by the unusual stimulation. It is indeed very possible to adopt in a poem the unmeaning repetitions, habitual phrases, and other blank counters which an unfurnished or confused understanding interposes at short intervals in order to keep hold of his subject, which is still slipping from him, and to give him time for recollection; or in mere aid of vacancy, as in the scanty companies of a country stage the same player pops backwards and forwards, in order to prevent the appearance of empty spaces, in the processions of *Macbeth* or *Henry VIII*. But what assistance to the poet, or ornament to the poem, these can supply, I am at a loss to conjecture. Nothing assuredly can differ either in origin or in mode more widely from the *apparent* tautologies of intense and turbulent feeling, in which the passion is greater and of longer endurance than to be exhausted or satisfied by a single representation of the image or incident exciting it. Such repetitions I admit to be a beauty of the highest kind; as illustrated by Mr Wordsworth himself from the song of Deborah.

At her feet he bowed, he fell, he lay down: at her feet he bowed, he fell: where he bowed, there he fell down dead.

Judges v, 27

From CHAPTER XXII

IF Mr Wordsworth has set forth principles of poetry which his arguments are insufficient to support, let him and those who have adopted his sentiments be set right by the confutation of those arguments, and by the substitution of more philosophical principles. And still let the due credit be given to the portion and importance of the truths which are blended with his theory: truths, the too exclusive attention to which had occasioned its errors, by tempting him to carry those truths beyond their proper limits. If his mistaken theory has at all influenced his poetic compositions, let the effects be pointed out, and the instances given. But let it likewise be shown how far the influence has acted; whether diffusively, or only by starts; whether the number and importance of the poems and passages thus infected be great or trifling compared with the sound portion; and lastly, whether they are inwoven into the texture of his works, or are loose and separable. The result of such a trial would evince beyond a doubt, what it is high time to announce decisively and aloud, that the *supposed* characteristics of Mr Wordsworth's poetry, whether admired or reprobated; whether they are simplicity or simpleness; faithful adherence to essential nature, or wilful selections from human nature of its meanest forms and under the least attractive associations; are as little the real characteristics of his poetry at large, as of his genius and the constitution of his mind. . . .

To these defects which, as appears by the extracts, are only occasional, I may oppose with far less fear of encountering the dissent of any candid and intelligent reader, the following (for the most part correspondent) excellences. First, an austere purity of language both grammatically and logically; in short a perfect appropriateness of the words to the meaning. Of how high value I deem this, and how particularly estimable I hold the example at the present day, has been already stated: and in part too the reasons on which I ground both the moral and intellectual importance of habituating ourselves to a strict accuracy of expression. It is noticeable, how limited an acquaintance with the masterpieces of art will suffice to form a correct and even a sensitive taste, where none but masterpieces have been seen and admired: while on the other hand, the most correct notions, and the widest acquaintance with the works of excellence of all ages and countries, will not perfectly secure us against the contagious familiarity with the far more numerous offspring of tastelessness or of a perverted taste. If this be the case, as it notoriously is, with the arts of music and painting, much more difficult will it be, to avoid the infection of multiplied and daily examples in the practice of an art, which uses words, and words only, as its instruments. In poetry, in which every line, every phrase, may pass the ordeal of deliberation and deliberate choice, it is possible, and barely possible, to attain that *ultimatum* which I have ventured to propose as the infallible test of a blameless style, namely, its *untranslateableness* in words of the same language without injury to the meaning. Be it observed, however, that I include in the *meaning* of a word not only its correspondent object, but likewise all the associations which it recalls. For language is framed to convey not the object alone, but likewise the character, mood and intentions of the person who is representing it. In poetry it is practicable to preserve the diction uncorrupted by the affectations and misappropriations, which promiscuous authorship, and reading not promiscuous only because it is disproportionally most conversant with the compositions of the day, have rendered general. Yet even to the poet, composing in his own province, it is an arduous work: and as the result and pledge of a watchful good sense, of fine and luminous distinction, and of complete self-possession, may justly claim all the honour which belongs to an attainment equally difficult and valuable, and the more valuable for being rare. It is at *all* times the proper food of the understanding; but in an age of corrupt eloquence it is both food and antidote.

In prose I doubt whether it be even possible to preserve our style wholly unalloyed by the vicious phraseology which meets us everywhere, from the sermon to the newspaper, from the harangue of the legislator to the speech from the convivial chair, announcing a *toast* or sentiment. Our chains rattle, even while we are complaining of them. The poems of Boetius rise high in our estimation when we compare them with those of his contemporaries, as Sidonius Apollinaris, &c. They might even be referred to a purer age, but that the prose in which they are set, as jewels in a crown of lead or iron, betrays the true age of the writer. Much however may be effected by education. I believe not only from grounds of reason, but from having in great measure assured myself of the fact by actual though limited experience, that to a youth led from his first boyhood to investigate the meaning of every word and the reason of its choice and position, logic presents itself as an old acquaintance under new names.

On some future occasion, more especially demanding such disquisition, I shall attempt to prove the close connection between veracity and habits of mental accuracy; the beneficial after-effects of verbal precision in the preclusion of fanaticism, which masters the feelings more especially by indistinct watch-words; and to display the advantages which language alone, at least which language with incomparably greater ease and certainty than any other means, presents to the instructor of impressing modes of intellectual energy so constantly, so imperceptibly, and as it were by such elements and atoms, as to secure in due time the formation of a second nature. When we reflect, that the cultivation of the judgement is a positive command of the moral law, since the reason can give the *principle* alone, and the conscience bears witness only to the *motive*, while the application and effects must depend on the judgement: when we consider, that the greater part of our success and comfort in life depends on distinguishing the similar from the same, that which is peculiar in each thing from that which it has in common with others, so as still to select the most probable, instead of the merely possible or positively unfit, we shall learn to value earnestly and with a practical seriousness, a mean, already prepared for us by nature and society, of teaching the young mind to think well and wisely by the same unremembered process and with the same never forgotten results, as those by which it is taught to speak and converse. Now how much warmer the interest is, how much more genial the feelings of reality and practicability, and thence how much stronger the impulses to imitation are, which a *contemporary* writer, and especially a contemporary *poet*, excites in youth and commencing manhood, has been treated of in the earlier pages of these sketches. I have only to add, that all the praise which is due to the exertion of such influence for a purpose so important, joined with that which must be claimed for the infrequency of the same excellence in the same perfection, belongs in full right to Mr Wordsworth. I am far however from denying that we have poets whose *general* style possesses the same excellence, as Mr Moore, Lord Byron, Mr Bowles, and in all his later and more important works our laurel-honouring Laureate. But there are none, in whose works I do not appear to myself to find more exceptions than in those of Wordsworth. Quotations or specimens would here be wholly out of place, and must be left for the critic who doubts and would invalidate the justice of this eulogy so applied.

The second characteristic excellence of Mr Wordsworth's works is: a correspondent weight and sanity of the thoughts and sentiments, – won, not from books, but – from the poet's own meditative observation. They are *fresh*, and have the dew upon them. His muse, at least when in her strength of wing, and when she hovers aloft in her proper element,

> Makes audible a linked lay of truth,
> Of truth profound a sweet continuous lay,
> Not learnt, but native, her own natural notes!

S. T. C.

Even throughout his smaller poems there is scarcely one, which is not rendered valuable by some just and original reflection.

See page 25, vol. ii (Star Gazers):* or the two following passages in one of his humblest compositions:

> O Reader! had you in your mind
> Such stores as silent thought can bring,
> O gentle Reader! you would find
> A tale in every thing.

and

> I have heard of hearts unkind, kind deeds
> With coldness still returning:
> Alas! the gratitude of men
> Has oftener left me mourning.

Simon Lee

Or in a still higher strain the six beautiful quatrains, page 134 (The Fountain):

> Thus fares it still in our decay:
> And yet the wiser mind
> Mourns less for what age takes away
> Than what it leaves behind.
>
> The Blackbird in the summer trees,
> The Lark upon the hill,
> Let loose their carols when they please,
> Are quiet when they will.
>
> With Nature never do *they* wage
> A foolish strife: they see
> A happy youth, and their old age
> Is beautiful and free!
>
> But we are pressed by heavy laws;
> And often, glad no more,
> We wear a face of joy, because
> We have been glad of yore.
>
> If there is one, who need bemoan
> His kindred laid in earth,
> The household hearts that were his own,
> It is the man of mirth.
>
> My days, my Friend, are almost gone,
> My life has been approved,
> And many love me; but by none
> Am I enough beloved.

or the Sonnet on Buonaparte, page 202, vol. ii; or finally (for a volume would scarce suffice to exhaust the instances), the last stanza of the poem on The Withered Celandine, vol. ii, p. 212.

* Page references are to Wordsworth's *Poems*, 2 vols., 1815.

> To be a prodigal's favourite – then, worse truth,
> A miser's pensioner – behold our lot!
> O man! that from thy fair and shining youth
> Age might but take the things youth needed not.

Both in respect of this and of the former excellence, Mr Wordsworth strikingly resembles Samuel Daniel, one of the golden writers of our golden Elizabethan age, now most causelessly neglected: Samuel Daniel, whose diction bears no mark of time, no distinction of age, which has been, and as long as our language shall last will be, so far the language of the to-day and for ever, as that it is more intelligible to us, than the transitory fashions of our own particular age. A similar praise is due to his sentiments. No frequency of perusal can deprive them of their freshness. For though they are brought into the full daylight of every reader's comprehension, yet are they drawn up from depths which few in any age are privileged to visit, into which few in any age have courage or inclination to descend. If Mr Wordsworth is not equally with Daniel alike intelligible to all readers of average understanding in all passages of his works, the comparative difficulty does not arise from the greater impurity of the ore, but from the nature and uses of the metal. A poem is not necessarily obscure, because it does not aim to be popular. It is enough, if a work be perspicuous to those for whom it is written, and

> Fit audience find, though few.

To the 'Ode on the Intimations of Immortality from Recollections of early Childhood' the poet might have prefixed the lines which Dante addresses to one of his own Canzoni –

> Canzone, i'credo, che saranno radi
> Color che tua ragione intendan bene:
> Tanto lor sei faticoso ed alto.

> O lyric song, there will be few, think I,
> Who may thy import understand aright:
> Thou art for *them* so arduous and so high!

But the ode was intended for such readers only as had been accustomed to watch the flux and reflux of their inmost nature, to venture at times into the twilight realms of consciousness, and to feel a deep interest in modes of inmost being, to which they know that the attributes of time and space are inapplicable and alien, but which yet cannot be conveyed, save in symbols of time and space. For such readers the sense is sufficiently plain, and they will be as little disposed to charge Mr Wordsworth with believing the platonic pre-existence in the ordinary interpretation of the words, as I am to believe, that Plato himself ever meant or taught it. . . .

Third (and wherein he soars far above Daniel) the sinewy strength and originality of single lines and paragraphs: the frequent *curiosa felicitas* of his diction, of which I need not here give specimens, having anticipated them in a preceding page. This beauty, and as eminently characteristic of Wordsworth's poetry, his rudest assailants have felt themselves compelled to acknowledge and admire.

Fourth; the perfect truth of nature in his images and descriptions as taken immediately from nature, and proving a long and genial intimacy with the very spirit which gives the physiognomic expression to all the works of nature. Like a green field reflected in a calm and perfectly transparent lake, the image is distinguished from the reality only by its greater softness and lustre. Like the moisture or the polish on a pebble, genius neither distorts nor false-colours its objects; but on the contrary brings out many a vein and many a tint, which escape the eye of common observation, thus raising to the rank of gems what had been often kicked away by the hurrying foot of the traveller on the dusty highroad of custom.

Let me refer to the whole description of skating, vol. i, page 42 to 47 (Influence of Natural Objects), especially to the lines

> So through the darkness and the cold we flew,
> And not a voice was idle: with the din
> Meanwhile the precipices rang aloud;
> The leafless trees and every icy crag
> Tinkled like iron; while the distant hills
> Into the tumult sent an alien sound
> Of melancholy, not unnoticed, while the stars
> Eastward were sparkling clear, and in the west
> The orange sky of evening died away.

Or to the poem on The Green Linnet, vol. i, p. 244. What can be more accurate yet more lovely than the two concluding stanzas?

> Upon yon tuft of hazel trees,
> That twinkle to the gusty breeze,
> Behold him perched in ecstacies,
>   Yet seeming still to hover,
> There! where the flutter of his wings
> Upon his back and body flings
> Shadows and sunny glimmerings
>   That cover him all over.

> While thus before my eyes he gleams,
> A brother of the leaves he seems:
> When in a moment forth he teems
>   His little song in gushes:
> As if it pleased him to disdain
> And mock the form which he did feign,
> While he was dancing with the train
>   Of leaves among the bushes.

Or the description of the blue-cap and of the noontide silence, p. 284;* or the poem to The Cuckoo, p. 299; or, lastly, though I might multiply the references to ten times the number, to the poem so completely Wordsworth's commencing

> Three years she grew in sun and shower.

Fifth: a meditative pathos, a union of deep and subtle thought with sensibility; a sympathy with man as man; the sympathy indeed of a contemplator, rather than a fellow-sufferer or co-mate (spectator, *haud particeps*), but of a contemplator, from whose view no difference of rank conceals the sameness of the nature; no injuries of wind or weather, of toil, or even of ignorance, wholly disguise the human face divine. The superscription and the image of the Creator still remain legible to *him* under the dark lines, with which guilt or calamity had cancelled or cross-barred it. Here the man and the poet lose and find themselves in each other, the one as glorified, the latter as substantiated. In this mild and philosophic pathos, Wordsworth appears to me without a compeer. Such he *is*: so he *writes*. See vol. i, page 134 to 136, ''Tis said that some have died for love', or that most affecting composition, the 'Affliction of Margaret — of —', page 165 to 168, which no mother, and if I may judge by my own experience, no parent can read without a tear. Or turn to that genuine lyric, in the former edition, entitled, the 'Mad Mother', page 174 to 178, of which I cannot refrain from quoting two of the stanzas, both of them for their pathos, and the former for the fine transition in the two concluding lines of the stanza, so expressive of that deranged state, in which from the increased sensibility the sufferer's attention is abruptly drawn off by every trifle, and in the same instant plucked back again by the one despotic thought, and bringing home with it, by the blending, *fusing* power of Imagination and Passion, the alien object to which it had been so abruptly diverted, no longer an alien but an ally and an inmate.

* In the poem called 'The Kitten and the Falling Leaves'.

Suck, little babe, oh suck again!
It cools my blood, it cools my brain:
Thy lips, I feel them, baby! they
Draw from my heart the pain away.
Oh! press me with thy little hand;
It loosens something at my chest;
About that tight and deadly band
I feel thy little fingers prest.
The breeze I see is in the tree!
It comes to cool my babe and me.
Thy father cares not for my breast,
'Tis thine, sweet baby, there to rest,
'Tis all thine own! – and, if its hue
Be changed, that was so fair to view,
'Tis fair enough for thee, my dove!
My beauty, little child, is flown,
But thou wilt live with me in love,
And what if my poor cheek be brown
'Tis well for me, thou canst not see
How pale and wan it else would be.

Lastly, and pre-eminently, I challenge for this poet the gift of *Imagination* in the highest and strictest sense of the word. In the play of *fancy*, Wordsworth, to my feelings, is not always graceful, and sometimes *recondite*. The *likeness* is occasionally too strange, or demands too peculiar a point of view, or is such as appears the creature of pre-determined research, rather than spontaneous presentation. Indeed his fancy seldom displays itself as mere and unmodified fancy. But in imaginative power, he stands nearest of all modern writers to Shakespeare and Milton; and yet in a kind perfectly unborrowed and his own. To employ his own words, which are at once an instance and an illustration, he does indeed to all thoughts and to all objects –

> . . . add the gleam,
> The light that never was on sea or land,
> The consecration, and the poet's dream.

Elegiac Stanzas on a Picture of Peele Castle

I shall select a few examples as most obviously manifesting this faculty; but if I should ever be fortunate enough to render my analysis of imagination, its origin and characters, thoroughly intelligible to the reader, he will scarcely open on a page of this poet's works without recognizing, more or less, the presence and the influences of this faculty.

From the poem on the 'Yew Trees', vol. i, pages 303, 304:

> But worthier still of note
> Are those fraternal four of Borrowdale,
> Joined in one solemn and capacious grove;
> Huge trunks! – and each particular trunk a growth
> Of intertwisted fibres serpentine
> Up-coiling, and inveterately convolved, –
> Not uninformed with phantasy, and looks
> That threaten the profane; – a pillared shade,
> Upon whose grassless floor of red-brown hue,
> By sheddings from the pinal umbrage tinged
> Perennially – beneath whose sable roof
> Of boughs, as if for festal purpose decked
> With unrejoicing berries, ghostly shapes
> May meet at noontide – Fear and trembling Hope,
> Silence and Foresight – Death, the skeleton,
> And Time, the shadow – there to celebrate,
> As in a natural temple scattered o'er
> With altars undisturbed of mossy stone,
> United worship; or in mute repose
> To lie, and listen to the mountain flood
> Murmuring from Glanamara's inmost caves.

The effect of the old man's figure in the poem of Resolution and Independence, vol. ii, page 33:

> While he was talking thus, the lonely place,
> The old man's shape, and speech, all troubled me:
> In my mind's eye I seemed to see him pace
> About the weary moors continually,
> Wandering about alone and silently.

Or the 8th, 9th, 19th, 26th, 31st, and 33rd, in the collection of Miscellaneous Sonnets – the Sonnet on the subjugation of Switzerland, page 210, or the last ode, from which I especially select the two following stanzas or paragraphs, page 349 to 350. ('On the Intimations of Immortality from Recollections of early Childhood.')

> Our birth is but a sleep and a forgetting:
> The soul that rises with us, our life's star
> Hath had elsewhere its setting,
>   And cometh from afar.
> Not in entire forgetfulness,
> And not in utter nakedness,
> But trailing clouds of glory do we come
> From God who is our home:

Heaven lies about us in our infancy!
Shades of the prison-house begin to close
    Upon the growing boy;
But he beholds the light, and whence it flows,
    He sees it in his joy!
The youth who daily further from the east
Must travel, still is nature's priest,
    And by the vision splendid
    Is on his way attended;
At length the man perceives it die away,
And fade into the light of common day.

And page 352 to 354 of the same ode:

O joy that in our embers
Is something that doth live,
That nature yet remembers
What was so fugitive!
The thought of our past years in me doth breed
Perpetual benedictions: not indeed
For that which is most worthy to be blest;
Delight and liberty, the simple creed
Of childhood, whether busy or at rest,
With new-fledged hope still fluttering in his breast: —
Not for these I raise
The song of thanks and praise;
But for those obstinate questionings
Of sense and outward things,
Fallings from us, vanishings;
Blank misgivings of a creature
Moving about in worlds not realized,
High instincts, before which our mortal nature
Did tremble like a guilty thing surprised!
But for those first affections,
Those shadowy recollections,
Which, be they what they may,
Are yet the fountain light of all our day,
Are yet a master light of all our seeing;
Uphold us – cherish – and have power to make
Our noisy years seem moments in the being
Of the eternal silence; truths that wake
To perish never:
Which neither listlessness, nor mad endeavour,
Nor man nor boy,
Nor all that is at enmity with joy
Can utterly abolish or destroy!

> Hence, in a season of calm weather,
> Though inland far we be,
> Our souls have sight of that immortal sea
> Which brought us hither,
> Can in a moment travel thither –
> And see the children sport upon the shore,
> And hear the mighty waters rolling evermore.

And since it would be unfair to conclude with an extract, which though highly characteristic, must yet from the nature of the thoughts and the subjects be interesting, or perhaps intelligible, to but a limited number of readers; I will add from the poet's last published work a passage equally Wordsworthian; of the beauty of which, and of the imaginative power displayed therein, there can be but one opinion, and one feeling (See The White Doe, page 5):

> Fast the church-yard fills; – anon
> Look again and they are gone;
> The cluster round the porch, and the folk
> Who sate in the shade of the prior's oak!
> And scarcely they have disappeared
> Ere the prelusive hymn is heard:
> With one consent the people rejoice,
> Filling the church with a lofty voice!
> They sing a service which they feel
> For 'tis the sun-rise of their zeal
> And faith and hope are in their prime
> In great Eliza's golden time.
>
> A moment ends the fervent din
> And all is hushed without and within;
> For though the priest more tranquilly
> Recites the holy liturgy,
> The only voice which you can hear
> Is the river murmuring near.
> When soft! – the dusky trees between
> And down the path through the open green,
> Where is no living thing to be seen;
> And through yon gateway, where is found,
> Beneath the arch with ivy bound,
> Free entrance to the church-yard ground;
> And right across the verdant sod
> Towards the very house of God;
> Comes gliding in with lovely gleam,
> Comes gliding in serene and slow,
> Soft and silent as a dream,

A solitary doe!
White she is as lily of June,
And beauteous as the silver moon
When out of sight the clouds are driven
And she is left alone in heaven!
Or like a ship some gentle day
In sunshine sailing far away –
A glittering ship that hath the plain
Of ocean for her own domain.

*

What harmonious pensive changes
Wait upon her as she ranges
Round and round this pile of state
Overthrown and desolate!
Now a step or two her way
Is through space of open day,
Where the enamoured sunny light
Brightens her that was so bright:
Now doth a delicate shadow fall,
Falls upon her like a breath
From some lofty arch or wall,
As she passes underneath.

The following analogy will, I am apprehensive, appear dim and
fantastic, but in reading *Bartram's Travels* I could not help transcribing
the following lines as a sort of allegory, or connected simile and meta-
phor of Wordsworth's intellect and genius. 'The soil is a deep, rich,
dark mould, on a deep stratum of tenacious clay; and that on a foun-
dation of rocks, which often break through both strata, lifting their
backs above the surface. The trees which chiefly grow here are the
gigantic black oak; magnolia grandiflora; fraxinus excelsior; platane;
and a few stately tulip trees.' What Mr Wordsworth *will* produce, it
is not for me to prophesy: but I could pronounce with the liveliest
convictions what he is capable of producing. It is the FIRST GENUINE
PHILOSOPHIC POEM.

The preceding criticism will not, I am aware, avail to overcome the
prejudices of those who have made it a business to attack and ridicule
Mr Wordsworth's compositions.

Truth and prudence might be imaged as concentric circles. The
poet may perhaps have passed beyond the latter, but he has confined
himself far within the bounds of the former, in designating these
critics, as too petulant to be passive to a genuine poet, and too feeble

to grapple with him; – 'men of palsied imaginations, in whose minds all healthy action is languid; – who therefore, feel as the many direct them, or with the many are greedy after vicious provocatives'.

Let not Mr Wordsworth be charged with having expressed himself too indignantly, till the wantonness and the systematic and malignant perseverance of the aggressions have been taken into fair consideration. I myself heard the commander-in-chief of this unmanly warfare make a boast of his private admiration of Wordsworth's genius. I have heard him declare, that whoever came into his room would probably find the *Lyrical Ballads* lying open on his table, and that (speaking exclusively of those written by Mr Wordsworth himself) he could nearly repeat the whole of them by heart. *But* a Review, in order to be a saleable article, must be *personal*, *sharp*, and *pointed*: and, *since then*, the poet has made himself, and with himself all who were, or were supposed to be, his friends and admirers, the object of the critic's revenge – how? by having spoken of a work so conducted in the terms which it deserved! I once heard a clergyman in boots and buckskin avow, that he would cheat his own father *in a horse*. A moral system of a similar nature seems to have been adopted by too many anonymous critics. As we used to say at school, in reviewing they *make*, being rogues: and he who complains is to be laughed at for his ignorance of *the game*. With the pen out of their hand they are *honourable men*. They exert indeed power (which is to that of the injured party who should attempt to expose their glaring perversions and mis-statements, as twenty to one) to write down, and (where the author's circumstances permit) to *impoverish* the man, whose learning and genius they themselves in private have repeatedly admitted. They knowingly strive to make it impossible for the man even to publish any future work without exposing himself to all the wretchedness of debt and embarrassment. But this is all *in their vocation*: and bating what they do in their *vocation*, 'who can say that black is the white of their eye?'

So much for the detractors from Wordsworth's merits. On the other hand, much as I might wish for their fuller sympathy, I dare not flatter myself, that the freedom with which I have declared my opinions concerning both his theory and his defects, most of which are more or less connected with his theory either as cause or effect, will be satisfactory or pleasing to *all* the poet's admirers and advocates. More indiscriminate than mine their admiration may be: deeper and more sincere it cannot be. But I have advanced no opinion either for praise or censure, other than as texts introductory to the reasons which compel me to form it. Above all, I was fully convinced that such a criticism was not only wanted; but that, if executed with adequate ability, it must conduce in no mean degree to Mr Wordsworth's *reputation*. His *fame* belongs to another age, and can neither be accelerated nor retarded. . . .

Extracts *from* LECTURES, NOTES, ETC.

DEFINITION OF POETRY

POETRY is not the proper antithesis to prose, but to science. Poetry is opposed to science, and prose to metre. The proper and immediate object of science is the acquirement, or communication, of truth; the proper and immediate object of poetry is the communication of immediate pleasure. This definition is useful; but as it would include novels and other works of fiction, which yet we do not call poems, there must be some additional character by which poetry is not only divided from opposites, but likewise distinguished from disparate, though similar, modes of composition. Now how is this to be effected? In animated prose, the beauties of nature, and the passions and accidents of human nature, are often expressed in that natural language which the contemplation of them would suggest to a pure and benevolent mind; yet still neither we nor the writers call such a work a poem, though no work could deserve that name which did not include all this, together with something else. What is this? It is that pleasurable emotion, that peculiar state and degree of excitement, which arises in the poet himself in the act of composition; – and in order to understand this, we must combine a more than ordinary sympathy with the objects, emotions, or incidents contemplated by the poet, consequent on a more than common sensibility, with a more than ordinary activity of the mind in respect of the fancy and the imagination. Hence is produced a more vivid reflection of the truths of nature and of the human heart, united with a constant activity modifying and correcting these truths by that sort of pleasurable emotion, which the exertion of all our faculties gives in a certain degree; but which can only be felt in perfection under the full play of those powers of mind, which are spontaneous rather than voluntary, and in which the effort required bears no proportion to the activity enjoyed. This is the state which permits the production of a highly pleasurable whole, of which each part shall also communicate for itself a distinct and conscious pleasure; and hence arises the definition, which I trust is now intelligible, that poetry, or rather a poem, is a species of composition, opposed to science, as having intellectual pleasure for its object, and as attaining its end by the use of language natural to us in a state of excitement, – but distinguished from other species of composition, not excluded by the former criterion, by permitting a pleasure from the whole consistent with a consciousness of pleasure from the component parts; – and the perfection of which is, to communicate from each part the greatest immediate pleasure compatible with the largest sum of pleasure on the whole. This, of course, will vary with the different modes of poetry; – and that splendour of particular lines, which would be worthy of admiration in an impassioned elegy, or a short indignant satire, would be a blemish and proof of vile taste in a tragedy or an epic poem.

It is remarkable, by the way, that Milton in three incidental words has implied all which for the purposes of more distinct apprehension, which at first must be slow-paced in order to be distinct, I have endeavoured to develop in a precise and strictly adequate definition. Speaking of poetry, he says, as in a parenthesis, 'which is simple, sensuous, passionate'. How awful is the power of words! – fearful often in their consequences when merely felt, not understood; but most awful when both felt and understood! – Had these three words only been properly understood by, and present in the minds of, general readers, not only almost a library of false poetry would have been either precluded or still-born, but, what is of more consequence, works truly excellent and capable of enlarging the understanding, warming and purifying the heart, and placing in the centre of the whole being the germs of noble and manlike actions, would have been the common diet of the intellect instead. For the first condition, simplicity, – while, on the one hand, it distinguishes poetry from the arduous processes of science, labouring towards an end not yet arrived at, and supposes a smooth and finished road, on which the reader is to walk onward easily, with streams murmuring by his side, and trees and flowers and human dwellings to make his journey as delightful as the object of it is desirable, instead of having to toil with the pioneers and painfully make the road on which others are to travel, – precludes, on the other hand, every affectation and morbid peculiarity; – the second condition, sensuousness, insures that framework of objectivity, that definiteness and articulation of imagery, and that modification of the images themselves, without which poetry becomes flattened into mere didactics of practice, or evaporated into a hazy, unthoughtful, daydreaming; and the third condition, passion, provides that neither thought nor imagery shall be simply objective, but that the *passio vera* of humanity shall warm and animate both.

To return, however, to the previous definition, this most general and distinctive character of a poem originates in the poetic genius itself; and though it comprises whatever can with any propriety be called a poem, (unless that word be a mere lazy synonyme for a composition in metre,) it yet becomes a just, and not merely discriminative, but full and adequate, definition of poetry in its highest and most peculiar sense, only so far as the distinction still results from the poetic genius, which sustains and modifies the emotions, thoughts, and vivid representations of the poem by the energy without effort of the poet's own mind, – by the spontaneous activity of his imagination and fancy, and by whatever else with these reveals itself in the balancing and reconciling of opposite or discordant qualities, sameness with difference, a sense of novelty and freshness with old or customary objects, a more than usual state of emotion with more than usual order, self-possession and judgement with enthusiasm and vehement feeling, – and which, while it blends and harmonizes the natural and the artificial, still subordinates art to nature, the manner to the matter, and our admiration of the poet to our sympathy with the images, passions, characters, and incidents of the poem. . . .

Lectures and Notes of 1818, Section I

THE ESSENCE OF POETRY

POETRY in essence is as familiar to barbarous as to civilized nations. The Laplander and the savage Indian are cheered by it as well as the inhabitants of London and Paris; – its spirit takes up and incorporates surrounding materials, as a plant clothes itself with soil and climate, whilst it exhibits the working of a vital principle within independent of all accidental circumstances. And to judge with fairness of an author's works, we ought to distinguish what is inward and essential from what is outward and circumstantial. It is essential to poetry that it be simple, and appeal to the elements and primary laws of our nature; that it be sensuous, and by its imagery elicit truth at a flash; that it be impassioned, and be able to move our feelings and awaken our affections. In comparing different poets with each other, we should inquire which have brought into the fullest play our imagination and our reason, or have created the greatest excitement and produced the completest harmony. If we consider great exquisiteness of language and sweetness of metre alone, it is impossible to deny to Pope the character of a delightful writer; but whether he be a poet, must depend upon our definition of the word; and, doubtless, if everything that pleases be poetry, Pope's satires and epistles must be poetry. This I must say, that poetry, as distinguished from other modes of composition, does not rest in metre, and that it is not poetry, if it make no appeal to our passions or our imagination. One character belongs to all true poets, that they write from a principle within, not originating in anything without; and that the true poet's work in its form, its shapings, and its modifications, is distinguished from all other works that assume to belong to the class of poetry, as a natural from an artificial flower, or as the mimic garden of a child from an enamelled meadow. In the former the flowers are broken from their stems and stuck into the ground; they are beautiful to the eye and fragrant to the sense, but their colours soon fade, and their odour is transient as the smile of the planter; – while the meadow may be visited again and again with renewed delight, its beauty is innate in the soul, and its bloom is of the freshness of nature.

Lectures of 1818, Section I

THE ENGLISH LANGUAGE

THE language, that is to say the particular tongue, in which Shakespeare wrote, cannot be left out of consideration. It will not be disputed, that one language may possess advantages which another does not enjoy; and we may state with confidence, that English excels all other languages in the number of its practical words. The French may bear the palm in the names of trades, and in military and diplomatic terms. Of the German it may be said, that, exclusive of many mineralogical words, it is incomparable in its metaphysical and psychological force: in another respect it nearly rivals the Greek:

> The learned Greek, rich in fit epithets,
> Blest in the lovely marriage of pure words;

I mean in its capability of composition – of forming compound words. Italian is the sweetest and softest language; Spanish the most majestic. All these have their peculiar faults; but I never can agree that any language is unfit for poetry, although different languages, from the condition and circumstances of the people, may certainly be adapted to one species of poetry more than to another.

Take the French as an example. It is, perhaps, the most perspicuous and pointed language in the world, and therefore best fitted for conversation, for the expression of light and airy passion, attaining its object by peculiar and felicitous turns of phrase, which are evanescent, and, like the beautifully coloured dust on the wings of a butterfly, must not be judged by the test of touch. It appears as if it were all surface and had no substratum, and it constantly most dangerously tampers with morals, without positively offending decency. As the language for what is called modern genteel comedy, all others must yield to French.

Italian can only be deemed second to Spanish, and Spanish to Greek, which contains all the excellences of all languages. Italian, though sweet and soft, is not deficient in force and dignity; and I may appeal to Ariosto, as a poet who displays to the utmost advantage the use of his native tongue for all purposes, whether of passion, sentiment, humour, or description.

But in English I find that which is possessed by no other modern language, and which, as it were, appropriates it to the drama. It is a language made out of many, and it has consequently many words, which originally had the same meaning; but in the progress of society those words have gradually assumed different shades of meaning. Take any homogeneous language, such as German, and try to translate into it the following lines:

> But not to one, in this benighted age,
> Is that diviner inspiration given,
> That burns in Shakspeare's or in Milton's page,
> The pomp and prodigality of heaven.
>
> Gray's Stanzas to Bentley

In German it would be necessary to say 'the pomp and *spendthriftness* of heaven', because the German has not, as we have, one word with two such distinct meanings, one expressing the nobler, the other the baser idea of the same action.

The monosyllabic character of English enables us, besides, to express more meaning in a shorter compass than can be done in any other language. In truth, English may be called the harvest of the unconscious wisdom of various nations, and was not the formation of any particular time, or assemblage of individuals. Hence the number of its passionate phrases – its metaphorical terms, not borrowed from poets, but adopted by them. Our commonest people, when excited by passion, constantly employ them: if a mother lose her child she is full of the wildest fancies, and the words she uses assume a tone of dignity; for the constant hearing and reading of the Bible and Liturgy clothes her thoughts not only in the most natural, but in the most beautiful forms of language.

Lectures, 1811–12

SHAKESPEARE OF NO AGE

SHAKESPEARE is of no age. It is idle to endeavour to support his phrases by quotations from Ben Jonson, Beaumont and Fletcher, &c. His language is entirely his own, and the younger dramatists imitated him. The construction of Shakespeare's sentences, whether in verse or prose, is the necessary and homogeneous vehicle of his peculiar manner of thinking. His is not the style of the age. More particularly, Shakespeare's blank verse is an absolutely new creation. Read Daniel – the admirable Daniel – in his *Civil Wars*, and *Triumphs of Hymen*. The style and language are just such as any very pure and manly writer of the present day – Wordsworth for example – would use; it seems quite modern in comparison with the style of Shakespeare. Ben Jonson's blank verse is very masterly and individual, and perhaps Massinger's is even still nobler. In Beaumont and Fletcher it is constantly slipping into lyricisms.

I believe Shakespeare was not a whit more intelligible in his own day than he is now to an educated man, except for a few local allusions of no consequence. As I said, he is of no age – nor, I may add, of any religion, or party, or profession. The body and substance of his works came out of the unfathomable depths of his own oceanic mind: his observation and reading, which was considerable, supplied him with the drapery of his figures.

March 15, 1834

SHAKESPEARE IS 'OUT OF TIME'

A FRIEND of mine well remarked of Spenser, that he is out of space: the reader never knows where he is, but still he knows, from the consciousness within him, that all is as natural and proper, as if the country where the action is laid were distinctly pointed out, and marked down in a map. Shakespeare is as much out of time, as Spenser is out of space; yet we feel conscious, though we never knew that such characters existed, that they might exist, and are satisfied with the belief in their existence.

This circumstance enabled Shakespeare to paint truly, and according to the colouring of nature, a vast number of personages by the simple force of meditation: he had only to imitate certain parts of his own character, or to exaggerate such as existed in possibility, and they were at once true to nature, and fragments of the divine mind that drew them. Men who see the great luminary of our system through various optical instruments declare that it seems either square, triangular, or round, when in truth it is still the sun, unchanged in shape and proportion. So with the characters of our great poet: some may think them of one form, and some of another; but they are still nature, still Shakespeare, and the creatures of his meditation.

When I use the term meditation, I do not mean that our great dramatist was without observation of external circumstances: quite the reverse; but mere observation may be able to produce an accurate copy, and even to furnish to other men's minds more than the copyist professed; but what is produced can only consist of parts and fragments, according to the means and extent of observation. Meditation looks at every character with interest, only as it contains something generally true, and such as might be expressed in a philosophical problem.

Lectures, 1811

SHAKESPEARE FOR THE NATION

O! WHEN I think of the inexhaustible mine of virgin treasure in our Shakespeare, that I have been almost daily reading him since I was ten years old, – that the thirty intervening years have been unintermittingly and not fruitlessly employed in the study of the Greek, Latin, English, Italian, Spanish, and German *belle lettrists*, and the last fifteen years in addition, far more intensely in the analysis of the laws of life and reason as they exist in man, – and that upon every step I have made forward in taste, in acquisition of facts from history or my own observation, and in knowledge of the different laws of being and their apparent exceptions, from accidental collision of disturbing forces, – that at every new accession of information, after every successful exercise of meditation, and every fresh presentation of experience, I have unfailingly discovered a proportionate increase of wisdom and intuition in Shakespeare; – when I know this, and know too, that by a conceivable and possible, though hardly to be expected, arrangement of the British theatres, not all, indeed, but a large, a very large, proportion of this indefinite all – (round which no comprehension has yet drawn the line of circumscription, so as to say to itself, 'I have seen the whole') – might be sent into the heads and hearts – into the very souls of the mass of mankind, to whom, except by this living comment and interpretation, it must remain for ever a sealed volume, a deep well without a wheel or a windlass; – it seems to me a pardonable enthusiasm to steal away from sober likelihood, and share in so rich a feast in the faery world of possibility! Yet even in the grave cheerfulness of a circumspect hope, much, very much, might be done; enough, assuredly, to furnish a kind and strenuous nature with ample motives for the attempt to effect what may be effected.

Lectures of 1818, Section I

SHAKESPEARE'S DISTINGUISHING
CHARACTERISTICS

THE stage in Shakespeare's time was a naked room with a blanket for a curtain; but he made it a field for monarchs. That law of unity, which has its foundations, not in the factitious necessity of custom, but in nature itself, the unity of feeling, is everywhere and at all times observed by Shakespeare in his plays. Read *Romeo and Juliet*; – all is youth and spring; – youth with all its follies, its virtues, its precipitancies; – spring with its odours, its flowers, and its transiency; it is one and the same feeling that commences, goes through, and ends the play. The old men, the Capulets and the Montagues, are not common old men; they have an eagerness, a heartiness, a vehemence, the effect of spring; with Romeo, his change of passion, his sudden marriage, and his rash death, are all the effects of youth: – whilst in Juliet love has all that is tender and melancholy in the nightingale, all that is voluptuous in the rose, with whatever is sweet in the freshness of spring; but it ends with a long deep sigh like the last breeze of the Italian evening. This unity of feeling and character pervades every drama of Shakespeare.

It seems to me that his plays are distinguished from those of all other dramatic poets by the following characteristics:

1. Expectation in preference to surprise. It is like the true reading of the passage; – 'God said, Let there be light, and there was *light*'; – not there *was* light. As the feeling with which we startle at a shooting star, compared with that of watching the sunrise at the pre-established moment, such and so low is surprise compared with expectation.

2. Signal adherence to the great law of nature, that all opposites tend to attract and temper each other. Passion in Shakespeare generally displays libertinism, but involves morality; and if there are exceptions

to this, they are, independently of their intrinsic value, all of them indicative of individual character, and, like the farewell admonitions of a parent, have an end beyond the parental relation. Thus the Countess's beautiful precepts to Bertram, by elevating her character, raise that of Helena her favourite, and soften down the point in her which Shakespeare does not mean us not to see, but to see and to forgive, and at length to justify. And so it is in Polonius, who is the personified memory of wisdom no longer actually possessed. This admirable character is always misrepresented on the stage. Shakespeare never intended to exhibit him as a buffoon: for although it was natural that Hamlet, – a young man of fire and genius, detesting formality, and disliking Polonius on political grounds, as imagining that he had assisted his uncle in his usurpation, – should express himself satirically, – yet this must not be taken as exactly the poet's conception of him. In Polonius a certain induration of character had arisen from long habits of business; but take his advice to Laertes, and Ophelia's reverence for his memory, and we shall see that he was meant to be represented as a statesman somewhat past his faculties, – his recollections of life all full of wisdom, and showing a knowledge of human nature, whilst what immediately takes place before him, and escapes from him, is indicative of weakness.

But as in Homer all the deities are in armour, even Venus; so in Shakespeare all the characters are strong. Hence real folly and dulness are made by him the vehicles of wisdom. There is no difficulty for one being a fool to imitate a fool: but to be, remain, and speak like a wise man and a great wit, and yet so as to give a vivid representation of a veritable fool, – *hic labor, hoc opus est.* A drunken constable is not uncommon, nor hard to draw; but see and examine what goes to make up a Dogberry.

3. Keeping at all times in the high road of life. Shakespeare has no innocent adulteries, no interesting incests, no virtuous vice: – he never renders that amiable which religion and reason alike teach us to detest, or clothes impurity in the garb of virtue, like Beaumont and Fletcher, the Kotzebues of the day. Shakespeare's fathers are roused by ingratitude, his husbands stung by unfaithfulness; in him, in short, the affections are wounded in those points in which all may, nay, must, feel. Let the morality of Shakespeare be contrasted with that of the writers of his own, or the succeeding, age, or of those of the present day, who boast their superiority in this respect. No one can dispute that the result of such a comparison is altogether in favour of Shakespeare: – even the letters of women of high rank in his age were often coarser

than his writings. If he occasionally disgusts a keen sense of delicacy, he never injures the mind; he neither excites, nor flatters, passion, in order to degrade the subject of it; he does not use the faulty thing for a faulty purpose, nor carries on warfare against virtue, by causing wickedness to appear as no wickedness, through the medium of a morbid sympathy with the unfortunate. In Shakespeare vice never walks as in twilight: nothing is purposely out of its place; – he inverts not the order of nature and propriety, – does not make every magistrate a drunkard or glutton, nor every poor man meek, humane, and temperate; he has no benevolent butchers, nor any sentimental ratcatchers.

4. Independence of the dramatic interest on the plot. The interest in the plot is always in fact on account of the characters, not *vice versa*, as in almost all other writers; the plot is a mere canvas and no more. Hence arises the true justification of the same stratagem being used in regard to Benedick and Beatrice, the vanity in each being alike. Take away from the *Much Ado About Nothing* all that which is not indispensable to the plot, either as having little to do with it, or, at best, like Dogberry and his comrades, forced into the service, when any other less ingeniously absurd watchmen and night-constables would have answered the mere necessities of the action; – take away Benedick, Beatrice, Dogberry, and the reaction of the former on the character of Hero, – and what will remain? In other writers the main agent of the plot is always the prominent character; in Shakespeare it is so, or is not so, as the character is in itself calculated, or not calculated, to form the plot. Don John is the mainspring of the plot of this play; but he is merely shown and then withdrawn.

5. Independence of the interest on the story as the groundwork of the plot. Hence Shakespeare never took the trouble of inventing stories. It was enough for him to select from those that had been already invented or recorded such as had one or other, or both, of two recommendations, namely, suitableness to his particular purpose, and their being parts of popular tradition, – names of which we had often heard, and of their fortunes, and as to which all we wanted was, to see the man himself. So it is just the man himself, the Lear, the Shylock, the Richard, that Shakespeare makes us for the first time acquainted with. Omit the first scene in *Lear*, and yet everything will remain; so the first and second scenes in the *Merchant of Venice*. Indeed it is universally true.

6. Interfusion of the lyrical – that which in its very essence is poetical – not only with the dramatic, as in the plays of Metastasio, where

at the end of the scene comes the *aria* as the *exit* speech of the character
– but also in and through the dramatic. Songs in Shakespeare are
introduced as songs only, just as songs are in real life, beautifully as
some of them are characteristic of the person who has sung or called
for them, as Desdemona's 'Willow', and Ophelia's wild snatches, and
the sweet carollings in *As You Like It*. But the whole of the *Mid-
summer Night's Dream* is one continued specimen of the dramatized
lyrical. And observe how exquisitely the dramatic of Hotspur; –

> Marry, and I'm glad on't with all my heart;
> I had rather be a kitten and cry – mew, &c.

melts away into the lyric of Mortimer; –

> I understand thy looks: that pretty Welsh
> Which thou pourest down from these swelling heavens,
> I am too perfect in, &c.

> *Henry IV, Part I, Act iii, Scene 1*

7. The characters of the *dramatis personae*, like those in real life, are
to be inferred by the reader; – they are not told to him. And it is well
worth remarking that Shakespeare's characters, like those in real life,
are very commonly misunderstood, and almost always understood by
different persons in different ways. The causes are the same in either
case. If you take only what the friends of the character say, you may
be deceived, and still more so, if that which his enemies say; nay, even
the character himself sees himself through the medium of his charac-
ter, and not exactly as he is. Take all together, not omitting a shrewd
hint from the clown or the fool, and perhaps your impression will be
right; and you may know whether you have in fact discovered the
poet's own idea, by all the speeches receiving light from it, and attest-
ing its reality by reflecting it.

Lastly, in Shakespeare the heterogeneous is united, as it is in nature.
You must not suppose a pressure or passion always acting on or in the
character; – passion in Shakespeare is that by which the individual is
distinguished from others, not that which makes a different kind of
him. Shakespeare followed the main march of the human affections.
He entered into no analysis of the passions or faiths of men, but
assured himself that such and such passions and faiths were grounded
in our common nature, and not in the mere accidents of ignorance or
disease. This is an important consideration, and constitutes our Shake-
speare the morning star, the guide and the pioneer, of true philosophy.

> *Lectures*, 1818

SHAKESPEARE'S JUDGEMENT
EQUAL TO HIS GENIUS

THUS then Shakespeare appears, from his *Venus and Adonis* and *Rape of Lucrece* alone, apart from all his great works, to have possessed all the conditions of the true poet. Let me now proceed to destroy, as far as may be in my power, the popular notion that he was a great dramatist by mere instinct, that he grew immortal in his own despite, and sank below men of second- or third-rate power, when he attempted aught beside the drama – even as bees construct their cells and manufacture their honey to admirable perfection; but would in vain attempt to build a nest. Now this mode of reconciling a compelled sense of inferiority with a feeling of pride, began in a few pedants, who having read that Sophocles was the great model of tragedy, and Aristotle the infallible dictator of its rules, and finding that the *Lear*, *Hamlet*, *Othello*, and other masterpieces, were neither in imitation of Sophocles nor in obedience to Aristotle, – and not having (with one or two exceptions) the courage to affirm, that the delight which their country received from generation to generation, in defiance of the alterations of circumstances and habits, was wholly groundless – took upon them, as a happy medium and refuge, to talk of Shakespeare as a sort of beautiful *lusus naturae*, a delightful monster, – wild, indeed, and without taste or judgement, but like the inspired idiots so much venerated in the East, uttering, amid the strangest follies, the sublimest truths. In nine places out of ten in which I find his awful name mentioned, it is with some epithet of 'wild', 'irregular', 'pure child of nature', &c. If all this be true, we must submit to it; though to a thinking mind it cannot but be painful to find any excellence, merely human, thrown out of all human analogy, and thereby leaving us neither rules for imitation, nor motives to imitate; – but if false, it is a dangerous falsehood; – for it affords a refuge to secret self-conceit, – enables a vain man at once to escape his reader's indignation by general swoln panegyrics, and merely by his *ipse dixit* to treat, as contemptible, what he has not intellect enough to comprehend, or soul to feel, without assigning any reason, or referring his opinion to any demonstrative principle; – thus leaving Shakespeare as a sort of Grand Lama, adored indeed, and his very excrements prized as relics, but with no authority or real influence. I grieve that every late voluminous edition of his works would enable me to substantiate the present charge with a variety of facts one-tenth of which would of themselves exhaust the time allotted to me. Every critic, who has or has not made a collection of black letter books – in itself a useful and respectable amusement, – puts on the seven-league boots of self-opinion, and strides at once from an illustrator into a supreme judge, and blind and deaf, fills his three-ounce phial at the waters of Niagara; and determines positively the greatness of the cataract to be neither more nor less than his three-ounce phial has been able to receive.

I think this a very serious subject. It is my earnest desire – my passionate endeavour, – to enforce at various times and by various arguments and instances the close and reciprocal connection of just taste with pure morality. Without that acquaintance with the heart of man, or that docility and childlike gladness to be made acquainted with it, which those only can have, who dare look at their own hearts – and that with a steadiness which religion only has the power of reconciling with sincere humility; – without this, and the modesty produced by it, I am deeply convinced that no man, however wide his erudition, however patient his antiquarian researches, can possibly understand, or be worthy of understanding, the writings of Shakespeare.

Assuredly that criticism of Shakespeare will alone be genial which is reverential. The Englishman, who without reverence, a proud and affectionate reverence, can utter the name of William Shakespeare, stands disqualified for the office of critic. He wants one at least of the very senses, the language of which he is to employ, and will discourse, at best, but as a blind man, while the whole harmonious creation of light and shade with all its subtle interchange of deepening and dissolving colours rises in silence to the silent *fiat* of the uprising Apollo. However inferior in ability I may be to some who have followed me, I own I am proud that I was the first in time who publicly demonstrated to the full extent of the position, that the supposed irregularity and extravagancies of Shakespeare were the mere dreams of a pedantry that arraigned the eagle because it had not the dimensions of the swan. In all the successive courses of lectures delivered by me, since my first attempt at the Royal Institution, it has been, and it still remains, my object, to prove that in all points from the most important to the most minute, the judgement of Shakespeare is commensurate with his genius, – nay, that his genius reveals itself in his judgement, as in its most exalted form. And the more gladly do I recur to this subject from the clear conviction, that to judge aright, and with distinct consciousness of the grounds of our judgement, concerning the works of Shakespeare, implies the power and the means of judging rightly of all other works of intellect, those of abstract science alone excepted.

It is a painful truth that not only individuals, but even whole nations, are ofttimes so enslaved to the habits of their education and immediate circumstances, as not to judge disinterestedly even on those subjects, the very pleasure arising from which consists in its disinterestedness, namely, on subjects of taste and polite literature. Instead of deciding concerning their own modes and customs by any rule of reason, nothing appears rational, becoming, or beautiful to them, but what coincides with the peculiarities of their education. In this narrow circle, individuals may attain to exquisite discrimination, as the French critics have done in their own literature; but a true critic can no more be such without placing himself on some central point, from which he may command the whole, that is, some general rule, which, founded in reason, or the faculties common to all men, must therefore apply to each, – than an astronomer can explain the movements of the solar system without taking his stand in the sun. And let me remark, that this will not tend to produce despotism, but, on the contrary, true tolerance, in the critic. He will, indeed, require, as the spirit and substance of a work, something true in human nature itself, and independent of all circumstances; but in the mode of applying it, he will estimate genius and judgement according to the felicity with which the imperishable soul of intellect shall have adapted itself to the age, the place, and the existing manners. The error he will expose lies in reversing this, and holding up the mere circumstances as perpetual, to the utter neglect of the power which can alone animate them. For art cannot exist without, or apart from, nature; and what has man of his own to give to his fellow-man, but his own thoughts and feelings, and his observations so far as they are modified by his own thoughts or feelings?

Let me, then, once more submit this question to minds emancipated alike from national, or party, or sectarian prejudice; – Are the plays of Shakespeare works of rude uncultivated genius, in which the splendour of the parts compensates, if aught can compensate, for the barbarous shapelessness and irregularity of the whole? – Or is the form equally admirable with the matter, and the judgement of the great poet not less deserving our wonder than his genius? – Or, again, to repeat the question in other words: – Is Shakespeare a great dramatic poet on account only of those beauties and excellencies which he possesses in common with the ancients, but with diminished claims to our love and honour to the full extent of his differences from them – Or are these very differences additional proofs of poetic wisdom, at once results and symbols of living power as contrasted with lifeless mechanism – of free and rival originality as contradistinguished from servile imitation, or, more accurately, a blind copying of effects, instead of a true imitation of the essential principles – Imagine not that I am about to oppose genius to rules. No! the comparative value of these rules is the very cause to be tried. The spirit of poetry, like all other living powers, must of necessity circumscribe itself by rules, were it only to unite power with beauty. It must embody in order to reveal itself; but a living body is of necessity an organized one; and what is organization but the connection of parts in and for a whole, so that each part is at once end and means? – This is no discovery of criticism; – it is a necessity of the human mind; and all nations have felt and obeyed it, in the invention of metre, and measured sounds, as the vehicle and *involucrum* of poetry – itself a fellow-growth from the same life, – even as the bark is to the tree!

No work of true genius dares want its appropriate form, neither indeed is there any danger of this. As it must not, so genius cannot, be lawless: for it is even this that constitutes it genius – the power of acting creatively under laws of its own origination. How then comes it that not only single *Zoili*, but whole nations have combined in unhesitating condemnation of our great dramatist, as a sort of African nature, rich in beautiful monsters, – as a wild heath where islands of fertility look the greener from the surrounding waste, where the loveliest plants now shine out among unsightly weeds, and now are choked by their parasitic growth, so intertwined that we cannot disentangle the weed without snapping the flower – In this statement I have had no reference to the vulgar abuse of Voltaire, save as far as his charges are coincident with the decisions of Shakespeare's own commentators and (so they would tell you) almost idolatrous admirers. The true ground of the mistake lies in the confounding mechanical regularity with organic form. The form is mechanic, when on any given material we impress a pre-determined form, not necessarily arising out of the properties of the material; – as when to a mass of wet clay we give whatever shape we wish it to retain when hardened. The organic form, on the other hand, is innate; it shapes, as it develops, itself from within, and the fulness of its development is one and the same with the perfection of its outward form. Such as the life is, such is the form. Nature, the prime genial artist, inexhaustible in diverse powers, is equally inexhaustible in forms; – each exterior is the physiognomy of the being within, – its true image reflected and thrown out from the concave mirror: – and even such is the appropriate excellence of her chosen poet, of our own Shakespeare, – himself a nature humanized, a genial understanding directing self-consciously a power and an implicit wisdom deeper even than our consciousness.

I greatly dislike beauties and selections in general; but as proof positive of his unrivalled excellence, I should like to try Shakespeare by this criterion. Make out your amplest catalogue of all the human faculties, as reason or the moral law, the will, the feeling of the coincidence of the two (a feeling *sui generis et demonstratio demonstrationum*) called the conscience, the understanding or prudence, wit, fancy, imagination, judgement, – and then of the objects on which these are to be employed, as the beauties, the terrors, and the seeming caprices of nature, the realities and the capabilities, that is, the actual and the ideal, of the human mind, conceived as an individual or as a social being, as in innocence or in guilt, in a play-paradise, or in a war-field of temptation; – and then compare with Shakespeare under each of these heads all or any of the writers in prose and verse that have ever lived! Who, that is competent to judge, doubts the result? – And ask your own hearts, – ask your own common sense – to conceive the possibility of this man being – I say not, the drunken savage of that wretched sciolist, whom Frenchmen, to their shame, have honoured before their elder and better worthies, – but the anomalous, the wild, the irregular, genius of our daily criticism! What! are we to have miracles in sport? – Or, I speak reverently, does God choose idiots by whom to convey divine truths to man?

Lectures, 1818

VITAL GENIUS AND MECHANICAL TALENT

... whilst I can never, I trust, show myself blind to the various merits of Jonson, Beaumont and Fletcher, and Massinger, or insensible to the greatness of the merits which they possess in common, or to the specific excellencies which give to each of the three a worth of his own, – I confess, that one main object of this Lecture was to prove that Shakespeare's eminence is his own, and not that of his age – even as the pineapple, the melon, and the gourd may grow on the same bed; – yea, the same circumstances of warmth and soil may be necessary to their full development, yet do not account for the golden hue, the ambrosial flavour, the perfect shape of the pineapple, or the tufted crown on its head. Would that those, who seek to twist it off, could but promise us in this instance to make it the germ of an equal successor!

What had a grammatical and logical consistency for the ear – what could be put together and represented to the eye – these poets took from the ear and eye, unchecked by any intuition of an inward impossibility; – just as a man might put together a quarter of an orange, a quarter of an apple, and the like of a lemon and a pomegranate, and make it look like one round diverse-coloured fruit. But nature, which works from within by evolution and assimilation according to a law, cannot do so, nor could Shakespeare; for he too worked in the spirit of nature, by evolving the germ from within by the imaginative power according to an idea. For as the power of seeing is to light, so is an idea in mind to a law in nature. They are correlatives, which suppose each other.

The plays of Beaumont and Fletcher are mere aggregations without unity; in the Shakespearian drama there is a vitality which grows and evolves itself from within, – a keynote which guides and controls the harmonies throughout. What is *Lear*? – It is storm and tempest – the thunder at first grumbling in the far horizon, then gathering around us, and at length bursting in fury over our heads, – succeeded by a breaking of the clouds for a while, a last flash of lightning, the closing in of night, and the single hope of darkness! And *Romeo and Juliet*? – It is a spring day, gusty and beautiful in the morn, and closing like an April evening with the song of the nightingale; – whilst *Macbeth* is deep and earthy, – composed to the subterranean music of a troubled conscience, which converts everything into the wild and fearful!

Doubtless from mere observation, or from the occasional similarity of the writer's own character, more or less in Beaumont and Fletcher and other such writers will happen to be in correspondence with nature, and still more in apparent compatibility with it. But yet the false source is always discoverable, first by the gross contradictions to nature in so many other parts, and secondly, by the want of the impression which Shakespeare makes, that the thing said not only might have been said, but that nothing else could be substituted, so as to excite the same sense of its exquisite propriety. I have always thought the conduct and expressions of Othello and Iago, in the last scene, when Iago is brought in prisoner, a wonderful instance of Shakespeare's consummate judgement:

> OTHELLO. I look down towards his feet; – but that's a fable.
> If that thou be'st a devil, I cannot kill thee.
> IAGO. I bleed, Sir; but not kill'd.
> OTHELLO. I am not sorry neither.

Think what a volley of execrations and defiances Beaumont and Fletcher would have poured forth here!

Indeed Massinger and Ben Jonson are both more perfect in their kind than Beaumont and Fletcher; the former in the story and affecting incidents; the latter in the exhibition of manners and peculiarities, whims in language, and vanities of appearance.

There is, however, a diversity of the most dangerous kind here. Shakespeare shaped his characters out of the nature within; but we cannot so safely say, out of his own nature as an individual person. No! this latter is itself but a *natura naturata*, – an effect, a product, not a power. It was Shakespeare's prerogative to have the universal, which is potentially in each particular, opened out to him, the *homo generalis*, not as an abstraction from observation of a variety of men, but as the substance capable of endless modifications, of which his own personal existence was but one, and to use this one as the eye that beheld the other, and as the tongue that could convey the discovery. There is no greater or more common vice in dramatic writers than to draw out of themselves. How I – alone and in the self-sufficiency of my study, as all men are apt to be proud in their dreams – should like to be talking *king*! Shakespeare, in composing, had no *I*, but the *I* representative. In Beaumont and Fletcher you have descriptions of characters by the poet rather than the characters themselves; we are told, and impressively told, of their being; but we rarely or never feel that they actually are.

1818

SHAKESPEARE'S WOMEN

'MOST women have no character at all', said Pope, and meant it for satire. Shakespeare, who knew man and woman much better, saw that it, in fact, was the perfection of woman to be characterless. Every one wishes a Desdemona or Ophelia for a wife, – creatures who, though they may not always understand you, do always feel you, and feel with you.

Table-Talk

September 27, 1830

ROMEO AND JULIET

IN a former lecture I endeavoured to point out the union of the Poet and the Philosopher, or rather the warm embrace between them, in the *Venus and Adonis* and *Lucrece* of Shakespeare. From thence I passed on to *Love's Labour Lost*, as the link between his character as a Poet, and his art as a Dramatist; and I showed that, although in that work the former was still predominant, yet that the germs of his subsequent dramatic power were easily discernible.

I will now, as I promised in my last, proceed to *Romeo and Juliet*, not because it is the earliest, or among the earliest of Shakespeare's works of that kind, but because in it are to be found specimens, in degree, of all the excellences which he afterwards displayed in his more perfect dramas, but differing from them in being less forcibly evidenced, and less happily combined: all the parts are more or less present, but they are not united with the same harmony.

There are, however, in *Romeo and Juliet* passages where the poet's whole excellence is evinced, so that nothing superior to them can be met with in the productions of his after years. The main distinction between this play and others is, as I said, that the parts are less happily combined, or to borrow a phrase from the painter, the whole work is less in keeping. Grand portions are produced: we have limbs of giant growth; but the production, as a whole, in which each part gives delight for itself, and the whole, consisting of these delightful parts, communicates the highest intellectual pleasure and satisfaction, is the result of the application of judgement and taste. These are not to be attained but by painful study, and to the sacrifice of the stronger pleasures derived from the dazzling light which a man of genius throws over every circumstance, and where we are chiefly struck by vivid and distinct images. Taste is an attainment after a poet has been disciplined by experience, and has added to genius that talent by which he knows what part of his genius he can make acceptable, and intelligible to the portion of mankind for which he writes.

In my mind it would be a hopeless symptom, as regards genius, if I found a young man with anything like perfect taste. In the earlier works of Shakespeare we have a profusion of double epithets, and sometimes even the coarsest terms are employed, if they convey a more vivid image; but by degrees the associations are connected with the image they are designed to impress, and the poet descends from the ideal into the real world so far as to conjoin both – to give a sphere of active operations to the ideal, and to elevate and refine the real.

In *Romeo and Juliet* the principal characters may be divided into two classes: in one class passion – the passion of love – is drawn and drawn truly, as well as beautifully; but the persons are not individualized farther than as the actor appears on the stage. It is a very just description and development of love, without giving, if I may so express myself, the philosophical history of it – without showing how the man became acted upon by that particular passion, but leading it through all the incidents of the drama, and rendering it predominant.

Tybalt is, in himself, a common-place personage. And here allow me to remark upon a great distinction between Shakespeare, and all who have written in imitation of him. I know no character in his plays (unless indeed Pistol be an exception), which can be called the mere portrait of an individual: while the reader feels all the satisfaction arising from individuality, yet that very individual is a sort of class character, and this circumstance renders Shakespeare the poet of all ages.

Tybalt is a man abandoned to his passions – with all the pride of family, only because he thought it belonged to him as a member of that family, and valuing himself highly, simply because he does not care for death. This indifference to death is perhaps more common than any other feeling: men are apt to flatter themselves extravagantly, merely because they possess a quality which it is a disgrace not to have, but which a wise man never puts forward, but when it is necessary.

Jeremy Taylor, in one part of his voluminous works, speaking of a great man, says that he was naturally a coward, as indeed most men are, knowing the value of life, but the power of his reason enabled him, when required, to conduct himself with uniform courage and hardihood. The good bishop, perhaps, had in his mind a story, told by one of the ancients, of a Philosopher and a Coxcomb, on board the same ship during a storm: the Coxcomb reviled the Philosopher for betraying marks of fear: 'Why are you so frightened? I am not afraid of being drowned: I do not care a farthing for my life.' – 'You are perfectly right,' said the Philosopher, 'for your life is not worth a farthing.'

Shakespeare never takes pains to make his characters win your esteem, but leaves it to the general command of the passions, and to poetic justice. It is most beautiful to observe, in *Romeo and Juliet*, that the characters principally engaged in the incidents are preserved

innocent from all that could lower them in our opinion, while the
rest of the personages, deserving little interest in themselves, derive it
from being instrumental in those situations in which the more im-
portant personages develop their thoughts and passions.

Look at Capulet – a worthy, noble-minded old man of high rank,
with all the impatience that is likely to accompany it. It is delightful
to see all the sensibilities of our nature so exquisitely called forth; as if
the poet had the hundred arms of the polypus, and had thrown them
out in all directions to catch the predominant feeling. We may see in
Capulet the manner in which anger seizes hold of everything that
comes in its way, in order to express itself, as in the lines where he
reproved Tybalt for his fierceness of behaviour, which led him to wish
to insult a Montague, and disturb the merriment.

> Go to, go to;
> You are a saucy boy. Is't so, indeed?
> This trick may chance to scath you; – I know what.
> You must contrary me! marry, 'tis time. –
> Well said, my hearts! – You are a princox: go:
> Be quiet or – More light, more light! – For shame!
> I'll make you quiet. – What! cheerly, my hearts!
>
> Act I, Scene 5

The line

> This trick may chance to scath you; – I know what,

was an allusion to the legacy Tybalt might expect; and then, seeing
the lights burn dimly, Capulet turns his anger against the servants.
Thus we see that no one passion is so predominant, but that it in-
cludes all the parts of the character, and the reader never has a mere
abstract of a passion, as of wrath or ambition, but the whole man is
presented to him – the one predominant passion acting, if I may so
say, as the leader of the band to the rest.

It could not be expected that the poet should introduce such a
character as Hamlet into every play; but even in those personages
which are subordinate to a hero so eminently philosophical, the pas-
sion is at least rendered instructive, and induces the reader to look
with a keener eye, and a finer judgement into human nature.

Shakespeare has this advantage over all other dramatists – that he
has availed himself of his psychological genius to develop all the
minutiae of the human heart: showing us the thing that, to common
observers, he seems solely intent upon, he makes visible what we
should not otherwise have seen: just as, after looking at distant objects

through a telescope, when we behold them subsequently with the naked eye, we see them with greater distinctness, and in more detail, than we should otherwise have done.

Mercutio is one of our poet's truly Shakespearian characters; for throughout his plays, but especially in those of the highest order, it is plain that the personages were drawn rather from meditation than from observation, or to speak correctly, more from observation, the child of meditation. It is comparatively easy for a man to go about the world, as if with a pocket-book in his hand, carefully noting down what he sees and hears: by practice he acquires considerable facility in representing what he has observed, himself frequently unconscious of its worth, or its bearings. This is entirely different from the observation of a mind, which, having formed a theory and a system upon its own nature, remarks all things that are examples of its truth, confirming it in that truth, and, above all, enabling it to convey the truths of philosophy, as mere effects derived from, what we may call, the outward watchings of life.

Hence it is that Shakespeare's favourite characters are full of such lively intellect. Mercutio is a man possessing all the elements of a poet: the whole world was, as it were, subject to his law of association. Whenever he wishes to impress anything, all things become his servants for the purpose: all things tell the same tale, and sound in unison. This faculty, moreover, is combined with the manners and feelings of a perfect gentleman, himself utterly unconscious of his powers. By his loss it was contrived that the whole catastrophe of the tragedy should be brought about: it endears him to Romeo, and gives to the death of Mercutio an importance which it could not otherwise have acquired.

I say this in answer to an observation, I think by Dryden (to which indeed Dr Johnson has fully replied), that Shakespeare having carried the part of Mercutio as far as he could, till his genius was exhausted, had killed him in the third Act, to get him out of the way. What shallow nonsense! As I have remarked, upon the death of Mercutio the whole catastrophe depends; it is produced by it. The scene in which it occurs serves to show how indifference to any subject but one, and aversion to activity on the part of Romeo, may be overcome and roused to the most resolute and determined conduct. Had not Mercutio been rendered so amiable and so interesting, we could not have felt so strongly the necessity for Romeo's interference, connecting it immediately, and passionately, with the future fortunes of the lover and his mistress.

But what am I to say of the Nurse? We have been told that her character is the mere fruit of observation – that it is like Swift's *Polite Conversation*, certainly the most stupendous work of human memory, and of unceasingly active attention to what passes around us, upon record. The Nurse in *Romeo and Juliet* has sometimes been compared to a portrait by Gerard Dow, in which every hair was so exquisitely painted, that it would bear the test of the microscope. Now, I appeal confidently to my hearers whether the closest observation of the manners of one or two old nurses would have enabled Shakespeare to draw this character of admirable generalization? Surely not. Let any man conjure up in his mind all the qualities and peculiarities that can possibly belong to a nurse, and he will find them in Shakespeare's picture of the old woman: nothing is omitted. This effect is not produced by mere observation. The great prerogative of genius (and Shakespeare felt and availed himself of it) is now to swell itself to the dignity of a god, and now to subdue and keep dormant some part of that lofty nature, and to descend even to the lowest character – to become everything, in fact, but the vicious.

Thus, in the Nurse you have all the garrulity of old age, and all its fondness; for the affection of old age is one of the greatest consolations of humanity. I have often thought what a melancholy world this would be without children, and what an inhuman world without the aged.

You have also in the Nurse the arrogance of ignorance, with the pride of meanness at being connected with a great family. You have the grossness, too, which that situation never removes, though it sometimes suspends it; and, arising from that grossness, the little low vices attendant upon it, which, indeed, in such minds are scarcely vices. – Romeo at one time was the most delightful and excellent young man, and the Nurse all willingness to assist him; but her disposition soon turns in favour of Paris, for whom she professes precisely the same admiration. How wonderfully are these low peculiarities contrasted with a young and pure mind, educated under different circumstances!

Another point ought to be mentioned as characteristic of the ignorance of the Nurse: – it is, that in all her recollections, she assists herself by the remembrance of visual circumstances. The great difference, in this respect, between the cultivated and the uncultivated mind is this – that the cultivated mind will be found to recall the past by certain regular trains of cause and effect; whereas, with the uncultivated mind, the past is recalled wholly by coincident images, or facts which happened at the same time. This position is fully exemplified in the following passages put into the mouth of the Nurse:

> Even or odd, of all days in the year,
> Come Lammas eve at night shall she be fourteen.
> Susan and she – God rest all Christian souls! –
> Were of an age. – Well, Susan is with God;
> She was too good for me. But, as I said,
> On Lammas eve at night shall she be fourteen;
> That shall she, marry: I remember it well.
> 'Tis since the earthquake now eleven years;
> And she was wean'd, – I never shall forget it, –
> Of all the days of the year, upon that day;
> For I had then laid wormwood to my dug,
> Sitting in the sun under the dove-house wall:
> My lord and you were then at Mantua. –
> Nay, I do bear a brain: – but, as I said,
> When it did taste the wormwood on the nipple
> Of my dug, and felt it bitter, pretty fool,
> To see it tetchy, and fall out with the dug!
> Shake, quoth the dove-house: 'twas no need, I trow,
> To bid me trudge.
> And since that time it is eleven years;
> For then she could stand alone.   Act I, Scene 3

She afterwards goes on with similar visual impressions, so true to the character. – More is here brought into one portrait than could have been ascertained by one man's mere observation, and without the introduction of a single incongruous point.

I honour, I love, the works of Fielding as much, or perhaps more, than those of any other writer of fiction of that kind: take Fielding in his characters of postillions, landlords, and landladies, waiters, or indeed, of anybody who had come before his eye, and nothing can be more true, more happy, or more humorous; but in all his chief personages, Tom Jones for instance, where Fielding was not directed by observation, where he could not assist himself by the close copying of what he saw, where it is necessary that something should take place, some words be spoken, or some object described, which he could not have witnessed (his soliloquies for example, or the interview between the hero and Sophia Western before the reconciliation) and I will venture to say, loving and honouring the man and his productions as I do, that nothing can be more forced and unnatural: the language is without vivacity or spirit, the whole matter is incongruous, and totally destitute of psychological truth.

On the other hand, look at Shakespeare: where can any character be produced that does not speak the language of nature? where does he not put into the mouths of his *dramatis personae*, be they high or low, Kings or Constables, precisely what they must have said? Where, from observation, could he learn the language proper to Sovereigns, Queens, Noblemen, or Generals? yet he invariably uses it. – Where, from observation, could he have learned such lines as these, which are put into the mouth of Othello, when he is talking to Iago of Brabantio?

> Let him do his spite:
> My services, which I have done the signiory,
> Shall out-tongue his complaints. 'Tis yet to know,
> Which, when I know that boasting is an honour,
> I shall promulgate, I fetch my life and being
> From men of royal siege; and my demerits
> May speak, unbonneted, to as proud a fortune
> As this that I have reach'd: for know, Iago,
> But that I love the gentle Desdemona,
> I would not my unhoused free condition
> Put into circumscription and confine
> For the sea's worth.

Act I, Scene 2

I ask where was Shakespeare to observe such language as this? If he did observe it, it was with the inward eye of meditation upon his own nature: for the time, he became Othello, and spoke as Othello, in such circumstances, must have spoken.

Another remark I may make upon *Romeo and Juliet* is, that in this tragedy the poet is not, as I have hinted, entirely blended with the dramatist, – at least, not in the degree to be afterwards noticed in *Lear*, *Hamlet*, *Othello*, or *Macbeth*. Capulet and Montague not unfrequently talk a language only belonging to the poet, and not so characteristic of, and peculiar to, the passions of persons in the situations in which they are placed – a mistake, or rather an indistinctness, which many of our later dramatists have carried through the whole of their productions.

When I read the song of Deborah, I never think that she is a poet, although I think the song itself a sublime poem; it is as simple a dithyrambic production as exists in any language; but it is the proper and characteristic effusion of a woman highly elevated by triumph, by the natural hatred of oppressors, and resulting from a bitter sense of wrong: it is a song of exultation on deliverance from these evils, a deliverance accomplished by herself. When she exclaims, 'The inhabitants of the villages ceased, they ceased in Israel, until that I, Deborah, arose, that I arose a mother in Israel', it is poetry in the highest sense: we have no reason, however, to suppose that if she had not been agitated by passion, and animated by victory, she would have been able so to express herself; or that if she had been placed in different circumstances, she would have used such language of truth and passion. We are to remember that Shakespeare, not placed under circumstances of excitement, and only wrought upon by his own vivid and vigorous imagination, writes a language that invariably, and intuitively becomes the condition and position of each character.

On the other hand, there is a language not descriptive of passion, nor uttered under the influence of it, which is at the same time poetic, and shows a high and active fancy, as when Capulet says to Paris,

> Such comfort as do lusty young men feel,
> When well-apparell'd April on the heel
> Of limping winter treads, even such delight
> Among fresh female buds, shall you this night
> Inherit at my house.
>
> Act I, Scene 2

Here the poet may be said to speak, rather than the dramatist; and it would be easy to adduce other passages from this play, where Shakespeare, for a moment forgetting the character, utters his own words in his own person.

In my mind, what have often been censured as Shakespeare's conceits are completely justifiable, as belonging to the state, age, or feeling of the individual. Sometimes, when they cannot be vindicated on these grounds, they may well be excused by the taste of his own and of the preceding age; as for instance, in Romeo's speech,

> Here's much to do with hate, but more with love: –
> Why then, O brawling love! O loving hate!
> O anything, of nothing first created!
> O heavy lightness! serious vanity!
> Misshapen chaos of well-seeming forms!
> Feather of lead, bright smoke, cold fire, sick health!
> Still-waking sleep, that is not what it is!
>
> Act I, Scene 1

I dare not pronounce such passages as these to be absolutely unnatural, not merely because I consider the author a much better judge than I can be, but because I can understand and allow for an effort of the mind, when it would describe what it cannot satisfy itself with the description of, to reconcile opposites and qualify contradictions, leaving a middle state of mind more strictly appropriate to the imagination than any other, when it is, as it were, hovering between images. As soon as it is fixed on one image, it becomes understanding; but while it is unfixed and wavering between them, attaching itself permanently to none, it is imagination. Such is the fine description of Death in Milton:

> The other shape,
> If shape it might be call'd, that shape had none
> Distinguishable in member, joint, or limb,
> Or substance might be call'd, that shadow seem'd,
> For each seem'd either: black it stood as night:
> Fierce as ten furies, terrible as hell,
> And shook a dreadful dart: what seem'd his head
> The likeness of a kingly crown had on.

> *Paradise Lost*, Book II

The grandest efforts of poetry are where the imagination is called forth, not to produce a distinct form, but a strong working of the mind, still offering what is still repelled, and again creating what is again rejected; the result being what the poet wishes to impress, namely, the substitution of a sublime feeling of the unimaginable for a mere image. I have sometimes thought that the passage just read might be quoted as exhibiting the narrow limit of painting, as compared with the boundless power of poetry: painting cannot go beyond a certain point; poetry rejects all control, all confinement. Yet we know that sundry painters have attempted pictures of the meeting between Satan and Death at the gates of Hell; and how was Death represented? Not as Milton has described him, but by the most defined thing that can be imagined – a skeleton, the dryest and hardest image that it is possible to discover; which, instead of keeping the mind in a state of activity, reduces it to the merest passivity, – an image compared with which a square, a triangle, or any other mathematical figure, is a luxuriant fancy.

It is a general but mistaken notion that, because some forms of writing, and some combinations of thought, are not usual, they are not natural; but we are to recollect that the dramatist represents his characters in every situation of life and in every state of mind, and there is no form of language that may not be introduced with effect by a great and judicious poet, and yet be most strictly according to nature. Take punning, for instance, which may be the lowest, but at all events is the most harmless, kind of wit, because it never excites envy. A pun may be a necessary consequence of association: one man, attempting to prove something that was resisted by another, might, when agitated by strong feeling, employ a term used by his adversary with a directly contrary meaning to that for which that adversary had resorted to it: it might come into his mind as one way, and sometimes the best, of replying to that adversary. This form of speech is generally produced by a mixture of anger and contempt, and punning is a natural mode of expressing them.

It is my intention to pass over none of the important so-called conceits of Shakespeare, not a few of which are introduced into his later productions with great propriety and effect. We are not to forget, that at the time he lived there was an attempt at, and an affectation of, quaintness and adornment, which emanated from the Court, and against which satire was directed by Shakespeare in the character of Osric in *Hamlet*. Among the schoolmen of that age, and earlier, nothing was more common than the use of conceits: it began with the revival of letters, and the bias thus given was very generally felt and acknowledged.

I have in my possession a dictionary of phrases, in which the epithets applied to love, hate, jealousy, and such abstract terms, are arranged; and they consist almost entirely of words taken from Seneca and his imitators, or from the schoolmen, showing perpetual antithesis, and describing the passions by the conjunction and combination of things absolutely irreconcilable. In treating the matter thus, I am aware that I am only palliating the practice in Shakespeare: he ought to have had nothing to do with merely temporary peculiarities: he wrote not for his own only, but for all ages, and so far I admit the use of some of his conceits to be a defect. They detract sometimes from his universality as to time, person, and situation.

If we were able to discover, and to point out the peculiar faults, as well as the peculiar beauties of Shakespeare, it would materially assist us in deciding what authority ought to be attached to certain portions of what are generally called his works. If we met with a play, or certain scenes of a play, in which we could trace neither his defects nor his excellences, we should have the strongest reason for believing that he had had no hand in it. In the case of scenes so circumstanced we might come to the conclusion that they were taken from the older plays, which, in some instances, he reformed or altered, or that they were inserted afterwards by some underhand, in order to please the mob. If a drama by Shakespeare turned out to be too heavy for popular audiences, the clown might be called in to lighten the representation; and if it appeared that what was added was not in Shakespeare's manner, the conclusion would be inevitable, that it was not from Shakespeare's pen.

It remains for me to speak of the hero and heroine, of Romeo and Juliet themselves; and I shall do so with unaffected diffidence, not merely on account of the delicacy, but of the great importance of the subject. I feel that it is impossible to defend Shakespeare from the most cruel of all charges – that he is an immoral writer – without entering fully into his mode of portraying female characters, and of displaying the passion of love. It seems to me, that he has done both with greater perfection than any other writer of the known world, perhaps with the single exception of Milton in his delineation of Eve.

When I have heard it said, or seen it stated, that Shakespeare wrote for man, but the gentle Fletcher for woman, it has always given me something like acute pain, because to me it seems to do the greatest injustice to Shakespeare: when, too, I remember how much character is formed by what we read, I cannot look upon it as a light question, to be passed over as a mere amusement, like a game of cards or chess. I never have been able to tame down my mind to think poetry a sport, or an occupation for idle hours.

Perhaps there is no more sure criterion of refinement in moral character, of the purity of intellectual intention, and of the deep conviction and perfect sense of what our own nature really is in all its combinations, than the different definitions different men would give of love. I will not detain you by stating the various known definitions, some of which it may be better not to repeat: I will rather give you one of my own, which, I apprehend, is equally free from the extravagance of pretended Platonism (which, like other things which super-moralize, is sure to demoralize) and from its grosser opposite.

Considering myself and my fellow-men as a sort of link between heaven and earth, being composed of body and soul, with power to reason and to will, and with that perpetual aspiration which tells us that this is ours for a while, but it is not ourselves; considering man, I say, in this two-fold character, yet united in one person, I conceive that there can be no correct definition of love which does not correspond with our being, and with that subordination of one part to another which constitutes our perfection. I would say therefore that –

'Love is a desire of the whole being to be united to some thing, or some being, felt necessary to its completeness, by the most perfect means that nature permits, and reason dictates.'

It is inevitable to every noble mind, whether man or woman, to feel itself, of itself, imperfect and insufficient, not as an animal only, but as a moral being. How wonderfully, then, has Providence contrived for us, by making that which is necessary to us a step in our exaltation to a higher and nobler state! The Creator has ordained that one should possess qualities which the other has not, and the union of both is the most complete ideal of human character. In everything the blending of the similar with the dissimilar is the secret of all pure delight. Who shall dare to stand alone, and vaunt himself, in himself, sufficient? In poetry it is the blending of passion with order that constitutes perfection: this is still more the case in morals, and more than all in the exclusive attachment of the sexes.

True it is, that the world and its business may be carried on without marriage; but it is so evident that Providence intended man (the only animal of all climates, and whose reason is pre-eminent over instinct) to be the master of the world, that marriage, or the knitting together of society by the tenderest, yet firmest ties, seems ordained to render him capable of maintaining his superiority over the brute creation. Man alone has been privileged to clothe himself, and to do all things so as to make him, as it were, a secondary creator of himself, and of his own happiness or misery: in this, as in all, the image of the Deity is impressed upon him.

Providence, then, has not left us to prudence only; for the power of calculation, which prudence implies, cannot have existed, but in a state which pre-supposes marriage. If God has done this, shall we suppose that He has given us no moral sense, no yearning, which is something more than animal, to secure that, without which man might form a herd, but could not be a society? The very idea seems to breathe absurdity.

From this union arise the paternal, filial, brotherly and sisterly relations of life; and every state is but a family magnified. All the operations of mind, in short, all that distinguishes us from brutes, originate in the more perfect state of domestic life. – One infallible criterion in forming an opinion of a man is the reverence in which he holds women. Plato has said, that in this way we rise from sensuality to affection, from affection to love, and from love to the pure intellectual delight by which we become worthy to conceive that infinite in ourselves, without which it is impossible for man to believe in a God. In a word, the grandest and most delightful of all promises has been expressed to us by this practical state – our marriage with the Redeemer of mankind.

I might safely appeal to every man who hears me, who in youth has been accustomed to abandon himself to his animal passions, whether when he first really fell in love, the earliest symptom was not a complete change in his manners, a contempt and a hatred of himself for having excused his conduct by asserting, that he acted according to the dictates of nature, that his vices were the inevitable consequences of youth, and that his passions at that period of life could not be conquered? The surest friend of chastity is love: it leads us, not to sink the mind in the body, but to draw up the body to the mind – the immortal part of our nature. See how contrasted in this respect are some portions of the works of writers, whom I need not name, with other portions of the same works: the ebullitions of comic humour have at times, by a lamentable confusion, been made the means of debasing our nature, while at other times, even in the same volume, we are happy to notice the utmost purity, such as the purity of love, which above all other qualities renders us most pure and lovely.

Love is not, like hunger, a mere selfish appetite: it is an associative quality. The hungry savage is nothing but an animal, thinking only of the satisfaction of his stomach: what is the first effect of love, but to associate the feeling with every object in nature? the trees whisper, the roses exhale their perfumes, the nightingales sing, nay the very skies smile in unison with the feeling of true and pure love. It gives to every object in nature a power of the heart, without which it would indeed be spiritless.

Shakespeare has described this passion in various states and stages beginning, as was most natural, with love in the young. Does he open his play by making Romeo and Juliet in love at first sight – at the first glimpse, as any ordinary thinker would do? Certainly not: he knew what he was about, and how he was to accomplish what he was about: he was to develop the whole passion, and he commences with the first elements – that sense of imperfection, that yearning to combine itself with something lovely. Romeo became enamoured of the idea he had formed in his own mind, and then, as it were, christened the first real being of the contrary sex as endowed with the perfections he desired. He appears to be in love with Rosaline; but, in truth, he is in love only with his own idea. He felt that necessity of being beloved which no noble mind can be without. Then our poet, our poet who so well knew human nature, introduces Romeo to Juliet, and makes it not only a violent, but a permanent love – a point for which Shakespeare has been ridiculed by the ignorant and unthinking. Romeo is first represented in a state most susceptible of love, and then, seeing Juliet, he took and retained the infection.

This brings me to observe upon a characteristic of Shakespeare, which belongs to a man of profound thought and high genius. It has been too much the custom, when anything that happened in his dramas could not easily be explained by the few words the poet has employed, to pass it idly over, and to say that it is beyond our reach, and beyond the power of philosophy – a sort of *terra incognita* for discoverers – a great ocean to be hereafter explored. Others have treated such passages as hints and glimpses of something now non-existent, as the sacred fragments of an ancient and ruined temple, all the portions of which are beautiful, although their particular relation to each other is unknown. Shakespeare knew the human mind, and its most minute and intimate workings, and he never introduces a word, or a thought, in vain or out of place: if we do not understand him, it is our own fault or the fault of copyists and typographers; but study, and the possession of some small stock of the knowledge by which he worked, will enable us often to detect and explain his meaning. He never wrote at random, or hit upon points of character and conduct by chance; and the smallest fragment of his mind not unfrequently gives a clue to a most perfect, regular, and consistent whole.

As I may not have another opportunity, the introduction of Friar Laurence into this tragedy enables me to remark upon the different manner in which Shakespeare has treated the priestly character, as compared with other writers. In Beaumont and Fletcher priests are represented as a vulgar mockery; and, as in others of their dramatic personages, the errors of a few are mistaken for the demeanour of the many: but in Shakespeare they always carry with them our love and respect. He made no injurious abstracts: he took no copies from the worst parts of our nature; and, like the rest, his characters of priests are truly drawn from the general body.

It may strike some as singular, that throughout all his productions he has never introduced the passion of avarice. The truth is, that it belongs only to particular parts of our nature, and is prevalent only in particular states of society; hence it could not, and cannot, be permanent. The Miser of Molière and Plautus is now looked upon as a species of madman, and avarice as a species of madness. Elwes, of whom everybody has heard, was an individual influenced by an insane condition of mind; but, as a passion, avarice has disappeared. How admirably, then, did Shakespeare foresee, that if he drew such a character it could not be permanent! he drew characters which would always be natural, and therefore permanent, inasmuch as they were not dependent upon accidental circumstances.

There is not one of the plays of Shakespeare that is built upon anything but the best and surest foundation; the characters must be permanent – permanent while men continue men, – because they stand upon what is absolutely necessary to our existence. This cannot be said even of some of the most famous authors of antiquity. Take the capital tragedies of Orestes, or of the husband of Jocasta: great as was the genius of the writers, these dramas have an obvious fault, and the fault lies at the very root of the action. In *Oedipus* a man is represented oppressed by fate for a crime of which he was not morally guilty; and while we read we are obliged to say to ourselves, that in those days they considered actions without reference to the real guilt of the persons.

There is no character in Shakespeare in which envy is portrayed, with one solitary exception – Cassius, in *Julius Caesar*; yet even there the vice is not hateful, inasmuch as it is counterbalanced by a number of excellent qualities and virtues. The poet leads the reader to suppose that it is rather something constitutional, something derived from his parents, something that he cannot avoid, and not something that he has himself acquired; thus throwing the blame from the will of man to some inevitable circumstance, and leading us to suppose that it is hardly to be looked upon as one of those passions that actually debase the mind.

Whenever love is described as of a serious nature, and much more when it is to lead to a tragical result, it depends upon a law of the mind, which, I believe, I shall hereafter be able to make intelligible, and which would not only justify Shakespeare, but show an analogy to all his other characters.

Lectures, 1811–12

ROMEO AND JULIET

How beautiful is the close! The spring and the winter meet; – winter assumes the character of spring, and spring the sadness of winter.

From Lectures, 1818

RICHARD II

I HAVE stated that the transitional link between the epic poem and the drama is the historic drama; that in the epic poem a pre-announced fate gradually adjusts and employs the will and the events as its instruments, whilst the drama, on the other hand, places fate and will in opposition to each other, and is then most perfect, when the victory of fate is obtained in consequence of imperfections in the opposing will, so as to leave a final impression that the fate itself is but a higher and a more intelligent will.

From the length of the speeches, and the circumstance that, with one exception, the events are all historical, and presented in their results, not produced by acts seen by, or taking place before, the audience, this tragedy is ill suited to our present large theatres. But in itself, and for the closet, I feel no hesitation in placing it as the first and most admirable of all Shakespeare's purely historical plays. For the two parts of *Henry IV* form a species of themselves, which may be named the mixed drama. The distinction does not depend on the mere quantity of historical events in the play compared with the fictions; for there is as much history in *Macbeth* as in *Richard*, but in the relation of the history to the plot. In the purely historical plays, the history forms the plot: in the mixed, it directs it; in the rest, as *Macbeth*, *Hamlet*, *Cymbeline*, *Lear*, it subserves it. But, however unsuited to the stage this drama may be, God forbid that even there it should fall dead on the hearts of jacobinized Englishmen! Then, indeed, we might say – *praeteriit gloria mundi!* For the spirit of patriotic reminiscence is the all-permeating soul of this noble work. It is, perhaps, the most purely historical of Shakespeare's dramas. There are not in it, as in the others, characters introduced merely for the purpose of giving a greater individuality and realness, as in the comic parts of *Henry IV*, by presenting, as it were, our very selves. Shakespeare avails himself of every opportunity to effect the great object of the historic drama, that, namely, of familiarizing the people to the great names of their country, and thereby of exciting a steady patriotism, a love of just liberty, and a respect for all those fundamental institutions of social life, which bind men together:

> This royal throne of kings, this scepter'd isle,
> This earth of majesty, this seat of Mars,
> This other Eden, demi-paradise;
> This fortress, built by nature for herself,
> Against infection, and the hand of war;
> This happy breed of men, this little world;
> This precious stone set in the silver sea,
> Which serves it in the office of a wall,
> Or as a moat defensive to a house,
> Against the envy of less happier lands;
> This blessed plot, this earth, this realm, this England,
> This nurse, this teeming womb of royal kings,
> Fear'd by their breed, and famous by their birth, &c.

Add the famous passage in *King John:*

> This England never did, nor ever shall,
> Lie at the proud foot of a conqueror,
> But when it first did help to wound itself.
> Now these her princes are come home again,
> Come the three corners of the world in arms,
> And we shall shock them: nought shall make us rue,
> If England to itself do rest but true.

And it certainly seems that Shakespeare's historic dramas produced a very deep effect on the minds of the English people, and in earlier times they were familiar even to the least informed of all ranks, according to the relation of Bishop Corbett. Marlborough, we know, was not ashamed to confess that his principal acquaintance with English history was derived from them; and I believe that a large part of the information as to our old names and achievements even now abroad is due, directly or indirectly, to Shakespeare.

Admirable is the judgement with which Shakespeare always in the first scenes prepares, yet how naturally, and with what concealment of art, for the catastrophe. Observe how he here presents the germ of all the after events in Richard's insincerity, partiality, arbitrariness, and favouritism, and in the proud, tempestuous, temperament of his barons. In the very beginning, also, is displayed that feature in Richard's character, which is never forgotten throughout the play – his attention to decorum, and high feeling of the kingly dignity. These anticipations show with what judgement Shakespeare wrote, and illustrate his care to connect the past and future, and unify them with the present by forecast and reminiscence. . . .

Ib. sc. 2.

> GAUNT. Heaven's is the quarrel; for heaven's substitute,
> His deputy anointed in his right,
> Hath caused his death: the which, if wrongfully,
> Let heaven revenge; for I may never lift
> An angry arm against his minister.

Without the hollow extravagance of Beaumont and Fletcher's ultra-royalism, how carefully does Shakespeare acknowledge and reverence the eternal distinction between the mere individual, and the symbolic or representative, on which all genial law, no less than patriotism, depends. The whole of this second scene commences, and is anticipative of, the tone and character of the play at large. . . .

Ib. sc. 4. This is a striking conclusion of a first act, – letting the reader into the secret; – having before impressed us with the dignified and kingly manners of Richard, yet by well managed anticipations leading us on to the full gratification of pleasure in our own penetration. In this scene a new light is thrown on Richard's character. Until now he has appeared in all the beauty of royalty; but here, as soon as he is left to himself, the inherent weakness of his character is immediately known. It is a weakness, however, of a peculiar kind, not arising from want of personal courage, or any specific defect of faculty, but rather an intellectual feminineness, which feels a necessity of ever leaning on the breast of others, and of reclining on those who are all the while known to be inferiors. To this must be attributed as its consequences all Richard's vices, his tendency to concealment, and his cunning, the whole operation of which is directed to the getting rid of present difficulties. Richard is not meant to be a debauchee: but we see in him that sophistry which is common to man, by which we can deceive our own hearts, and at one and the same time apologize for, and yet commit, the error. Shakespeare has represented this character in a very peculiar manner. He has not made him amiable with counterbalancing faults; but has openly and broadly drawn those faults without reserve, relying on Richard's disproportionate sufferings and gradually emergent good qualities for our sympathy; and this was possible, because his faults are not positive vices, but spring entirely from defect of character. . . .

Ib. sc. 2.

> QUEEN. To please the king I did; to please myself
> I cannot do it; yet I know no cause
> Why I should welcome such a guest as grief,
> Save bidding farewell to so sweet a guest
> As my sweet Richard: yet again, methinks,
> Some unborn sorrow, ripe in sorrow's womb,
> Is coming toward me; and my inward soul
> With nothing trembles: at something it grieves,
> More than with parting from my lord the king.

It is clear that Shakespeare never meant to represent Richard as a vulgar debauchee, but a man with a wantonness of spirit in external show, a feminine *friendism*, an intensity of woman-like love of those immediately about him, and a mistaking of the delight of being loved by him for a love of him. And mark in this scene Shakespeare's gentleness in touching the tender superstitions, the *terrae incognitae* of presentiments, in the human mind: and how sharp a line of distinction he commonly draws between these obscure forecastings of general experience in each individual, and the vulgar errors of mere tradition. Indeed, it may be taken once for all as the truth, that Shakespeare, in the absolute universality of his genius, always reverences whatever arises out of our moral nature; he never profanes his muse with a contemptuous reasoning away of the genuine and general, however unaccountable, feelings of mankind.

The amiable part of Richard's character is brought full upon us by his queen's few words –

> . . . so sweet a guest
> As my sweet Richard; –

and Shakespeare has carefully shown in him an intense love of his country, well knowing how that feeling would, in a pure historic drama, redeem him in the hearts of the audience. Yet even in this love there is something feminine and personal:

> Dear earth, I do salute thee with my hand, –
> As a long parted mother with her child
> Plays fondly with her tears, and smiles in meeting;
> So weeping, smiling, greet I thee, my earth,
> And do thee favour with my royal hands.

With this is combined a constant overflow of emotions from a total incapability of controlling them, and thence a waste of that energy, which should have been reserved for actions, in the passion and effort of mere resolves and menaces. The consequence is moral exhaustion, and rapid alternations of unmanly despair and ungrounded hope, – every feeling being abandoned for its direct opposite upon the pressure of external accident. And yet when Richard's inward weakness appears to seek refuge in his despair, and his exhaustion counterfeits repose, the old habit of kingliness, the effect of flatterers from his infancy, is ever and anon producing in him a sort of wordy courage which only serves to betray more clearly his internal impotence. The second and third scenes of the third act combine and illustrate all this. . . .

I would once more remark upon the exalted idea of the only true loyalty developed in this noble and impressive play. We have neither the rants of Beaumont and Fletcher, nor the sneers of Massinger; – the vast importance of the personal character of the sovereign is distinctly enounced, whilst, at the same time, the genuine sanctity which surrounds him is attributed to, and grounded on, the position in which he stands as the convergence and exponent of the life and power of the state.

The great end of the body politic appears to be to humanize, and assist in the progressiveness of, the animal man; – but the problem is so complicated with contingencies as to render it nearly impossible to lay down rules for the formation of a state. And should we be able to form a system of government, which should so balance its different powers as to form a check upon each, and so continually remedy and correct itself, it would, nevertheless, defeat its own aim; – for man is destined to be guided by higher principles, by universal views, which can never be fulfilled in this state of existence, – by a spirit of progressiveness which can never be accomplished, for then it would cease to be. Plato's *Republic* is like Bunyan's Town of Man-Soul, – a description of an individual, all of whose faculties are in their proper subordination and inter-dependence; and this it is assumed may be the prototype of the state as one great individual. But there is this sophism in it, that it is forgotten that the human faculties, indeed, are parts and not separate things; but that you could never get chiefs who were wholly reason, ministers who were wholly understanding, soldiers all wrath, labourers all concupiscence, and so on through the rest. Each of these partakes of, and interferes with, all the others.

Lectures, 1818

THE TEMPEST

The Tempest is a specimen of the purely romantic drama, in which the interest is not historical, or dependent upon fidelity of portraiture, or the natural connection of events, – but is a birth of the imagination, and rests only on the coaptation and union of the elements granted to, or assumed by, the poet. It is a species of drama which owes no allegiance to time or space, and in which, therefore, errors of chronology and geography – no mortal sins in any species – are venial faults, and count for nothing. It addresses itself entirely to the imaginative faculty; and although the illusion may be assisted by the effect on the senses of the complicated scenery and decorations of modern times, yet this sort of assistance is dangerous. For the principal and only genuine excitement ought to come from within, – from the moved and sympathetic imagination; whereas, where so much is addressed to the mere external senses of seeing and hearing, the spiritual vision is apt to languish, and the attraction from without will withdraw the mind from the proper and only legitimate interest which is intended to spring from within.

The romance opens with a busy scene admirably appropriate to the kind of drama, and giving, as it were, the keynote to the whole harmony. It prepares and initiates the excitement required for the entire piece, and yet does not demand anything from the spectators, which their previous habits had not fitted them to understand. It is the bustle of a tempest, from which the real horrors are abstracted; – therefore it is poetical, though not in strictness natural – (the distinction to which I have so often alluded) – and is purposely restrained from concentering the interest on itself, but used merely as an induction or tuning for what is to follow.

In the second scene, Prospero's speeches, till the entrance of Ariel, contain the finest example I remember of retrospective narration for the purpose of exciting immediate interest, and putting the audience in possession of all the information necessary for the understanding of the plot. Observe, too, the perfect probability of the moment chosen by Prospero (the very Shakespeare himself, as it were, of the tempest) to open out the truth to his daughter, his own romantic bearing, and how completely anything that might have been disagreeable to us in the magician, is reconciled and shaded in the humanity and natural feelings of the father. In the very first speech of Miranda the simplicity and tenderness of her character are at once laid open; it would have been lost in direct contact with the agitation of the first scene. The opinion once prevailed, but, happily, is now abandoned, that Fletcher alone wrote for women; – the truth is, that with very few, and those partial, exceptions, the female characters in the plays of Beaumont and Fletcher are, when of the light kind, not decent; when heroic, complete viragos. But in Shakespeare all the elements of womanhood are holy, and there is the sweet, yet dignified feeling of all that *continuates* society, as sense of ancestry and of sex, with a purity unassailable by sophistry, because it rests not in the analytic processes, but in that sane equipoise of the faculties, during which the feelings are representative of all past experience, – not of the individual only, but of all those by whom she has been educated, and their predecessors even up to the first mother that lived. Shakespeare saw that the want of prominence, which Pope notices for sarcasm, was the blessed beauty of the woman's character, and knew that it arose not from any deficiency, but from the more exquisite harmony of all the parts of the moral being constituting one living total of head and heart. He has drawn it, indeed, in all its distinctive energies of faith, patience, constancy, fortitude, – shown in all of them as following the heart, which gives its results by a nice tact and happy intuition, without the intervention of the discursive faculty, – sees all things in and by the light of the affections, and errs, if it ever err, in the exaggerations of love alone. In all the Shakespearian women there is essentially the same foundation and principle; the distinct individuality and variety are merely the result of the modification of circumstances, whether in Miranda the maiden, in Imogen the wife, or in Katharine the queen. . . .

In this play are admirably sketched the vices generally accompanying a low degree of civilization; and in the first scene of the second act Shakespeare has, as in many other places, shown the tendency in bad men to indulge in scorn and contemptuous expressions, as a mode of getting rid of their own uneasy feelings of inferiority to the good, and also, by making the good ridiculous, of rendering the transition of others to wickedness easy. Shakespeare never puts habitual scorn into the mouths of other than bad men, as here in the instances of Antonio and Sebastian. The scene of the intended assassination of Alonzo and Gonzalo is the exact counterpart of the scene between Macbeth and his lady, only pitched in a lower key throughout, as designed to be frustrated and concealed, and exhibiting the same profound management in the manner of familiarizing a mind, not immediately recipient, to the suggestion of guilt, by associating the proposed crime with something ludicrous or out of place, – something not habitually matter of reverence. By this kind of sophistry the imagination and fancy are first bribed to contemplate the suggested act, and at length to become acquainted with it. Observe how the effect of this scene is heightened by contrast with another counterpart of it in low life, – that between the conspirators Stephano, Caliban, and Trinculo in the second scene of the third act, in which there are the same essential characteristics.

In this play and in this scene of it are also shown the springs of the vulgar in politics, – of that kind of politics which is inwoven with human nature. In his treatment of this subject, wherever it occurs, Shakespeare is quite peculiar. In other writers we find the particular opinions of the individual; in Massinger it is rank republicanism; in Beaumont and Fletcher even *jure divino* principles are carried to excess; – but Shakespeare never promulgates any party tenets. He is always the philosopher and the moralist, but at the same time with a profound veneration for all the established institutions of society, and for those classes which form the permanent elements of the state – especially never introducing a professional character, as such, otherwise than as respectable. If he must have any name, he should be styled a philosophical aristocrat, delighting in those hereditary institutions which have a tendency to bind one age to another, and in that distinction of ranks, of which, although few may be in possession, all enjoy the advantages. Hence, again, you will observe the good nature with which he seems always to make sport with the passions and follies of a mob, as with an irrational animal. He is never angry with it, but hugely content with holding up its absurdities to its face; and sometimes you may trace a tone of almost affectionate superiority, something like that in which a father speaks of the rogueries of a child. See the good-humoured way in which he describes Stephano passing from the most licentious freedom to absolute despotism over Trinculo and Caliban. The truth is, Shakespeare's characters are all *genera* intensely individualized; the results of meditation, of which observation supplied the drapery and the colours necessary to combine them with each other. He had virtually surveyed all the great component powers and impulses of human nature, – had seen that their different combinations and subordinations were in fact the individualizers of men, and showed how their harmony was produced by reciprocal disproportions of excess or deficiency. The language in which these truths are expressed was not drawn from any set fashion, but from the profoundest depths of his moral being, and is therefore for all ages.

If a doubt could ever be entertained whether Shakespeare was a great poet, acting upon laws arising out of his own nature, and not without law, as has sometimes been idly asserted, that doubt must be removed by the character of Ariel. The very first words uttered by this being introduce the spirit, not as an angel, above man; not a gnome, or a fiend, below man; but while the poet gives him the faculties and the advantages of reason, he divests him of all mortal character, not positively, it is true, but negatively. In air he lives, from air he derives his being, in air he acts; and all his colours and properties seem to have been obtained from the rainbow and the skies. There is nothing about Ariel that cannot be conceived to exist either at sunrise or sunset: hence all that belongs to Ariel belongs to the delight the mind is capable of receiving from the most lovely external appearances. His answers to Prospero are directly to the question, and nothing beyond; or where he expatiates, which is not unfrequently, it is to himself and upon his own delights, or upon the unnatural situation in which he is placed, though under a kindly power and to good ends.

Shakespeare has properly made Ariel's very first speech characteristic of him. After he has described the manner in which he had raised the storm and produced its harmless consequences, we find that Ariel is discontented – that he had been freed, it is true, from a cruel confinement, but still that he is bound to obey Prospero, and to execute any commands imposed upon him. We feel that such a state of bondage is almost unnatural to him, yet we see that it is delightful for him to be so employed. – It is as if we were to command one of the winds in a different direction to that which nature dictates, or one of the waves, now rising and now sinking, to recede before it bursts upon the shore: such is the feeling we experience, when we learn that a being like Ariel is commanded to fulfil any mortal behest.

When, however, Shakespeare contrasts the treatment of Ariel by Prospero with that of Sycorax, we are sensible that the liberated spirit ought to be grateful, and Ariel does feel and acknowledge the obligation; he immediately assumes the airy being, with a mind so elastically correspondent, that when once a feeling has passed from it, not a trace is left behind.

Is there anything in nature from which Shakespeare caught the idea of this delicate and delightful being, with such child-like simplicity, yet with such preternatural powers? He is neither born of heaven, nor of earth; but, as it were, between both, like a May-blossom kept suspended in air by the fanning breeze, which prevents it from falling to the ground, and only finally, and by compulsion, touching earth. This reluctance of the Sylph to be under the command even of Prospero is kept up through the whole play, and in the exercise of his admirable judgement Shakespeare has availed himself of it, in order to give Ariel an interest in the event, looking forward to that moment when he was to gain his last and only reward – simple and eternal liberty.

Another instance of admirable judgement and excellent preparation is to be found in the creature contrasted with Ariel – Caliban; who is described in such a manner by Prospero, as to lead us to expect the appearance of a foul, unnatural monster. He is not seen at once: his voice is heard; this is the preparation: he was too offensive to be seen first in all his deformity, and in nature we do not receive so much disgust from sound as from sight. After we have heard Caliban's voice he does not enter, until Ariel has entered like a water-nymph. All the strength of contrast is thus acquired without any of the shock of abruptness, or of that unpleasant sensation, which we experience when the object presented is in any way hateful to our vision.

The character of Caliban is wonderfully conceived: he is a sort of creature of the earth, as Ariel is a sort of creature of the air. He partakes of the qualities of the brute, but is distinguished from brutes in two ways: – by having mere understanding without moral reason; and by not possessing the instincts which pertain to absolute animals. Still, Caliban is in some respects a noble being: the poet has raised him far above contempt: he is a man in the sense of the imagination: all the images he uses are drawn from nature, and are highly poetical; they fit in with the images of Ariel. Caliban gives us images from the earth, Ariel images from the air. Caliban talks of the difficulty of finding fresh water, of the situation of morasses, and of other circumstances which even brute instinct, without reason, could comprehend. No mean figure is employed, no mean passion displayed, beyond animal passion, and repugnance to command. . . .

Many, indeed innumerable, beautiful passages might be quoted from this play, independently of the astonishing scheme of its construction. Everybody will call to mind the grandeur of the language of Prospero in that divine speech, where he takes leave of his magic art; and were I to indulge myself by repetitions of the kind, I should descend from the character of a lecturer to that of a mere reciter. Before I terminate, I may particularly recall one short passage, which has fallen under the very severe, but inconsiderate, censure of Pope and Arbuthnot, who pronounce it a piece of the grossest bombast. Prospero thus addresses his daughter, directing her attention to Ferdinand:

> The fringed curtains of thine eye advance,
> And say what thou seest yond.

Act I, Scene 2

Taking these words as a periphrase of – 'Look what is coming yonder', it certainly may to some appear to border on the ridiculous, and to fall under the rule I formerly laid down, – that whatever, without injury, can be translated into a foreign language in simple terms, ought to be in simple terms in the original language; but it is to be borne in mind, that different modes of expression frequently arise from difference of situation and education: a blackguard would use very different words, to express the same thing, to those a gentleman would employ, yet both would be natural and proper; difference of feeling gives rise to difference of language: a gentleman speaks in polished terms, with due regard to his own rank and position, while a blackguard, a person little better than half a brute, speaks like half a brute, showing no respect for himself, nor for others.

But I am content to try the lines I have just quoted by the introduction to them; and then, I think, you will admit, that nothing could be more fit and appropriate than such language. How does Prospero introduce them? He has just told Miranda a wonderful story, which deeply affected her, and filled her with surprise and astonishment, and for his own purposes he afterwards lulls her to sleep. When she awakes, Shakespeare has made her wholly inattentive to the present, but wrapped up in the past. An actress, who understands the character of Miranda, would have her eyes cast down, and her eyelids almost covering them, while she was, as it were, living in her dream. At this moment Prospero sees Ferdinand, and wishes to point him out to his daughter, not only with great, but with scenic solemnity, he standing before her, and before the spectator, in the dignified character of a great magician. Something was to appear to Miranda on the sudden, and as unexpectedly as if the hero of a drama were to be on the stage at the instant when the curtain is elevated. It is under such circumstances that Prospero says, in a tone calculated at once to arouse his daughter's attention,

> The fringed curtains of thine eye advance,
> And say what thou seest yond.

Turning from the sight of Ferdinand to his thoughtful daughter, his attention was first struck by the downcast appearance of her eyes and eyelids; and, in my humble opinion, the solemnity of the phraseology assigned to Prospero is completely in character, recollecting his preternatural capacity, in which the most familiar objects in nature present themselves in a mysterious point of view. It is much easier to find fault with a writer by reference to former notions and experience, than to sit down and read him, recollecting his purpose, connecting one feeling with another, and judging of his words and phrases, in proportion as they convey the sentiments of the persons represented. . . .

Lectures, 1818

TROILUS AND CRESSIDA

. . . INDEED, there is no one of Shakespeare's plays harder to characterize. The name and the remembrances connected with it, prepare us for the representation of attachment no less faithful than fervent on the side of the youth, and of sudden and shameless inconstancy on the part of the lady. And this is, indeed, as the gold thread on which the scenes are strung, though often kept out of sight and out of mind by gems of greater value than itself. But as Shakespeare calls forth nothing from the mausoleum of history, or the catacombs of tradition, without giving, or eliciting, some permanent and general interest, and brings forward no subject which he does not moralize or intellectualize, – so here he has drawn in Cressida the portrait of a vehement passion, that, having its true origin and proper cause in warmth of temperament, fastens on, rather than fixes to, some one object by liking and temporary preference.

> There's language in her eye, her cheek, her lip,
> Nay, her foot speaks; her wanton spirits look out
> At every joint and motive of her body.

This Shakespeare has contrasted with the profound affection represented in Troilus, and alone worthy the name of love; – affection, passionate indeed, – swoln with the confluence of youthful instincts and youthful fancy, and growing in the radiance of hope newly risen, in short enlarged by the collective sympathies of nature; – but still having a depth of calmer element in a will stronger than desire, more entire than choice, and which gives permanence to its own act by converting it into faith and duty. Hence with excellent judgement, and with an excellence higher than mere judgement can give, at the close of the play, when Cressida has sunk into infamy below retrieval and beneath hope, the same will, which had been the substance and the basis of his love, while the restless pleasures and passionate longings, like sea-waves, had tossed but on its surface, – this same moral energy is represented as snatching him aloof from all neighbourhood with her dishonour, from all lingering fondness and languishing regrets, whilst it rushes with him into other and nobler duties, and deepens the channel, which his heroic brother's death had left empty for its collected flood. Yet another secondary and subordinate purpose Shakespeare has inwoven with his delineation of these two characters, – that of opposing the inferior civilization, but purer morals, of the Trojans to the refinements, deep policy, but duplicity and sensual corruptions, of the Greeks.

To all this, however, so little comparative projection is given, – nay the masterly group of Agamemnon, Nestor, and Ulysses, and, still more in advance, that of Achilles, Ajax, and Thersites, so manifestly occupy the foreground, that the subservience and vassalage of strength and animal courage to intellect and policy seems to be the lesson most often in our poet's view, and which he has taken little pains to connect with the former more interesting moral impersonated in the titular hero and heroine of the drama. But I am half inclined to believe, that Shakespeare's main object, or shall I rather say, his ruling impulse, was to translate the poetic heroes of paganism into the not less rude, but more intellectually vigorous, and more *featurely*, warriors of Christian chivalry, – and to substantiate the distinct and graceful profiles or outlines of the Homeric epic into the flesh and blood of the romantic drama, – in short, to give a grand history-piece in the robust style of Albert Dürer.

The character of Thersites, in particular, well deserves a more careful examination, as the Caliban of demagogic life; – the admirable portrait of intellectual power deserted by all grace, all moral principle, all not momentary impulse; – just wise enough to detect the weak head, and fool enough to provoke the armed fist of his betters; – one whom malcontent Achilles can inveigle from malcontent Ajax, under the one condition, that he shall be called on to do nothing but abuse and slander, and that he shall be allowed to abuse as much and as purulently as he likes, that is, as he can; – in short, a mule, – quarrelsome by the original discord of his nature, – a slave by tenure of his own baseness, – made to bray and be brayed at, to despise and be despicable. 'Aye, sir, but say what you will, he is a very clever fellow, though the best friends will fall out. There was a time when Ajax thought he deserved to have a statue of gold erected to him, and handsome Achilles, at the head of the Myrmidons, gave no little credit to his *friend Thersites*!'

Lectures, 1818

A MIDSUMMER NIGHT'S DREAM

. Act ii, sc. 1. Theobald's edition.

> *Through* bush, *through* briar –
> . . .
> *Through* flood, *through* fire –

What a noble pair of ears this worthy Theobald must have had! The eight amphimacers or cretics,

> Ovĕr hĭll, ōvĕr dāle,
> Thōrŏ' būsh, thōrŏ' brīar,
> Ovĕr pārk, ōvĕr pāle,
> Thōrŏ' flood, thōrŏ' fīre –

have a delightful effect on the ear in their sweet transition to the trochaic,

> Ĭ dŏ wănděr ēv'ry wherĕ
> Swĭftěr thăn thĕ mōōnĕs sphērĕ, &c.

The last words as sustaining the rhyme, must be considered, as in fact they are, trochees in time.

It may be worth while to give some correct examples in English of the principal metrical feet:

PYRRHIC or DIBRACH, ◡ ◡ = bŏdў, spĭrĭt.
TRIBRACH, ◡ ◡ ◡ = nŏbŏdў, *hastily pronounced.*
IAMBUS ◡ — = dĕlīght.
TROCHEE, — ◡ = līghtlў.
SPONDEE, — — = Gōd spāke.

The paucity of spondees in single words in English and, indeed, in the modern languages in general, makes, perhaps, the greatest distinction, metrically considered, between them and the Greek and Latin.

DACTYL, — ◡ ◡ = mērrĭlў.
ANAPAEST, ◡ ◡ — = ă prŏpōs, *or the first three syllables of*
cĕrĕmōny.
AMPHIBRACHYS, ◡ — ◡ = dĕlīghtfŭl.
AMPHIMACER, — ◡ — = ōvĕr hĭll.
ANTIBACCHIUS, ◡ — — = thĕ Lōrd Gōd.
BACCHIUS, — — ◡ = Hĕlvēllўn.
MOLOSSUS, — — — = Jōhn Jāmes Jōnes.

These simple feet may suffice for understanding the metres of Shakespeare, for the greater part at least;—but Milton cannot be made harmoniously intelligible without the composite feet, the Ionics, Paeons, and Epitrites. . . .

Ib. sc. 2.

> PUCK. Now the hungry lion roars,
> And the wolf behowls the moon;
> Whilst the heavy ploughman snores
> All with weary task foredone, &c.

Very Anacreon in perfectness, proportion, grace, and spontaneity! So far it is Greek;—but then add, O! what wealth, what wild ranging, and yet what compression and condensation of, English fancy! In truth, there is nothing in Anacreon more perfect than these thirty lines, or half so rich and imaginative. They form a speckless diamond.

HAMLET

THE seeming inconsistencies in the conduct and character of Hamlet have long exercised the conjectural ingenuity of critics; and, as we are always loth to suppose that the cause of defective apprehension is in ourselves, the mystery has been too commonly explained by the very easy process of setting it down as in fact inexplicable, and by resolving the phenomenon into a misgrowth or *lusus* of the capricious and irregular genius of Shakespeare. The shallow and stupid arrogance of these vulgar and indolent decisions I would fain do my best to expose. I believe the character of Hamlet may be traced to Shakespeare's deep and accurate science in mental philosophy. Indeed, that this character must have some connection with the common fundamental laws of our nature may be assumed from the fact, that Hamlet has been the darling of every country in which the literature of England has been fostered. In order to understand him, it is essential that we should reflect on the constitution of our own minds. Man is distinguished from the brute animals in proportion as thought prevails over sense: but in the healthy processes of the mind, a balance is constantly maintained between the impressions from outward objects and the inward operations of the intellect; – for if there be an overbalance in the contemplative faculty, man thereby becomes the creature of mere meditation, and loses his natural power of action. Now one of Shakespeare's modes of creating characters is, to conceive any one intellectual or moral faculty in morbid excess, and then to place himself, Shakespeare, thus mutilated or diseased, under given circumstances. In Hamlet he seems to have wished to exemplify the moral necessity of a due balance between our attention to the objects of our senses, and our meditation on the workings of our minds, – an *equilibrium* between the real and the imaginary worlds. In Hamlet this balance is disturbed: his thoughts, and the images of his fancy, are far more vivid than his actual perceptions, and his very perceptions, instantly passing through the *medium* of his contemplations, acquire, as they pass, a form and a colour not naturally their own. Hence we see a great, an almost enormous, intellectual activity, and a proportionate aversion to real action consequent upon it, with all its symptoms and accompanying qualities. This character Shakespeare places in circumstances, under which it is obliged to act on the spur of the moment: – Hamlet is brave and careless of death; but he vacillates from sensibility, and procrastinates from thought, and loses the power of action in the energy of resolve.

Thus it is that this tragedy presents a direct contrast to that of *Macbeth*; the one proceeds with the utmost slowness, the other with a crowded and breathless rapidity.

The effect of this overbalance of the imaginative power is beautifully illustrated in the everlasting broodings and superfluous activities of Hamlet's mind, which, unseated from its healthy relation, is constantly occupied with the world within, and abstracted from the world without, – giving substance to shadows, and throwing a mist over all common-place actualities. It is the nature of thought to be indefinite; – definiteness belongs to external imagery alone. Hence it is that the sense of sublimity arises, not from the sight of an outward object, but from the beholder's reflection upon it; – not from the sensuous impression, but from the imaginative reflex. Few have seen a celebrated waterfall without feeling something akin to disappointment: it is only subsequently that the image comes back full into the mind, and brings with it a train of grand or beautiful associations. Hamlet feels this; his senses are in a state of trance, and he looks upon external things as hieroglyphics. His soliloquy –

> O! that this too too solid flesh would melt, &c.

springs from that craving after the indefinite – for that which is not – which most easily besets men of genius; and the self-delusion common to this temper of mind is finely exemplified in the character which Hamlet gives of himself:

> It cannot be
> But I am pigeon-liver'd, and lack gall
> To make oppression bitter.

He mistakes the seeing his chains for the breaking them, delays action till action is of no use, and dies the victim of mere circumstance and accident. . . .

Compare the easy language of common life, in which this drama commences, with the direful music and wild wayward rhythm and abrupt lyrics of the opening of *Macbeth*. The tone is quite familiar; – there is no poetic description of night, no elaborate information conveyed by one speaker to another of what both had immediately before their senses – (such as the first distich in Addison's 'Cato', which is a translation into poetry of 'Past four o'clock and a dark morning!'); – and yet nothing bordering on the comic on the one hand, nor any striving of the intellect on the other. It is precisely the language of sensation among men who feared no charge of effeminacy, for feeling what they had no want of resolution to bear. Yet the armour, the dead silence, the watchfulness that first interrupts it, the welcome relief of the guard, the cold, the broken expressions of compelled attention to bodily feelings still under control – all excellently accord with, and prepare for, the after gradual rise into tragedy; – but, above all, into a tragedy, the interest of which is as eminently *ad et apud intra*, as that of *Macbeth* is directly *ad extra*.

In all the best attested stories of ghosts and visions, as in that of Brutus, of Archbishop Cranmer, that of Benvenuto Cellini recorded by himself, and the vision of Galileo communicated by him to his favourite pupil Torricelli, the ghost-seers were in a state of cold or chilling damp from without, and of anxiety inwardly. It has been with all of them as with Francisco on his guard, – alone, in the depth and silence of the night; – ''twas bitter cold, and they were sick at heart, and *not a mouse stirring*'. The attention to minute sounds, – naturally associated with the recollection of minute objects, and the more familiar and trifling, the more impressive from the unusualness of their producing any impression at all – gives a philosophic pertinency to this last image; but it has likewise its dramatic use and purpose. For its commonness in ordinary conversation tends to produce the sense of reality, and at once hides the poet, and yet approximates the reader or spectator to that state in which the highest poetry will appear, and in its component parts, though not in the whole composition, really is, the language of nature. If I should not speak it, I feel that I should be thinking it; – the voice only is the poet's, – the words are my own. That Shakespeare meant to put an effect in the actor's power in the very first words – 'Who's there?' – is evident from the impatience expressed by the startled Francisco in the words that follow – 'Nay, answer me: stand and unfold yourself.' A brave man is never so peremptory, as when he fears that he is afraid. Observe the gradual transition from the silence and the still recent habit of listening in Francisco's – 'I think I hear them' – to the more cheerful call out, which a good actor would observe, in the – 'Stand ho! Who is there?' Bernardo's inquiry after Horatio, and the repetition of his name and in his own presence, indicate a respect or an eagerness that implies him as one of the persons who are in the foreground; and the scepticism attributed to him,

> Horatio says, 'tis but our fantasy;
> And will not let belief take hold of him –

prepares us for Hamlet's after eulogy on him as one whose blood and judgement were happily commingled. The actor should also be careful to distinguish the expectation and gladness of Bernardo's 'Welcome, Horatio!' from the mere courtesy of his 'Welcome, good Marcellus!'

Now observe the admirable indefiniteness of the first opening out of the occasion of all this anxiety. The preparation informative of the audience is just as much as was precisely necessary, and no more; – it begins with the uncertainty appertaining to a question:

MARCELLUS. What, has *this thing* appear'd again to-night? –

Even the word 'again' has its *credibilizing* effect. Then Horatio, the representative of the ignorance of the audience, not himself, but by Marcellus to Bernardo, anticipates the common solution – ''tis but our fantasy!' upon which Marcellus rises into

This dreaded sight, twice seen of us –

which immediately afterwards becomes 'this apparition', and that, too, an intelligent spirit, that is, to be spoken to! Then comes the confirmation of Horatio's disbelief;

Tush! tush! 'twill not appear! –

and the silence, with which the scene opened, is again restored in the shivering feeling of Horatio sitting down, at such a time, and with the two eye-witnesses, to hear a story of a ghost, and that, too, of a ghost which had appeared twice before at the very same hour. In the deep feeling which Bernardo has of the solemn nature of what he is about to relate, he makes an effort to master his own imaginative terrors by an elevation of style, – itself a continuation of the effort, – and by turning off from the apparition, as from something which would force him too deeply into himself, to the outward objects, the realities of nature, which had accompanied it:

BERNADO. Last night of all,
　　When yon same star, that's westward from the pole,
　　Had made his course to illume that part of heaven
　　Where now it burns, Marcellus and myself,
　　The bell then beating one – –

This passage seems to contradict the critical law that what is told, makes a faint impression compared with what is beholden; for it does indeed convey to the mind more than the eye can see; whilst the interruption of the narrative at the very moment, when we are most intensely listening for the sequel, and have our thoughts diverted from the dreaded sight in expectation of the desired, yet almost dreaded, tale – this gives all the suddenness and surprise of the original appearance;

MARCELLUS. Peace, break thee off; look, where it comes again! –

Note the judgement displayed in having the two persons present, who, as having seen the Ghost before, are naturally eager in confirming their former opinions, – whilst the sceptic is silent, and after having been twice addressed by his friends, answers with two hasty syllables – 'Most like', – and a confession of horror:

– It harrows me with fear and wonder.

O heaven! words are wasted on those who feel, and to those who do not feel the exquisite judgement of Shakespeare in this scene, what can be said? – Hume himself could not but have had faith in this Ghost dramatically, let his anti-ghostism have been as strong as Samson against other ghosts less powerfully raised.

Act i, sc. 1.

MARCELLUS. Good now, sit down, and tell me, he that knows,
    Why this same strict and most observant watch, &c.

How delightfully natural is the transition to the retrospective narrative! And observe, upon the Ghost's reappearance, how much Horatio's courage is increased by having translated the late individual spectator into general thought and past experience, – and the sympathy of Marcellus and Bernardo with his patriotic surmises in daring to strike at the Ghost; whilst in a moment, upon its vanishing, the former solemn awe-stricken feeling returns upon them:

We do it wrong, being so majestical,
To offer it the show of violence. –

Ib. Horatio's speech:
                I have heard,
The cock, that is the trumpet to the morn,
Doth with his lofty and shrill-sounding throat
Awake the god of day, &c.

No Addison could be more careful to be poetical in diction than Shakespeare in providing the grounds and sources of its propriety. But how to elevate a thing almost mean by its familiarity, young poets may learn in this treatment of the cock-crow.

Ib.

HAMLET. A little more than kin, and less than kind.
KING. How is it that the clouds still hang on you?
HAMLET. Not so, my lord, I am too much i' the sun.

Hamlet opens his mouth with a playing on words, the complete absence of which throughout characterizes *Macbeth*. This playing on words may be attributed to many causes or motives, as either to an exuberant activity of mind, as in the higher comedy of Shakespeare generally; – or to an imitation of it as a mere fashion, as if it were said – 'Is not this better than groaning?' – or to a contemptuous exultation in minds vulgarized and overset by their success, as in the poetic instance of Milton's Devils in the battle; – or it is the language of resentment, as is familiar to every one who has witnessed the quarrels of the lower orders, where there is invariably a profusion of punning invective, whence, perhaps, nicknames have in a considerable degree sprung up; – or it is the language of suppressed passion, and especially of a hardly smothered personal dislike. The first, and last of these combine in Hamlet's case; and I have little doubt that Farmer is right in supposing the equivocation carried on in the expression 'too much i' the sun', or son. . . .

Ib. sc. 4. The unimportant conversation with which this scene opens is a proof of Shakespeare's minute knowledge of human nature. It is a well established fact, that on the brink of any serious enterprise, or event of moment, men almost invariably endeavour to elude the pressure of their own thoughts by turning aside to trivial objects and familiar circumstances: thus this dialogue on the platform begins with remarks on the coldness of the air, and inquiries, obliquely connected, indeed, with the expected hour of the visitation, but thrown out in a seeming vacuity of topics, as to the striking of the clock and so forth. The same desire to escape from the impending thought is carried on in Hamlet's account of, and moralizing on, the Danish custom of wassailing: he runs off from the particular to the universal, and, in his repugnance to personal and individual concerns, escapes, as it were, from himself in generalizations, and smothers the impatience and uneasy feelings of the moment in abstract reasoning. Besides this, another purpose is answered; – for by thus entangling the attention of the audience in the nice distinctions and parenthetical sentences of this speech of Hamlet's, Shakespeare takes them completely by surprise on the appearance of the Ghost, which comes upon them in all the suddenness of its visionary character. Indeed, no modern writer would have dared, like Shakespeare, to have preceded this last vistation by two distinct appearances, – or could have contrived that the third should rise upon the former two in impressiveness and solemnity of interest.

But in addition to all the other excellencies of Hamlet's speech concerning the wassail-music – so finely revealing the predominant idealism, the ratiocinative meditativeness, of his character – it has the advantage of giving nature and probability to the impassioned continuity of the speech instantly directed to the Ghost. The *momentum* had been given to his mental activity; the full current of the thoughts and words had set in, and the very forgetfulness, in the fervour of his argumentation, of the purpose for which he was there, aided in preventing the appearance from benumbing the mind. Consequently, it acted as a new impulse, – a sudden stroke which increased the velocity of the body already in motion, whilst it altered the direction. The co-presence of Horatio, Marcellus, and Bernardo is most judiciously contrived; for it renders the courage of Hamlet and his impetuous eloquence perfectly intelligible. The knowledge, – the unthought-of consciousness, – the sensation, – of human auditors, – of flesh and blood sympathists – acts as a support and a stimulation *a tergo*, while the front of the mind, the whole consciousness of the speaker, is filled, yea, absorbed, by the apparition. Add too, that the apparition itself has by its previous appearances been brought nearer to a thing of this world. This accrescence of objectivity in a Ghost that yet retains all its ghostly attributes and fearful subjectivity, is truly wonderful.

Ib. sc. 5. Hamlet's speech:

> O all you host of heaven! O earth! What else?
> And shall I couple hell? –

I remember nothing equal to this burst unless it be the first speech of Prometheus in the Greek drama, after the exit of Vulcan and the two Afrites. But Shakespeare alone could have produced the vow of Hamlet to make his memory a blank of all maxims and generalized truths, that 'observation had copied there', – followed immediately by the speaker noting down the generalized fact,

> That one may smile, and smile, and be a villain!

Ib.

> MARCELLUS. Hilli, ho, ho, my lord!
> HAMLET. Hillo, ho, ho, boy! come bird, come, &c.

This part of the scene after Hamlet's interview with the Ghost has been charged with an improbable eccentricity. But the truth is, that after the mind has been stretched beyond its usual pitch and tone, it must either sink into exhaustion and inanity, or seek relief by change. It is thus well known that persons conversant in deeds of cruelty, contrive to escape from conscience, by connecting something of the ludicrous with them, and by inventing grotesque terms and a certain technical phraseology to disguise the horror of their practices. Indeed, paradoxical as it may appear, the terrible by a law of the human mind always touches on the verge of the ludicrous. Both arise from the perception of something out of the common order of things – something, in fact, out of its place; and if from this we can abstract danger, the uncommonness will alone remain, and the sense of the ridiculous be excited. The close alliance of these opposites – they are not contraries – appears from the circumstance, that laughter is equally the expression of extreme anguish and horror as of joy: as there are tears of sorrow and tears of joy, so is there a laugh of terror and a laugh of merriment. These complex causes will naturally have produced in Hamlet the disposition to escape from his own feelings of the overwhelming and supernatural by a wild transition to the ludicrous, – a sort of cunning bravado, bordering on the flights of delirium. For you may, perhaps, observe that Hamlet's wildness is but half false; he plays that subtle trick of pretending to act only when he is very near really being what he acts.

THE PLAYERS' SCENE

Ib.

> The rugged Pyrrhus – he whose sable arms, &c.

This admirable substitution of the epic for the dramatic, giving such a reality to the impassioned dramatic diction of Shakespeare's own dialogue, and authorized, too, by the actual style of the tragedies before his time (*Porrex and Ferrex*, *Titus Andronicus*, &c.) – is well worthy of notice. The fancy, that a burlesque was intended, sinks below criticism: the lines, as epic narrative, are superb.

In the thoughts, and even in the separate parts of the diction, this description is highly poetical: in truth, taken by itself, this is its fault that it is too poetical! – the language of lyric vehemence and epic pomp, and not of the drama. But if Shakespeare had made the diction truly dramatic, where would have been the contrast between *Hamlet* and the play in *Hamlet*?

LADY MACBETH

ACT i, sc. 5. Macbeth is described by Lady Macbeth so as at the same time to reveal her own character. Could he have everything he wanted, he would rather have it innocently; – ignorant, as alas! how many of us are, that he who wishes a temporal end for itself, does in truth will the means; and hence the danger of indulging fancies. Lady Macbeth, like all in Shakespeare, is a class individualized: – of high rank, left much alone, and feeding herself with day-dreams of ambition, she mistakes the courage of fantasy for the power of bearing the consequences of the realities of guilt. Hers is the mock fortitude of a mind deluded by ambition; she shames her husband with a super-human audacity of fancy which she cannot support, but sinks in the season of remorse, and dies in suicidal agony. Her speech:

> Come, all you spirits
> That tend on mortal thoughts, unsex me here, &c.

is that of one who had habitually familiarized her imagination to dreadful conceptions, and was trying to do so still more. Her invocations and requisitions are all the false efforts of a mind accustomed only hitherto to the shadows of the imagination, vivid enough to throw the everyday substances of life into shadow, but never as yet brought into direct contact with their own correspondent realities. . . .

Act ii, sc. 2. Now that the deed is done or doing – now that the first reality commences, Lady Macbeth shrinks. The most simple sound strikes terror, the most natural consequences are horrible, whilst previously everything, however awful, appeared a mere trifle. . . .

Ib. Macbeth's speech:

> Be innocent of the knowledge, dearest chuck,
> Till thou applaud the deed.

This is Macbeth's sympathy with his own feelings, and his mistaking his wife's opposite state.

LEONTES AND OTHELLO

THE idea of this delightful drama* is a genuine jealousy of disposition, and it should be immediately followed by the perusal of *Othello*, which is the direct contrast of it in every particular. For jealousy is a vice of the mind, a culpable tendency of the temper, having certain well-known and well-defined effects and concomitants, all of which are visible in Leontes, and, I boldly say, not one of which marks its presence in *Othello*; – such as, first, an excitability by the most inadequate causes, and an eagerness to snatch at proofs; secondly, a grossness

---

* A Winter's Tale.

of conception, and a disposition to degrade the object of the passion by sensual fancies and images; thirdly, a sense of shame of his own feelings exhibited in a solitary moodiness of humour, and yet from the violence of the passion forced to utter itself, and therefore catching occasions to ease the mind by ambiguities, equivoques, by talking to those who cannot, and who are known not to be able to, understand what is said to them – in short, by soliloquy in the form of dialogue, and hence a confused, broken, and fragmentary, manner; fourthly, a dread of vulgar ridicule, as distinct from a high sense of honour, or a mistaken sense of duty; and lastly, and immediately, consequent on this, a spirit of selfish vindictiveness. . . .

Finally, let me repeat that Othello does not kill Desdemona in jealousy, but in a conviction forced upon him by the almost superhuman art of Iago, – such a conviction as any man would and must have entertained who had believed Iago's honesty as Othello did. We, the audience, know that Iago is a villain from the beginning; but in considering the essence of the Shakespearian Othello, we must perseveringly place ourselves in his situation, and under his circumstances. Then we shall immediately feel the fundamental difference between the solemn agony of the noble Moor, and the wretched fishing jealousies of Leontes, and the morbid suspiciousness of Leonatus, who is, in other respects, a fine character. Othello had no life but in Desdemona: – the belief that she, his angel, had fallen from the heaven of her native innocence, wrought a civil war in his heart. She is his counterpart; and, like him, is almost sanctified in our eyes by her absolute unsuspiciousness, and holy entireness of love. As the curtain drops, which do we pity the most?

Lectures, 1818

THE CHARACTER OF IAGO

ACT i, sc. 1.* Admirable is the preparation, so truly and peculiarly Shakespearian, in the introduction of Roderigo, as the dupe on whom Iago shall first exercise his art, and in so doing display his own character. Roderigo, without any fixed principle, but not without the moral notions and sympathies with honour, which his rank and connections had hung upon him, is already well fitted and predisposed for the purpose; for very want of character and strength of passion, like wind loudest in an empty house, constitute his character. The first three lines

* Othello.

happily state the nature and foundation of the friendship between him and Iago, – the purse, – as also the contrast of Roderigo's intemperance of mind with Iago's coolness, – the coolness of a preconceiving experimenter. The mere language of protestation –

> If ever I did dream of such a matter,
> Abhor me, –

which falling in with the associative link, determines Roderigo's continuation of complaint –

> Thou told'st me, thou didst hold him in thy hate –

elicits at length a true feeling of Iago's mind, the dread of contempt habitual to those, who encourage in themselves, and have their keenest pleasure in, the expression of contempt for others. Observe Iago's high self-opinion, and the moral, that a wicked man will employ real feelings, as well as assume those most alien from his own, as instruments of his purposes:

> And, by the faith of man,
> I know my place, I am worth no worse a place.

I think Tyrwhitt's reading of 'life' for 'wife' –

> A fellow almost damn'd in a fair *wife* –

the true one, as fitting to Iago's contempt for whatever did not display power, and that intellectual power. In what follows, let the reader feel how by and through the glass of two passions, disappointed vanity and envy, the very vices of which he is complaining, are made to act upon him as if they were so many excellencies, and the more appropriately, because cunning is always admired and wished for by minds conscious of inward weakness; – but they act only by half, like music on an inattentive auditor, swelling the thoughts which prevent him from listening to it.

Ib. Iago's speech:

> Virtue? a fig! 'tis in ourselves, that we are thus, or thus, &c.

This speech comprises the passionless character of Iago. It is all will in intellect; and therefore he is here a bold partisan of a truth, but yet of a truth converted into a falsehood by the absence of all the necessary modifications caused by the frail nature of man. And then comes the last sentiment,

> Our raging motions, our carnal stings, our unbitted lusts, whereof I take this, that you call – love, to be a sect or scion!

Here is the true Iagoism of, alas! how many! Note Iago's pride of mastery in the repetition of 'Go, make money!' to his anticipated dupe, even stronger than his love of lucre: and when Roderigo is completely won –

> I am changed. I'll go sell all my land.

when the effect has been fully produced, the repetition of triumph –

> Go to; farewell; put money enough in your purse!

The remainder – Iago's soliloquy – the motive-hunting of a motiveless malignity – how awful it is! Yea, whilst he is still allowed to bear the divine image, it is too fiendish for his own steady view, – for the lonely gaze of a being next to devil, and only not quite devil, – and yet a character which Shakespeare has attempted and executed, without disgust and without scandal!

Lectures, 1818

LEAR

OF all Shakespeare's plays *Macbeth* is the most rapid, *Hamlet* the slowest, in movement. *Lear* combines length with rapidity, – like the hurricane and the whirlpool, absorbing while it advances. It begins as a stormy day in summer, with brightness; but that brightness is lurid and anticipates the tempest.

It was not without forethought, nor is it without its due significance, that the division of Lear's kingdom is in the first six lines of the play stated as a thing already determined in all its particulars, previously to the trial of professions, as the relative rewards of which the daughters were to be made to consider their several portions. The strange, yet by no means unnatural, mixture of selfishness, sensibility, and habit of feeling derived from, and fostered by, the particular rank and usages of the individual; – the intense desire of being intensely beloved, – selfish, and yet characteristic of the selfishness of a loving and kindly nature alone; – the self-supportless leaning for all pleasure on another's breast; – the cravings after sympathy with a prodigal disinterestedness, frustrated by its own ostentation, and the mode and nature of its claims; – the anxiety, the distrust, the jealousy, which more or less accompany all selfish affections, and are amongst the surest contradistinctions of mere fondness from true love, and which originate Lear's eager wish to enjoy his daughter's violent professions, whilst the inveterate habits of sovereignty convert the wish into claim and positive right, and an incompliance with it into crime and treason; – these facts, these passions, these moral verities, on which the whole tragedy is founded, are all prepared for, and will to the retrospect be found implied, in these first four or five lines of the play. They let us know that the trial is but a trick; and that the grossness of the old king's rage is in part the natural result of a silly trick suddenly and most unexpectedly baffled and disappointed.

It may here be worthy of notice, that *Lear* is the only serious performance of Shakespeare, the interest and situations of which are derived from the assumption of a gross improbability; whereas Beaumont and Fletcher's tragedies are, almost all of them, founded on some out of the way accident or exception to the general experience of mankind. But observe the matchless judgement of our Shakespeare. First, improbable as the conduct of Lear is in the first scene, yet it was an old story rooted in the popular faith, – a thing taken for granted already, and consequently without any of the effects of improbability. Secondly, it is merely the canvas for the characters and passions, – a mere occasion for, – and not, in the manner of Beaumont and Fletcher, perpetually recurring as the cause, and *sine qua non* of, – the incidents and emotions. Let the first scene of this play have been lost, and let it only be understood that a fond father had been duped by hypocritical professions of love and duty on the part of two daughters to disinherit the third, previously, and deservedly, more dear to him; – and all the rest of the tragedy would retain its interest undiminished, and be perfectly intelligible. The accidental is nowhere the groundwork of the passions, but that which is catholic, which in all ages has been, and ever will be, close and native to the heart of man, – parental anguish from filial ingratitude, the genuineness of worth, though coffined in bluntness, and the execrable vileness of a smooth iniquity. Perhaps I ought to have added *The Merchant of Venice*; but here too the same remarks apply. It was an old tale; and substitute any other danger than that of the pound of flesh (the circumstance in which the improbability lies), yet all the situations and the emotions appertaining to them remain equally excellent and appropriate. Whereas take away from the *Mad Lover* of Beaumont and Fletcher the fantastic hypothesis of his engagement to cut out his own heart, and have it presented to his mistress, and all the main scenes must go with it. . . .

To return to Lear. Having thus in the fewest words, and in a natural reply to as natural a question, – which yet answers the secondary purpose of attracting our attention to the difference or diversity between the characters of Cornwall and Albany, – provided the premisses and *data*, as it were, for our after insight into the mind and mood of the person, whose character, passions, and sufferings are the main subject-matter of the play; – from Lear, the *persona patiens* of his drama, Shakespeare passes without delay to the second in importance, the chief agent and prime mover, and introduces Edmund to our acquaintance, preparing us with the same felicity of judgement, and in the same easy and natural way, for his character in the seemingly casual communication of its origin and occasion. From the first drawing up of the curtain Edmund has stood before us in the united strength and beauty of earliest manhood. Our eyes have been questioning him. Gifted as he is with high advantages of person, and further endowed by nature with a powerful intellect and a strong energetic will, even without any concurrence of circumstances and accident, pride will necessarily be the sin that most easily besets him. But Edmund is also the known and acknowledged son of the princely Gloster: he, therefore, has both the germ of pride, and the conditions best fitted to evolve and ripen it into a predominant feeling. Yet hitherto no reason appears why it should be other than the not unusual pride of person, talent, and birth, – a pride auxiliary, if not akin, to many virtues, and the natural ally of honourable impulses. But alas! in his own presence his own father takes shame to himself for the frank avowal that he is his father, – he has 'blushed so often to acknowledge him that he is now brazed to it!' Edmund hears the circumstances of his birth spoken of with a most degrading and licentious levity, – his mother described as a wanton by her own paramour, and the remembrance of the animal sting, the low criminal gratifications connected with her wantonness and prostituted beauty, assigned as the reason, why 'the whoreson must be acknowledged!' This, and the consciousness of its notoriety; the gnawing conviction that every show of respect is an effort of courtesy, which recalls, while it represses, a contrary feeling; – this is the ever trickling flow of wormwood and gall into the wounds of pride, – the corrosive *virus* which inoculates pride with a venom not its own, with envy, hatred, and a lust for that power which in its blaze of radiance would hide the dark spots on his disc, – with pangs of shame personally undeserved and therefore felt as wrongs, and with a blind ferment of vindictive working towards the occasions and causes, especially towards a brother, whose stainless birth and lawful honours were the constant remembrancers of his own debasement, and were ever in the way to prevent all chance of its being unknown, or overlooked and forgotten. Add to this, that with excellent judgement, and provident for the claims of the moral sense, – for that which, relatively to the drama, is called poetic justice, and as the fittest means for reconciling the feelings of the spectators to the horrors of Gloster's after sufferings, – at least, of rendering them somewhat less unendurable; – (for I will not disguise my conviction, that in this one point the tragic in this play has been urged beyond the outermost mark and *ne plus ultra* of the dramatic) – Shakespeare has precluded all excuse and palliation of the guilt incurred by both the parents of the base-born Edmund, by Gloster's confession that he was at the time a married man, and already blest with a lawful heir of his fortunes. The mournful alienation of brotherly love, occasioned by the law of primogeniture in noble families, or rather by the unnecessary distinctions engrafted thereon, and this in children of the same stock, is still almòst proverbial on the continent, – especially, as I know from my own observation, in the south of Europe, – and appears to have been scarcely less common in our own island before the Revolution of 1688, if we may judge from the characters and sentiments so frequent in our elder comedies. There is the younger brother, for instance, in Beaumont and Fletcher's play of *The Scornful Lady*, on the one side, and Oliver in Shakespeare's *As You Like It*, on the other. Need it be said how heavy an aggravation, in such a case, the stain of bastardy must have been, were it only that the younger brother was liable to hear his own dishonour and his mother's infamy related by his father with an excusing shrug of the shoulders, and in a tone betwixt waggery and shame!

By the circumstances here enumerated as so many predisposing causes, Edmund's character might well be deemed already sufficiently explained; and our minds prepared for it. But in this tragedy the story or fable constrained Shakespeare to introduce wickedness in an outrageous form in the persons of Regan and Goneril. He had read nature too heedfully not to know, that courage, intellect, and strength of character, are the most impressive forms of power, and that to power in itself, without reference to any moral end, an inevitable admiration and complacency appertains, whether it be displayed in the conquests of a Buonaparte or Tamerlane, or in the foam and the thunder of a cataract. But in the exhibition of such a character it was of the highest importance to prevent the guilt from passing into utter monstrosity, – which again depends on the presence or absence of causes and temptations sufficient to account for the wickedness, without the necessity of recurring to a thorough fiendishness of nature for its origination. For such are the appointed relations of intellectual power to truth, and of truth to goodness, that it becomes both morally and poetically unsafe to present what is admirable, – what our nature compels us to admire – in the mind, and what is most detestable in the heart, as co-existing in the same individual without any apparent connection, or any modification of the one by the other. That Shakespeare has in one instance, that of Iago, approached to this, and that he has done it successfully, is, perhaps, the most astonishing proof of his genius, and the opulence of its resources. But in the present tragedy, in which he was compelled to present a Goneril and a Regan, it was most carefully to be avoided; – and therefore the only one conceivable addition to the inauspicious influences on the preformation of Edmund's character is given, in the information that all the kindly counteractions to the mischievous feelings of shame, which might have been derived from co-domestication with Edgar and their common father, had been cut off by his absence from home, and foreign education from boyhood to the present time, and a prospect of its continuance, as if to preclude all risk of his interference with the father's views for the elder and legitimate son:

> He hath been out nine years, and away he shall again.

Act i, sc. 1.

> CORDELIA. Nothing, my lord.
> LEAR. Nothing?
> CORDELIA. Nothing.
> LEAR. Nothing can come of nothing: speak again.
> CORDELIA. Unhappy that I am, I cannot heave
> My heart into my mouth: I love your majesty
> According to my bond; nor more, nor less.

There is something of disgust at the ruthless hypocrisy of her sisters, and some little faulty admixture of pride and sullenness in Cordelia's 'Nothing'; and her tone is well contrived, indeed, to lessen the glaring absurdity of Lear's conduct, but answers the yet more important purpose of forcing away the attention from the nursery-tale, the moment it has served its end, that of supplying the canvas for the picture. This is also materially furthered by Kent's opposition, which displays Lear's moral incapability of resigning the sovereign power in the very act of disposing of it. Kent is, perhaps, the nearest to perfect goodness in all Shakespeare's characters, and yet the most individualized. There is an extraordinary charm in his bluntness, which is that only of a nobleman arising from a contempt of overstrained courtesy; and combined with easy placability where goodness of heart is apparent. His passionate affection for, and fidelity to, Lear act on our feelings in Lear's own favour: virtue itself seems to be in company with him.

Ib. sc. 2. Edmund's speech:

> Who, in the lusty stealth of nature, take
> More composition and fierce quality
> Than doth, &c.

Warburton's note upon a quotation from Vanini.

Poor Vanini! Any one but Warburton would have thought this precious passage more characteristic of Mr Shandy than of atheism. If the fact really were so (which it is not, but almost the contrary), I do not see why the most confirmed theist might not very naturally utter the same wish. But it is proverbial that the youngest son in a large family is commonly the man of the greatest talents in it; and as good an authority as Vanini has said – *incalescere in venerem ardentius, spei sobolis injuriosum esse.*

In this speech of Edmund you see, as soon as a man cannot reconcile himself to reason, how his conscience flies off by way of appeal to nature, who is sure upon occasions never to find fault, and also how shame sharpens a predisposition in the heart to evil. For it is a profound moral, that shame will naturally generate guilt; the oppressed will be vindictive, like Shylock, and in the anguish of undeserved ignominy the delusion secretly springs up, of getting over the moral quality of an action by fixing the mind on the mere physical act alone.

Ib. Edmund's speech:

This is the excellent foppery of the world! that, when we are sick in fortune (often the surfeit of our own behaviour), we make guilty of our disasters, the sun, the moon, and the stars, &c.

Thus scorn and misanthropy are often the anticipations and mouthpieces of wisdom in the detection of superstitions. Both individuals and nations may be free from such prejudices by being below them, as well as by rising above them.

Ib. sc. 3. The Steward should be placed in exact antithesis to Kent, as the only character of utter irredeemable baseness in Shakespeare. Even in this the judgement and invention of the poet are very observable; – for what else could the willing tool of a Goneril be? Not a vice but this of baseness was left open to him.

Ib. sc. 4. In Lear old age is itself a character, – its natural imperfections being increased by life-long habits of receiving a prompt obedience. Any addition of individuality would have been unnecessary and painful; for the relations of others to him, of wondrous fidelity and of frightful ingratitude, alone sufficiently distinguish him. Thus Lear becomes the open and ample play-room of nature's passions.

KNIGHT. Since my young lady's going into France, Sir; the fool hath much pin'd away.

The Fool is no comic buffoon to make the groundlings laugh – no forced condescension of Shakespeare's genius to the taste of his audience. Accordingly the poet prepares for his introduction, which he never does with any of his common clowns and fools, by bringing him into living connection with the pathos of the play. He is as wonderful a creation as Caliban; his wild babblings, and inspired idiocy, articulate and gauge the horrors of the scene.

The monster Goneril prepares what is necessary, while the character of Albany renders a still more maddening grievance possible, namely, Regan and Cornwall in perfect sympathy of monstrosity. Not a sentiment, not an image, which can give pleasure on its own account, is admitted; whenever these creatures are introduced, and they are brought forward as little as possible, pure horror reigns throughout. In this scene and in all the early speeches of Lear, the one general sentiment of filial ingratitude prevails as the mainspring of the feelings; – in this early stage the outward object causing the pressure on the mind, which is not yet sufficiently familiarized with the anguish for the imagination to work upon it.

Ib.

> GONERIL. Do you mark that, my lord?
> ALBANY. I cannot be so partial, Goneril,
> To the great love I bear you.
> GONERIL. Pray you, content, &c.

Observe the baffled endeavour of Goneril to act on the fears of Albany, and yet his passiveness, his *inertia*; he is not convinced, and yet he is afraid of looking into the thing. Such characters always yield to those who will take the trouble of governing them, or for them. Perhaps, the influence of a princess, whose choice of him had royalized his state, may be some little excuse for Albany's weakness.

Ib. sc. 5.

> LEAR. O let me not be mad, not mad, sweet heaven!
> Keep me in temper! I would not be mad! –

The mind's own anticipation of madness! The deepest tragic notes are often struck by a half sense of an impending blow. The Fool's conclusion of this act by a grotesque prattling seems to indicate the dislocation of feeling that has begun and is to be continued.

Act ii, sc. 1. Edmund's speech:

> He replied,
> Thou unpossessing bastard! &c.

Thus the secret poison in Edmund's own heart steals forth; and then observe poor Gloster's –

> Loyal and *natural* boy!

as if praising the crime of Edmund's birth!

Ib. Compare Regan's –

> What, did *my father's* godson seek your life?
> He whom *my father* named?

with the unfeminine violence of her –

> All vengeance comes too short, &c.

and yet no reference to the guilt, but only to the accident, which she uses as an occasion for sneering at her father. Regan is not, in fact, a greater monster than Goneril, but she has the power of casting more venom.

Ib. sc. 2. Cornwall's speech:

> This is some fellow
> Who, having been praised for bluntness, doth affect
> A saucy roughness, &c.

In thus placing these profound general truths in the mouths of such men as Cornwall, Edmund, Iago, &c., Shakespeare at once gives them utterance, and yet shows how indefinite their application is.

Ib. sc. 3. Edgar's assumed madness serves the great purpose of taking off part of the shock which would otherwise be caused by the true madness of Lear, and further displays the profound difference between the two. In every attempt at representing madness throughout the whole range of dramatic literature, with the single exception of Lear, it is mere lightheadedness, as especially in Otway. In Edgar's ravings Shakespeare all the while lets you see a fixed purpose, a practical end in view; – in Lear's, there is only the brooding of the one anguish, an eddy without progression.

Ib. sc. 4. Lear's speech:

> The king would speak with Cornwall; the dear father
> Would with his daughter speak, &c.
>
> .   .   .   .
>
> No, but not yet: may be he is not well, &c.

The strong interest now felt by Lear to try to find excuses for his daughter is most pathetic.

Ib. Lear's speech:

> – – Beloved Regan,
> Thy sister's naught; – O Regan, she hath tied
> Sharp-tooth'd unkindness, like a vulture, here.
> I can scarce speak to thee; – thou'lt not believe
> Of how depraved a quality – O Regan!
> REGAN. I pray you, Sir, take patience; I have hope,
> You less know how to value her desert,
> Than she to scant her duty.
> LEAR. Say, how is that?

Nothing is so heart-cutting as a cold unexpected defence or palliation of a cruelty passionately complained of, or so expressive of thorough hard-heartedness. And feel the excessive horror of Regan's 'O, Sir, you are old!' – and then her drawing from that universal object of reverence and indulgence the very reason for her frightful conclusion –

> Say, you have wrong'd her!

All Lear's faults increase our pity for him. We refuse to know them otherwise than as means of his sufferings, and aggravations of his daughter's ingratitude.

Ib. Lear's speech:

> O, reason not the need: our basest beggars
> Are in the poorest thing superfluous, &c.

Observe that the tranquillity which follows the first stunning of the blow permits Lear to reason.

Act iii, sc. 4. O, what a world's convention of agonies is here! All external nature in a storm, all moral nature convulsed, – the real madness of Lear, the feigned madness of Edgar, the babbling of the Fool, the desperate fidelity of Kent – surely such a scene was never conceived before or since! Take it but as a picture for the eye only, it is more terrific than any which a Michel Angelo, inspired by a Dante, could have conceived, and which none but a Michel Angelo could have executed. Or let it have been uttered to the blind, the howlings of nature would seem converted into the voice of conscious humanity. This scene ends with the first symptoms of positive derangement; and the intervention of the fifth scene is particularly judicious, – the interruption allowing an interval for Lear to appear in full madness in the sixth scene.

Ib. sc. 7. Gloster's blinding:

What can I say of this scene – There is my reluctance to think Shakespeare wrong, and yet –

Act. iv, sc. 6. Lear's speech:

Ha! Goneril! – with a white beard! – They flattered me like a dog: and told me, I had white hairs in my beard, ere the black ones were there. To say *Ay* and *No* to every thing I said! – Ay and No too was no good divinity. When the rain came to wet me once, &c.

The thunder recurs, but still at a greater distance from our feelings. Ib. sc. 7. Lear's speech:

Where have I been? Where am I? – Fair daylight? –
I am mightily abused. – I should even die with pity
To see another thus, &c.

How beautifully the affecting return of Lear to reason, and the mild pathos of these speeches prepare the mind for the last sad, yet sweet, consolation of the aged sufferer's death!

BEN JONSON

A CONTEMPORARY is rather an ambiguous term, when applied to authors. It may simply mean that one man lived and wrote while another was yet alive, however deeply the former may have been indebted to the latter as his model. There have been instances in the literary world that might remind a botanist of a singular sort of parasite plant, which rises above ground, independent and unsupported, an apparent original; but trace its roots, and you will find the fibres all terminating in the root of another plant at an unsuspected distance, which, perhaps, from want of sun and genial soil, and the loss of sap, has scarcely been able to peep above the ground. – Or the word may mean those whose compositions were contemporaneous in such a sense as to preclude all likelihood of the one having borrowed from the other. In the latter sense I should call Ben Jonson a contemporary of Shakespeare, though he long survived him; while I should prefer the phrase of immediate successors for Beaumont and Fletcher, and Massinger, though they too were Shakespeare's contemporaries in the former sense.

Ben Jonson is original; he is, indeed, the only one of the great dramatists of that day who was not either directly produced, or very greatly modified, by Shakespeare. In truth, he differs from our grea master in everything – in form and in substance – and betrays no tokens of his proximity. He is not original in the same way as Shakespeare is original; but after a fashion of his own, Ben Jonson is most truly original.

The characters in his plays are, in the strictest sense of the term, abstractions. Some very prominent feature is taken from the whole man, and that single feature or humour is made the basis upon which the entire character is built up. Ben Jonson's *dramatis personae* are almost as fixed as the masks of the ancient actors; you know from the first scene – sometimes from the list of names – exactly what every one of them is to be. He was a very accurately observing man; but he cared only to observe what was external or open to, and likely to impress, the senses. He individualizes, not so much, if at all, by the exhibition of moral or intellectual differences, as by the varieties and contrasts of manners, modes of speech and tricks of temper; as in such characters as Puntarvolo, Bobadill, &c.

I believe there is not one whim or affectation in common life noted in any memoir of that age which may not be found drawn and framed in some corner or other of Ben Jonson's dramas; and they have this merit, in common with Hogarth's prints, that not a single circumstance is introduced in them which does not play upon, and help to bring out, the dominant humour or humours of the piece. Indeed I ought very particularly to call your attention to the extraordinary skill shown by Ben Jonson in contriving situations for the display of his characters. In fact, his care and anxiety in this matter led him to do what scarcely any of the dramatists of that age did – that is, invent his plots. It is not a first perusal that suffices for the full perception of the elaborate artifice of the plots of *The Alchemist* and *The Silent Woman*; – that of the former is absolute perfection for a necessary entanglement, and an unexpected, yet natural, evolution.

Ben Jonson exhibits a sterling English diction, and he has with great skill contrived varieties of construction; but his style is rarely sweet or harmonious, in consequence of his labour at point and strength being so evident. In all his works, in verse or prose, there is an extraordinary opulence of thought; but it is the produce of an amassing power in the author, and not of a growth from within. Indeed a large proportion of Ben Jonson's thoughts may be traced to classic or obscure modern writers, by those who are learned and curious enough to follow the steps of this robust, surly, and observing dramatist.

Lectures, 1818

SHAKESPEARE'S MORAL DELICACY

BEAUMONT and Fletcher always write as if virtue or goodness were a sort of talisman, or strange something, that might be lost without the least fault on the part of the owner. In short, their chaste ladies value their chastity as a material thing, – not as an act or state of being; and this mere thing being imaginary, no wonder that all their women are represented with the minds of strumpets, except a few irrational humourists, far less capable of exciting our sympathy than a Hindoo, who has had a basin of cow-broth thrown over him; – for this, though a debasing superstition, is still real, and we might pity the poor wretch, though we cannot help despising him. But B. and F.'s Lucinas are clumsy fictions. It is too plain that the authors had no one idea of chastity as a virtue, but only such a conception as a blind man might have of the power of seeing, by handling an ox's eye. In *The Queen of Corinth*, indeed, they talk differently; but it is all talk, and nothing is real in it but the dread of losing a reputation. Hence the frightful contrast between their women (even those who are meant for virtuous) and Shakespeare's. So, for instance, *The Maid in the Mill*: – a woman must not merely have grown old in brothels, but have chuckled over every abomination committed in them with a rampant sympathy of imagination, to have had her fancy so drunk with the *minutiae* of lechery as this icy chaste virgin evinces hers to have been.

It would be worth while to note how many of these plays are founded on rapes, – how many on incestuous passions, and how many on mere lunacies. Then their virtuous women are either crazy superstitions of a merely bodily negation of having been acted on, or strumpets in their imaginations and wishes, or, as in this *Maid in the Mill*, both at the same time. In the men, the love is merely lust in one direction, – exclusive preference of one object. The tyrant's speeches are mostly taken from the mouths of indignant denouncers of the tyrant's character, with the substitution of 'I' for 'he', and the omission of the prefatory 'he acts as if he thought' so and so. The only feelings they can possibly excite are disgust at the Aeciuses, if regarded as sane loyalists, or compassion, if considered as Bedlamites. So much for their tragedies. But even their comedies are, most of them, disturbed by the fantasticalness, or gross caricature, of the persons or incidents. There are few characters that you can really like, – (even though you should have had erased from your mind all the filth, which bespatters the most likeable of them, as Piniero in *The Island*

Princess for instance,) – scarcely one whom you can love. How different this from Shakespeare, who makes one have a sort of sneaking affection even for his Barnardines; – whose very Iagos and Richards are awful, and, by the counteracting power of profound intellects, rendered fearful rather than· hateful; – and even the exceptions, as Goneril and Regan, are proofs of superlative judgement and the finest moral tact, in being left utter monsters, *nulla virtute redemptae*, and in being kept out of sight as much as possible, – they being, indeed, only means for the excitement and deepening of noblest emotions towards the Lear, Cordelia, &c., and employed with the·severest economy! But even Shakespeare's grossness – that which is really so, independently of the increase in modern times of vicious associations with things indifferent, – (for there is a state of manners conceivable so pure, that the language of Hamlet at Ophelia's feet might be a harmful rallying, or playful teasing, of a shame that would exist in Paradise) – at the worst, how diverse in kind is it from Beaumont and Fletcher's! In Shakespeare it is the mere generalities of sex, mere words for the most part, seldom or never distinct images, all head-work, and fancy-drolleries; there is no sensation supposed in the speaker. I need not proceed to contrast this with B. and F.

Notes on Beaumont and Fletcher's *Valentinian*, 1818

SPENSER

THERE is this difference, among many others, between Shakespeare and Spenser:–Shakespeare is never coloured by the customs of his age; what appears of contemporary character in him is merely negative; it is just not something else. He has none of the fictitious realities of the classics, none of the grotesquenesses of chivalry, none of the allegory of the middle ages; there is no sectarianism either of politics or religion, no miser, no witch, – no common witch, – no astrology – nothing impermanent of however long duration; but he stands like the yew tree in Lorton vale, which has known so many ages that it belongs to none in particular; a living image of endless self-reproduction, like the immortal tree of Malabar. In Spenser the spirit of chivalry is entirely predominant, although with a much greater infusion of the poet's own individual self into it than is found in any other writer. He has the wit of the southern with the deeper inwardness of the northern genius.

No one can appreciate Spenser without some reflection on the nature of allegorical writing. The mere etymological meaning of the word, allegory, – to talk of one thing and thereby convey another, – is too wide. The true sense is this, – the employment of one set of agents and images to convey in disguise a moral meaning, with a likeness to the imagination, but with a difference to the understanding, – those agents and images being so combined as to form a homogeneous whole. This distinguishes it from metaphor, which is part of an allegory. But allegory is not properly distinguishable from fable, otherwise than as the first includes the second, as a genus its species; for in a fable there must be nothing but what is universally known and acknowledged, but in an allegory there may be that which is new and not previously admitted. The pictures of the great masters, especially of the Italian schools, are genuine allegories. Amongst the classics, the multitude of their gods either precluded allegory altogether, or else made everything allegory, as in the Hesiodic Theogonia; for you can scarcely distinguish between power and the personification of power. The Cupid and Psyche of, or found in, Apuleius, is a phenomenon. It is the platonic mode of accounting for the fall of man. The 'Battle of the Soul' by Prudentius is an early instance of Christian allegory.

Narrative allegory is distinguished from mythology as reality from symbol; it is, in short, the proper intermedium between person and personification. Where it is too strongly individualized, it ceases to be allegory; this is often felt in the *Pilgrim's Progress*, where the characters are real persons with nicknames. Perhaps one of the most curious warnings against another attempt at narrative allegory on a great scale, may be found in Tasso's account of what he himself intended in and by his *Jerusalem Delivered*.

As characteristic of Spenser, I would call your particular attention in the first place to the indescribable sweetness and fluent projection of his verse, very clearly distinguishable from the deeper and more inwoven harmonies of Shakespeare and Milton. This stanza is a good instance of what I mean:

> Yet she, most faithfull ladie, all this while
> Forsaken, wofull, solitarie mayd,
> Far from all peoples preace, as in exile,
> In wildernesse and wastfull deserts strayd
> To seeke her knight; who, subtily betrayd
> Through that late vision which th' enchaunter wrought,
> Had her abandoned; she, of nought affrayd,
> Through woods and wastnes wide him daily sought,
> Yet wished tydinges none of him unto her brought.

F. Qu., B. I, c. 3, st. 3

2. Combined with this sweetness and fluency, the scientific construction of the metre of the *Faery Queene* is very noticeable. One of Spenser's arts is that of alliteration, and he uses it with great effect in doubling the impression of an image:

> In *w*ildernesse and *w*astful deserts, –
>
> . . . .
>
> Through *w*oods and *w*astnes *w*ilde, –
>
> . . . .
>
> They passe the bitter waves of Acheron,
> Where many soules sit *w*ailing *w*oefully,
> And come to *f*iery *f*lood of *Ph*legeton,
> Whereas the damned ghosts in torments fry,
> And with *sh*arp, *sh*rilling *sh*rieks doth bootlesse cry, &c.

He is particularly given to an alternate alliteration, which is, perhaps, when well used, a great secret in melody:

> A *r*amping lyon *r*ushed suddenly, –
>
> . . . .
>
> And *s*ad to *s*ee her *s*orrowful constraint,
>
> . . . .
>
> And on the grasse her *d*aintie *l*imbes *d*id *l*ay, – &c.

You cannot read a page of the *Faerie Queene*, if you read for that purpose, without perceiving the intentional alliterativeness of the words; and yet so skilfully is this managed, that it never strikes any unwarned ear as artificial, or other than the result of the necessary movement of the verse.

3. Spenser displays great skill in harmonizing his descriptions of external nature and actual incidents with the allegorical character and epic activity of the poem. Take these two beautiful passages as illustrations of what I mean:

> By this the northerne wagoner had set
> His sevenfold teme behind the stedfast starre
> That was in ocean waves yet never wet,
> But firme is fixt, and sendeth light from farre
> To all that in the wide deepe wandring arre;
> And chearefull chaunticlere with his note shrill
> Had warned once, that Phoebus' fiery carre
> In hast was climbing up the easterne hill,
> Full envious that Night so long his roome did fill;

When accursed messengers of hell,
That feigning dreame, and that faire-forged spright
Came, &c. –

B. I, c. 2, st. 1

*

At last! the golden orientall gate
Of greatest Heaven gan to open fayre;
And Phoebus, fresh as brydegrome to his mate,
Came dauncing forth, shaking his deawie hayre;
And hurld his glistring beams through gloomy ayre.
Which when the wakeful Elfe perceiv'd, streightway
He started up, and did him selfe prepayre
In sunbright armes and battailons array;
For with that Pagan proud he combat will that day.

Ib., c. 5, st. 2

Observe also the exceeding vividness of Spenser's descriptions. They are not, in the true sense of the word, picturesque; but are composed of a wondrous series of images, as in our dreams. Compare the following passage with anything you may remember *in pari materia* in Milton or Shakespeare:

His haughtie helmet, horrid all with gold,
Both glorious brightnesse and great terrour bredd,
For all the crest a dragon did enfold
With greedie pawes, and over all did spredd
His golden winges; his dreadfull hideous hedd,
Close couched on the bever, seemd to throw
From flaming mouth bright sparkles fiery redd,
That suddeine horrour to faint hartes did show;
And scaly tayle was stretcht adowne his back full low.

Upon the top of all his loftie crest
A bounch of haires discolourd diversly,
With sprinkled pearle and gold full richly drest,
Did shake, and seemed to daunce for jollitie;
Like to an almond tree ymounted hye
On top of greene Selinis all alone,
With blossoms brave bedecked daintily,
Whose tender locks do tremble every one
At everie little breath that under heaven is blowne.

Ib., c. 7, st. 31–2

4. You will take especial note of the marvellous independence and true imaginative absence of all particular space or time in the *Faerie Queene*. It is in the domains neither of history or geography; it is

298

ignorant of all artificial boundary, all material obstacles; it is truly in land of Faery, that is, of mental space. The poet has placed you in a dream, a charmed sleep, and you neither wish, nor have the power, to inquire where you are, or how you got there. It reminds me of some lines of my own:

> Oh! would to Alla!
> The raven or the sea-mew were appointed
> To bring me food! – or rather that my soul
> Might draw in life from the universal air!
> It were a lot divine, in some small skiff,
> Along some ocean's boundless solitude,
> To float for ever with a careless course,
> And think myself the only being alive!

Remorse, Act IV, Scene 3

Indeed Spenser himself, in the conduct of his great poem, may be represented under the same image, his symbolizing purpose being his mariner's compass:

> As pilot well expert in perilous wave,
> That to a stedfast starre his course hath bent,
> When foggy mistes or cloudy tempests have
> The faithfull light of that faire lampe yblent,
> And coverd Heaven with hideous dreriment;
> Upon his card and compas firmes his eye,
> The maysters of his long experiment,
> And to them does the steddy helme apply,
> Bidding his winged vessell fairely forward fly.

B. II, c. 7, st. 1

So the poet through the realms of allegory.

5. You should note the quintessential character of Christian chivalry in all his characters, but more especially in his women. The Greeks, except, perhaps, in Homer, seem to have had no way of making their women interesting, but by unsexing them, as in the instances of the tragic Medea, Electra, &c. Contrast such characters with Spenser's Una, who exhibits no prominent feature, has no particularization, but produces the same feeling that a statue does, when contemplated at a distance:

> From her fayre head her fillet she undight,
> And layd her stole aside: her angels face,
> As the great eye of Heaven, shyned bright,
> And made a sunshine in the shady place;
> Did never mortal eye behold such heavenly grace.

B. I, c. 3, st. 4

6. In Spenser we see the brightest and purest form of that nationality which was so common a characteristic of our elder poets. There is nothing unamiable, nothing contemptuous of others, in it. To glorify their country – to elevate England into a queen, an empress of the heart – this was their passion and object; and how dear and important an object it was or may be, let Spain, in the recollection of her Cid, declare! There is a great magic in national names. What a damper to all interest is a list of native East Indian merchants! Unknown names are non-conductors; they stop all sympathy. No one of our poets has touched this string more exquisitely than Spenser; especially in his chronicle of the British Kings (B. II, c. 10), and the marriage of the Thames with the Medway (B. IV, c. 11), in both which passages the mere names constitute half the pleasure we receive. To the same feeling we must in particular attribute Spenser's sweet reference to Ireland:

> Ne thence the Irishe rivers absent were;
> Sith no lesse famous than the rest they be, &c. – *Ib.*

> *

> And Mulla mine, whose waves I whilom taught to weep. – *Ib.*

And there is a beautiful passage of the same sort in the 'Colin Clout's Come Home Again':

> 'One day,' quoth he, 'I sat, as was my trade,
> Under the foot of Mole,' &c.

Lastly, the great and prevailing character of Spenser's mind is fancy under the conditions of imagination, as an ever present but not always active power. He has an imaginative fancy, but he has not imagination, in kind or degree, as Shakespeare and Milton have; the boldest effort of his powers in this way is the character of Talus. Add to this a feminine tenderness and almost maidenly purity of feeling, and above all, a deep moral earnestness which produces a believing sympathy and acquiescence in the reader, and you have a tolerably adequate view of Spenser's intellectual being.

MILTON

IF we divide the period from the accession of Elizabeth to the Protectorate of Cromwell into two unequal portions, the first ending with the death of James I, the other comprehending the reign of Charles and the brief glories of the Republic, we are forcibly struck with a difference in the character of the illustrious actors, by whom each period is rendered severally memorable. Or rather, the difference in the characters of the great men in each period, leads us to make this division. Eminent as the intellectual powers were that were displayed in both; yet in the number of great men, in the various sorts of excellence, and not merely in the variety but almost diversity of talents united in the same individual, the age of Charles falls short of its predecessor; and the stars of the Parliament, keen as their radiance was, in fulness and richness of lustre, yield to the constellation at the court of Elizabeth; – which can only be paralleled by Greece in her brightest moment, when the titles of the poet, the philosopher, the historian, the statesman and the general not seldom formed a garland round the same head, as in the instances of our Sidneys and Raleighs. But then, on the other hand, there was a vehemence of will, an enthusiasm of principle, a depth and an earnestness of spirit, which the charms of individual fame and personal aggrandizement could not pacify, – an aspiration after reality, permanence, and general good, – in short, a moral grandeur in the latter period, with which the low intrigues, Machiavellic maxims, and selfish and servile ambition of the former, stand in painful contrast.

The causes of this it belongs not to the present occasion to detail at length; but a mere allusion to the quick succession of revolutions in religion, breeding a political indifference in the mass of men to religion itself, the enormous increase of the royal power in consequence of the humiliation of the nobility and the clergy – the transference of the papal authority to the crown, – the unfixed state of Elizabeth's own opinions, whose inclinations were as popish as her interests were protestant – the controversial extravagance and practical imbecility of her successor – will help to explain the former period; and the persecutions that had given a life and soul interest to the disputes so imprudently fostered by James, – the ardour of a conscious increase of power in the commons, and the greater austerity of manners and maxims, the natural product and most formidable weapon of religious disputation not merely in conjunction, but in closest combination, with newly awakened political and republican zeal, these perhaps account for the character of the latter era.

In the close of the former period, and during the bloom of the latter, the poet Milton was educated and formed; and he survived the latter, and all the fond hopes and aspirations which had been its life; and so in evil days, standing as the representative of the combined excellence of both periods, he produced the *Paradise Lost* as by an after-throe of nature. 'There are some persons (observes a divine, a contemporary of Milton's) of whom the grace of God takes early hold, and the good spirit inhabiting them carries them on in an even constancy through innocence into virtue, their Christianity bearing equal date with their manhood, and reason and religion, like warp and woof, running together, make up one web of a wise and exemplary life. This (he adds) is a most happy case, wherever it happens; for besides that there is no sweeter or more lovely thing on earth than the early buds of piety, which drew from our Saviour signal affection to the beloved disciple, it is better to have no wound than to experience the most sovereign balsam, which, if it work a cure, yet usually leaves a scar behind.' Although it was and is my intention to defer the consideration of Milton's own character to the conclusion of this Lecture, yet I could not prevail on myself to approach the *Paradise Lost* without impressing on your minds the conditions under which such a work was in fact producible at all, the original genius having been assumed as the immediate agent and efficient cause; and these conditions I find in the character of the times and in his own character. The age in which the foundations of his mind were laid, was congenial to it as one golden era of profound erudition and individual genius; – that in which the superstructure was carried up, was no less favourable to it by a sternness of discipline and a show of self-control, highly flattering to the imaginative dignity of an heir of fame, and which won Milton over from the dear-loved delights of academic groves and cathedral aisles to the anti-prelatic party. It acted on him, too, no doubt, and modified his studies by a characteristic controversial spirit (his presentation of God is tinted with it) – a spirit not less busy indeed in political than in theological and ecclesiastical dispute, but carrying on the former almost always, more or less, in the guise of the latter. And so far as Pope's censure of our poet, – that he makes God the Father a school divine – is just, we must attribute it to the character of his age, from which the men of genius, who escaped, escaped by a worse disease, the licentious indifference of a Frenchified court.

Such was the *nidus* or soil, which constituted, in the strict sense of the word, the circumstances of Milton's mind. In his mind itself there were purity and piety absolute; an imagination to which neither the past nor the present were interesting, except as far as they called forth and enlivened the great ideal, in which and for which he lived; a keen love of truth, which, after many weary pursuits, found a harbour in a

sublime listening to the still voice in his own spirit, and as keen a love
of his country, which, after a disappointment still more depressive,
expanded and soared into a love of man as a probationer of immor-
tality. These were, these alone could be, the conditions under which
such a work as the *Paradise Lost* could be conceived and accomplished.
By a life-long study Milton had known –

> What was of use to know,
> What best to say could say, to do had done.
> His actions to his words agreed, his words
> To his large heart gave utterance due, his heart
> Contain'd of good, wise, fair, the perfect shape;

and he left the imperishable total, as a bequest to the ages coming, in
the *Paradise Lost*.*

... The language and versification of the *Paradise Lost* are peculiar
in being so much more necessarily correspondent to each than those
in any other poem or poet. The connection of the sentences and the
position of the words are exquisitely artificial; but the position is
rather according to the logic of passion or universal logic, than to the
logic of grammar. Milton attempted to make the English language
obey the logic of passion as perfectly as the Greek and Latin. Hence
the occasional harshness in the construction.

Sublimity is the pre-eminent characteristic of the *Paradise Lost*. It is
not an arithmetical sublime like Klopstock's, whose rule always is to
treat what we might think large as contemptibly small. Klopstock
mistakes bigness for greatness. There is a greatness arising from images
of effort and daring, and also from those of moral endurance; in
Milton both are united. The fallen angels are human passions, invested
with a dramatic reality.

The apostrophe to light at the commencement of the third book is
particularly beautiful as an intermediate link between Hell and
Heaven; and observe, how the second and third book support the
subjective character of the poem. In all modern poetry in Christen-
dom there is an under consciousness of a sinful nature, a fleeting away
of external things, the mind or subject greater than the object, the
reflective character predominant. In the *Paradise Lost* the sublimest
parts are the revelations of Milton's own mind, producing itself and

* Not perhaps here, but towards, or as, the conclusion, to chastize the
fashionable notion that poetry is a relaxation or amusement, one of the super-
fluous toys and luxuries of the intellect! To contrast the permanence of poems
with the transiency and fleeting moral effects of empires. and what are called,
great events. – S. T. C.

evolving its own greatness; and this is so truly so, that when that which is merely entertaining for its objective beauty is introduced, it at first seems a discord.

Lectures, 1818

THE reader of Milton must be always on his duty: he is surrounded with sense; it rises in every line; every word is to the purpose. There are no lazy intervals; all has been considered, and demands and merits observation. If this be called obscurity, let it be remembered that it is such an obscurity as is a compliment to the reader; not that vicious obscurity, which proceeds from a muddled head.

From a Notebook, 1796

CHAUCER

I TAKE unceasing delight in Chaucer. His manly cheerfulness is especially delicious to me in my old age. How exquisitely tender he is, and yet how perfectly free from the least touch of sickly melancholy or morbid drooping! The sympathy of the poet with the subjects of his poetry is particularly remarkable in Shakespeare and Chaucer; but what the first effects by a strong act of imagination and mental metamorphosis, the last does without any effort, merely by the inborn kindly joyousness of his nature. How well we seem to know Chaucer! How absolutely nothing do we know of Shakespeare!

I cannot in the least allow any necessity for Chaucer's poetry, especially the *Canterbury Tales*, being considered obsolete. Let a few plain rules be given for sounding the final *è* of syllables, and for expressing the termination of such words as *ocëan*, and *natiön*, &c., as dissyllables, – or let the syllables to be sounded in such cases be marked by a competent metrist. This simple expedient would, with a very few trifling exceptions, where the errors are inveterate, enable any reader to feel the perfect smoothness and harmony of Chaucer's verse. As to understanding his language, if you read twenty pages with a good glossary, you surely can find no further difficulty, even as it is; but I should have no objection to see this done: – Strike out those words which are now obsolete, and I will venture to say that I will replace every one of them by words still in use out of Chaucer himself, or Gower his disciple. I don't want this myself: I rather like to see the significant terms which Chaucer unsuccessfully offered as candidates for admission into our language; but surely so very slight a change of the text may well be pardoned, even by black-*letterati*, for the purpose of restoring so great a poet to his ancient and most deserved popularity.

Table-Talk

March 15, 1834

SWIFT

IN Swift's writings there is a false misanthropy grounded upon an inclusive contemplation of the vices and follies of mankind, and this misanthropic tone is also disfigured or brutalized by his obtrusion of physical dirt and coarseness. I think *Gulliver's Travels* the great work of Swift. In the voyages to Lilliput and Brobdingnag he displays the littleness and moral contemptibility of human nature; in that to the Houyhnhnms he represents the disgusting spectacle of man with the understanding only, without the reason or the moral feeling, and in his horse he gives the misanthropic ideal of man – that is, a being virtuous from rule and duty, but untouched by the principle of love.

Lecture, 1818

ROBINSON CRUSOE

THE wise only possess ideas; the greater part of mankind are possessed by them. Robinson Crusoe was not conscious of the master-impulse, even because it was his master, and had taken, as he says, full possession of him. When once the mind, in despite of the remonstrating conscience, has abandoned its free power to a haunting impulse or idea, then whatever tends to give depth and vividness to this idea or indefinite imagination, increases its despotism, and in the same proportion renders the reason and free will ineffectual. Now, fearful calamities, sufferings, horrors, and hair-breadth escapes will have this effect, far more than even sensual pleasure and prosperous incidents. Hence the evil consequences of sin in such cases, instead of retracting or deterring the sinner, goad him on to his destruction. This is the moral of Shakespeare's *Macbeth*, and the true solution of this paragraph, – not any overruling decree of divine wrath, but the tyranny of the sinner's own evil imagination, which he has voluntarily chosen as his master.

Compare the contemptuous Swift with the contemned De Foe, and how superior will the latter be found! But by what test? – Even by this; that the writer who makes me sympathize with his presentations with the whole of my being, is more estimable than he who calls forth, and appeals but to, a part of my being – my sense of the ludicrous, for instance. De Foe's excellence it is, to make me forget my specific class, character, and circumstances, and to raise me while I read him, into the universal man.

P. 80. I smiled to myself at the sight of this money: 'O drug!' said I aloud, &c. *However, upon second thoughts, I took it away;* and wrapping all this in a piece of canvass, &c.

Worthy of Shakespeare! – and yet the simple semicolon after it, the instant passing on without the least pause of reflex consciousness, is more exquisite and masterlike than the touch itself. A meaner writer, a Marmontel, would have put an (!) after '*away*', and have commenced a fresh paragraph. 30th July, 1830. . . .

One excellence of De Foe, amongst many, is his sacrifice of lesser interest to the greater because more universal. Had he (as without any improbability he might have done) given his Robinson Crusoe any of the turn for natural history, which forms so striking and delightful a feature in the equally uneducated Dampier; – had he made him find out qualities and uses in the before (to him) unknown plants of the island, discover, for instance a substitute for hops, or describe birds, &c. – many delightful pages and incidents might have enriched the book; – but then Crusoe would have ceased to be the universal representative, the person for whom every reader could substitute himself. But now nothing is done, thought, suffered, or desired, but what every man can imagine himself doing, thinking, feeling, or wishing for. Even so very easy a problem as that of finding a substitute for ink, is with exquisite judgement made to baffle Crusoe's inventive faculties. And in what he does, he arrives at no excellence; he does not make basket-work like Will Atkins; the carpentering, tailoring, pottery, &c., are all just what will answer his purposes, and those are confined to needs that all men have, and comforts that all men desire. Crusoe rises only to the point to which all men may be made to feel that they might, and that they ought to, rise in religion – to resignation, dependence on, and thankful acknowledgement of, the divine mercy and goodness.

Marginalia, 1830

RICHARDSON

I CONFESS it has cost, and still costs, my philosophy some exertion not to be vexed that I must admire, aye, greatly admire, Richardson. His mind is so very vile a mind, so oozy, hypocritical, praise-mad, canting, envious, concupiscent! But to understand and draw *him* would be to produce a work almost equal to his own; and, in order to do this, '*down, proud Heart, down*' (as we teach little children to say to themselves, bless them!) all hatred down! and, instead thereof, charity, calmness, a heart fixed on the good part, though the understanding is surveying all. Richardson felt truly the defect of Fielding, or what was not his excellence, and made that his *defect* – a trick of uncharitableness often played, though not exclusively, by contemporaries. Fielding's talent was observation, not meditation. But Richardson was not philosopher enough to know the difference – say, rather, to understand and develop it.

Notebooks, 1805

ON PROSE STYLE

FROM the common opinion that the English style attained its greatest perfection in and about Queen Anne's reign I altogether dissent; not only because it is in one species alone in which it can be pretended that the writers of that age excelled their predecessors; but also because the specimens themselves are not equal, upon sound principles of judgement, to much that had been produced before. The classical structure of Hooker – the impetuous, thought-agglomerating flood of Taylor – to these there is no pretence of a parallel; and for mere ease and grace, is Cowley inferior to Addison, being as he is so much more thoughtful and full of fancy? Cowley, with the omission of a quaintness here and there, is probably the best model of style for modern imitation in general. Taylor's periods have been frequently attempted by his admirers; you may, perhaps, just catch the turn of a simile or single image, but to write in the real manner of Jeremy Taylor would require as mighty a mind as his. Many parts of Algernon Sidney's treatises afford excellent exemplars of a good modern practical style; and Dryden in his prose works is a still better model, if you add a stricter and purer grammar. It is, indeed, worthy of remark that all our great poets have been good prose writers, as Chaucer,

Spenser, Milton; and this probably arose from their just sense of metre. For a true poet will never confound verse and prose; whereas it is almost characteristic of indifferent prose writers that they should be constantly slipping into scraps of metre. Swift's style is, in its line, perfect; the manner is a complete expression of the matter, the terms appropriate, and the artifice concealed. It is simplicity in the true sense of the word.

After the Revolution, the spirit of the nation became much more commercial than it had been before; a learned body, or clerisy, as such, gradually disappeared, and literature in general began to be addressed to the common miscellaneous public. That public had become accustomed to, and required, a strong stimulus; and to meet the requisitions of the public taste, a style was produced which by combining triteness of thought with singularity and excess of manner of expression, was calculated at once to soothe ignorance and to flatter vanity. The thought was carefully kept down to the immediate apprehension of the commonest understanding, and the dress was as anxiously arranged for the purpose of making the thought appear something very profound. The essence of this style consisted in a mock antithesis, that is, an opposition of mere sounds, in a rage for personification, the abstract made animate, far-fetched metaphors, strange phrases, metrical scraps, in every thing, in short, but genuine prose. Style is, of course, nothing else but the art of conveying the meaning appropriately and with perspicuity, whatever that meaning may be, and one criterion of style is that it shall not be translatable without injury to the meaning. Johnson's style has pleased many from the very fault of being perpetually translatable; he creates an impression of cleverness by never saying any thing in a common way. The best specimen of this manner is in Junius, because his antithesis is less merely verbal than Johnson's. Gibbon's manner is the worst of all; it has every fault of which this peculiar style is capable. Tacitus is an example of it in Latin; in coming from Cicero you feel the *falsetto* immediately.

In order to form a good style, the primary rule and condition is, not to attempt to express ourselves in language before we thoroughly know our own meaning: – when a man perfectly understands himself, appropriate diction will generally be at his command either in writing or speaking. In such cases the thoughts and the words are associated. In the next place preciseness in the use of terms is required, and the test is whether you can translate the phrase adequately into simpler terms, regard being had to the feeling of the whole passage.

Try this upon Shakespeare, or Milton, and see if you can substitute other simpler words in any given passage without a violation of the meaning or tone. The source of bad writing is the desire to be something more than a man of sense, – the straining to be thought a genius; and it is just the same in speech-making. If men would only say what they have to say in plain terms, how much more eloquent they would be! Another rule is to avoid converting mere abstractions into persons. I believe you will very rarely find in any great writer before the Revolution the possessive case of an inanimate noun used in prose instead of the dependent case, as 'the watch's hand', for 'the hand of the watch'. The possessive or Saxon genitive was confined to persons, or at least to animated subjects. And I can not conclude this Lecture without insisting on the importance of accuracy of style as being near akin to veracity and truthful habits of mind; he who thinks loosely will write loosely, and, perhaps, there is some moral inconvenience in the common forms of our grammars which give our children so many obscure terms for material distinctions. Let me also exhort you to careful examination of what you read, if it be worthy any perusal at all; such an examination will be a safeguard from fanaticism, the universal origin of which is in the contemplation of phenomena without investigation into their causes.

Lectures, 1818

INDEX OF FIRST LINES

READ MORE IN PENGUIN

In every corner of the world, on every subject under the sun, Penguin represents quality and variety – the very best in publishing today.

For complete information about books available from Penguin – including Puffins, Penguin Classics and Arkana – and how to order them, write to us at the appropriate address below. Please note that for copyright reasons the selection of books varies from country to country.

In the United Kingdom: Please write to *Dept. JC, Penguin Books Ltd, FREEPOST, West Drayton, Middlesex UB7 OBR.*

If you have any difficulty in obtaining a title, please send your order with the correct money, plus ten per cent for postage and packaging, to *PO Box No. 11, West Drayton, Middlesex UB7 OBR*

In the United States: Please write to *Consumer Sales, Penguin USA, P.O. Box 999, Dept. 17109, Bergenfield, New Jersey 07621-0120.* VISA and MasterCard holders call 1-800-253-6476 to order all Penguin titles

In Canada: Please write to *Penguin Books Canada Ltd, 10 Alcorn Avenue, Suite 300, Toronto, Ontario M4V 3B2*

In Australia: Please write to *Penguin Books Australia Ltd, P.O. Box 257, Ringwood, Victoria 3134*

In New Zealand: Please write to *Penguin Books (NZ) Ltd, Private Bag 102902, North Shore Mail Centre, Auckland 10*

In India: Please write to *Penguin Books India Pvt Ltd, 706 Eros Apartments, 56 Nehru Place, New Delhi 110 019*

In the Netherlands: Please write to *Penguin Books Netherlands bv, Postbus 3507, NL-1001 AH Amsterdam*

In Germany: Please write to *Penguin Books Deutschland GmbH, Metzlerstrasse 26, 60594 Frankfurt am Main*

In Spain: Please write to *Penguin Books S. A., Bravo Murillo 19, 1° B, 28015 Madrid*

In Italy: Please write to *Penguin Italia s.r.l., Via Felice Casati 20, I–20124 Milano*

In France: Please write to *Penguin France S. A., 17 rue Lejeune, F–31000 Toulouse*

In Japan: Please write to *Penguin Books Japan, Ishikiribashi Building, 2–5–4, Suido, Bunkyo-ku, Tokyo 112*

In Greece: Please write to *Penguin Hellas Ltd, Dimocritou 3, GR–106 71 Athens*

In South Africa: Please write to *Longman Penguin Southern Africa (Pty) Ltd, Private Bag X08, Bertsham 2013*

PENGUIN AUDIOBOOKS

A Quality of Writing that Speaks for Itself

Penguin Books has always led the field in quality publishing. Now you can listen at leisure to your favourite books, read to you by familiar voices from radio, stage and screen. Penguin Audiobooks are ideal as gifts, for when you are travelling or simply to enjoy at home. They are produced to an excellent standard, and abridgements are always faithful to the original texts. From thrillers to classic literature, biography to humour, with a wealth of titles in between, Penguin Audiobooks offer you quality, entertainment and the chance to rediscover the pleasure of listening.

You can order Penguin Audiobooks through Penguin Direct by telephoning (0181) 899 4036. The lines are open 24 hours every day. Ask for Penguin Direct, quoting your credit card details.

Published or forthcoming:

Emma by Jane Austen, read by Fiona Shaw

Persuasion by Jane Austen, read by Joanna David

Pride and Prejudice by Jane Austen, read by Geraldine McEwan

The Tenant of Wildfell Hall by Anne Brontë, read by Juliet Stevenson

Jane Eyre by Charlotte Brontë, read by Juliet Stevenson

Villette by Charlotte Brontë, read by Juliet Stevenson

Wuthering Heights by Emily Brontë, read by Juliet Stevenson

The Woman in White by Wilkie Collins, read by Nigel Anthony and Susan Jameson

Heart of Darkness by Joseph Conrad, read by David Threlfall

Tales from the One Thousand and One Nights, read by Souad Faress and Raad Rawi

Moll Flanders by Daniel Defoe, read by Frances Barber

Great Expectations by Charles Dickens, read by Hugh Laurie

Hard Times by Charles Dickens, read by Michael Pennington

Martin Chuzzlewit by Charles Dickens, read by John Wells

The Old Curiosity Shop by Charles Dickens, read by Alec McCowen

PENGUIN AUDIOBOOKS

Crime and Punishment by Fyodor Dostoyevsky, read by Alex Jennings

Middlemarch by George Eliot, read by Harriet Walter

Silas Marner by George Eliot, read by Tim Pigott-Smith

The Great Gatsby by F. Scott Fitzgerald, read by Marcus D'Amico

Madame Bovary by Gustave Flaubert, read by Claire Bloom

Jude the Obscure by Thomas Hardy, read by Samuel West

The Return of the Native by Thomas Hardy, read by Steven Pacey

Tess of the D'Urbervilles by Thomas Hardy, read by Eleanor Bron

The Iliad by Homer, read by Derek Jacobi

Dubliners by James Joyce, read by Gerard McSorley

The Dead and Other Stories by James Joyce, read by Gerard McSorley

On the Road by Jack Kerouac, read by David Carradine

Sons and Lovers by D. H. Lawrence, read by Paul Copley

The Fall of the House of Usher by Edgar Allan Poe, read by Andrew Sachs

Wide Sargasso Sea by Jean Rhys, read by Jane Lapotaire and Michael Kitchen

The Little Prince by Antoine de Saint-Exupéry, read by Michael Maloney

Frankenstein by Mary Shelley, read by Richard Pasco

Of Mice and Men by John Steinbeck, read by Gary Sinise

Travels with Charley by John Steinbeck, read by Gary Sinise

The Pearl by John Steinbeck, read by Hector Elizondo

Dr Jekyll and Mr Hyde by Robert Louis Stevenson, read by Jonathan Hyde

Kidnapped by Robert Louis Stevenson, read by Robbie Coltrane

The Age of Innocence by Edith Wharton, read by Kerry Shale

The Buccaneers by Edith Wharton, read by Dana Ivey

Mrs Dalloway by Virginia Woolf, read by Eileen Atkins

READ MORE IN PENGUIN

POETRY LIBRARY

Arnold	Selected by Kenneth Allott
Blake	Selected by W. H. Stevenson
Browning	Selected by Daniel Karlin
Burns	Selected by Angus Calder and William Donnelly
Byron	Selected by A. S. B. Glover
Clare	Selected by Geoffrey Summerfield
Coleridge	Selected by Richard Holmes
Donne	Selected by John Hayward
Dryden	Selected by Douglas Grant
Hardy	Selected by David Wright
Herbert	Selected by W. H. Auden
Jonson	Selected by George Parfitt
Keats	Selected by John Barnard
Kipling	Selected by James Cochrane
Lawrence	Selected by Keith Sagar
Milton	Selected by Laurence D. Lerner
Pope	Selected by Douglas Grant
Rubáiyát of Omar Khayyám	Translated by Edward FitzGerald
Shelley	Selected by Isabel Quigley
Tennyson	Selected by W. E. Williams
Wordsworth	Selected by Nicholas Roe
Yeats	Selected by Timothy Webb

READ MORE IN PENGUIN

A SELECTION OF POETRY

American Verse
British Poetry since 1945
Caribbean Verse in English
A Choice of Comic and Curious Verse
Contemporary American Poetry
Contemporary British Poetry
Contemporary Irish Poetry
English Poetry 1918–60
English Romantic Verse
English Verse
First World War Poetry
German Verse
Greek Verse
Imagist Poetry
Irish Verse
Japanese Verse
Love Poetry
The Metaphysical Poets
Modern African Poetry
New Poetry
Penguin Book of Homosexual Verse
Poetry of the Thirties
Scottish Verse
Spanish Verse
Women Poets

READ MORE IN PENGUIN

A SELECTION OF POETRY

James Fenton Out of Danger

A collection wonderfully open to experience – of foreign places, differences, feelings and languages.

U. A. Fanthorpe Selected Poems

She is an erudite poet, rich in experience and haunted by the classical past ... fully at home in the world of the turbulent NHS, the decaying academies, and all the draughty corners of the abandoned Welfare State' – *Observer*

Yehuda Amichai Selected Poems
Translated by Chana Bloch and Stephen Mitchell

'A truly major poet ... there's a depth, breadth and weighty momentum in these subtle and delicate poems of his' – Ted Hughes

Czesław Miłosz Collected Poems 1931–1987
Winner of the 1980 Nobel Prize for Literature

'One of the greatest poets of our time, perhaps the greatest' – Joseph Brodsky

Joseph Brodsky To Urania
Winner of the 1987 Nobel Prize for Literature

Exiled from the Soviet Union in 1972, Joseph Brodsky has been universally acclaimed as the most talented Russian poet of his generation.

Paul Celan Selected Poems
Winner of the first European Translation Prize, 1990

'The English reader can now enter the hermetic universe of a German–Jewish poet who made out of the anguish of his people, things of terror and beauty' – *The Times Literary Supplement*

Geoffrey Hill Collected Poems

'Sternly formal, wry, grand, sensually direct: the contraries of a major poet' – *Observer*, Books of the Year